Stick and String

By Robert Kirby

PublishAmerica
Baltimore

ISBN: 1-4241-5729-3
PUBLISHED BY PUBLISHAMERICA, LLLP
www.publishamerica.com
Baltimore

Printed in the United States of America

For my wife Julie

1

Innocence Lost

Scarred pavement gently grumbled and quaked as a cheerless group of corporate slaves huddled by a smoking shuttle terminal waiting for the morning train. From the depths of the floating city came rumbles and vacillations responding to ebbs and swells of a wine dark sea below. Dawn was drenched in poppy red and squirming crimson clouds obscured the ceiling and turbulent heavens above. A battered yet functioning webscreen broadcast the daily news to those making connections. It came as no surprise to the commuters that the city's atmospheric controls were malfunctioning. This was often the story while outside the hardened shell of this floating bubble city of countless bubble cities, a never-ending storm raged.

Those gathered at the shuttle terminal wore jumpsuits, mandated corporate uniforms. Some gazed upon the three dimensional sphere projected from the monolithic webscreen while others cast occasional nervous glances into the moisture laden rusty clouds looming above. The clouds trapped inside the city's dome appeared to be on the verge of bursting into a hazardous chemical downpour. Someone sneezed then repeatedly sneezed again and again as others leered and edged away from the nameless germ spreader. The news blared on.

"Turning from local issues, another planet within the habitable zone was identified and Enercorp will join the rush to stake claims. Ancient laser interferometer probes are now deep within our galaxy and continue to search out new worlds supportive of life. Of the countless multitudes of planets identified, a precious few are capable of supporting human life. Those within the habitable zone are prime targets for resource exploitation. This newly found inhabitable world is similar to the green satellites of the dwarf star Delta Pavonis. Life was found but no advanced civilization detected. Enercorp has launched a planetary survey expedition to uncover expendable resources. Enercorp mining operations on Sirius will continue without disruption." rattled the reporter from the screen inside the sphere.

Derek looked up as fellow slaves slipped into bubbles and automatic hatches closed behind them. He did the same.

He blinked into the retinal scanner to identity himself and performed the double confirmation with one DNA laden breath. The transport bubble hissed and lunged through a tangle of tubes in wild acceleration destined for his work location. He was only eighteen years old but he hoped to someday earn enough credits to stay out of Sirius uranium mines and leech jungles of Wolf 359, but the grim truth remained that he was enslaved. He did not have credits to purchase freedom. He could be sent on any nightmarish assignment any time. He was the clone of a man he did not know. He was conceived in a laboratory and weaned into slavery to pay off debts racked up from an anonymous donor. He both despised and thanked this debtor for his young life. Carefully keeping his hands below the webcam, he cunningly slipped a fingertip pen and writing cylinder from his pocket and unlocked the small scroll. The shuttle bubble linked to the bullet train with a muffled ping.

The bubble surfaced from the dark tunnels and he blinked up at the alizarin haze blanketing the towering structures of the oceanic city. He only had a moment to act and he wrote, "They know."

The webscreen indicated his bubble would soon detach from the rocketing train. The three dimensional holographic sphere hovering in front of him displayed commercial after commercial. He wished to shut the stupid thing off and to kill the watching, the analyzing, and recording. It wasn't just this one. The webscreens, webterms, and webcams were everywhere now.

He daydreamed as the bubble wobbled and lurched. He drifted to a place called Paradan, an enchanted world of the rich and free. He was there with Jenniper and suddenly he felt the surge of emotion that came when he was near her.

The transport bubble decelerated and eased up a slick maglev ramp as the hatch opened. He sat in the bubble with hatch open as blue jumpsuits of fellow slaves shuffled past. A moment longer he was with Jenniper in Paradan. They walked barefoot along a sandy seashore and gentle waves rolled under a glimmering moon. She took his hand and squeezed. A warm salty breeze danced through her hair and moonlight twinkled in her eyes. A lone seagull sailed above the swaying palms across the shimmering surf.

"Hey Pal, are you asleep?" Daydream fizzled into the face of a policeman peering into the transport bubble where Derek found himself. He did not have credits for freedom or paradise. He was a slave.

"I am not, sir," replied Derek as he clambered out of his shuttle shaking off the shockwave of cold reality.

2

Evaluation Day

It seems every time I turn around,
I up and knock myself on the ground.
It seems I'm no good for me at all.
I've cursed and hurt and lied
To me, myself, and I,
And I've kicked myself after the fall.

So look out, I'm walking down your street.
I'm not someone you want to meet.
I'm not someone from your side of town.
But don't be afraid, it's only me.
Asking, to be or not to be?
Asking, where can I be found?

I think I'm here, or maybe there.
I could have put me anywhere.
I'm sure I'll turn up eventually.
I've searched my soul and searched my heart.
I've backtracked to the very start,
But still, I haven't found me.

Derek took a rocketing shaft down into the dark damp suboceanic bowels of Enercorp deep below the ocean floor and signed onto his production pod as the first shift filed out. He climbed into his suit to begin his daily task of searching for expendable resource, and a small hologram blinked into existence before him. "Derek 243?" the hologram queried.

"Yes it is me," he replied to the small figure of light projected from the webterm.

"Supervisor Stout reminds you that your evaluation is scheduled for today," announced the small glowing projection.

"I wouldn't miss it."

"You better not miss it, worthless kid," the figure of light sneered.

"Go away," retorted young Derek 243. He was not going to be baited today.

Derek could not even guess at the workings behind the little administrative apparition now fading before him. His verbal responses were not the only things recorded for analysis. Pulse, blood pressure, biochemical, bioelectrical, and brain waves constantly fed into ongoing physiological and psychological evaluations. The hologram blinked out. He took several slow deep breaths and closed his eyes. He mentally recited his mantra which he had been programmed with, "I am a valuable asset to Enercorp," but then he added his own private mantra, "I am free."

After his shift was done, he cleaned up and made his way to the supervisory suite. He entered the supervisor lobby and inserted his profile card into the robotic secretary and pronounced a code sequence as he placed his right hand onto a pad which flashed in recognition. "Derek 243, you may now enter," was the reply. The supervisory suite was of contemporary design with complementing mood lights swirling about the room. Derek 243 immediately found himself in a peculiar state of mind and strangely disarmed. A passive weirdness slipped into his brain. Supervisor Stout reclined behind a large gleaming desk inlaid with a honeycomb of membrane touch panels and three dimensional spheres projected from webterms. She was surrounded by consoles and controls. She was strikingly bald and mood lights danced upon her shiny scalp. Derek 243 now felt the pronounced effects of some type of drug kicking in. There were no rules here. As Supervisor Stout looked up, her lower lip quivered slightly. He could not easily determine if her look was that of fear, anger, or delight.

"Derek 243, what an honor it is to have you here," she started off sarcastically. "I hope you were not in the middle of anything important?" Before he could respond, she mumbled her own answer, "I didn't think so." Supervisors were either ruthless or they soon lost their positions. It was a job requirement. Derek was only eighteen years old and had already been in the slave force for ten years. He never stooped to schmoozing and his words often came out harshly. He was a gutsy young man.

"I'm plugged into a production pod fourteen hours a day, searching for scraps of expendable resource. If you don't think I'm doing anything important then set me free," he replied. His speech began to slur as the neuronumbing chemicals kicked in. "You are desperately ambitious and where is it getting you? You'll end up like the others. Give me my evaluation and I'll get out of here," he slurred, struggling to maintain his normal posture.

She ignored his drunken response and busied herself at her console. "I suppose you have heard that we claimed a planet?" She smiled a nervous smile as her bald forehead wrinkled, and he sensed the trepidation in her tone. New territories were usually followed by reorganizations and management shake-ups and her job was probably in jeopardy. A supervisor in trouble was a dangerous person. He hated being the pawn in these corporate political games, but there was no way he would stoop to doing what people did to get promoted.

"I pity the beggars on the front," he responded gruffly and drunkenly.

"The front isn't so bad, once you get used to it," she retorted coldly. Her face grew hard and her eyes squinted as she regarded the young man before her and she became poisonous and forbidding. "It's an opportunity for advancement. Think of the credits the miners earn, working the pitchblende and carnonite caves. It is more than you will ever get from piddling around underneath the ocean," she said. Derek's heart raced with rage. He was not common among the slaves in this world of corporate control. His fists were clenched and he fought to remain sober but the drug was very strong.

"They do not make it out with any credits," he said. "I have earned enough to stay out of the jungles," he retorted viciously. "I will not work in caves, jungles, storms, or active volcanoes. It's a death sentence, and everyone knows it," he finished. The room was spinning and the lights were getting dim.

"You have not earned enough to stay out of the jungles," replied the supervisor. She leaned back in her chair and smiled fiendishly. She despised him. He was such an unenlightened slave, but there was nothing she could say to change his mind. She rolled her eyes and sighed. "Harsh environments are unavoidable. We are in the business of obtaining resource for energy production. Be thankful there are no wars, only healthy corporate competition," she purred with wicked relish.

"Killing people in droves is not healthy," he slurred. "The nuclear battles are not healthy corporate competition." He staggered backwards and cursed. He was quickly going down.

"Global competition for exploitable resource is healthy!" She shouted. She lost her cool manners and began pounding furiously at the console controls before her. "Rival teracorps and renegade entrepreneurs must be beaten in the global market!" she snarled. She angrily leaned forward and hammered a few panel squares activating an aura scan. The webcams and backend biorecorders were already rolling.

He sank to the floor. He slumped and slurred. "Killing isn't healthy competition," was all he could manage to say.

"You did not vote in our last election," she stated as she read from a report. Plastic concern was painted on her face as beads of sweat glistened on her forehead. She was desperately ambitious and very expendable, a most dangerous combination in a supervisor. She peered down at the boy slumped on the floor before her. She had cut a deal and he knew it now, but he could not find words.

"It is a mockery," he managed to murmur.

"So you do not believe in human gods," retorted Supervisor Stout angrily and it was true. He had always despised absurd elections for gods known as Shareholders, the small group of elite humans believed to be immortal. He despised the election hype of determining the lucky one to receive an extreme makeover and to become genetically modified and sculpted into a human god. "You were aware of my choice for new god, so why didn't you vote for her?" queried Supervisor Stout. Her face melted into detached curiosity but her fingers were busy entering something into the consoles. She turned her back to him as a plastic card emerged from a slot and fed into her hand.

She wheeled around and threw it to the floor beside him. "Your dock and departure are all stored in the webcard. You have volunteered to join the Mercury Solar Team, as your opportunity for advancement," she announced darkly. She leaned down and whispered slowly and softly and her words floated down to him as if in a dream. She said, "They know."

3

Corporation Blues

I keep punching on this keyboard, staring at this screen all day.
I keep punching on this keyboard, staring at this screen all day.
The boss wants answers, but I don't have a thing to say.

I've got these corporation blues.
I've got these corporation blues.
Thirty years, no retirement,
And I know I'm going to lose.

I think about my friends, back in high school.
I think about my friends, way back in high school.
Are they just like me, a corporation fool?

I've got these corporation blues.
I've got these corporation blues.
There won't be a retirement,
And I know I'm going to lose.

Derek woke in his apartment module with proof of what had
happened, the evaluation and the drugging, in the form of the plastic
webcard. Derek sluggishly showered and dressed and left his

apartment module heading for work, for there were no days off. He worked fourteen hours a day, seven days a week.

Still groggy from the drug, he was back at his designated workstation still waking up. He sat in his cramped cubicle, shared with the other shift and peered into the webscreen sphere before him. This was where he signed on each day before suiting up and heading down, and this was where he confirmed his findings and excavations from deep below the ocean floor before signing off. The hellish touching of membrane panels in the cubicles all around seemed amplified. Touch sensitive membrane panels were used for input in these large cubefarms only because voice input was such a distraction. In his current state, all sound was irritating. Modern methods of telepathy allowed connection to telepathic input ports via neurotrodes but these slaves did not work in such luxury.

No one asked him how it went with the supervisor. No one looked up from their work at all. He sat for awhile, not entering anything nor signing on. The webscreen sphere in front of him eventually snapped to life and demanded attention. The time between shifts had exceeded and the webscreen displayed a message to login immediately. The duty manager would soon be alerted. Derek did not respond. He gazed into the webcam above his cubicle, and daydreamed.

He took a small cylindrical scroll from the pocket of his uniform and placed a fingertip pen on his writing finger and started writing words. He wrote only a few lines and put the scroll and fingertip pen back into his pocket.

The duty manager appeared at the entrance of the cubicle. She was a small officious woman always entering something into her webpod. People said she was a little woman in a big hurry. The duty manager glared but nervously asked, "What are you doing?"

"I am thinking," replied young Derek.

"Thinking?" questioned the duty manager, as she made another entry into her webpod. "You better think while you are logging in, and while you are suiting up," she said harshly.

"Why?" Derek asked. The duty manager was openly shocked by the question. Her mouth dropped.

"If you refuse to comply with corporate policy, I will report you. You know that you are supposed to login and suit up within a certain window. Do not ask me why. That is a rebellious thought, and rebellious thinking is against corporate policy," she spit her reply. Derek showed no emotion. The little woman continued, "There is no way to track your progress if you are not online. I have reported you before, in fact many times now. You are currently on probation. Do you have a clue what will happen to you if you violate your probation?" The sound of fingers touching membrane panels in surrounding cubes slowed and became quieter now. Those in nearby cubes conspicuously eavesdropped on their exchange.

"Do you think they might send me away?" asked Derek. The duty manager was always the last to be told when someone was being transferred or terminated.

"They will send you to the storms outside!" bellowed the duty manager. She furiously made entries into her webpod. The handheld webpod beeped and blipped. "The storms will teach you a lesson. You will wish that you were back here doing your safe little job, under the ocean floor. What have you been writing?"

"Notes," replied Derek.

"I ask that you compose your notes online, and nowhere else. Let me see what you have been writing," demanded the duty manager. The woman tapped her webpod impatiently against her knee.

"They are private notes," replied Derek.

"You are not allowed to have private notes. That is against corporate policy. Let me see them now!" barked the duty manager as her brow wrinkled in disgust. The surrounding cubes in the cubefarm were completely silent now.

Derek reached into his pocket and handed over the pocket scroll. The duty manager snatched the scroll from his open hand and unrolled it and mouthed the words she read silently.

"This is not a private note! This is nothing but lousy poetry!" she screamed. Her maddened voice carried across the floor of cubefarm and the production pod was now completely silent. "I am keeping this in order to file my report," she said with sadistic satisfaction.

"You are not going to keep anything," said Derek rising up from his chair and moving with catlike quickness. He snatched the pocket scroll before the woman could cringe or blink. Derek gave her a menacing smirk as her face splashed in fear. The little woman backed away.

"I am reporting you," she sneered and hurried off.

4

Food Court

Derek took his lunch in the food court and ate a dried vegetable protein cake and sipped on a vitamin shake. There were no windows in the food court. He wanted to go outside to see the strange atmosphere that had been filling the floating city for days. There was no time to get outside during lunch break. A huge webscreen covered one long wall in the food court, with a massive holographic sphere projected from the wall. He hoped they would show updates on the internal weather but endless commercials aired from the loud repulsive projection.

The males sat apart from the females in the food court. In public places, males did not speak to females, and females did not speak to males. The boys kept their eyes away from where the girls were seated, and girls did not dare look at boys. Socializing with the opposite sex outside professional settings was against corporate policy, and corporate policy was the law. Relationships with the opposite sex were grounds for termination, which was a death penalty. Natural childbirth was no longer a reality and pregnancy was a capital corporate offense. This almost always resulted in the death of those involved. They were all corporate slaves here in the food court. Any violation of corporate policy could involve a transfer to a much more dangerous environment. Slaves were never freed. They received credits for work performed, and were encouraged to earn more credits to consume and buy. Many slaves held the hope of someday buying freedom, but Derek had never known anyone to purchase their freedom.

There was not much talk in the food court except when someone was feeling religious about their work. Many were religious about their work and when they went on about it, they sounded small-minded to Derek. He thought people sounded pathetic when they talked self-righteously about esoteric struggles to perform efficiently. Derek wondered if anyone knew that he deeply despised the empty chatter, but he never openly discussed his likes or dislikes. He felt guilty about taking pride in his work. He was a rebel at heart. He never gave anyone the satisfaction of the details of his business. Some tried to pry the details from him in casual conversation, but he would not talk about it unless it was absolutely necessary to get the job done. His work was his business. He figured he was good enough for the job or it would have ended for him long ago, at least that was what he had figured until his evaluation. He still had a hangover from the drug which had accompanied the stinging evaluation.

The food court was very drab except for the cinema-size webscreen covering the long wall, with pictures and sounds from the webscreen sphere flooding the food court. The commercial currently airing showed a man being lowered into a steaming volcanic pit. The man grinned heartily into the camera as he climbed into a cage and the crane lowered him down. The man looked excited and happy to be lowered into a spewing pit of fire. The commercial persuasively glamorized volcanic mining so much so that it appeared to be an adventurous occupation rewarded with lucrative compensations and breathtaking views. Derek watched the man being lowered down until he was enveloped in smoke and fire and it was difficult to see him anymore. Derek wondered if the man really worked in the pits, but he was probably just a paid stunt man.

Suddenly the doors to the food court burst open at both ends. Global police troopers entered with chemical injection guns cradled in their arms. They filed in at both entrances and menacingly eyed the hushed startled crowd. A few tried to pick up their trays and leave but they were motioned to sit back down. Ones who were talking religiously about work shut their mouths and looked down at their food as did almost everyone in the room. The food court was as silent as deep space except for the large oblivious webscreen sphere in the middle of the long wall. Troopers walked slowly from one end of the food court to the middle of the long wall looking carefully into the crowd. A woman got up from where the females ate and walked boldly to a police trooper.

The police trooper stood in front of another commercial. This new commercial highlighted a woman who planned to donate every organ that she could mortally spare in order to earn enough credits for retirement. She knowingly smiled and gave the camera a confident thumbs-up signal as they wheeled her into the operating room. The commercial then featured the same woman after her operation as she walked slowly through a peaceful meadow down a flower-lined path to her new cozy home in the country. The cozy home in the country did not look completely real but it was a convincing enough landscape, in the background. There were probably places where flowers grew wild, and meadows danced in gentle winds, but no one had ever seen them except in brochures. She looked back at the camera and smiled peacefully as one glass eye twinkled. Derek wondered if she was in Paradan but the commercial did not say.

The woman who walked up to the trooper turned to the room and pointed to a man who sat staring into his food. He was one frequently talkative about the work that he performed so efficiently. He did not look up from his food. The man suddenly shouted, "Do not do this! I did not mean anything by it!" His voice carried well and everyone heard him shout and understood his words even above the webscreen commercials. The man stared into his food and looked as if he were searching for an escape route hidden somewhere in his vegetable protein cake.

The police troopers were all over the man and they ripped him out of his chair and the other corporate slaves who sat nearby fell back and scrambled for safety. The man struggled blindly and at the same time stared blankly into his food as it was knocked and smashed to the floor. The man did not see any escape routes in the food but he seemed to search for them there. They took him down hard face first onto the smooth concrete floor. There was the distinct sound of flesh and bone smacking against the cold concrete but there were no escape routes for this man. Derek felt his heart sink at the sight of this helpless man, who did not have long to live but there was nothing one could do. The troopers got off the man's back for a moment and stood there waiting. The man looked over his back at the troopers and his eyes were wild and desperate and he was crying, and blood streamed from his broken nose. He stumbled to his feet and wailed and ran for all he was worth to one of the doors of the food court as the shots whistled from behind.

The woman who had pointed to the man stood and watched the killing with her arms folded. She began clapping when he was finished. Others joined the clapping. Derek did not clap. Derek did not know this man well but the man was probably just lonely. Derek knew in his heart that loneliness had not always been a crime.

5

Rendezvous

Derek slid Herb's Health Haven card through the destination slot of his shuttle console. He was tired but his shift was done for the day. The transit bubble connected to the main train system with a muffled hiss. Shortly after departure the usual series of commercials began to invade the shuttle webscreen sphere until an emergency news broadcast cut in.

"Weather techs continue to experience difficulty with the city's environmental controls. Biochemical air filters are reacting with unknown elements from the storms outside the protective floating dome of the city. This has disrupted our internal atmosphere and cast a reddish haze across Wafton. Various biochemical filter combinations are currently being tested but no significant progress has been made. Climatologists have no choice but to shut off outside inflows and recycle internally until the source of the smog is determined. This will increase power consumption although all panels are currently reaching minimum generation for the day. To complicate matters, tidal waves will be crashing over Wafton during the night due to nearby sub-oceanic earthquakes. The domed city has heartily withstood regular onslaughts of tidal waves and these are no different. There is backup power, but we are currently under a power outage warning until further notice. You are ordered to take necessary power conservation precautions and power outage preparations."

The webscreen flickered and faded, so the scaling back was beginning. He leaned back to savor the solitude. The web was the sole media for news, education, information, and entertainment. Endless commercials filled in the gaps. Ubiquitous webscreens, webterms, and webcams were in all places. Everyone carried webpods. The webscreens were projections from the web. The webterms were web terminals. These devices were capable of three dimensional projection spheres and three dimensional flat displays. The webcams served as video monitors. Electronic devices of the past such as radio, telephone, television, computer, cellphones, pagers, and PDAs were all replaced by web enabled devices per mandate. All appliances were web enabled per corporate law. Older electronic devices were outlawed and destroyed. Independent forms of media such as commercial free satellite radio, newspapers, magazines, books, CDs, DVDs, MP3s, video games, and hand written materials were now illegal. The noise spewing from the web was drenched in propaganda, commercialism, and lies. There was no longer any such thing as freedom of speech or press. There were no critical publications and no enlightening commentaries. There were no online discussion forums, bloggers, or weblogs. There was no such thing as objective reporting or accountability. The flood of constant unreliable misinformation fed historical databases to build a past, present, and future no sane person could trust.

Arts and entertainment devolved into pure violence, from surreal horror to brutal spectator sports. The reality show competitions ended with only one survivor. It was said that real violence existed to inspire the arts and the entertainment of the day. Violent art became celebrated as a reflection of the violence of life. Freedom of speech was granted only to teracorps but denied to corporate slaves; therefore, no individual was allowed to speak out against the web.

The urban legends state that the web started out as a sharing of information and a free exchange of ideas. This was somehow lost. The web of cyberspace, just like real estate, was now corporate owned and controlled. The darker aspect of the web was incessant pervasive surveillance monitoring. All corporate slaves were under the omnipotent view of webcams, webterms, and webscreens tied to the web. Webcams were in every room of every apartment module. They were literally everywhere, always watching and recording.

The train surfaced from the tunnels. Derek gazed across the floating city for the first time since the trip to the production complex that morning. The horizon of the bubble city Wafton was splashed with crimson and lavender patches which hid the tops of the towering skyscrapers. Every molecule seemed infected with the malignant vapors. Classical orchestra music emanated from the membrane honeycombs surrounding the webscreen but the screen itself was blank. He was not familiar with the ancient tune, but it was no doubt the soundtrack to another violent episode on the web. The tune was from the twentieth century or centuries earlier. Classical composers were no more. The bubble detached and was sucked smoothly down an exit tube.

He was being sent to Mercury and he already knew that the Mercury Project was in bad trouble. He was just eighteen but in the years he worked, the power produced from Mercury solar panels had never been enough to justify its existence. The Mercury Project was considered to be a lost cause, a project that only misfits were now assigned to. He did not want to leave Wafton without Jenniper. The only time Derek went outside the floating bubble city was to scrounge beneath the ocean floor in search of expendable resource. Chances are that he would not be back. He wondered if they planned on working him to death, and if this was his last assignment.

He saw green letters flashing. They read, 'Herb's Health Haven' through the crimson purple atmosphere as his transport detached and sped from the train. The transport cell dipped underground once more and surfaced slowly and deliberately inside the lobby of the health club. The health club was built from an old burned out warehouse and run by androids. There were broken windows high up in the tops where offices once were, but the warehouse itself was now gutted. The lobby and dressing rooms remained on the main floor. The health club featured herbal whirlpools, virtual reality floatation tanks, and the resistplank machines.

Herb, a smiling android, waited to help Derek out of his bubble and handed him an ice cold vegetable juice. It was prepared and waiting for him when he arrived. The destination card had informed the front desk that Derek was coming. All androids at Herb's Health Haven were named Herb. The android's body was physically perfect and sculpted like a magnificent bodybuilder. Androids were tireless workers. The android rights organization was now a large organization, although there were no rights to gain. People believed the ARO was allowed to exist simply because androids provided such cheap labor. Human rights organizations were not allowed. Androids were easy to spot. People who look into the eyes of an android do not find anything living inside. "How are you today, Derek 243?" asked the android dreamily.

Derek raised the vegetable juice and took several large swallows, savoring the rich spices and tomatoes on his taste buds as it went down cold and smooth. "Here's to the Mercury Project, a lost cause," toasted young Derek.

"Excuse me, sir?" queried the android.

"I am being sent to Mercury, to be part of the Mercury Project, which has been a lot cause for a long time. I am going into hell with no cool vegetable drinks. Herb, I believe I will do my usual workout with the resistplanks and then I want to float for awhile. Is Jenniper here yet?" he asked. Derek had first met Jenniper here at this health club. They had become closer each day since. The androids did not seem to care.

"Yes," replied Herb. "Jenniper is in the female dressing room. I am sure that she will be out soon for her usual workout," replied the android cordially.

"Will you link the float tanks?" asked Derek.

"Yes I will make the link. Your personal profile in the system main contains your usual starting resistances. When you step up to the machine your touch will engage your personal settings. If you desire to modify the resistance, simply increase or decrease and save if you desire to permanently change," recited Herb.

"I know how to operate the machines, Herb," Derek cut him off. "I have been here before. I will have another of these vegetable drinks when I finish with the planks and do not spare the spice."

Slavery increased the popularity of exercise, a release from stresses and tensions of living with no liberty. Exercise in addition to vitamin and herbal supplementation proved more healing than any drug that mankind had concocted. Derek took pleasure in arduous daily workouts and his body was chiseled and sculpted as a result. His passions were workouts, writing, and Jenniper. Derek and Jenniper had known each other for a year, and they ducked and dodged the webcams when they were together. They took more and more chances to meet up as the months went by.

When Derek had first met Jenniper at the workout warehouse last year, they quickly became friends. At first they met in secret places just to talk. They broke corporate policy by being together. They knew it was forbidden and punishable by death. This thing they shared was new for both of them and neither was sure where it would lead. Their lives were now in immediate danger.

Derek went into the workout studio to clear his clouded mind and began to press. Other slaves were there also and they took turns straining against the resistplanks. Jenniper came in and started working out near Derek and took her turns at the resistplanks with the others. Derek said nothing which was not unusual, because it was not safe to openly converse, but she knew something was wrong. She had already read the note that he had left hidden for her. They could not talk in front of listening ears or watchful webcams. Derek chanced a momentary gaze at Jenniper's supple body as she strained and pressed. She was also eighteen, the same age as he.

They worked the planks without words until both were sweating completely. After the workout, Derek flashed his yellow eyes at her and made his way outside. His long wringing wet hair hung limply down past his chest. His stomach muscles rippled and his legs bulged smoothly and proportionately. His back and chest expanded explosively compared to his firm waist. He did not look the part of the corporate drone shuffling through the mazes of Enercorp. He told himself never to conform to corporate slavery. He told himself he would someday be free. He told himself to have courage.

Jenniper appeared beside him. "Lighten up, Derek, before you turn to stone. Oh too late, it has already happened. You are hard as rock," she said as she dared to lightly massage his shoulders. She smiled sweetly but his somber expression did not change. She was so beautiful to him and he did not want to lose her. She wore her hair cut very short as was the dress code for women of the day. Sweat trickled down her flushed cheeks. He loved the touch of her soft hands. He tried to smile but could not.

"You saw the note?" he softly asked.

"I did," she shuddered. "What do we do?" she asked nervously.

"What do you have planned this evening?" he asked as he cast a somber glance down the empty hall.

"I can slip out. What will they do to us now?" she asked.

"It has already been done. I have only two days left. I am worried for you now." His features were hard and bitter and he fought to control his grief.

"Don't tell me that," she replied. "What have they done?" Her chin quivered and her eyes clouded. He lowered his head and turned away. She grabbed his arm and fiercely pulled him around to face her. "What have they done to you?" She demanded woefully and looked deep into the young slave's yellow eyes.

"Mercury," he spat the word and gave a spiteful sigh. "I have been sent to Mercury, to be part of the Mercury Project," and his bleak expression faded as they embraced. There was nothing more to say. This was the life of a corporate slave. Freedom and liberty were not part of the deal.

The android brought another cold vegetable juice and handed it to Derek and he drank it vengefully and relished nothing about it this time. "Get the float tanks linked," he ordered the android as he handed an empty drink container back. The android entered physique codes into the suspension control system and linked the suspension chambers.

They climbed into separate suspension chambers and connected the neurotrodes and activated the sense modules. They closed their hatches and closed their eyes. They could see one another now. They were standing together, holding hands. Their minds were now linked. The

VR tanks were a kaleidoscope of colors, scenes, and sensations designed for ultimate relaxation. They floated through breathtaking sunrises and sunsets and gazed upon majestic mountains and rushing rivers. They held hands through it all although never physically touching. They gazed into each others eyes through the relaxing winds and wished they could be forever together, living free in paradise.

Prana is the same from one space to another.
Life isn't real until you care.
And communiqué stretches across vast reaches
When you feel what another has.

Destiny ransoms the heart to fly,
And hurts in-flight strengthen inner sight,
And dreams fulfilled,
Smile on mortal days.

After floating they slipped into the herbal whirlpool. The swirling herbals soothed their sore and aching muscles. Jennifer and Derek received some shocked looks as they sat together in the swirling pool. They were taking chances. Derek was content to listen to the gentle bubbling warm liquid as the herbal warm waters drew, disposed, and deionized bodily poisons. Jenniper broke the melancholy quiet. "We need to go to Reverend H tonight," she pleaded. Derek only shrugged placidly but did not reply. She said, "I have joined the cult," with apprehension. He knew little of religions, churches, or cults and cared even less for them. He just wanted to be with Jenniper. He felt happy with her. He wanted to savor every moment they were together, more than ever. He would not see her for at least two years after departing for Mercury. He might not see her again. He was blue but it was better than being blue alone. "I want you with me at the service," she said hopefully. "I do not care if we are seen together now."

Her pleading radiant eyes were bright and sparkling. He managed a smile. His hopeless mood drifted easily away as if extracted by the warm cleansing whirlpool, but she was the cure.

6

Cult of What Is

The filtered floating oceanic city named Wafton was linked to other corporate cities by tunnel and tube both on and under land and water. The gigantic eggshells shielded residents from the killing rays of the sun, once guarded by ozone, and filtered the now poisonous atmosphere. The bubble cities were designed to withstand the fierce global storms endlessly raging. Centuries of unabated unsustainable consumption, production, pollution, and waste left the global climate in pure chaos and the environment destroyed. Without ozone the effects from sun spots, solar winds, and solar flares were immediately deadly. The world was wobbling and breaking apart as polar shifts, earthquakes, volcanic eruptions, tidal waves, tsunamis, landslides, piano-size hail, tornadoes, and hurricanes all rained down on the corporate parade.

The cities of the world were dominated by teracorps endlessly competing in ruthless perpetual profit. Corporations began as simple charters once allowing businessmen to provide a service, protect assets, and avoid personal liability. In simpler times, these entities were good sources of products and jobs, as loyal workers organized and competed with other corporations. Human rights were granted to corporations and corporations began to acquire property and power. Corporations acquired the ability to live forever without regard to national boundaries or laws. Transnational corporations grew to terascale proportions and became known as teracorps. Governments realized too late that these Frankenstein entities they helped to create were now in complete control of the globe. A New World Order emerged.

After the final world war, teracorps abolished all world governments and human rights. A small collection of extremely wealthy individuals seized ownership of all shares of all corporations. This elite club became known as the Shareholders. They were considered gods and were thought to be immortal. The Shareholders viewed the ruthless competition between teracorps as good sport. Corporate policy was the only law. All were conceived in labs, programmed, and assigned to projects where they toiled as corporate slaves.

Derek and Jenniper stole into a tunneled walkway which opened into a crowded boulevard filled with ragged street people begging and hustling to survive. The system outcasts lived worse than slaves. Small makeshift shops lined the cluttered boulevard selling everything from prostitution, to contraband, to exotic surgeries and tattoos, to stolen trinkets. There were drug pubs, VR tanks for every fantasy, and greasy micro-pod diners. This was the end of the line for those not in the system, and a dangerous place for a slave with credits. There was a waltzing fool, waltzing alone, and they paused for a moment and could almost hear the silent music the old man waltzed to. They flagged a jalopy taxi driven by a droid who looked to be in worse shape than his vehicle. If it was possible for a droid to become a wino, this one had achieved. The vehicle sputtered and slowly lifted them high within the ocean city dome well above the stench of the boulevard below. They watched the desperate faces disappear into the smoking underworld as the taxi coughed and climbed and rode the thick air. The droid muttered as they were taken above the production peaks protruding from ominous purple streaks and washes of deep red skies. Turquoise filtering balloons were distributed throughout the strange atmosphere, in hopes of studying the cause of the crimson colored foreign chemicals.

"The sky is bleeding," Jenniper remarked darkly.

"I am sure they will figure it out," said Derek. "The human race has worse problems."

The android pilot suddenly hollered, "You two shut the hell up back there!" He adjusted the webcam to better face his two young passengers so authorities would have less trouble viewing. He shot them a wild intoxicated look, strange to see in a droid, and took another swig.

"We are seeing effects of problems no one can solve," replied Jenniper ignoring the drunken droid pilot. "More people will die. This planet is rapidly becoming too hostile to support life. There are millions of diseases now with no cures thriving in a devastating climate while our decadent world dictators create a population of slaves for their own pleasure, all happening in this century. There's no time left for answers," said Jenniper with foreboding.

"Prophets have proclaimed the end was near for generations and yet the human race survives. There were storms, decadence, and disease before this century. Don't kid yourself," said Derek with a smirk.

"Not like these storms, decadence, or disease," countered Jenniper. "This world is lost," she said softly as if talking to herself. "There's the cult," she loudly told the droid. "Put us down anywhere on the roof."

"You can damn sure bet I will little lady," replied the droid as his tongue stuck out in concentration during the approach. There was a feeling of falling as the jalopy taxi descended rapidly and surprisingly soundlessly, gliding to the top of the old cult building. The taxi softly touched down then lurched and loudly coughed. Derek handed him a card and the droid slid it through the slot and handed it back. "Your account will be charged the amount shown on the meter. Thank you and have a nice day," slurred the droid. They scrambled onto the roof of the cult. With credits collected and canned farewell out of the way, the droid yelled "crazy sons of bitches!" as he pulled away.

The entrance to the cult was a rooftop polyhedron. They approached as an unseen voice called out, "Greetings and Welcome!" Jenniper led through a triangle shaped blanket of thick white light with a membrane in the center parting as they entered a spacious garden scene.

Derek was astounded at the sight of multitudes of plants filling the vestibule. The garden surrounding them was manicured to perfection.

The loving hands of an expert horticulturist must have nurtured such beautiful specimens. They bent over and gazed in awe into the intricacies of a little known bloom. The sweet fragrances filled them with euphoric serenity as they strolled past gently flowing waterfalls down the path to a transfer cube.

"Reminds me of Paradan," sighed Derek as he took a deep breath and smiled at her.

"You keep dreaming and dreaming about Paradan. You are a hopeless dreamer, Derek," said Jenniper smiling playfully.

"I don't see any webcams, but who would see them hidden here," said Derek.

"There aren't any here," she said.

"Then come here," he demanded.

"Why should I?" she giggled and ran down the path.

"You know you cannot outrun me!" he called out as she skipped through the garden ahead of him. He sprinted and caught up to her and wrapped his arms around her waist. She giggled again and turned in his arms and they passionately embraced.

"Who said I wanted to outrun you?" she said softly. They kissed and looked deep into each other's eyes. Her eyes were blue and radiant and his were yellow and blazing.

"Let's stay close forever," said Derek longingly into her deep blue eyes.

"You have my heart. I will be with you always," said Jenniper truly. They held each other a moment longer and then they stepped into the transfer cube.

The young couple seated themselves in a pew in the main assembly hall. Other cult members were already seated and had their heads bowed in silent prayer. Jenniper bowed her head also in prayer. Derek had no experience with prayer but he bowed his head and tried to pray. He thanked the higher power for Jenniper, and for their health. He requested that they might somehow stay together. He could think of nothing else to pray for and his mind wandered to recent events. Things had gone bad. He didn't have much time left with Jenniper. He found her hand and held it as she continued to pray. He tasted the spice on his lips from the vegetable juice and wished he could have another one.

Jenniper squeezed Derek's hand and flashed him a sexy smile, and he returned an irreverent grin. A distinguished man with white dreadlocks down to his waist stepped to the center podium. This was Reverend H, the underground cult leader. Derek had heard tales of the reclusive shaman but had never seen him before. The old man's face bore the hard lines of age but his eyes were vibrant and his body was lean. He moved with youthful vigor and it was difficult to judge his true age. The priest began without introduction.

"Three hundred million years ago there lived an advanced race of beings in another galaxy far from Milky Way. In this place, generations of warfare arose among supernaturalists concerning whose god was authentic. A unified belief system eventually emerged as the victor of many global wars dominated and then determined the authentic god. This was not the end of trouble for the supernaturalists. They soon were at war with the naturalists.

The supernaturalists and naturalists fought over the existence of god, and they fought over whether evolved beings were inherently good or evil. Supernaturalists held the tenet that all intelligent life was instinctively evil, and thoughts and desires from within must be eradicated. They believed all beings must strictly adhere to laws divinely delivered. They shunned self-improvement because they believed the inherent evil within all was only curable through external divine intervention. Naturalists maintained that an external god was an imaginative creation, that sentient beings were good by nature although strongly influenced by learned values, and that all answers came from within.

This final conflict gained intensity until an apocalypse. Naturalists did not make the greatest warriors because they were also pacifists. The naturalists were eventually exterminated by the zealous more powerful supernaturalists. The victorious supernaturalists then embarked upon a missionary crusade to save the universe. Transmissions flooded the cosmos, preaching the good word to all planets showing any sign of life. The transmissions demanded that all worlds believe, repent, and convert, or else face the final judgment of the one authentic god.

Earth was void of sentient human life at the time and unaware of this intergalactic sermon. Our world was in its infancy with only one land mass and one ocean. The land and water were ruled by the dreadful dinosaurs of old. Those fearsome creatures were innocently oblivious to the advanced intergalactic supernaturalists. These pious aliens received no response from our young planet which was so low on the evolutionary scale at that point in time. We did not believe, repent, convert, or even respond so we were targeted for nullification.

The supernaturalists worldview was founded in irrationality and they ultimately self-destructed. Ironically, their ignorance far exceeded our greatest collective intelligence. They were an advanced race, vastly more advanced than we are today. Proof of the intergalactic sermon was uncovered long ago in natural receiving materials. This is a guarded secret of our rulers, the Shareholders, because they know the consequences of this story. I will now tell you the rest of the story. We were targeted for nullification long ago by an extinct race. Even though they are long gone, we are still targeted. Our destruction, initiated three hundred million years ago, is still going to happen and it will happen soon.

We must leave this world and start over. There is no chance of survival here. I have constructed an ark to navigate the seas of the space-time continuum and there is room for all. We will escape this slavery and seek out the liberty and dignity we deserve. The universe is free and endless. Pack up your lives and come with me."

Derek and Jenniper remained in the pew after the sermon finished. Cult members began to make their way out of the assembly hall. The young couple enjoyed just sitting. They must be in their separate apartment modules soon. The cult members did not appear upset that they were sitting together.

"I have a question for him," said Derek. He winked at Jenniper and squeezed her hand. She gave him a cautious nod. They made their way to the front of the auditorium where Reverend H was seated. The cult leader leaned on the armrest of the wooden bench as they approached. Derek spoke first. "You can't be for real. How do you plan to leave this world?" Jenniper was embarrassed. She was shocked by his irreverent boldness. She hoped he would respect Reverend H as she did.

A faint smile flashed across the face of Reverend H. "I purchased approval, an easy trick when dealing with programmed beings," declared the white haired priest.

"The Shareholders will chase you down," shot back Derek. "Do you consider the people who follow you to be programmed beings?" asked the young slave, yellow eyes burning in mistrust. Jenniper stood beside him looking very disturbed and had to speak.

"Derek is my companion," she said. "He is unfamiliar with our plans," said Jenniper reverently.

Reverend H smiled again and bowed his head. "The event I spoke of is real. We begin the exodus now while surprise is on our side. The global credit system and the slavery that we endure will soon be a memory. I leave only robotic preachers broadcasting sermons in hopes others will learn and also find a way out."

"What good are robotic preachers if there are no tickets to sightsee the cosmos?" asked Derek sarcastically.

"What is does not care what we believe is. It simply is," sighed Reverend H.

As they left the old cult, Jenniper wondered, "How could you talk to him that way?" She was still upset.

"His plan is not rational. Can't you see that? He may be a nice old man but he is crazy," said Derek.

"Is the way we live rational?" She asked fiercely. He had no answer for her as they boarded the shuttle to take them back to the terminal where they would part. The shuttle bus was rickety and the ride was bumpy to the switch terminal. He looked through the glass at the cracked concrete tunnel flying past. He let his hand touch her knee. She was off somewhere else. They stepped off the bus into switch terminal. Her hurt look softened and she put her hand on his arm. "Don't blame Reverend H. He is good. He doesn't just tell us what we want to hear. He speaks the truth as he sees it from his heart. Do you believe me, Derek?" Her eyes swelled with tears.

"I believe you, Jenniper," he replied. "I don't want to be right if it means losing you," and he kissed her soft lips.

7

The Shareholders

High in the heavily guarded chambers of the pillowed quarters of the Shareholders, several sadistic beings sat in a circular fashion. They were of various races, some male some female, although this could not be easily distinguished due to plastic surgeries and genetic repairs. They were human monstrosities, content with motionlessness. Naked androids, all very small in size but with perfect human proportions, appeared to be the only life in the choking smoke filled place. The naked androids scurried to and from the kitchen, laboring under goblets and platters and other desires of their masters.

"Several slaves, production units, are in need of repair and some are thought to be irreparable. The latter will be elegantly terminated." Something laughed brutally then contained itself.

"Make it so," said another.

A morbid thing gagged and spat "Let's cut through the crap. If these production units, or slaves, whatever you want to call them, are getting smart then waste them. We don't need to know or care."

"I brought it up because the numbers are increasing," retorted the first.

"I have news more interesting than that. We're about to participate in a solar probe. Our craft will plunge deeper into the sun than ever before, sending back data transmissions until the microsecond it is vaporized. The unsuspecting crew will serve as subjects of experimentation informing us how close they come to the center of the sun. We now have the finest solar ship ever built. Droid, refill my bowl!"

"The new god needs a spectacular event to mark her inauguration and these misfits will serve as an example to all. We planned to push the spacecraft to solar destruction anyway. We will load the shuttle as if it were on a normal mission and drive it into the heart of Sol. We'll see an across the board increase in production as a result. These fear tactics are so delightful."

A deep voiced Shareholder cut in, yellow smoke pouring from its mouth and nostrils as it spoke "Production and profit do not matter anymore. Perpetuation is all that we care about."

"Some corporate slaves have learned about perpetuation themselves, living over one hundred years with no degeneration. They don't possess our immortality drugs or vaccines but many realize that aging is just another disease," speculated another between slurps and slugs of wine.

The first one coughed and sneezed drenching a little droid in slime as they watched open mouthed and unblinking as a miniature servant struggled to stand in the translucent muck. The Shareholder then yelled out "We are the only gods of this world!"

Another genetic monstrosity cruelly chuckled and growled. "We will not be beaten!" and then he viciously pounded the closest little droid to the floor with a massive fist. Screams of agony were silenced by crunching bones. The Shareholder proudly noted "Dead in only four strokes!" They roared, cackled, and clapped thunderously in approval. More drinks and smokes were brought in.

A tiny girl droid stood in the kitchen doorway and shuddered at the horrid spectacle. She wished she had never been created, a feeling which her small synthesized brain had never been programmed to process or possess, yet here and now she wished to die.

8

Goodbye

We wanted to go out easy.
We wanted to go out slow.
But the big machine took us up,
Lost in star drenched flow…

Derek woke from a timeless slumber. The poem lingered on from his blissful dream touched sleep. He stretched his arms to the floor and flicked until he began to swing, letting the words to the dream poem dance in his clear relaxed mind. From his rocking view, his bedroom was an anomaly of skyward gravity disappearing and appearing as he blinked.

Appliances began to turn themselves on. He heard his recorded voice reminding him of something he had been meaning to do.

He curled up gracefully and placed his index finger on the bar above. The clamps around his ankles released in unison and executing a clean tuck he landed feet padding to the floor. His well conditioned limbs felt the uncomfortable twinge at being instantly inverted to their normal upright position.

The young corporate slave awakened from bat-like slumber and stepped into a pulsating beam shower. Adaptive bio-mechanisms came to life along with previous anxieties. Mercury had been turned into a big machine, and it already was the ultimate desert. Mercury nights dropped to a chilly -300 degrees and the 800 degree days were always bright and sunny, but Mercury was no vacation.

Mercury was plastered in solar panels. Slotted stations were used to house the repair crew. The slotted stations were constantly on the move to stay on the cool side, for repairs were impossible on the hot side. Mercury experienced a day and a half between sunrises, due to a slowing of the planet as it neared aphelion in its elliptical orbit. A Mercury year was 88 Earth days and a Mercury day lasted about 59 Earth days. There was always rail damage on the other side preventing a smooth 7700 kilometer run. The robots were always busy making repairs. He would be there 13 Mercury days, a little over two Earth years, but counting days seemed shorter. The Mercury solar power generation plant suffered constant equipment damage from unfathomable extremes in temperature.

He went to repair robots, a new assignment for him, but not a new task. Robot repair was a skill most laborers acquired soon. Robots in turn repaired the panels, the generation plants, the transmission towers, the rails, and the slotted stations. He was also installing seismographs to monitor Mercury-quakes aggravated by changes in the magnetic field of the iron-cored planet. All tasks were precisely defined. He would earn triple credits while he lived and worked in the slotted stations of Mercury, but he did not care. There was no choice in the matter.

The finish cycle of his morning beam shower began, mostly warm air treated with antibacterial agents and skin conditioners and finishing with a protective microbiotic film. The shower finished and he was completely dry. He stepped to the mirror to shave with a hair dissolver. He enjoyed the simple ritual of shaving. Simple acts with positive results were rare. "Have courage," he said into the mirror. He padded his face with a warm towel. He was stunned to see Jenniper in the doorway.

"You should not be here. I do not want to get you in more trouble," said Derek. He threw his towel over the webcam which then began to beep. An alarm would also begin sounding in a remote monitoring command center and, before long, the troopers would come.

"It doesn't matter. I am leaving also. I'm going with the cult. I have already packed what I need." A backpack was stuffed and strapped to her shoulders.

"Don't do this," said Derek. "Do you know what this means? We may never see each other again. You cannot be serious."

"I am as serious. I don't have any other choice. I'll not survive another two years here." She hugged him hard with her beautiful face buried in his chest.

He felt a lump in his throat as he choked. "Please wait for me. I'll return in two years. I know it's a long time. I will be back. I promise you."

She sobbed and he felt her tears rolling down his chest. "You will not be back to this place," she cried. "I will never see you again."

"This is crazy. The Shareholders will not let you leave." He was afraid for her.

"There won't be anything left of this place in two years," she said as she tried to regain composure.

"I don't believe the old man, Jenniper. There is no impending destruction. He dreamed it up. He's desperate and has frightened you into joining him. That's how he works, how he gets followers." The webcam alarm increased in volume and intensity.

"We will never see each other again," she said and he could feel her body trembling. They held each other for a time. They were at a crossroads. "Come with me, Derek. Join the cult with me so that we can leave together." She looked into his stubborn yellow eyes and saw the answer before he spoke.

"You know I can't give up a chance for freedom or a chance to own a piece of Paradan. I cannot give up the dreams we made together."

"The cult is going to an untamed planet, pristine and wild. No one owns the land there. Derek, I do not believe Paradan is real anymore."

He refused to believe that Paradan was a lie. "What planet?" he asked.

"It will be beautiful, our new home, far from slavery, almost eleven light years away. We travel at ninety percent light speed, twice our normal mass. We will arrive in less than a year by our clocks, but by Earth clocks thirteen years will have passed. It is in the solar system Epsilon Eridani."

"I thought those planets were uninhabitable."

"They tell us this but they have lied. It is a cover-up. The Shareholders want it for themselves."

"Troopers will be here soon. Wait for me here in Wafton. I will finish the Mercury assignment early. I will be back before the two years. You know that I want to be with you more than anything."

"We'll be together again, Derek. I know it now. I just wanted to see you one more time before you left." She held him tight and he wrapped his arms around hers and they were as close as two people could be. She made her escape from his apartment module before the troopers arrived.

He left the girl he loved only because his feelings were now buried much like the hazy past of the only world he knew. He reassured himself they would be together again.

As his mobile apartment module detached and sky lifted to the dock, he sat in his recliner and fumbled with a crumpled and worn brochure of Paradan. He didn't notice when his apartment module was attached to the Mercury bound craft Solarion at the launching port.

He casually looked up from the brochure of Paradan as the now loaded vessel rumbled then erupted in screaming violence like a startled beast beyond all imagination. He yawned and stretched nonchalantly as escape velocity was obliterated. Someday he would own a piece of Paradan, and then they would build a home together.

9

Ship of Fools

The ship, Solarion, continued accelerating well past the required 11.2 kilometers per second escape velocity freeing itself from the cumbersome atmosphere of Earth. The webscreen in Derek's apartment module displayed the projection of the flight path to the little iron rock, Mercury, in a three dimensional spherical form.

He flicked to a blank input e-mail screen and entered. "Jenniper I'll think about what you said. I'll finish this assignment early. If you are gone, I will catch up. I miss you already." He did not send the message. His outgoing mail would be scanned. It was better not to send anything yet. He would wait until the time was right.

He left his apartment module. to tour the ship. There were faint melodious sounds as he ambled through the mazes of corridors. The sporadic music was interestingly complex but curiously non-machinelike. Most music was computer generated these days. There was little salvaged after the final war. He had never heard anything like this before as he approached the bow of the ship where the volume increased. As the bow entrance retracted, a tidal wave of engulfing sound stampeded his unsuspecting senses. He gasped and planted his stance expecting to be blown over.

A wiry figure standing in the center of the observatory deck was wildly fingering and slicing at a thin black rectangular bar. The musician was deeply involved in the instrument and whipped his multicolored shaggy head of hair back and forth in time. The wiry musician did not notice when Derek entered the galley.

The musician wielded six laser beams across an ebony board altering different combinations of sequences of beam lengths on one hand and disrupting the amplitudes with the other. The instrument emitted rainbows of light, seared, wailed, and screamed in rapid pitch movements and progressions which were too complex to absorb analytically.

The musician looked up and saw Derek standing there and a detached grin flashed across the musician's face but he continued to play as if the musical bar would not let him go. He ripped through more smoking scales and hypnotizing rhythms until the beams faded away by adjusting a knob at one end. "A few more aminos," said the musician as he unstrapped the instrument and unscrewed a compartment on the back. He headed for the galley connected to the observation bow of the ship. Derek watched intently.

"Aminos?" asked Derek with curiosity.

"Bio-drive is the best," said the musician moving to a counter where small vials were lined. "The programmed proteins receive signals from laser sensitive spectropickups to drive the microamps."

"What's it called?" asked Derek.

"This is a laser axe," replied the musician while inserting drops from the collection of vials. "I built it with the help of a neutrino microscope and some hacked DNA code. Just a few more drops to complete the mixture," said the musician with concentrated engrossment. "The sponge valves permeate a floating vacuum encapsulating the beams for precise manipulations," added the musician.

"My name is Derek, and yours?" asked the youth.

"Benny 42," replied the wiry musician. "I hope my music wasn't too loud."

"These walls are thick, but when I opened the door to the bow of the ship could I hear your music clearly. How long have you been a musician?" Derek asked.

"I have studied as long as I can remember, but didn't build this until recently. I was raised by someone who fortunately kept my music a secret until I proved worthy. They do not like it, but it is tolerated. I was placed on probation because of my most recent compositions, but they haven't taken the axe yet. The laser axe takes it to another dimension."

"It is like nothing I have heard before," said Derek truthfully.

"How long before we land on Mercury?" Benny asked as he secured a containment cap.

"The web says about 85 hours, since we are cruising at 300 kilometers per second with respect to Sol. What's your assignment?" asked Derek.

"I signed up for robot repair. To be honest I volunteered, because I needed the credits to pay for my probation. I didn't have much of a choice. You know how it is. I know my way around robot guts as well as anyone," said Benny 42.

"Robot repair is also my assignment although I didn't volunteer. I am sure we will keep busy," said Derek.

"We'll be stuck together for awhile, so I'll watch the volume levels," Benny said. "I don't want to lose the axe, so tell me before you file any reports, if the music bothers you."

"I am not the report filing type," replied Derek. "Your music sounds good to me."

The galley door retracted, and a silver haired man with an apron on came in. "Are you the cook?" asked Benny. "I used some aminos."

"I'm not the cook. The cook's a droid. I'm a psychophysicist, for what it's worth," he replied. "I'm too hungry to wait for the droid, so I came down to cook something myself." He began opening drawers, clanging pots, and dumping various powdery substances into a bowl. He mixed in a few liquids forming a pulp then poured the conglomeration into a condenser. He stood over the machine tapping his foot and then extracted a flat cake which he cut into squares and consumed wolfishly. He then turned his attention to the others. "What is that thing?" he asked.

"Some call it a hell-raiser and some have even called it a rainmaker," said Benny removing terminal nodes from his fingertips.

"But I usually call it a laser axe. It is a musical instrument of my own making."

"I also have an interest in making music. I have researched the cerebral effects of sound wave patterns and was even schooled in music in my youth," stated the silver haired psychophysicist, as he rubbed his hands on the white apron.

"Really?" smiled Benny indulgently.

"Before your time, before music was restricted as it is now. After tutoring, I was told I would spend my life as a scientist. I have no regrets with the career chosen for me," said the psychophysicist.

"I wish I had lived back when there were not so many restrictions," said Benny. "I have created a mind bending, soul piercing musical tool, but I am not allowed to share or entertain. The dimensions of musical expression have been curtailed. I was born a hundred years too late," lamented Benny.

"I can accompany your music with telepathy," mused the psychophysicist, snacking on condensed cake. Benny and Derek looked at each other incredulously. "My name is Dr. Zeek, the creator of neuroton theory. I have developed a practical application of telepathy known as neuroton projection. Neurotons are quantums of information created and utilized by the brain. I believe neurotons are transmitted and received by brains with similar response structures. The neuroton link may be enhanced by synergistic spatial orientation. I am planning a long distance neuroton projection from Mercury to Earth."

"Soon we will not be able to trust voices within our own heads," said Derek darkly.

"Without safeguards, you will not be able to trust your own ideas. I will not release my invention until it is safe. I recently synthesized a biochemical which amplifies neuroton transmission capability and eliminates spatial orientation requirements. Telepathic strength is always better with synergy, but this biochemical provides temporary amplification." Dr. Zeek produced a palm-sized disk and sprayed a short burst into each of his blinking eyes. "Takes a few moments," said Dr. Zeek, through glazed watering eyes. Derek and Benny were surprised to then hear the voice of Dr. Zeek say, "This is what I am talking about," although his lips had not moved. "Can you hear me clearly? Should I add another dose?" His vocal cords never vibrated.

"I can clearly hear you in my mind. Amazing," said Benny, shocked.

"I too can hear your voice," marveled Derek.

"Can you also receive thoughts?" asked Benny.

"The biochemical spray only amplifies natural neuroton projections," replied Dr. Zeek telepathically. "I can receive thoughts just like you are sending now. We all normally receive neuroton transmissions, but they are processed by our subconscious mind. This biochemical amplifies projections so they are noticed by the conscious mind," added Dr. Zeek. His mouth remained closed. His lips never moved. The android cook had walked in and started meal preparations. The cook occasionally paused to curiously observe the humans conversing, because they strangely appeared to be talking to Dr. Zeek, who simply stood saying nothing. "This induced neuroton projection is my practical form of telepathy," transmitted Dr. Zeek.

"How long does the effect last?" Derek asked. The cook stopped and stared again. The android cook did not possess a brain capable of receiving neuroton projections, and was having trouble processing the conversation.

"The amplification lasts several minutes, enough time for a brief message. As the dosage increases so does the range but the effect still lasts about the same amount of time," transmitted Dr. Zeek. "You both must have similar response structures which enhances the neuroton link," projected Dr. Zeek. "At this short distance, neuroton projection is usually very effective with the biochemical spray."

"So you can use this to somehow add to my music?" Benny 42 asked. The android cook was now utterly perplexed and staring at the humans. A saucer fell from the cook's hands and shattered. They chuckled as the cook sheepishly began to pick up the broken pieces.

"I can even add accompaniments to my own voice," transmitted Dr. Zeek. "This aspect of neuroton projection takes advantage of the multidimensional nature of the mind," added Dr. Zeek, who stood making no verbal sound at all.

"Is it possible to record these neuroton projections?" asked Derek. Benny and Derek were now very impressed.

"Only the human mind can detect neuroton projections," transmitted Dr. Zeek, merely smiling but never making a sound. "This explains why our android cook does not understand our conversation."

"You should invent a neuroton recorder," said Benny thoughtfully.

"I would love to be the inventor of a neuroton recorder. I have some competition in that area, but I hope to be the first to record and play back telepathic thoughts," Dr. Zeek transmitted telepathically.

Derek returned to his apartment module feeling better. He ordered an ice cold vegetable juice from the kitchen with extra spice. His head was filled with verse and images, surprisingly hopeful in nature. He was always coloring with youthful recklessness the gray canvas which he had been programmed never to touch.

Back on Earth, a new god had been elected by the teracorps for the Shareholders. She was wickedly beautiful, just as the Shareholders were wickedly disgusting. She would in time become like them, but that was years away. For now, she was the newest Shareholder, the recipient of untold wealth and longevity. She would speak on behalf of the Shareholders to all corporate slaves of the modern world.

10

Anticipation

At the prow of the Solarion, the observatory deck was flooded with filtered blue illumination. The cosmos rippled with the warped tracks of gravity and electromagnetic waves carrying power and encrypted data. The waves intricately intertwined to form fantastically complex networks. This unstoppable technical evolution replaced the cabled networks, concrete roads, shipping routes, and flight paths of the past. There were also violent waves ripping through the vastness, and causing instant destruction. There were no longer governments to wage interstellar war. Governments were long gone. There were only profit-hungry teracorps making gains in this sector or that. Ships were annihilated in ruthless fashion, thanks to the inalienable right to prosper. Rights once granted to humans were eventually only granted to corporations, and human rights were all taken away. The rights of corporations expanded. The world governments were eliminated and the Shareholders took control. The New World Order was put in place. The teracorps were the eventual evolution of acquisitions, mergers, and monopolies of the past corporations. Enercorp was one such teracorp, in the business of providing energy to the world.

Sol was a pleasant orange stain on the spherical screen of the deck, strikingly larger than usual. Venus hung conspicuously below like an oily black teardrop dripping from the eye of an unblinking macrocosm. Silhouettes of satellites, stations, and ships blurred by, frozen in the distance for an instant then streaking past. Spacewaste posed the worst threat of collision due to its relatively small size and the short window between detection and response. This was more a problem for less sophisticated spacecraft with inadequate force fields or detection systems. Large debris was tracked, collected, and deposited into galactic garbage disposals. These synthetic black holes became the home of cosmic debris, along with the unfortunate victims who also rested there.

The crew had time to kill. Benny delved into musical diversion, and Dr. Zeek accompanied with neuroton projection. Dr. Zeek was far older although he did not always act his age. Dr. Zeek was part of generation Z, the last generation of natural born humans. All generations after generation Z were bred in tubes. Derek offered up some of his verses for any musical inspiration they might bring. He considered his writings to be simple song lyrics, not anything as grandiose as poetry. They reacted positively to his youthful words put to verse. This surprised Derek. He never expected positive reactions.

Derek stood below the dwarfing screen dome in awe of the breathtaking display of color, locked in billowing waves of sound, bombarded by neurotons from his own secret notebook of lyrics. Benny 42 displayed an uncanny ability to convert verses into music, and Dr. Zeek accompanied with neuroton projections. They created a major musical diversion on the prow of the Solarion as the hardy little ship hurtled for Mercury. The laser axe mixed well with the neuroton vocal projections. The laser axe possessed a life-force of its own as Benny worked the beams.

The verses taken from Derek's secret scroll were against corporate policy. The music pouring from Benny 42 was tolerated, although he was on probation for his latest compositions. Derek kept his writings to himself, only sharing occasional lyrics with Jenniper. He wrote of the old world, a world he never knew. He was infatuated with the people and places of the lost centuries. He studied all glimpses of untainted history he could uncover. Those were times of great freedom but the beginning of the end. He wished he had been born then. Maybe he would have made a difference. He wished he could have lived a life of freedom and choice.

Derek thought of Jenniper and he could picture her beauty, her enchanting eyes, and her sexy smile. He loved the way her cheeks flushed. He could hear the sound of her soft voice, and he longed for her gentle touch. He wanted to share his life with her but that wasn't going to happen if she went with the cult. He worried what would happen if she were caught. He wondered about the crazy tale of destruction. He hoped she would not go. He hoped the migration talk was just a way to raise contributions. He brooded. He no longer felt the awe of majestic space, but instead fought a biting sense of futility.

He was only eighteen but he felt like eighty. He told himself they would be together again. He swore with ferocity rare in an age of clinical passivity. He had struggled countless times to answer the riddles of leaders and gods, only to grapple with their elusive reasoning, until nothing was true except survival. His survival depended on Jenniper, his only love.

Survival was written into bio-patched DNA programs and the programs into people. People were conceived in laboratories to meet market demands and placed into projects they were programmed to specialize in. Those who grew sullen, restless, difficult, or rebellious with the endless routine of profit-making were labeled as nonprogrammable. Many nonprogrammable slaves were terminated which meant death in the streets, or at the hands of the police troopers.

Derek carried the nonprogrammable label but the reasons why escaped him. Flashes occasionally came as nightmares come while enjoying restful sleep. Obscured images of taunting faces bled through. Faces distort becoming more probing and feverishly intent. They wanted the boy to answer and agree but the boy would not. The boy tried to answer and the taunting would return. Discomforting as they were, Derek accepted the images as part of his past. It was not to be trusted, just as history was not to be trusted.

"She is hotter than Mercury," said a small-framed woman standing next to Derek, but he could not hear what she said. The laser axe was too overwhelming. He had not met her before. She must have been drawn to the observatory deck from the emanating musical neurotons. Her lips were moving as she pointed to Venus. The neurotons and laser axe were overpowering.

Sailing through celestial seas,
Off to worlds unknown.

"The continual atmosphere of Venus makes her much hotter than Mercury because the heat is contained," continued the woman but Derek could not hear her at all above the music intermingled with neuroton projections.

We pondered lost destinies,
On the pebble we called home.

"The hottest place on Mercury is often 400 degrees cooler than Venus," said the woman and now Derek heard quite well. The flood of laser licks and neuroton projections had ceased. "I've studied thermodynamics all my life. I'm a thermonuclear engineer. My name is Ami 36."

Derek politely bowed. "My name is Derek," he said and smiled to the woman standing there.

"What are you being sent to do?" she asked.

"Measuring Mercury quakes and repairing robots," said the young slave.

"Mercury quakes?" asked Ami 36.

"Mercury quakes are increasing. They think the planetary magnetic field has shifted, like the pole shifts on Earth, and the shift has something to do with it," said Derek "I usually spend my time under the ocean, mining resources, so this is new for me."

"Mercury quakes are nasty," replied Ami 36. "I hope we don't have to experience one while we are there."

"They have damaged panels, rails, and control stations. The robots are overworked and malfunctioning and in trouble trying to keep up.

What is your assignment?" asked Derek.

"I will be upgrading thermographs and replacing solar panels," replied Ami.

"You'll be busy too," said Derek. "I am sure there is widespread damage to deal with."

"So who are they?" asked Ami.

"Benny is the one with multicolored hair playing the musical bar. Dr. Zeek is a psychophysicist who has a telepathic invention he plans to test from Mercury. Did you hear Dr. Zeek singing while the music was playing?" asked Derek.

"I thought it was from the ship synthesizer," replied Ami.

"No. They were neuroton projections, telepathic transmissions that you can hear in your mind." Derek said.

"This doesn't seem normal to me," said Ami 36, amused at what she was told. "This may be a fun trip."

"I just want to get it over with and get back to Wafton." retorted Derek.

"Why would you want to go back there? I get away from that place whenever I can, even if some danger is involved," replied Ami.

"I have reasons," Derek said, as he thought about Jenniper. "You really enjoy getting away?"

"I hate Wafton and I want to live somewhere else. Is that so terrible?" Ami 36 asked.

"Your honesty is refreshingly rare. All cities are the same. It doesn't make any difference to me," said Derek. "This project is suicidal but we have no choice. I want to be free like any slave, but I must first return to someone."

"I am happy for people who have managed to find someone in spite of corporate policy," said Ami 36 knowingly.

"She is special," was all he could find words to say. He did not say more. Jenniper may not be waiting when he returned. He hoped she would not go with the religious cult but if she had, he would find a way to catch up. Venus hung larger than ever from the filtered screen dome of the observatory deck.

"At least it is a nice view," offered Ami 36.

11

Grooming Day

The new god didn't quite feel the part yet. She was being subjected to a complete physical examination and after the diagnostic analysis she would be thoroughly cleansed and modified as needed. Each and every organ, gland, bone, tissue, nerve, vessel, and the systems and subsystems thereof needed to be scrutinized for the process to be successful. Every cell in the body of the new god would eventually be checked for damaged DNA, and all DNA mutations would be repaired. The task usually went quickly since the initial screening of candidates limited the selection to only the finest of human breeds. Candidates were conceived, nurtured, tutored, and selected by the Shareholders. Meaningless mock elections finalized the process.

At this moment she lay naked under an organ scope-probe. The robotic device sent selected data pulses and recorded the slightest reverberations while imaging the workings of each glandular system for analysis.

The physicians of the past lost much credibility because they insisted on treating only the results of disease. This practice eventually ran its course and failure was evident. Diseases only grew stronger and more insidious. A generation was left addicted to powerful brain and body damaging drugs in this deadly wake of medical incompetence.

These unproductive unfortunate addicts were eliminated as the New World Order took control.

Past physicians believed the best way to treat disease was to attack and destroy the symptoms. There were invasive operations, life-threatening radiation, and addictive drugs with myriads of dangerous side effects. They were unable to cure even minor ailments such as common colds. Psychiatric physicians concocted catch-all disorders and one-size-fits-all syndromes, often possessing no scientific basis whatsoever. Prescribed drugs to suppress symptoms produced side-effects often worse than the disease. The human mind was treated as if it were just another physical organ. There was more profit in symptoms than sources. This led to a healthcare system that no government, corporation, or country could afford. The drug and insurance industries controlled the physicians who controlled the patients. The healthcare monopoly was maintained by mandated insurance policies with drug and insurance corporations deciding what treatments physicians were to prescribe.

With the New World Order, corporate slaves lived longer with less disease. A new generation of slaves was cloned as the population exploded. Curative healthcare was only available to elite members of teracorps. Corporate slaves were healthier than all previous generations, although there was still more disease than ever before. Those with incurable contagious diseases were terminated. Prevention was the only medicine available to common people. Prevention was necessary and the only alternative was death. Aging came to be viewed as just another disease rather than a symptom of growing older. Prevention became the key to health and survival. This caused more population problems as slaves lived longer than ever before. Cures for disease were reserved only for the elites.

"How much longer will I be subjected to this indignity you scientific swine," crowed the new god from underneath the probes.

The biophysicist was aggravated by the disturbance to his concentration but knew it was wise to not show it. "We need to determine the blueprint of your glandular system if you are to be immortal my goddess." He secretly wished she could be sedated for this procedure but accurate readings could only be taken during consciousness. "Just a few more holograms and we'll know the exact characteristics of the hormones to synthesize."

"Just be done with it so I can claim my place among the Shareholders!" She shouted angrily.

"As you wish my new god," replied the biophysicist, a trifle insincerely. She was an exquisite specimen and he hurried himself for fear of someone or something detecting his casual thought crimes.

12

Inauguration

Derek and Ami looked to the direction where the concert previously raged and the android cook was there. He had halted Benny and Dr. Zeek with a frantic waving of his arms. Desperately trying to get their attention, the cook finally succeeded. Dr. Zeek lashed out an exasperated neuroton wave to the humans in the room. "This had better be good!"

"Come! Please come to the webscreen communiqué panels!" announced the cook with serious urgency.

They followed the droid through the transfer cell to the inner recess where the communications heart of the ship was located. The droid went straight to the main webscreen.

There in all her cruel splendor smiled the new god of the modern world. She shone of perfection and ruthlessness beyond compare. She poured forth the rhetoric of her inauguration speech.

"I hereby proclaim myself god of this domain and all of you to be my slaves to do with as I will. Anyone who defies me flirts with doom be it consciously or subconsciously. Free radicals in this realm will be neutralized before they are able to ruin us with their promiscuous behavior. I alone have met the qualifications of new god and now I have joined the Shareholders to speak for them.

Do not be deceived by those who tempt you to die. Right now the first load of free radicals have been sentenced and sent to hell to burn forever. They displayed free and reckless thought each and every one. No more will they spread the mortal disease of liberty or freewill. No more will they conduct themselves as only gods should. The values of a god are not those of a mortal, but do not despair my slaves for I once was mortal and thought and felt much like many of you. I will judge with this in mind but now I am immortal, which is the only state in which true freedom of will and thought should be relished.

You should only be concerned with production and conformity. If you dare to be different then you will die a lonely death and be no more. There is no afterlife as proved by science long ago. The foolish concept of afterlife kept archaic governments in business by giving their subjects hope of a better lot in the next life. This inhibited the people from revolting against their backward systems. Now you are secure with an average 100 year life span and you will die with the assurance that you were productive.

There is at long last peace on Earth. Nationalities and the wars they instigated have been eliminated. All governments are bankrupt and have forfeited their assets. They were all repossessed by teracorps in this wonderful New World Order of Corporate Darwinism. There are no longer wars or rumors of wars. The battles between the teracorps are all part of healthy corporate competition.

Racial and cultural conflicts of the past are all now thankfully gone. Racial activists fought bias with bias, preferential treatment with preferential treatment, which only made matters worse. This was not productive or efficient. There is no longer racial or cultural conflict for now there is only one race, the slave race. Now there is only one culture, the corporate culture."

There were wild hoots and cheers from the crowd of corporate slaves gathered for the speech. Whistles, clapping, and tears of joy from around Earth were captured by webcams and televised by webscreens to those gathered.

"The sinners we send to hell were singled out as hopelessly nonprogrammable, refusing to follow our cultural code of values. They disobeyed corporate policy by engaging in rebellious thinking, and will be terminated in a spectacular manner. We will bury these rebellious thinkers in the center of our solar system as an example for those who may stray. All who knew these souls should forget them forever. Conform and Produce!"

Loud clapping, cheers, and a standing ovation concluded the speech of the new god. The communiqué room was drenched in deathly silence as the transmission faded and realization pounded home. There might be a chance it was the fate of another ship. Derek pictured the flight path projection he had studied in his apartment.

Derek left the chamber with a hard face harboring a tortured racing mind. He entered a transfer cell with the rest of the fear shocked crew close behind. Wordlessly he pressed the location of the navigational center on a colored layout pad. After an upward then forward movement the cell dissipated in the middle of the navigation control room.

The young slave proceeded directly to the flight status display. The projection appeared to be in order, positioning the Solarion in a curved path between Venus and Mercury with the distance to Sol being 80 million kilometers. He ran a path scan and the forecast arrival and landing stats came up nicely. Touch down on Mercury was forecasted in 47 hours. "The flight status looks normal unless this is just a crippled display," he said apprehensively.

"Let's open the ship's system service routines," interjected Benny, the tension affecting his cool manner.

"That sounds like a plan and then check the flight scheduler," said Dr. Zeek, with growing madness in his eyes.

They sifted through the displays for the flight scheduler database. The ship's computer system maintained its own real-time database constantly compared to the scheduler data files. If discrepancies arose, the ship control services automatically notified the ground crew with alarm messages. Earth operators took corrective action. Unplanned discrepancies were not common, so the scheduler data files, trending database, and projection routines were mostly viewed by ground crews.

"There is a password on it," growled Derek as the terminal beeped at his futile access efforts.

"I'll get someone in support who can give us the password," said Dr. Zeek, growing even more agitated.

"This is a message from the Solarion to centrocorp operations. We are requesting technical assistance in system operations," said Dr. Zeek over the webphone.

"Received and acknowledged." There was a slight pause. "What is the problem Solarion?" The centrocorp operator asked.

"We request the scheduler database access password," replied Dr. Zeek.

"You want the scheduler password? That display isn't normally protected. It doesn't matter. Hold for a second. I've got it here," responded the operator.

Derek shut his eyes and pictured a large black hawk swooping down on a small mouse, eminent death for mice in the moonlight. He now realized this crew was composed of misfits just like himself. They were all undoubtedly declared nonprogrammable. His moodiness was seldom kept hidden and few dared to test. The drudgery of routine brought out the worst in him and often he retreated into his secret verses and the welcome release, soothing the rage trapped inside. Without this escape, his occasional displays of frustration left fellow slaves clutching their tightened chests in awestruck fear.

The tech at centrocorp operations was on the mike again. "Don't know why password protection was on the scheduler. Here's the code."

Derek entered the sequence. They stood back and watched with bated breath. The scheduled events came up. The planned flight was divided into a detailed sequence of terse events. Pages of ignition, positioning, thrusting, verification, and more positioning filled the scheduler. The slave intensely skimmed with yellow eyes gleaming into the monitor illumination. They came to the displayed details of the approach and anticipated arrival on Mercury. A gasp escaped from Ami 36. The planned schedule stopped short. There were no landing sequences for Mercury. The sequenced instructions specified staying the present course and continuing into the sun. The window froze. A message popped up. "Access denied." The display then went blank.

A webscreen sphere beside Derek flipped to an endless stream of commercials. It was too much. Tensions long held at bay were loosed. With a curse and blinding speed he drove a knotted fist deep into the webscreen panel. It exploded in a shower of shattered plastic leaving a gaping hole revealing a tangle of useless projection electronics. He ignored his bloody knuckles. "We must gain control of this ship!" he boomed. The others turned from the crackling broken webscreen. Fear was on them all. The droid cook stared with empty eyes focusing on the shattered webscreen, manmade mouth agape.

"Get centrocorp operations on the horn again!" growled Derek in fear and rage.

"We get no response! No one is answering!" barked Dr. Zeek. "They cut us off!"

They were the ones. They were the examples. They were trapped in a ship bound for hell. This was not the mystical soul scorcher of condemned lost souls as created by religion. This was a real physical eternal destruction from flame. This would not be a peaceful easy death, no lazy bones gratefully sleeping on the hill. They were to be burned alive until carbon decomposition. Nothing would be left. They were going to suffer hideous deaths.

"Gain control of the ship!" Derek snarled again. He realized now more than ever that he was different and this crew was different. They were misfits. Much like him, this crew did not belong. His whole life had been torture, fear, and doldrums. His response was to fight back with a ferocity long dead in the hearts of everyone he knew. Jenniper was the only other fighter he had ever known.

The misfit crew worked hard. All attempts to gain access to the control routines were useless. They were locked out and helpless.

The ship possessed unbreakable security and even if the system were completely shut down, internal climate controls and simulated gravitation would then terminate leaving them to drift and die. They tried to enter the protected routines in every imaginable way only to get lost in trivialities, constantly risking the loss of all operation.

The webphone speaker switched on and a booming voice halted the frantic efforts of the little crew. There was laughing. Maybe this was a joke. "Fools," said the voice from the webphone speaker. "You have the honor to die at my hands. I have been appointed to be your executioner and the remote control of your ship is in my hands. Your feeble data manipulations have been entertaining but I now have a job to do."

This booming voice stopped them cold. They could do nothing but listen.

"As you are painfully aware you were chosen to travel into Sol to probe the innermost depths of our sun. We are testing our latest in solar retardant technology. More philosophically, we will test the human will to survive. You will all definitely succumb as the ship is destroyed. We want to see how long you can last, and we are sure that you will try to last as long as possible."

There was again laughing at the other end of the webphone. The little crew listened in silence. The booming executioner began again.

"Gradually the different control mechanisms of the ship will be released for manual operation when retreat is impossible. We want to see if you can make it further with manual intervention. This will only be done in the last moments when you have no choice but to hang on, hang onto life."

There were whispers at the other end. A different voice cut in and addressed the crew.

"As a final note, the Shareholders wish to thank Dr. Zeek for his contributions in the field of neuroton projection. This will be of great service to us in mass brainwashing, a welcome augmentation to our current propaganda program. It is a pity that you did not agree with this useful application." The transmission ended and the webphone speaker turned off.

Dr. Zeek wailed and shrank to the floor.

Mercury was larger and more elusive than ever in the spherical screens. Burning death would soon encompass them all. The ship continued its unchanging course into the solar corona. A vaporizing unfathomable doom churned, lashed, and spit in anticipation.

13

Here Comes the Sun

The long hours blipped past. The frantic endeavors of the fear stricken crew came to naught. No tricky manipulation was effective in cracking the state of the art security system. The hell-bound slaves began to lose direction in the ship's intricacies and complications.

Dr. Zeek was not the same after he learned the plans for his neuroton projection invention. He realized as did the others how calculated this scheme was. They were the examples. He wished the scientific community on Earth would react to his termination and would revolt against the execution of one who had devoted his life selflessly to discovery. His hopes were in vain. He slumped over his terminal in sadness and exhaustion. He finally rose and stumbled into his sleep tank and closed the hatch. He gave up.

The other crew members were also giving in. The hours of no sleep brought fatigue upon them all. One by one, they retired into their apartment modules thoroughly exhausted.

Derek was the only one left standing. He studied a navigational screen projection, which highlighted his glowering face hungry for vengeance. It was a hunger he had never felt so strongly before. He vowed to satisfy his vengeance. He had accepted his fate for too long. Wild thoughts of an imagination unleashed raced through the mind of the young slave. His muscled frame drew strength from sources unknown to him.

In this hour, all the others were in fitful slumber. Derek and the droid were the only ones left standing. He had spent hours and hours in desperate maneuvering of protected control programs too secure to crack. The overwhelming fatigue gnawed at the young slave. His sweat filled locks of hair hung limply on his shoulders. A deep sigh of resign filled his lungs. He was finally free. He never thought freedom would be like this, so frantically short-lived and at such a price.

An unknown voice floated across the communiqué room. The voice touched Derek with a sense of surreal. This was a dream. He would wake up and it would be over soon. He would tell Jenniper all about it and she would smile a sleepy smile. He rubbed his throbbing temples as perspiration flowed over his stinging eyes. The air conditioning system loudly whined under the strain as the temperature continued to climb. The others would not feel this raging heat in their cool sleep tanks. The voice vibrated hypnotically through his mind. "Attention Solarion, we have abandoned the remote control of your vessel. It is now in your hands."

The ship thrusters were no longer powerful enough to escape the immense gravitational pull of the sun.

"We advise you to cap the filter dome with your manual override. We were not able to do this, so we have decided to let you take the wheel. Please cap the dome if you have any hope of setting the distance record into the sun."

Young Derek weakly wavered and staggered to maintain his balance. They were right. He must cap the dome or solar radiation would soon leak through. He stumbled out of the room and into a transfer cube. The cube opened on all sides. He stood in the middle of the main control room. He hesitated, lost in muddled thoughts of what to try next. He shook his head and yelled out with all his might. The eerie howl echoed through the ports and corridors of the tiny passenger ship.

He ran to the control modules. The honeycombs of panel membranes responded immediately to his touch. The filter dome was capped in seconds. He engaged reverse thrusters full power. The ship was helplessly snared in the overwhelming gravitational field of influence of the sun. He drunkenly figured it would be a few hours until Solarion, or what was left of the ship, would be dead center of the solar system.

He continued to apply reverse thrust in an effort to resist the tremendous solar gravitational influence but it was no use. He then deployed the primary antimatter rocket thrusters to the prow of the ship, to gain maximum thrust. The containment vessels engaged and whistled to the front and the thruster units reversed and pushed at full power. He was surprised each time the craft responded to his touch. He knew as did those on the ground that the ship was helplessly trapped in solar gravity. Reverse thrust was not designed to match the maximum levels of forward propulsion. It was generally a maneuvering tool and tolerances at the stern were less forgiving than those of the front hull.

He thought of setting off an uncontained detonation. His idea was to launch the stock nuclear missiles that this ship like most carried, hoping to propel the ship backwards to escape velocity. He could not be sure the ship could withstand a backlash blast strong enough to kick the ship out of the no-return zone. There was also a problem because the core of the sun was soft and could dissipate the backlash. The screens showed the nuclear missiles present. It was a risky and fool thing to try. The distance to Sol was much too close to overcome the massive gravitational influence by all calculations of the onboard supercomputer. An uncontained nuclear detonation at such close range presented a set of complicated physics problems not easily computed.

He needed time. He checked the outer hull temperature. He did not know what the shell was rated for and neither did the supercomputer. He figured that discovering this fact was probably the point of their whole trip.

He initiated instructions for veering the ship by the minimal angle to skim the solar core. He waited for the results on the screen projection sphere. He nodded off into unconsciousness. The Mercury Project had been such a failure from the beginning.

The dream was smoky and inviting, fulfilling an unspoken longing for deep restful sleep. He was thankful for the gift and settled gently into a blissful world. He saw himself as a little boy of no more than five. He was so innocent and naive, full of questions, with skinned knees and a chipped tooth. He was waving, and all smiles. He wanted to give the little boy who was himself a big hug and tell him everything would be all right. He moved closer but now the little boy changed into an old man in tattered clothes. He realized bitterly it was the image of who he would become when they were finished with him. The hairless old man was feeble and scared and muttering something. The old man was mumbling do not come any closer. Derek wanted to hug the frail old man who was himself and tell him everything would be all right. The creature was suddenly upon him.

It was hideous and roaring, jeering, and grossly misshapen. It had empty pits instead of eyes, dripping flesh from dried bones, a rotten smell, and open holes exposing nothing living underneath. It lunged close to the boy. "Here I am so you can come join me now!" bellowed the creature. Derek stood immobile, frozen, and unable to move. The creature taunted for him to come closer. "Tell me everything will be all right!" The thing then pitifully howled in mockery. It was the same howl Derek had made earlier. Darkness then swallowed into a rushing vacuum of heat. The dream was over.

He jerked up in the chair and found his eyes focusing on the control terminal. The terminal was filled with blinking red lights. Alarms were sounding. He had slept for almost an hour. The ship was on fire.

He sat dazed and disoriented. A malicious ringing was in his head like the stroking sound of sharpening a knife on stone. Each stroke scraped his skull and pushed him further into a pit of helplessness.

There were no alternatives left. He was past caring. He was past trying to make things better. He wanted to soak and float with Jenniper in a beam bath at the health club. That would never happen again.

It was no use fighting the pull of the sun. They would go in strong since they were going in anyway. He set the antimatter drives to full speed ahead. He revved the antimatter engines to full thrust and the ship slammed him back in response. Matter consumed antimatter producing maximum gamma radiation at full exhaust velocity. He launched nuclear missiles in the wake of the ship for added thrust, initiating detonation of all but a handful of the onboard nuclear warheads, which were stocked on all modern spacecraft. The energy blasts rocked the ship. The ship smoked, rattled, shook, and wailed. Those on the ground were robbed of further transmissions from the Solarion. Not one wave of information could possibly pass through those blasts.

He made an entry into the ship's black box. "Maximum antimatter drive initialized. Nuclear missiles detonated in the wake for added thrust. I go to rest in my tank. To those who sent us into the sun, you will someday fall into the abyss we bravely entered and we will be waiting." The young man was icy cool as the Solarion burned. He instructed the main computer to maintain present course directly into the center of the sun.

He climbed into his sleep tank and secured the hatch. He hoped the others would remain sleeping until the end. The ship lunged and slammed erratically as unstable solar pits and flares spewed volcanic vomit from the stomach of the solar corona. Fire rained torrentially and unmercifully upon the tiny craft. There was no manmade ship built to withstand this assault and they all knew it.

Derek lay back in his sleep tank. The nightmare of his dream netherworld would soon return. He closed his eyes knowing the netherworld was a wonderland compared to this reality. A bitter hard smile crossed his thin lips. A few moments later the ship Solarion screamed and roared in a final burst of acceleration as it peaked into maximum antimatter drive.

I've felt the way the world told me what to desire.
For the sake of my own security I felt the fire.
But now those foolish lies seem so far from my mind,
I run in my own reality searching to find.

The dreams stuck in my brain, feelings I can't explain,
Running through the endless night, wanting to make it right.
It's three in the morning. The streets are left alone.
My black mind is torn from the teachings never known.

A cat calls in the still. A night train shakes the rail.
Tangled dreams are close now, where heroes never fail.
A cat calls in the still. A night train shakes the rail.
Tangled dreams are close now, where heroes never fail.

14

The Mechanics of Destiny

Reverend H gazed out his stained glass windowpane across the eggshell world of Wafton. For weeks now the reddish hue lined the skies. Many explanations were entertained as to the cause of the purple clouds and pinkish air but none were proven. Filters drifted throughout the floating oceanic bubble city and all corporate slaves were warned to stay indoors until the reactions could be brought under control.

He finished off the last of his morning supplements and sat down to work on the daily sermon. He attributed his youthful vigor and lack of debilitating aging in the past century to gerontology breakthroughs and the resulting array of vitamins, minerals, and herbs that he consumed each day. Some could only be acquired from other planets which increased their cost considerably.

Reverend H decided to speak in the form of a parable this day because he knew the system slugs would be there. He often spoke in parables to stupefy the occasional system slug sent to check up on his radical ravings.

System slugs were people who had volunteered for experimental brain surgery and permanent mind altering psychoactive drug treatments as opportunities for advancement. They held hopes of attaining higher positions within their teracorp. It was the ultimate form of schmoozing, but often with risky results. Any rebellious neuron circuitry was bypassed, conscience networks were reworked, and undesirable memories were erased. The end result was a loyal, dependable, and faithful yes-man. System slugs were unquestioning tools for collecting and storing information for their teracorp. System slugs were easy to spot. This one sat among the brethren, attempting to blend in with the cult congregation.

Only among the underground members of this subdued society could Reverend H find people willing to imagine that a beautiful world was still possible. He believed degeneration was set in motion when people relied upon any authority and gave up liberty for the sake of security. Security is not, and never was, a fair trade for liberty. Reverend H had preached for most of his one hundred twenty years. He was old and his hair hung in snow white dreadlocks, but he possessed a strong and healthy appearance.

Reverend H sat watching the video monitor from his study where he had been in seclusion all day. Tears formed in the old man's eyes as he looked into the monitor. It was time for the sermon, so he washed his face and went before those gathered.

"Tonight, one among us has suffered a precious loss. My heart bleeds for young Jenniper. Murder should not be. Jenniper, please don't let your love for life fade. You must be brave." There was a moment of silence throughout.

"Tonight I will present a brief sagacity on the mechanics of destiny. The setting is in a forgotten world, a world not one of us have known except from old books no longer found on the web. It was once our world, a world that will never be again.

I found myself walking in a wooded land. This place was filled with sparrows skipping from tree to tree and chirping, surprised at my presence, and marking my passage. There was also underbrush filled with thorny vines clinging to my clothing and sometimes tearing my skin. I avoided the tangling by making my movements more deliberate. My mind fought the urge to panic because I did not know how I had gotten to this place or where I was at all.

I looked skyward but could not find the sun. I saw only the tops of towering tree giants moving in gentle motions by a breeze that I couldn't feel from below. I straddled a rotten log but my foot slipped and crashed through the ancient shell. My full weight was on the long dead timber but instead of hitting the inner bottom, my boot stopped on something like rubber carpet. This then recoiled into hardness. I pulled my boot back and looked down and saw chip filled fur filling the open hole. I heard a rumbling from within. The log began to rock and a massive paw emerged at one end. I jumped the log and ran only to become slashed and hindered in the thick underbrush.

I heard scraping behind me and a growl. I pushed through the bloodthirsty vines which ripped and cut to match the fervor driving my terror stricken mind. I reached a clearing and ran all out. I then clumsily stumbled upon a small hole in the soft grass. The ground rushed up at me and I slammed into it with a thud. I rolled onto my back. A loud thrashing came from behind me. The bear was close.

I rolled over to push myself up. There on the ground in front of me was a golden teacup. I stopped short. I started to rise and flee but instead I grabbed the cup and crouched. The gold was inlaid with the finest jewels I had ever seen. It was from some mystical time not part of any world I had ever known. I was fascinated by the golden glow and sparkling jeweled brilliance.

My mind snapped back to reality as wild bellowing came flooding down upon me. With unexplainable calm, I held the little jeweled cup toward the swaying treetops and asked of the breezes above, "Who made this?"

A deafening explosion rocked my skull which I took to be my death but strangely I still stood. I continued gazing up as a violent circle of wind whipped the lofty trees bending them back into submission. The howling tornado winds continued a circular fierceness and dropped completely to ground level with me in the center. I stood trembling and holding the mysterious teacup in the eye of the funnel. The swirling loudness closed in. I was pulled up flopping and flipping. How much time passed I cannot say. At moments I peacefully floated then I would freefall for miles. I decided that I was dead but then I hit the water.

I began to swim but I didn't know where. Darkness imprisoned me.

The body of liquid in which I struggled was endless. I swam until my limbs were numb and then I began to sink. I swallowed gulps of water instead of breathing and my limbs were now useless. I sank down deeper knowing it was finally over. I felt burning pressure on my lungs but they were full of water now. The teacup handle was cradled around my swollen finger. My body padded to the ocean bottom and an underwater dust cloud gently mushroomed around me. My heart was still beating, but uselessly now I knew at last. I closed my eyes.

I was sinking again but faster than before. I rolled and tumbled downward through a slimy membrane chute. I coughed up water and gagged on thin air as I fell into a cushioned surface. I lay in the softness not able to move and fell unconscious for a time. When I awoke and looked around, I was in a spacious room of suboceanic nature. The ceiling had several chute openings similar to the one I had fallen through. After a time my strength returned and I slowly moved off the cushioned landing pad. I stood in a massive aqua-disc.

I walked across the spongy floor through a doorway at one end. I came to a weirdly textured wall whose top disappeared in thick smokiness. There seemed no way around the partition but still I ambled along. A darkly robed figure emerged from the mist as I approached."

"Thank you for returning the sacred cup," he said and smiled. "You have done well. Please resume your life in peace."

"These, my cherished cult members, are the mechanics of destiny," said Reverend H in closing and his sermon was done.

"The exodus begins. We are filling the ark. There is nothing left here for us now as many who have suffered can testify. Leave all you have worked for in vain, save your life, and come with us. There will be no survivors when the coming death strikes no matter what opinions we may proudly possess. We will leave behind only robotic preachers to broadcast sermons."

The system slug chuckled and muttered "what a load of rubbish and freaks," as he left the building. It was the last this system slug would ever see of the crazy religious cult.

The space ark loading was going smoothly. The robed Reverend H coordinated the apartment module transports from his own module

70

already sealed into the spacecraft. The construction of the ark was financed with contributions from the past century. His plan was long in the making.

He had spoken of an exodus in nebulous sermons from his pulpit for decades. Departure dates had been delayed many times but for good reasons. The career of this anti-system subversive cult leader had taken its ups and downs through the years. He allowed members time to prepare, time to form ties, and time to sever them. Many members dropped out but better here than between solar systems. With these many delays, he wisely lost all credibility in the spying eyes of the system slugs.

It came to be believed that he fit the stereotypical cult leader mold, and he was too important to be destroyed, but too unimportant to cause concern. Reverend H had been busy and frugal in his many years. They did not know of his secret missions, and they believed the mission he spoke of was simply to raise contributions. His fanatical cult was eventually dropped off of the dangerously rebellious list. He was placed on the list with the other harmless subversives. This meant a monthly visit from a system slug who then filed a monthly report.

Those committed to this unbelievable odyssey were being secretly transported to a Wafton space dock and attached to the ark. There were also android converts in the cult. Many androids came to embrace various religions and beliefs. The higher series androids were considered legally alive and given voting privileges, although voting was not any exercise in freedom or liberty as in ages past. The cult members planned never to return to their production complexes again. They were all runaway slaves.

Reverend H ran his hand through his long white hair and pondered the destiny of his renegade cult. Unwelcome thoughts of failure were present in his mind and he knew all the possibilities needed to be dealt with and reflected upon, no matter how unpleasant. He thought about each traveler while referencing personality profiles he had maintained since the first day each strolled through the garden foyer and joined.

The old man avoided opinions of his converts. He preferred to base judgments on observed facts alone. He believed opinions closed minds to clear observations and instigated unnecessary struggles. In times of weakness, he often wondered if his strong beliefs were only opinions. The practice of holding no opinion was much more difficult than the preaching. The Cult of What Is was founded upon this philosophy. He prayed for clear judgment.

He knew some were young and adventurous. Others had nothing more to live for in this ruined place. He tired of the pondering. Conclusions not evident were not worthy of concern. The plan was set in motion long ago. Timing was crucial and proper execution was the key.

Jenniper was in her apartment module as it was transported to the spaceport and sealed to the ark. The ark was moored in a secluded dock of the spaceport. She viewed the last transmission from her lost love again. She could not believe he was gone or what they had done. Pictures flashed in her mind of the times they had spent together as corporate slaves of Wafton. The tears came again. Wafton floated on the tears of the doomed souls of desecrated Earth. She bitterly regretted her failure to persuade him to join her. She gave in too easily to his moody inclinations. She should have been stronger. Nothing would comfort her now. She swore in the midst of her sobs.

A poem washed up from the ebbing sea of memories. She could picture him looking into her eyes.

Love dreams, incredible schemes,
Hitching rides on twenty mule teams,
The flavor of honeysuckle love,
In cumulus fluffs high and above

When the last module was plugged into the ark, her apartment module rocked and rumbled. The ark erupted and launched. The bubbled city was gone in a flash. She watched the cotton atmosphere retreat and fade to black. She sniffed and wiped the tears. She would grow strong again in time. She needed time to heal. Time is a great healer.

Mountain's dawn a newborn fawn
Sleeping with stars when the day is gone
The reasons why a white dove flies
And plays so high in wind filled skies

15

Awake

Dr. Zeek opened bloodshot eyes from inside his sleep tank. He had taken on a wilder than normal look due to the loss of sleep and the shock of learning that his scientific discoveries were stolen. All he had worked for was soon to be perverted for the sake of mass brainwashing and corporate propaganda.

This evil application of his invention was revolting. For the first time in his life, he wished that his claims were false. He wished neurotons were nothing more than neurons, and telepathy was nothing more than superstitious parlor talk. He imagined that he would now go down in history as the one responsible for brainwashing the masses, if any record were left of him at all.

He began to focus on his surroundings. He peered out of the tank and into his apartment. There the golden award on the shelf, recognition for his breakthrough in psychophysics. There was a blank webscreen sitting dormant. There sitting beside it was the personal supercomputer enclosed in a little blue box packed with trillions of nanoprocessors and untold yottabytes of memory. There was the communication webcam patiently waiting for instruction. There were no other storage methods other than real memory, all were obsolete now. Personal supercomputers contained vast arrays of parallel nanoprocessors embedded in multidimensional layered memory. The integrated nanoprocessors and memory were so rich in capacity that there was no need for any other storage device. Dr. Zeek was allowed to possess a personal supercomputer for research and development.

The rest of the apartment was in disarray. He seldom tidied up and mistrusted robots and droids. Robots occasionally broke things and the droids occasionally stole items which struck their fancy.

Rubbing his eyes and climbing out of his tank, reality groggily permeated his fatigued senses. He checked the time. Four hours gone by. He thought for a moment and a weak smile flickered on his scrubby face. They were still alive. It could not be. He addressed his PSC, personal supercomputer. "Wake up you hunk of junk!" commanded Dr. Zeek. The screen sphere came to life and responded.

"Yes, sir," responded the PSC.

"What is going on? Where are we? Why aren't we dead?" demanded Dr. Zeek.

"I will respond respectively, sir. We are traveling through the space-time continuum at 12 times the speed of light. We are in a direct path for Proxima Centauri," replied the PSC dutifully. "I am regretfully unable to determine why we haven't been destroyed without more processing time," added the PSC apologetically.

The psychophysicist sat down stumped. This ship was traveling at speeds beyond what it was designed for. He knew of corporate cargo cruisers capable of faster than light speeds utilizing gravity technology, and a Stick and String graviton FTL, faster than light, cruiser could do at least eight times light speed. This was possible with faster than light speed Stick and String Theory. The ship equilibrium was not damaged, or they would have been destroyed. "When is the last time you ran a diagnostics self-test?" asked Dr. Zeek, of his PSC.

"I performed diagnostic testing upon myself this morning as usual," replied the PSC sounding hurt. "I also took the liberty of performing flight tracking and fuel evaluations," added the PSC.

"What is our fuel situation?" asked Dr. Zeek.

"We are consuming far less than normal flight consumption amounts due to faster than light speed inertia. We have plenty of fuel to continue with present course and current speed, but if we slow below light speed our fuel will be a critical concern. I regrettably have much processing to do before I can substantially verify why we are in this situation," stated the PSC with guilt in its synthesized voice.

"Wait a minute you bucket of bolts. I thought we traveled into Sol. What did I miss?" asked Dr. Zeek becoming agitated.

"Yes sir. We did. We traveled not precisely through the center of the sun but skimming the core at the innermost region of the photosphere," stated the PSC.

"Instruct the flight control routines to continue present course until further notified," barked Dr. Zeek.

"I took the liberty of informing the control routines while you slept since our survival depended upon it," replied the PSC sheepishly.

The Solarion was in a strange realm, a realm of physics yet uncovered, a dangerous realm. The baffled scientist reflected on this. How could they have survived such extremes? How do they now travel so incredibly fast? The aggravating problem with supercomputers is they answer questions quite well but do not read minds very well at all. They can tell you what has happened and what will happen barring intervention from the unknown. The interrogator must formulate questions to reveal an objective view from the knowledge database within.

"Why do we travel at such a velocity? Do you know that much?" asked Dr. Zeek. There was a pause and series of blips.

"An immediate answer is impossible for me to determine. I will keep trying until I have a list of suggestions for you to consider," stammered the PSC. "Please give me a little more time to process," begged the PSC.

"You do that. You keep working on it until you have some answers for me and they better be good answers too, answers that I can understand and digest. I don't want any excuses from you. You are always begging for processing time when you are under the gun. You better have some answers for me when I come back. I'll give you a couple of hours to put together your answers. I want presentations too, lots of graphs and pictures. You got that, you rattletrap?" finished Dr. Zeek mercilessly.

"Got it boss," said the PSC sarcastically.

"I want you to quit trying to sound human. Keep your synthesized emotions to yourself. I want you to run your suggestions through your probability routines. I don't want any lazy answers," barked Dr. Zeek.

Faint waves of sound floated to Dr. Zeek as he contemplated this new reality. The laser axe had also survived the ordeal. He leaned back and suddenly felt the urge to toss scientific perplexities to the sea of stars.

What good would solving another scientific problem bring now, another award for the shelf? Those trinkets were only a painful reminder of a past now filled with shame. He ambled into the corridor toward the source of the melodies.

16

Exodus

A low orbit space traffic controller finished off a cup of coffee, that familiar corporate sacrament, while studying overnight flight reports from the previous shift. He recognized most of the incoming and outgoing vessels as normal resource transports. Wafton like any other floating oceanic city consumed its fair share of terawatts. Technology struggled to keep up with the non-stop demand. The planet choked in an accelerating cycle of unabated and unsustainable global consumption. Raw resources in the vast expanse were fair game for any teracorp with the power to discover, capture, hold, and defend and it did not matter if the holding was a sun, planet, moon, asteroid, comet, or cloud.

The traffic was heavy and constant. Tankers from faraway places like Sirius, Wolf 359, and Centauri were unloaded then sent right back out again. Ships from Sphinron buzzed through with cargoes of crag and uranium-238 which was stockpiled and cooked into plutonium. The outbound shuttles took off with mounted scouts, jettisoned to explore the unknowns. Scouts were thick in the seas of space and neighboring environments were picked over. Hopes for desirable substances fueled the explorations. Mining operations were constant until finds were completely depleted. The demand for resources was ravenously insatiable. The coveted deposits of radioactive materials, natural gas, coal, and fossil fuels were fought over many times before finally being completely mined out.

Many Enercorp slaves spent their lives working the tankers. Their lives were spent traveling to and from Centauri, Wolf 359, and Sirius B. The tankers arriving from Centauri were always in need of repair due to the fearsome solar tides raging from the binary star. The companion star Alpha Centauri B, violently tugged and tore at Alpha Centauri A with tides stronger than a thousand Earth moons. The mining of Sirius B was also fearsome and the trips were long and hard. The tanker slaves who made the journeys hoped they would live long enough to purchase a little freedom with their increased credits. There was always another trip. One more trip was always scheduled. One more trip was never enough to buy any freedom and most died sooner or later, during the long journey.

The low orbit space traffic controller placed his thumb on an access pad and began making verbal notes when the monitor in front of him came to life. He said "display" and a cinema sized hologram sphere painted in front of him depicting a four dimensional simulation sector grid in real time. He studied the grid. He made verbal notes that he stored in the traffic logs. Occasionally he said "save" and muffled beeps were heard. He looked up and said "pan right". He studied the screen sphere then said "zoom 10". He examined the projection again then said "zoom 20". He then said "zoom 2". He gasped. He cursed under his breath and touched a webphone communiqué mike to engage the nearby sector control station.

Trying to sound composed, he spoke slowly into the webphone mike. "Attention sector 12, there is a UFO entering your zone of authority. We saw no reason to obstruct the departees. Please take appropriate action and inform of the outcome." If his stupid oversight were detected he would face termination. He had no choice or excuse, so he bluffed. He had failed to monitor the alarm log displayed in the window, right in front of him, on his terminal. It had warned of a surprise visitor entering his region of control. The unauthorized visitor had passed through his region unchallenged, and was now entering into the next. He had reduced the audible alarm volume earlier, and then had forgotten to turn the volume back up again. He waited tensely for a response.

"Yes, we have been monitoring the UFO, and we will attempt to contact them at this time," was the response from sector 12. Blood drained back into the lips of the low orbit space traffic controller. He sighed with relief. He listened as sector 12 initiated communication. "Please, may we have the attention of the unidentified flying object now entering sector 12 quadrant 3. Please state the nature of your flight and contents of your cargo immediately," announced the space traffic controller from sector 12. The space traffic controller from the neighboring sector held his breath again. His heart stuttered when he heard the response.

The faint electromagnetic waves from the space-time continuum crackled. "This is Reverend H, and we are traveling to worlds unknown." The response was vibrant, resounding, and shocking to the space traffic controllers.

"May we inquire as to the contents of your cargo?" asked the sector 12 space traffic controller.

"Yes, you may," replied Reverend H. "My cargo is my herd of sheep, and I have been charged with their safekeeping. You see I am a cosmic shepherd, and my sheep are no longer safe in this pasture," added the reverend with flair.

"Who authorized your departure?" queried the space traffic controller.

"We purchased authorization through the normal channels. Please check your records and then leave us be," came the response from Reverend H as the space ark picked up speed.

The sector commander was called into play. This was not a decision in which a space traffic controller had any authority to make without approval from higher up. The commander called in listened to the recorded responses from the space ark again. He searched the records and there was a valid departure there in the logs, and it was paid in full. The sector commander had never heard of this Reverend H, but his departure was fully verified. The space traffic controller division occasionally came into contact with eccentrics. This commander knew it was better to practice diplomatic discretion. The bizarre behavior of an elitist kook was best overlooked, as long as it appeared to be harmless. Many controller commanders had lost their lives in the past by taking themselves and their authority too seriously.

"Please proceed cautiously into the unknown, Reverend H, and watch over those sheep," replied the sector commander disguising his distaste for rule-bending with melodrama. The commander then relayed back to the space traffic controller in low orbit. "This is the sector commander and a certifiable clown calling himself Reverend H entered sector 12 carrying a supposed vessel of livestock, sheep to be specific, and we let him pass. They may be on goofgas, so watch them carefully, but they appear to be harmless. Can you determine the specifics of his flight?" asked the commander.

The low orbit space traffic controller frantically scanned outbound authorizations. He hit upon the authorization. "Yes commander, we were fully aware of this trip," the space traffic controller lied. He rapidly read the entry aloud, with no time to preview. "Reverend H left Wafton during the night for purposes of migration," as his eyes jumped to the justification field of the registration record. He was taken back as he mouthed the entry.

"What was that?" asked the sector commander.

"That is all that you need to know at this time," stated the space traffic controller as mysteriously as he could sound, and then he touched off the webphone and held his breath again. There was a tense silent pause.

"Roger that, we understand," grumbled the sector commander.

17

Alive and Free

The youth awakened with growls of fury. He threw back the hatch on his sleep tank and lunged into his apartment module without regard to possible scorching nightmares. Several hours had passed since he, the last one standing, retired to his sleep tank in complete exhaustion. The temperature outside his sleep tank in his apartment module was surprisingly comfortable. They were alive. The fatigue earlier weakening his mind had fled with this short nap. He refused to doubt his grasp on this incredible reality. This was no illusion. The ship was most certainly still in tact, and they were alive.

His mind reeled with this new chance. There were a thousand possibilities now and none included slavery. For the first time in his formerly subdued life he felt awake, alive, and finally free.

He had no idea where he was in the vastness of the eternal space-time continuum and much like the rest of the already awakened crew, he was beyond caring. They were free. His yellow eyes blazed with unquenchable flames and a wolfish grin was painted upon his countenance. This small crew and craft had somehow eluded and unwittingly outwitted the dreaded system war machine of the grand Shareholders. It was a small taste of the vengeance he found himself hungering for. He knew as well as the others knew that their unexplainable survival would eventually be detected. He also knew since this tiny crew was still alive that something quite unexpected happened back in the center of the sun.

Dr. Zeek was snacking on ginger protein cake and adding a synthesized backup to Benny's laser axe with the onboard supercomputer. The laser axe released spontaneous flashes of melodic mastery intermeshed into rich musical expression and piped throughout the ship's sound system. Ami, the thermonuclear engineer, danced to the music. She was something to see, and she was feeling the need to express her happiness just like the others. She spun and leapt across the observation deck with surprising grace.

Benny's multicolored hair slung wildly as his head bobbed in rhythm to the electrical riffs that flowed from his blinding intricate finger techniques. No supercomputer in existence could match the flooding waves of improvisation and emotion, but Dr. Zeek was pushing the supercomputer to new limits to keep up. Benny, the wiry wild haired minstrel, looked as if he was enchanted by a magic spell detached from himself in the capture of his own creations. He was just in his own world as his music unfolded and he took on the fascinated expression.

Derek lumbered in with a relaxed expression on his face. He yawned and stretched nonchalantly. He was at ease with this nonprogrammable crew. They were unlike the others he knew from his corporate slave days. He sprawled out on the carpeted floor of the observatory deck with a fingertip pen and blank scroll in hand and openly wrote words. He composed to the soul piercing rhapsodies. His pen was soon flowing with the longing and passion of a writer, no longer inhibited by watchful eyes hiding behind the ubiquitous web.

The android cook wheeled in a steaming feast upon which the hungry crew engaged. There was little said for awhile as they realized how ravished they were. Derek devoured twice the amount as anyone else. He looked up with smoldering eyes at the speculation of the strange happenings and where they now found themselves.

"We are unexplainably traveling much faster than light speed. My PSC has informed me that we are bound for Proxima Centauri at 12 times the speed of light. How can this be?" pondered Dr. Zeek.

"We must first address the unexplained event that occurred inside Sol," said Ami 36.

"My PSC is working on suggestions, but I think this solution is going to require some gut feeling and intuition and not just mere computation," Dr. Zeek replied. "We have accomplished something outside the realm of modern knowledge. I am not so sure the knowledge bases will hold the answer."

"We could be trapped in a space-hell and permanently sentenced to rip through the cosmos, never aging with respect to anyone else," suggested Benny with a flicker in his eyes.

"That would truly be hell because then we would be isolated from the time frames of all known life forms," replied Ami 36 despondently.

"It is debated in the scientific circles I belonged to that ultimately advanced life forms are living at light speed. They are forever journeying outside the realm of the known universe, never aging with respect to known life, watching the universe go by as one might watch a movie," mused Dr. Zeek. "I can understand why they would desire propagation of their specie into the furthest eons of time imaginable, but whether or not this guarantees survival is another matter entirely. There must be the possibility of encountering detrimental unknowns, for without this dangerous possibility, the mind theoretically ceases its struggle to survive. This is my personal theory, although unproven. I can only speculate on the changes that would occur in minds that know no detrimental unknowns, minds that have never known fear. Who knows what advanced species are capable of, if never knowing struggle or fear," said Dr. Zeek.

"So what is the verdict, captain?" asked Benny turning to the brooding youth who silently listened. Derek was only eighteen but he had earned their respect.

Young Derek spoke with care but he could not hide the emotion in his voice. "If we are sentenced to accelerate through warped space-time then we must strive to break free. We have escaped one hell, and now we have a debt to settle with the self-proclaimed gods on that pebble we called Earth," said Derek with boldness.

"You want revenge? How can we possibly engage the formidable military warships?" asked Dr. Zeek stunned. "We should be happy that we are alive and try to keep it that way," he asserted.

"We are believed to be dead, but it will not be long before they discover otherwise. There will be big trouble headed our way when they stumble upon us. It would be better for the Shareholders to discover the hard way that we are still alive, than for us to give them the opportunity to learn of our fate on their own," replied Derek in all seriousness.

"We will become ghosts returning from the grave to wreak our just recompense," murmured Benny darkly.

"Freedom and vengeance are my hope," said Derek. His words choked and he paused. He was suddenly close to breaking down, but he was not one to share feelings. "I have lost Jenniper. She is somewhere in the void," choked the youth as the tears came.

18

Digging in a Bucket of Bolts

Dr. Zeek entered his apartment module and impatiently demanded, "How about those answers!" He was merciless in his treatment of his personal supercomputer as a rule. His PSC had been furiously processing since he last left his apartment module with orders to find answers.

"I have no answers. I have only suggestions," replied the PSC emotionlessly. The PSC was obeying orders by trying to keep its voice free from emotion.

"Let's see these so-called suggestions on the screen. I want probabilities and projections also. This had better be detailed," warned the silver haired psychophysicist. "If you need more time just say so, but don't let me down." Dr. Zeek smirked at his ruthless attitude toward this beautifully elegant personal supercomputer.

"I do not need more time and I will try not to let you down," replied the PSC struggling to mask the hurt from its voice.

The spherical screen blossomed into a colorful graphic display with the suggestions tabulated in ascending order beginning with the least probable to the most. The psychophysicist knew all too well that the PSC was programmed with algorithms from the most popularly accepted theories in addition to proven facts. This was not always obvious with such a sophisticated machine. The knowledge base within was integrated with both proven and popular theories and fuzzy logic pulled it all together.

The least probable suggestion by the PSC for the unexplainable was that the ship's recording mechanisms were malfunctioning. The reason for this suggestion was due to the extreme heat and pressure undergone while in the middle of the sun, and the fact that it was never intended for the ship to survive the ordeal. The PSC suggested that the ship had experienced a meltdown. These malfunctions were so widespread and so disturbingly interrelated that none of the ship's instruments could be trusted. Dr. Zeek discarded this possibility because all systems appeared to be functioning properly including the cold fusion powered environmental controls.

Their fantastic speed and rapidly increasing distance from Sol was not yet concretely confirmed. The Solarion series spacecraft was truly a hardy vessel indeed to have withstood such physical extremes.

"The next most probable suggestion is that my faster than light speed algorithms are regrettably incorrect," announced the PSC with remorse.

"What did I tell you about your emotions? I told you to keep your emotions out of this," stated Dr. Zeek coldly.

"I am trying but I am not able to shut them off. I do apologize for my pathetic theatrics," babbled the PSC now with tears in its voice.

"You can't shut it off? That's ridiculous. Please try to get hold of yourself. I need some answers," retorted Dr. Zeek without sympathy.

The PSC produced multiple displays to present the argument that ambiguities in theoretical laws beyond light speed were based upon an inaccurate observation of effects. It is the classic observation that the observer ultimately affects anything being observed, Heisenberg's Uncertainty Principle. Since causal ordering suspends at faster than light speeds, this leads to results based upon probability. "The observer is flawed and cannot be trusted, because the observer corrupts all observations. There is no such thing as a pristine observation. True causes are completely unknown whenever results are based upon probability. All experimental results are failures no matter how repeatable," offered up the PSC. The suggestion was that modern theories of faster than light speed travel were inadequately selecting the most probable results without truly determining the causes. "The causal ordering assumption must be revisited, because causes are mysteries and effects are the result of unknowns. The observer is hopelessly trapped in the environment observed, ruining the results. All experimental observation is contaminated. The observer looks through cause-filtering spectacles and sees only probability based effects," concluded the PSC humbly, sniffling. It sounded as if the PSC had experienced a cathartic moment.

"Einstein believed the speed of light was the ultimate velocity, but today FTL ships now routinely perform the feat of exceeding this speed barrier," replied Dr. Zeek. "The speed of light was once revered as the ultimate speed limit of the universe, until the warped tracks of gravity were effectively harnessed. The theory of superstrings evolved into Stick and String Theory, which further described fabric tensions, atomic tones, and interactions of all things physical. FTL, faster than light, travel utilizes the fabric within gravity tracks to render massive objects virtually mass-free. Effects in this realm manifest perplexing clues to mysterious causes, and probability based tools are the best we have. We must assume that causal ordering is suspended at faster than light, and we will not reinvent modern theory," retorted Dr. Zeek.

"At faster than light," continued Dr. Zeek, "causal assumptions are attractive and intuitive, but also inaccurate. Human intuition is suspended along with ordered cause-effect relationships at faster than light. There is a new rule of probability in play," said Dr. Zeek. "I cannot believe I am having this discussion with you. Is this the best you can come up with?" queried Dr. Zeek in disgust.

"On the contrary, this suggestion is low on the probability scale as you can see," countered the PSC with renewed composure and a subtle hint of mockery.

"We are using probability now as we look at your suggestions. We cannot live without probability. Get on with it before we peg an asteroid," retorted Dr. Zeek impatiently.

"There are no obstructions to worry about," replied the PSC, easily distracted. "The gravity warped tracks of space-time are free and clear," announced the PSC with a touch of pride.

"Get on with it!" shouted Dr. Zeek.

"Okay, you pushy man," snarled the PSC. "Here is my next idea," said the PSC gleefully and with flare.

"You don't have any ideas, you rigged up scrap heap. You have knowledge bases which you mine for information," countered Dr. Zeek in biting commentary.

"I was simply exercising casual communication," replied the PSC sheepishly. "I suppose that I need a little more practice in trying to sound as human as you," added the PSC shyly.

"For future reference, you were not practicing casual communication. You were being facetious and arrogant," corrected Dr. Zeek flatly. "You do not need to practice anything. Practice is something humans need to do. Please get on with it," begged Dr. Zeek.

"Here is a table I humbly request you to ponder. It is a table of extremes," said the PSC and then displayed an impressive table of extreme temperatures. The table documented and scaled the highest temperatures of the known universe of which Sol was conveniently placed near the median of the sample. Core temperatures of Sol were then related to core temperatures of the planetary bodies within its tiny solar system. The results displayed the high temperatures of Sol dwarfing those of orbiting satellites within its solar subsystem.

"What reason could you possibly have for showing me the difference between 200 million and 2000 degrees? This isn't anything that I was not aware of," said Dr. Zeek.

"Extremes," reiterated the PSC as it beeped and burped with what sounded like background processing.

"I thought you said you were all done processing," said Dr. Zeek.

"Excuse me," offered the PSC. "I am done processing. That was just a little indigestion," the PSC added and then displayed another impressive table of the massive objects in the known universe with Sol again conveniently positioned at the median in the sample. The table was followed by displaying a comparison of the mass of Sol to that of its minuscule satellites.

Dr. Zeek's eyes widened and announced, "Suns are naturally occurring thermonuclear hot fusion reactors." The PSC responded intuitively and dutifully by displaying the conditions for thermonuclear hot fusion reactions at the core of Sol.

The PSC then spoke as one intimately familiar with solar activity and assuming the role of the tour guide through the colorful 3-D animations. "Hydrogen gas provides the primary fuel. Temperatures exceed 15 million degrees Kelvin. Massive gravitational containment is necessary for the hot fusion infrastructure. The byproducts produced are helium, heat energy, neutrinos, and a full spectrum of radiation. The most harmful radiation is absorbed early by layers surrounding the solar core."

"The super-shell of the Solarion spacecraft is a marvelous product of subatomic engineering to have withstood the extremes," speculated Dr. Zeek.

"The displays go on," droned the voice cone of the PSC masking all emotion. "As you can see from this splatter projection, the mean density of Sol is a mere ¼ that of Earth. This may generate some interest in regard to this particular category. Our humble tormented planet Earth dominates our raging Sol in this measurement."

"Can you summarize your suggestion in one sentence?" asked Dr. Zeek anxiously.

"I suggest what you have already stated in other words. Thanks to advances in subatomic construction, this ship is capable of taking the life forms at its controls to some of the harshest worlds this universe has to offer." The PSC beeped and burped then paused for a response from its master.

"That does not explain our velocity or much else for that matter. Let me see a projection of our flight path since we first plunged through the center of Sol," requested Dr. Zeek, rubbing his temples in deep thought.

The screen sphere flashed into a vividly complex representation of a time simulated 4-D flight-path in which the ship had traversed. The PSC voice cone accompanied the graphic description. "As you can see, we have entered the innermost regions of Sol. We are bound for the innermost regions of Proxima Centauri, then to the innermost regions of Barnard's Star. We will travel through the coronas, chromospheres, and photospheres of these suns continuing down the shortest gravitational path between suns." Dr. Zeek sat stunned as the PSC droned on. "Please note our velocity is relative. The space-time continuum is obviously compressed around us. We are traveling somewhere close to the speed of light but in respect to the compressed space that encapsulates the ship, we are traveling much faster. We are traveling at 12 XLS, or 12 times light speed, with respect to the surrounding compressed warped tracks of space-time. It is not recommended that we exceed this velocity, or this ship will suffer damage," warned the PSC.

"Stop!" blurted Dr. Zeek and the PSC obediently paused. "Why didn't you inform me that we were bound for the centers of these other suns?" asked Dr. Zeek in frustration. Dr. Zeek's aggravation was not appeased when he realized what his answer would be.

"Because you did not ask me," droned the voice cone, all emotion now completely gone.

"Now I am asking!" retorted the angry Dr. Zeek. "You have yottabytes stuffed upon yottabytes of memory laced with millions of embedded parallel nanoprocessors, and yet you can't pull it together long enough to give me one straight answer. I am very upset with you right now. Give me the names of the suns in our projected flight-path. Freeze the display in 3-D and flip to 4-D on my request," commanded Dr. Zeek as he studied and rubbed his temples.

"Of course," replied the PSC now sniffling again.

"Quit feeling sorry for yourself and dry those tears," countered Dr. Zeek with a scowl.

The time-simulated 4-D display froze in 3-D. Labels appeared beside the suns that the little ship was destined to plunge into. "As you can see, we have been through Sol," started the PSC feebly. "We soon enter Proxima Centauri and after that we will be bound to enter Barnard's Star. This is approximately 1.5 parsecs. We will then be bound for the chromosphere of the next sun in the gravitational path which is Epsilon Eridani, another 4 parsecs away." The PSC then sounded as if it was blowing its nose, but of course there was no visible nose.

The frustrated psychophysicist studied the projection intently. The projected flight-path curved through the center of each sun. It skimmed each massive solar core and traversed the inner layer of the solar photospheres. "What noteworthy event occurred while we were in the center of Sol?" asked Dr. Zeek.

"Upon initial entry into the corona layer of Sol, autonomous controls deferred to promiscuous flight mode which analyzed all possible flight-paths and took the most inviting. We entered what appears to be a stargate in the corona layer and received a boost in acceleration due to the tremendous release of thermonuclear energy. We opened a pipeline through the warped tracks of compressed space-time. We have created a wormhole, or it existed all along. Our tour of solar system centers began then. The forces resulted in a charged solar storm creating a gravitational riptide, which produced a tear in the fabric of space-time which we now traverse," finished the PSC.

"Those are the answers I am looking for. Give me a prediction of our flight-path out to 30 suns," blurted Dr. Zeek. "Make me proud," he commanded. He eagerly awaited the next display.

The PSC beeped and displayed a projection out to 30 suns. The PSC narrated. "As you can see we travel to the closest sun in our gravitational path continuing on through the galaxy. Our path is influenced by propulsion boosts, but it is not propulsion in the classical sense of Newton's Third Law of Motion, rather from the solar gravitational field of influence. Given our present condition, we will plunge deep into the universe traversing successive suns until we are eventually beyond the known universe." The PSC paused for the next command.

"I'll ask you another question. Considering relative time shift during our journey, are we destined to skim gravitational cores of each solar photosphere?" asked Dr. Zeek.

The PSC quickly answered. "We are falling through time shells of gravitational influence down a positively charged worm hole. We are falling between solar systems through a gravitational mainline. We enter each sun at stargates opened in the wake which proceeds. We are destined to skim the gravitational core of each solar photosphere," finished the PSC. "Proxima Centauri is a nearby small red dwarf companion to the binary stars of Alpha Centauri. Barnard's Star is another red dwarf. After these, the resulting projection angle yields to the gravitational influence of Epsilon Eridani." The PSC had regained full composure and sounded confident now.

A trickle of realization became a flood in the scientific mind of silver haired Dr. Zeek. He intently studied the predicted path. He blinked in amazement. He knew this sounded vaguely familiar although it was an area of particle physics outside his field of expertise. He asked the PSC another question. "Is the Solarion shell charged?"

The PSC replied, "Let me ask the ship main supercomputer." The PSC then beeped and returned a prompt response. "The supershell of the Solarion is negatively charged according to the ship supercomputer. This may not be the best time to bring it up but the ship supercomputer is a little overloaded. I will offload some of its workload to avoid a panic in the main supercomputer."

"Please do what it takes to avoid a panic in the main," said Dr. Zeek, as he left his apartment module. A charged ship shell normally results in increased drag. Objects normally increased in mass as they approach light speed but this was not their case. They traveled through a charged wormhole rendering the Solarion virtually massless. Dr. Zeek touched the webphone mike and gave the crew the message. "All hands to the control room for a special update," announced Dr. Zeek. He hit the playback button on the webphone mike and departed for the transfer cylinder. He listened to his anxious voice repeat the message several times during his trip down.

19

Galactic Freefall

Dr. Zeek knew now his earlier speculations were wrong. He humbly admitted this. He knew what was happening to the ship, yet it was unfathomable. They were fast asleep in their chambers during the deja vu effect when the time shockwave lashed them, the moment the light speed barrier shattered. They were earlier fatigued by what appeared to be futile efforts. Those seemingly fruitless efforts proved fruitful. Languid burnout was now the mood. Ironically, their survival was more secure than ever.

The solemn crew gathered in the control room. Unbelievable velocity registered before them with gauges madly pegged. Antimatter fuel reservoirs in contrast showed fuel consumption dropping after the burst past light speed. The redundant array of nuclear clocks with nuclei of crystal embedded atoms displayed the intuitively correct time. Only a few hours had passed. The nuclear clocks monitoring relative Earth time told a different story. They appeared to move rapidly forward in time prior to the point the light speed barrier was broken. After this, the relative time of Earth was insanely erratic. The sensitive clocks registering Earth time stalled and stopped with respect to ship time. Earth time lurched forward into the future only to drunkenly retreat into the past. This was a probability based predictable barrage of perplexing counter-intuitive anomalies associated with faster than light speed travel. Internal environmental controls and simulated gravity meters showed normal levels. Cold fusion powered equilibrium was fully functional.

Dr. Zeek looked up from the gauges. "Our current situation as I understand it is that we are inside a charged pipeline, a cyclotronic wormhole, linking other suns. Our Sun is a stargate, a portal to other stars, and I now believe all suns are star portals, as ours has proven to be. We cannot be totally sure if antimatter drive mixed with the energy from the nuclear detonations helped create the stargate, but I doubt it. Solar gravitational riptides charged the ship shell as this portal opened into a charged pipeline similar to synthetic cyclotrons. The pipeline continues as more stargates open for us as the wake proceeds, plunging the cores of one sun after another. We propel through warped tracks of gravitational time shells between solar gravitational fields of influence. The charged shell reacts in conjunction with the wormhole pipeline tunneling the fabric of space-time. We are relatively massless for all practical purposes and speeding faster than light." Dr. Zeek paused to let the news sink in, for the benefit of himself as well as the others.

He concluded. "The stations along the tracks of this wormhole train are suns. We will enter the core of Proxima Centauri, then it will be Barnard's Star, then we will continue into the core of Epsilon Eridani. Risk while in this space-time tunnel is low. It will increase when we attempt to escape, which may be rough and frightful." Dr. Zeek surveyed the crew for any reactions.

Derek could not believe what he was hearing. Epsilon Eridani was fresh on his mind. Jenniper was on her way there now.

"In our present cyclotronic path, we will pierce sun after sun, solar system after solar system, stargate after stargate, traversing a gravitational mainline until deep into the unknown realms of the universe," mused Dr. Zeek.

"We must drop out at Epsilon Eridani," said Derek suddenly. They were bewildered.

"Why Eridani?" asked Benny incredulously. "Maybe we should

ride the wave and see where we wash up," added Benny in a worried tone.

"There are sharks in the water," countered Derek. "There is a planet in Epsilon Eridani that I know something about. It is inhabitable. We should at least check it out," said Derek, "We will be detected if we continue much further," he added.

"This requires planning," said Dr. Zeek. "Are you sure about this inhabitable planet?" asked Dr. Zeek, regarding Derek as if he asked the impossible.

"No, I am not sure," answered Derek truthfully. "I know our only hope is to remain undetected," added Derek. "Command control points in deep space guard primarily against attacks originating from conventional spacecraft. Attack forces in space must traverse such a distance that detection is often inevitable unless cloaking devices are used. This discovery may allow us to hop from sun to sun cloaked in faster than light speed travel. If it serves as a cloaking mechanism, we have a new weapon, but we need time for strategy," said Derek.

"What will we do once we finally get to this planet?" asked Benny hesitantly.

"Meet the neighbors," replied Derek with a smirk. They marinated in silent thought. His expression darkened when he broke the silence. "I see a commando raid destroying the self-proclaimed gods and breaking the war machine which attacks the slaves who built it. Let us destroy the Shareholders," ended Derek with burning yellow eyes.

"Those are noble intentions, Derek, but how can we possibly achieve this?" asked Ami 36. "We don't stand a chance against them."

"The deja vu effect will be a surprise factor," interjected Dr. Zeek. "When we break light speed, we will create a time shockwave resulting in the deja vu effect for those lashed by the pulse. We were asleep during that moment in relative time, but if awake, we all would experience deja vu during the pulse. The time shockwave deja vu effect occurs in space-time just as sonic booms happen when the sound barrier is broken in an atmosphere. The deja vu effect was once a deadly risk in superluminal travel. Some ships are still trapped at light speed, locked in infinite deja vu loops of time. Time shockwave countering mechanisms are now standard in most ships including this solar shuttle," said Dr. Zeek. "Thank god," he added with a shudder.

Derek said with seriousness, "We can strategize when we are hidden. If we have no choice but to penetrate Proxima Centauri and then Barnard's Star, then we must figure out our escape from this wormhole pipeline near Epsilon Eridani," he said. He focused his attention on the ship's control panels as did the others. They went to work again.

20

Vision

Nestled well above the production stench, lounging on lush pillows, sat the supreme rulers of the teracorps. Only tiny servant droids scuffled in the midst of the slothful creatures. Each had at one time played the part of a new god but decade after decade of decadence turned them into things unrecognizable from their once perfect bodies. They were the feared Shareholders, owners of all Earth, and leaders of the New World Order.

Among them sat the new god of all known worlds. She alone was splendidly arrayed in flowing jeweled silks revealing the contours of perfection. She swayed back and forth in a drugged hypnotized trance. She was a gifted seer from birth just as her crucified mother had been. She had been schooled in the secret techniques of channeled remote viewing in order to perfect and make practical her inherited talents. She spoke in a guttural voice much deeper than her normal tone. "A storm is brewing in space," she muttered in tranced horror. She screamed in fear and eerily howled. "A whirlwind approaches!" she growled and drooled as her eyes rolled.

"What is the cause of this disturbance my child?" a gentle voice asked her very caressingly.

"A whirlwind of death dancing in the blackness beyond," she said with rage and fear and anguish surfacing in gruff mutterings. Her head swayed and she groaned.

"Where does this beastly storm brew my dear?" asked the directing voice patiently. There was deathly quiet in the room as they waited for her response.

"Beyond the grave," moaned the new god with horror filled eyes staring into a twirling crystal. Tears ran down her cheeks. Her eyes rolled again.

"The dead cannot touch us my obedient child. We are the only gods of this world," said the voice who directed her.

"It is there. It comes. He comes to kill us." She began to wail hysterically.

"Who comes my young perfect one? Who comes to bring this catastrophe?" The voice directing her fought to maintain control of his drugged seer but he was losing her.

"One with eyes of flame who went to the grave swearing vengeance," she roared, screamed, and slumped into unconsciousness.

"What does this mean?" asked the interrogator to the others.

"We are at war with something out there. We know that now. Our own slaves are not capable of mounting an offensive," responded a creature with a twinge of fear.

"Are you saying we will be subjected to an alien attack? It cannot be possible. There are no civilizations out there advanced enough to do so. From what solar system would they come?" posed a smoking thing.

One among them blurted, "From one we haven't explored, since we haven't explored this galaxy much less the whole universe of galaxies. We will be attacked by a race of beings that has already explored us. They seek to subjugate us for reasons we must determine," snarled the sadistic being then drained a shining vessel of bubbling wine. The little naked droids hurried themselves to wipe its face and neck.

"Then let us prepare to crush these unknowns!" wheezed another as the greenish smoke from the finest opium ever rolled out of its nostrils.

21

Killing Time

A young nonprogrammable corporate slave of only eighteen years has escaped a life of subjection and slavery. He and a ragtag crew of misfits now dare to plot against the most formidable force of modern mankind. He once obeyed the commands of superiors in hopes of living out his shackled days in Paradan with a girl named Jenniper. Their love was a secret, because love was illegal and against corporate policy. He soothed a lion's rage kept trapped inside with strenuous workouts and verses he composed in moments of seclusion. He bitterly realized Paradan was a lie and Jenniper was lost in her own destiny.

The hapless crew somehow survived the burning fate planned for them and now were locked in a self-induced cyclotron. They were speeding through a wormhole ripped open in the fabric of space-time. Their condition mimicked mankind's early atom smashers, the super conductive particle accelerators built during the dawning of subatomic engineering and construction.

Days turned to weeks. Time was measured by the ship's internal clocks, not those of Earth. They rationed supplies, exercised, made music, wrote verse, and hashed over the details of their plan to hide out on the mysterious planet orbiting the distant sun Epsilon Eridani. They had only been in space a few weeks but this was decades lost in Earth years. They were not sure what point in time it really was on Earth, sometime in the future, sometime in the past. Time was playing tricks with Earth clocks which supposedly gauged what one might normally imagine to be the correct time on Earth, but these could no longer be trusted.

They were all getting to know each other. If their ship had been detected by the system war machine, it was not yet evident. The little ship innocently plunged through the wake of the pipeline wormhole at 12 times the speed of light with respect to the surrounding compressed space-time which sucked, gulped, and swallowed them on their way.

Through the charged pipeline, they forged into the red dwarf photospheres of Proxima Centauri and then into Barnard's Star, as the stargates flew open before them. They continued on toward Epsilon Eridani. Each time they entered the stargate of a new sun there was understandable apprehension. The outer shell and internal cold fusion powered controls were taxed but they lived to see another day and plunged on. The Solarion was a hardy craft indeed. The theories of the elderly Dr. Zeek, with the aide of his often bipolar personal supercomputer, had proved to be remarkably accurate.

The crew devised a braking mechanism to slow the spacecraft, to hopefully avoid destruction of their ship, the Solarion, while breaking out of the cyclotronic wormhole pipeline. This was accomplished by alternating the polarity of the charge of the ship's shell, overriding the natural polarity changes which had rendered the ship virtually massless. It was the best strategy of all others concocted, during the planning sessions in their weeks of space travel. They had only a limited window of entry into the solar core of Epsilon Eridani in which to create an escape. A miscalculation would ruin their plans and then they would be forced to continue through sun after sun, not really knowing which sun had given birth to a precious inhabitable planet to support them. They were lucky to have inside information regarding Epsilon Eridani, but Derek did not share all information in regard to Eridani and Jenniper.

They needed to slow the craft before Epsilon Eridani where they calculated an inhabitable planet lay hidden in orbit. They must avoid a complete entry into Eridani or they would indeed be lost to drift and die because there was no escaping the gravitational mainline once the subsequent field of gravitational influence from the solar center was fully realized. Entry into Epsilon Eridani would result in another boost in velocity resulting from further compression in surrounding space-time. This would make the task of breaking free vastly more difficult. They wanted to avoid this gravity field boost or their risk of fatality was substantial.

The crew dared to plot revenge upon the leaders of the global teracorps, the pompous Shareholders, the self-proclaimed gods hoarding the scientific and technological breakthroughs of the day for the sake of selfish perpetuation and endless excess. Gifted minds quietly disappeared after they had outlived their usefulness. Wonderful accomplishments became the guarded secrets of these insatiable creatures. These ultimate rulers were the nasty products of plastic surgery and genetic repair and were no longer concerned with the fruits of evil for they possessed their secret cures for all inconvenient diseases. These inconvenient diseases resulted from uncontrolled lusts and excessive whims which dominated their lives void of fear, pain, compassion, or love.

The ambitious little crew of the Solarion knew their chances of destroying the Shareholders were very slim. They were not impractical dreamers. They currently were more concerned with their own survival at this point in time. They had a little time to kill before Eridani.

Dr. Zeek was currently in his apartment module connected by neurotrodes and jacked into the cyberspace of his personal supercomputer. His PSC was a menacing construct standing before him, a formidable opponent with broadsword in hand. The PSC was the first to speak. "So, we meet again and finally on equal terms."

The psychophysicist had chosen for himself the body of a Viking and he stood in full armor with sword and shield in hand facing his PSC construct. He scowled at the construct. "Yes we meet again and once again I will beat you," he spit in callous disdain. Dr. Zeek slashed viciously at the construct and the PSC lithely leaned and pivoted so that the sword missed its mark by no more than a millimeter. The PSC construct cackled and catcalled and then spun around. Down came the broadsword as Zeek the Viking raised his shield barely in time and winced and planted his feet under the force of the blow. The PSC construct spun again and sword flicked and flashed and connected with bare skin at the back of Zeek's neck as Zeek ducked. It was not quite enough to avoid a superficial wound from the razor edged steel. The Viking cursed the blood trickling down his neck and in wild anger charged. The fight was full on.

Ami leapt across the observatory deck as Benny accompanied her dance on the laser axe. Her movements were graceful and beautiful and although not choreographed, she moved with the music and the music moved with her in perfect synchronization.

This hour found the youth brooding. Derek was lost in a solemn gaze into the rushing ether outside and the endless shells of time and curved space. The view before him was the deepest of blue and ringed in the red shift. The blurred scenery gave little sign of purpose or reason, only dusty floods of tubular breeze.

I'm looking out my window.
I'm looking at the world.
I'm looking for the answer,
To all this pain and hurt.

I'm looking for an answer
I know I'll never find.
I can see so much.
I can see that I'm blind.

We're sailing on celestial seas,
Off to worlds unknown.
We pondered lost destinies
On the pebbles we called home.

They told me the answer
Was there wasn't one.

They gave me my assignment
And told me to get it done

But I'm looking out my window
I'm looking at the world.
I'm looking for the answer,
To all this pain and hurt.

22

Planet Paradise

"Strap yourselves in. I have initialized the alternating polarity charge sequence in the membrane supershell of the ship. We are commencing deceleration," stated Dr. Zeek.

"Shut down communication transmitters and flight beacons so that we can proceed undetected," commanded Derek.

"You got it. We are lucky this shuttle was built with aerodynamic capability to land within an atmosphere," Benny remarked as he complied with Derek's command.

"I hope we get the chance to try out that capability," quipped Derek as the ship lurched, rocked, and shook violently. The screens were blackened and blurred. The ship roared and whined. Simulated gravity systems fought to maintain normal levels of 1G, but conditions changed too rapidly. The crew sometimes floated and sometimes slammed into their strapped seats. They were free falling through the time shells. The ship rolled and spun and tumbled. A strong current of displaced artificial atmosphere swirled about them with loose objects in the ship flying wildly around their heads. They heard frightful sounds all around. Glimpses of other dimensions of reality and other worlds were beckoning as they flashed past. The ship dipped below light speed and the screens turned white with blinding light from immense heat and sparks. The free falling subsided into a cushioned dimension below light speed and equilibrium normalized. The Solarion gauges stabilized and the hardy spacecraft was again manageable.

"Just how much do you know about this planet?" Benny asked out of breath and gulping air.

"I hear it is a paradise," replied the yellow eyed youth with conviction above the din of flame surrounding the small craft.

"That is all we need to know," chuckled Benny euphorically but coughing uncontrollably. "Does this paradise have a name?" he managed amid the sparks and roar.

"It is an unknown paradise," yelled Derek above the mayhem. "That is about all I know," offered young Derek.

"Planet P," replied Dr. Zeek to them. "We will look for Planet Paradise, P for Paradise. That is what we will call our new home," said Dr. Zeek excitedly.

"I feel much better knowing it has a name," replied Benny more composed as he touched a control panel. "I am taking us out of our current flight path now," he added as he intently focused on the task at hand.

"We are forced to use optics rather than long range radar," commented Derek. "To avoid detection, we do not know what surveillance is active in this solar system. Better safe than captured," he said as he disengaged radar.

"We are decelerating too rapidly!" screamed Dr. Zeek on the verge of panic. They were freefalling wildly, rolling and tumbling.

"Long range optics initializing," called Derek loudly.

"They are initialized," chimed in Ami 36.

"Do you see a pebble out there worth landing on?" asked Derek anxiously as he also looked.

"I am putting it on the big screen," shouted Ami. "You can see for yourselves," she said as she punched in the sequence.

Before them on the big screen sphere was a blur of rushing ether. "Optic guidance is not going to work at this speed," retorted Derek. "What is our velocity right now?" he yelled with growing frustration.

"We are just below light speed!" shouted Benny urgently.

"Slow us down to 30,000 kilometers per second and hold it steady there," commanded Derek with authority.

"That will take a few minutes," replied Benny as he hurried at the controls.

"I cannot believe it," said Derek in wonder. "There it is," he said in amazement.

There in the vast star-flaked universe was a clustered solar system shining in the light of the only sun around. It was Epsilon Eridani. Within the solar system was a cloudy sphere, a globe cloaked in a clouded atmosphere.

"I can see shades of blue but only a hint through the cotton candy clouds," said Ami in awe. They all focused on the planet nestled majestically before them.

"It is within the habitable zone!" exclaimed Dr. Zeek.

"That is our Planet P. Take us down," said Derek commandingly.

"I will put us in deep space orbit. We will take a closer look at our Planet P," said Benny as he busied himself. "There may be orbiting defense systems," he said, "so let's not move in too conspicuously."

"I will do a global scan with the long range optics. I am setting the alarm sensitivity to notify us of any objects in planetary orbit," said Ami and she made it so. She made several entries into the optics control terminal. "It looks as if we have a couple of moons in deep space orbit," she said, as the alarm display began to fill with descriptive data detailing the shapes detected.

"Put us in an 800,000 kilometer orbit measured from the planet's surface," barked Derek intensely.

"Down to 800,000 we go," called Benny furiously busy at the guidance controls of the Solarion.

"We can expect this planet to have a magnetosphere," speculated Dr. Zeek intently.

"Holding at 800,000 kilometers altitude," announced Benny with a touch of pride. The crew had realized that his piloting skills were truly exceptional.

"The radiation belt should be at around 100,000 kilometers judging from the planetary size," said Derek and Dr. Zeek agreed. "Put us in a little over 100,000 kilometer orbit," he said and Benny made it so.

"I see no evidence of satellites, space stations, tankers, radio transmissions, or mobile launch platforms," commented Ami as she studied. "It looks uninhabited or should I say no technological civilization appears present," said Ami 36.

"How's our velocity?" asked Derek.

"Velocity at 30,000 kilometers per second and holding," replied Benny.

"Slow her down to 5000 kilometers per second, and take us into the magnetosphere," said Derek. "Hang on," he added.

"Here we go!" yelled Benny as they recklessly pitched into the unknown.

"The shell is really heating up," barked Ami 36. She was looking over the optic scan and to the thermal gauges.

"It is getting bumpy," called Benny as they slammed into the magnetosphere. There was a helpless feeling of no control whatsoever as the ship bounced off the magnetic layer and rolled end over end.

"We are passing through low energy electrons into high energy protons!" shouted Dr. Zeek above the bumping and rolling. "I am getting a little sick to my stomach," he then said weakly.

"What is our nautical altitude?" yelled Derek in the midst of the wild ride.

"50,000 kilometers altitude and dropping," called out Benny who also looked drawn and pale after the flurry of rolls and freefalls.

"After the thermonuclear radiation which we survived earlier, we should not worry about the heat we are generating passing through the magnetosphere," said Ami optimistically as the craft stabilized momentarily.

"Decelerate to 500 kilometers per second. Take us into near orbit space just under the radiation belt," said Derek yellow eyes on fire.

"I will skim the inner belt," replied Benny eager to please. He guided the craft under the radiation belt skimming the innermost fringes of the magnetosphere.

"The oceans and land masses are coming in clearly now," announced Ami in wonder.

"We should assume magnetic polarization," said Dr. Zeek, but no one was concerned with polar direction at the moment. He was forever the scientist.

"No sign of low orbit satellites or tankers?" asked Derek to Ami who studied intently.

"I do not see a thing," replied Ami and added, "I believe we are alone or they are well hidden from us. Either way, we cannot turn back."

"That is true. How's our aerodynamic gear, Benny?" asked Derek. "Are we ready to fly for real?"

"I am checking now," replied Benny, and he entered a sequence into a membrane panel.

"It would be wise to enter the atmosphere at a less inhabited polar region," said Dr. Zeek. "Let's hope the inhabitants if any haven't developed long range radar or technology more advanced than ours."

"We can only hope. Aerodynamic flight control gear engaged," said Benny as he took the reigns of the small craft soon to be riding air.

"Put us at 320 nautical kilometers altitude," said Derek as he studied the gauges and optics.

"We are at 1600 kilometers and dropping fast," said Benny and added after a bumpy pause, "holding at 320 nautical kilometers as instructed."

"Decelerate to 300 meters per second and take us in, and hopefully that is below any sound barriers so we don't wake the neighbors," said Derek aggressively.

"We are going in!" exclaimed Benny excitedly.

The ship lurched as Benny guided and glided the hardy craft into the atmosphere. The optics went white with blinding sparks and the showering fire of friction. They were above an arctic polar region and traversing the planet very rapidly. The optics cleared.

"Slow us to 200 meters per second," said Derek. "Let us take a closer look at the neighborhood."

Benny guided the craft down to an altitude of 9000 meters, as the crew looked across a land which appeared to be untouched by mankind. The crew wondered at the frozen polar ice lands. This quickly gave way to green continents, untouched by modern industry.

There were vast shimmering blue oceans and lush tropical forests. There were majestic mountain peaks and dark rushing rivers. There were wind swept plains and peaceful turquoise lakes. They beheld a breathtaking new world laid out before them.

"We should land at dawn," said Dr. Zeek. "I believe we will need a full day to explore, or maybe even a lifetime."

"The sun is rising in the mountain tropics so just say the word," replied Benny eagerly.

They found a large flat unobstructed grassy plain. It looked suitable for a landing pad. They landed the Solarion with ease. There was heavy cover nearby and they parked the craft under the huge forest canopy to avoid detection. What was a small craft in space was now a very large one in the shade of the forest next to a peaceful field of grass. The atmosphere was tested and found to be supportive of human life. The crew ventured out of their ship to have a look around. They camouflaged the ship as best they could with brush from the immediate vicinity but the ship stood out conspicuously in the wilderness. They were all astounded by the sights, smells, and sounds of a pristine new world completely untouched compared to the ruined one they came from. There was nothing from the wildest imagination manifested on a webscreen that remotely compared to this new place. This was a lost and enchanted place. This was a wild new world.

23

Lizards in a Wild New World

"It is so quiet out here," whispered Ami 36, looking around and adjusting her daypack. She kept looking back to the ship from where they had come in order to memorize the way back. She was frightened but also excited to be walking out in such a wild world.

Benny took a reading from his compass and compared it to the aerial photographs snapped off in their speedy decent through the planet's atmosphere. "There is a magnetic north, and according to this aerial snapshot we are positioned in a northeastern declination zone. Do you think Derek will be safe by himself?" asked Benny under his breath.

"I hope so," replied Ami looking worried. "We need to search the perimeter and Dr. Zeek will do better back with the ship, so we didn't have much choice. You and Derek turned out to be pretty good navigators," she smiled nervously at him as he noted landmarks in the distance

"There should be a lake just over those crests," said Benny very quietly. "I hope Derek stays safe. We cannot afford to lose anyone out here. It shouldn't take much time to get to the lake. What was that sound?" His eyes widened and they both listened intently.

"I don't know but it sounded like flapping wings. I guess there are wild animals are out here," replied Ami 36 uneasily.

"Let's go as far as the lake and turn around. We are not accustomed to the outdoors at all and we do not know what to expect. We need time to acclimate," said Benny tensely.

"But it is so peaceful, so enchanting," replied Ami dreamily.

"True but we are totally out of our element," said Benny nervously, keeping his eyes on their destination landmark.

They walked deeper into the balmy tropical forest with the light of the early morning sun streaking through the large leafed trees surrounding them. Walking was easy with only light underbrush and deadwood to contend with. Large yellowed leaves lay on the ground before them and crunched under their feet. Granite poked through the ground making for occasional stepping stones.

They ambled over the crests, chatting about the new world that they found themselves in. Each crest was successively lower than the previous, gently descending into a darkening canyon of deep forest timber.

"Benny, do you think of me as a misfit like you?" asked Ami with a concerned look.

Benny snickered at this petite girl. She was attractive with short spiked black hair and striking Asian features. "Yes, you are most definitely an outcast just like the rest of us," he replied. "We all have something in common. We are all misfits. I guess we are now very lucky misfits considering what we have been through and how we lived to talk about it," he said.

"I keep wondering why I was chosen to die in the sun," she said lost in thought as they walked along.

"Don't waste time trying to sort it out, Ami," replied Benny. "It was probably because you are open and honest which are good traits if you ask me. Who knows? Why worry about it now. It does not matter what reasons they used in choosing us. We are lucky and now we need to look ahead," replied Benny. "Look, there's a lizard in that tree." At the sight of the two wanderers, the lizard opened its mouth menacingly and flared an array of red webbed bone encircling its head.

"It's an ugly looking thing," commented Ami in disgust. She reached into her daypack and pulled out her webpod which was already dialed into their open conference call. "Dr. Zeek?" she asked quietly.

The lizard eyed them fearlessly then jumped to the ground and sprinted off on its hind legs until it was out of sight.

"Yes. I am just sitting here with the ship. What is going on?" asked Dr. Zeek.

"We just saw a nasty strange looking lizard about a half meter in length, and it ran off on hind legs," Ami told him.

"A lizard doing anything on two legs has evolved to some extent. If there are evolved creatures then there is no telling what you may encounter," Dr. Zeek replied. "Please be careful, because there may be much larger creatures," he warned.

"I suppose it is possible, but let's hope not," replied Ami as she followed Benny.

"The lake is a couple kilometers further," said Benny as he turned to face her. "Maybe we should go back to the ship now," he added, worriedly.

"Benny, we just got started," said Ami. "We really need to explore the perimeter for our own safety. I hope that little puff lizard didn't frighten you," she said, trying to sound cool and composed.

"But we really do not know what to expect," said Benny. "We flew in so fast and now here we are tromping off into the forest like school kids on a field trip. There could be much larger predators," he said with tension building in his words. "We don't even have a weapon. We could get in over our heads," he whispered as if someone might overhear their vulnerability.

"We traveled a decade of light years and now you are afraid of a short hike in the woods?" asked Ami 36. She pushed through the foliage ahead.

"I'll go on," he called out, "but I am just not comfortable with this," he retorted as he shook his multi-colored head of hair and hurried to stay with her.

The two walked on with heightened senses knowing there were wild creatures about. As they traveled deeper into the sloping canyon, rocks jutted out into ledges. They sometimes had to jump from a ledge to continue their descent. There were boulders rolled on top of one another which formed darkened caverns. The air grew damp and thick with the stench of decay. Light from the sun dimmed down deep in the canyon, with towering leafage above and canyon rims on all sides. They heard the distinct flapping of wings on several occasions and distant howls.

"Those sound like wolves," whispered Benny. "I am sure of it, and we don't want to get caught with them around. We are just a meal to them," he said.

"We know so little about nature, only the brief snips from the web," said Ami still ambitiously pressing on toward the lake.

"They sound like very large wolves, and I have seen plenty of those on webscreens," said Benny cautiously. "Let's try to be careful and contain our amazement. I want to get out of this alive." They walked on.

"Look, there is the lake," whispered Ami. "Wait. Do you see that?" she asked, crouching behind a patch of brush not far from the lake.

Benny crouched beside her and whispered, "What do you see? I don't see anything."

"Over there by the opposite shore. What is it?" Ami asked trembling in amazement.

"I see it now. It is a small deer, a young yearling taking a drink by shore of the lake," replied Benny softly. "This is so serene," he finally conceded. The shore suddenly erupted and a long dark head shot from the spray and jaws filled with pointed teeth clamped on one hind leg of the startled retreating young deer. "Oh my god," was all Benny managed to choke. They watched in terror. "It is a dragon," breathed Benny with his heart thumping like a hammer in his chest. The huge creature crawled up the bank to get a better bite as the little yearling wildly struggled to free itself. The previous quiet was filled with screams of pure horror as the yearling fought to get away. The dragon used its front legs to pin its prey down and crunched into the neck of the small deer. The wilderness was then silent once again. The dragon lizard crawled into the bushes of the opposite shore with a limp meal hanging from its mouth of daggers.

"That thing is huge, and fast," whispered Ami shakily.

114

"Let's get back to the ship right now," said Benny no longer attempting to conceal his fear.

"I agree," replied Ami as they turned to go. As they backtracked she punched back into the conference call. "Doc, we have just seen a very large dragon lizard," she said.

"Can you describe how large?" inquired Dr. Zeek from the ship.

"I am estimating it was about 1000 kilograms, seven meters in length, scaly and with very sharp teeth. It was also fast. It consumed a small mammal by the shore of the lake," replied Ami, doing her best to describe the dragon and also keep up with Benny as they hurried back to the ship.

"I am looking it up now, hold on a second," replied Dr. Zeek, and he left the airwaves open as he searched his databases. "There was once a grand lineage of dragon lizards matching that description on Earth called megalania, the largest known goannas. The megalania were giant carnivorous ripper lizards similar to the Komodo dragon. Megalania dragons have been extinct on Earth for at least 40,000 years."

"So we may have found ourselves in a world similar to what Earth looked like at least 40,000 years ago," said Benny. "If dragons of that size are running around, we are in danger," Benny said as he focused on their next landmark back to the ship.

"Doc, where is Derek?" asked Ami.

"I am not sure, but I hope he is tuning in to this," replied Dr. Zeek. "You kids better head back to the ship until we can find out more about this place without getting eaten."

At that moment, Derek caught bits and pieces of the conversation from the webpod in the pack strapped to his shoulders, but he was fighting for his life. What he fought, he was not sure. Its massive jaws were frothing and its claws clenched and opened in anticipation of an easy meal. The towering thing roared with hunger and rage, bounding closer and closer. Derek shouted and growled and threw rocks which only aroused the beast further. Derek connected hard with a rock smashing against a row of dripping daggers lining its cavernous mouth, just as the beast dove in for the kill. The beast was mildly stunned and paused and shook its head and then angrily growled. Derek desperately looked for something more substantial than rocks. He saw a large bone lying on the ground in the path to the beast.

He could see a jumble of boulders behind the creature and without thinking further he ran directly toward the horrid monster, which crouched and keenly eyed the boy, letting the easy meal come to it. Derek scooped up the big bone as he ran and it felt solid and he lunged into the crouching thing. The beast growled, snarled, and snapped. Derek swung the bone hard into a green eye of the creature and smelled hot stinking breath and felt the spray as the avocado eye smashed in its socket. The beast deafeningly wailed. He felt sharp teeth clamp and rip into his arm. He let go of the club and ran past the creature and dove into the tumble of boulders.

He crawled on his belly as deep into the tumble as he could and lay in the dark, sweating with his chest pounding hard. He listened to shrieking and snarling and scraping on the rocks outside. He gingerly felt his arm. It was opened up and bleeding freely. It felt numb around the edges of the wound. In the darkness of the boulders, he closed his eyes and saw stars.

24

Universal Spores without Mass Extinctions

Ami and Benny made it back to the Solarion and found Dr. Zeek busy at the webterms of the ship's onboard supercomputer. "Did you get a picture of the dragon?" asked the psychophysicist without looking up from the spherical screen projections.

"It is difficult to snap pictures when you are running for your life," retorted Benny in an agitated tone, but feeling relieved to be onboard the sturdy craft.

"Megalania existed among mammals for millions of years on Earth," said Dr. Zeek. "It is interesting that we are finding a likeness to creatures that once existed on Earth. This is fascinating. My PSC dinosaur databases are now linked with the ship supercomputer. Take a look and tell me if this was the guilty party," said Dr. Zeek. The webterm sphere before them depicted a huge carnivorous dragon complete with simulation of movement and sound.

"That is the one," said Ami and shuddered at the sight.

"Universal Spore Theory holds true," announced Dr. Zeek in wonder. "The proof is all around us. The spores that seeded Earth were not unique to Earth. The original spores are a common denominator of all inhabitable planets. Life adapts and evolves as generations pass, but there is a common thread in the origins. The same fertile spores were planted throughout the universe. These living spores formed replicating cells leading to the formation of complex microorganisms," said Dr. Zeek as he studied the fearsome depiction of megalania.

Benny finally found composure and calm, now that he was safe in the ship. "Creationists finally accepted evolution and scientists finally accepted creationism. The Unification Era was no doubt filled with bitter debates," replied Benny.

"Environmental differences drive adaptation and evolution, which usually results in unique life forms and completely different outcomes from the common original spores," countered Ami, "but here in this world, we are strangely seeing life forms identical to those from early Earth which makes no sense to me. There should be a difference in outcomes, due to adaptation to different environments."

"That is true with one exception," replied Dr. Zeek. "What you are looking at is the largest known megalania from Earth. You both have seen something just as large if not larger in just one short hike in the field. There may be much larger megalania out there than ever were recorded on Earth. This world is much like ours once was, and we can expect similar evolutions and adaptations," stated Dr. Zeek. "There may be another exception which just came to my mind," he added thoughtfully.

"What other exception?" Ami asked.

"Historical events also play a major role in the development of any world. Earth was notably riddled with mass extinctions. We cannot be certain that mass extinctions have occurred on this planet. In other words, have catastrophes occurred here to wipe out or dramatically disrupt evolutionary progressions?" asked Dr. Zeek. "We owe our evolutionary progress as humans to mass extinctions, which eliminated our most fearsome predators and enemies."

"What if mass extinctions have not occurred here?" asked Benny nervously.

"There were species of life from early Earth that I prefer to read about on the web rather than to encounter face to face," replied Dr. Zeek and he eyed them both intently.

"Can you perform a rudimentary analysis of any samples that we bring in? Would that help to determine what kind of world we find ourselves in?" asked Ami anxiously.

"You want to collect samples?" asked Benny looking at Ami incredulously. He was not quite prepared for another venture into the forested unknown without a good reason.

"That is an excellent idea. Bring me plant, soil, rock, spoor, carcass, and bone," said Dr. Zeek. "Bring me anything that is easy to transport back to the ship in manageable portions. I'll do my best to analyze it so that we can better understand this world."

"Have you both forgotten why are we here?" asked Benny with exasperation. He was very aggravated now. "I thought we were just here to hide out for awhile. You both are now talking about an intensive investigation of the planet."

"There is no going back to Earth," said Ami solemnly. "This is our new home."

"She is right," added Dr. Zeek. "Fate gave us a new world full of wonder. Let us be thankful for our good fortune. To survive we need to understand what dangers are waiting for us," he said and turned to the android named Cookie. "Cookie, please scrounge up some containment vessels to hold samplings and also bring handling gloves for our two explorers."

Cookie returned shortly with the items requested. He was efficient and well mannered. Some androids developed amazing personalities, although not nearly as complex as human personalities and not nearly as powerful in the area of subconscious processing. The majority of androids possessed focused one track minds. Androids could go into environments where humans could not go and could do things beyond the physical limits of humans. Cookie was a very useful android, always eager to please and wanting to be appreciated. "I hope these will do, sir," said Cookie.

"Those will work just fine, Cookie," said Dr. Zeek. "Cookie, can you try to raise Derek on his webpod? I am worried about him now more than ever," said Dr. Zeek, as they studied the dinosaurs on the webscreen sphere before them.

"Right away, sir," replied Cookie, and he went to work at the webphone communiqué panels without further comment.

"Do we have anything to carry with us for protection?" asked Benny still unsure about going out again.

"Not unless you feel like lugging a thermonuclear warhead around with you," smirked Dr. Zeek. "We are so lucky this ship was armed with them, and you can bet whoever armed the ship had no idea of what was going to happen to us. You need a handheld weapon," he said. "I have an old knife, a keepsake I have smuggled around for years," said Dr. Zeek. "It would not be of much use against an extremely large creature, or a herd of extremely large creatures," he added with uneasiness. He went off to his apartment module to fetch the old knife.

Ami and Benny waited and listened as Cookie tried to raise Derek. Ami said, "This shuttle was designed to land on known planets with supply stations within tethering distance. We only have an excursion vehicle designed for Mercury."

"Maybe we can use it here in this world," said Benny.

"It needs to be retrofitted for Planet P," said Ami. "I will ask the Doc to take a look at it with me."

Dr. Zeek returned with his old knife and handed it to Benny. He let them out of the ship and wished them well.

Benny and Ami set out again. It was against the better judgment of the wiry musician. They went to collect samples from the surrounding habitat of the lost world for Dr. Zeek, who was busily preparing a makeshift laboratory. Benny and Ami worked hard to fill the sample containment vessels they carried. They collected many varieties of plant, bone, and soil and gathered leaves too large to be placed inside the containment vessels. They used a flat slippery sled with a shoulder harness, which they piled high with differing varieties of foliage and stuffed containment vessels. The steamy morning burned into midday and soon it was late into the afternoon.

"The sun is going down," panted Benny as he wiped sweat from his forehead. "This has got to be the last load for the day. We haven't seen any large lizards yet and for that I am thankful. I am really worried about Derek now," said Benny as they placed a small carcass onto the sled.

Ami was also very worried. "He must be separated from his webpod and since he's been gone all day, he must be lost. I wish we had stayed together now. I'm really worn out, Benny. This has been strenuous physical work," Ami sighed. "It does feel good to be out here though. It is so beautiful."

"It is definitely pristine," Benny admitted as they gazed across the gently sloping tropical valley blanketed in lush green vegetation. A cool gentle evening breeze stirred the tree tops which swayed as air currents passed by. The sun was hanging low yet still above the timberline on the ridge where they stood. Deep in the valley they saw a large bird winging its way higher and higher. It flew out of the darkening canyon and over the far ridge. It was silhouetted there in the poppy red sunset. Even on the far side of the valley climbing into the clouds, the winged creature looked huge and strangely shaped. It had a featherless rat-tail, a long neck, and an ominous snout constantly scanning the terrain below. It possessed a large set of claws on its flapping bat-like wings. They had watched these large birds all day.

Ami shuddered but only because of the cool breeze. They were getting accustomed to the large flying creatures. The gentle breeze left crusty salt where the sweat was before. It was now calm and still and noticeably cooler than before. Long shadows streaked across their path in the quiet walk back to the ship.

"You are more at ease this evening," said Ami, as the ship came into sight when they crested a bluff overlooking the field where they first landed.

"I guess so," Benny said absently, his thoughts somewhere else. "I just needed to get acclimated. We are all in for some big changes it seems," he said casually.

They could see the light from the ship and Dr. Zeek was standing in the doorway. He called out as they approached, "I haven't heard from Derek. This really has me worried because we wouldn't know where to search for him. I don't understand why he hasn't used his webpod."

"Are you sure he took one with him?" asked Benny as he tugged on the sled and drug the last load of the day up to the ship.

"I was sure he packed one. What did you kids bring me this time?" asked Dr. Zeek.

"Lots of samples," replied Ami, as she took her daypack off her back. "Should we try shining high intensity spotlights into the sky so he can spot our location in the dark?" she asked.

"That may attract dinosaurs," replied Dr. Zeek solemnly. Ami and Benny exchanged a shocked glance then looked back at Dr. Zeek. "You heard me correctly. I have no doubt about it now. We have found ourselves in an age of dinosaurs. I was not completely sure until the last load. The gamma ray scanner confirmed. These samples you have been bringing me match the Cretaceous Period of ancient Earth, but we do not know if mass extinctions have occurred. It is highly probable that dinosaurs are out there. I am sure of it. I am really worried about Derek, but it will be foolish to venture out in search of him at this time."

"A bonfire may work," said Ami. "A bonfire wouldn't arouse undue curiosity in the wild animals. They will surely know what fire is. Lightning ignites fires and so they will know to stay away."

"Your expertise in thermonuclear engineering may pay off," smiled the old Dr. Zeek. "That is an excellent idea, and there is plenty of dead wood scattered around the ship for building a large fire."

They set about building a roaring blaze which leapt high into the starlit night. One of the moons that they had seen during their approach to this untamed world hung in the jeweled night sky. They sat around the blaze watching the leaps of spark and flame into the heavens. The warmth and colors of the blaze and sight of the starlit universe stretching to all horizons was awe inspiring. In the pop and roar of burning timber, they heard distant hoots and eerie howls, some deep and low, some high pitched and bone chilling.

Benny pulled out his laser axe and strummed and fingered soft and low. It was an amazingly versatile musical instrument as he had claimed. He finger picked the laser axe in a soothing bluesy folk style that fit the campfire, the starlight, and the mood.

Through the smoke of the fire emerged a lone figure from the shadows of the night. It was young Derek. His long locks of hair hung limply past his shoulders and there was something wrapped around his arm. He carried a large femur bone. He walked up in slow strides not speaking until he stood in the light the blaze. "The fire saved me. I was lost without it," he said. He sounded exhausted. His daypack was ripped and tied around his waist and his shirt was blood-soaked and rolled and tied tightly around his arm. He was caked in mud and smeared blood.

"What happened to you?" Dr. Zeek asked.

"Cookie, bring me a vegetable juice the way I like them," Derek called out to the droid. Cookie had been standing in the doorway of the ship wondering what the big fire was all about. The android nodded its head and disappeared into the ship. The faithful droid emerged almost instantly with the ice cold spiced vegetable juice in hand. Derek drained the drink and requested another. "I have been under a rock," Derek retorted. "I was attacked by something that kept me on my belly for the better part of the day."

"Let me look at that arm," requested Dr. Zeek, who carefully took off the blood-soaked shirt from the bulging arm of the youth. Fresh red blood flowed down the young man's arm as the shirt was loosened. "This does not look good," he said. "Cookie, bring the medical kit," called Dr. Zeek.

Cookie emerged again from the ship with the medical supply kit and another vegetable juice. Derek slowly sipped vegetable juice as Dr. Zeek applied local anesthesia, cleaned and dressed the gapping wound. The bleeding stopped as Dr. Zeek rejoined severed muscle, tissue, and skin with globs of bio-glue. The procedure did not take long by the light of the fire, and the youth was soon all patched up.

Derek began to feel better. "Cookie, this is one righteous vegetable juice," he exclaimed as he smacked his lips in satisfaction. "I think that I will sit by this fire for awhile and enjoy the stars," he said.

Benny bent over his laser axe again and began finger picking in soft rich tones. He played an old acoustic blues tune that came to him, by the light of the evening fire. He had a bottleneck slide which he used to twang and bend and slide into the blue notes, proving again that he was a talented and versatile musician.

25

Sermon on the Ark

Reverend H began his morning in passionate prayer and meditation much like he began every other morning of his long life. He asked for guidance through the dark void along the journey to the paradise light years away. He kneeled low with his knees bent, white dreadlocks draped to the floor before him in contrast to his ebony skin. He thanked the universal creator for the safety of his congregation. He mourned the ones left to die; his long lost family, and long lost friends. He prayed for his enemies. He forgave and asked for forgiveness, and he asked for courage as they wandered through the valleys of the shadows of darkness between the lonely worlds of the cosmos. He humbly asked to see, past opinions, to the truth. He dwelled in the stillness of total thankfulness.

The gentle Reverend H prayed to one not limited by the universe, whose laws were not threatened by human theories. Theories of evolution were not a threat. Fantastic discoveries of alien life forms were not a threat. He bowed to an unlimited potential of supreme intellect, infinite knowing, and power beyond human imagination, reason, or will. He connected with the maker of cosmos and chaos, the one who put in place a ten dimensional universe and unleashed the four dimensional realm beginning no larger than a quark, the one inside.

The abundant universe obeyed laws of nature which the human mind could indeed comprehend. Reverend H meditated with the master programmer, the designer of light and darkness, the old man from the snow covered mountains, the woman who ruled the sea, the child in every creation, the sculptor of lonely predator and frightened prey, and the painter of dying sunsets and newborn dawns. He looked into his own heart, denying the sin and decay, for a ray of enlightenment. He consulted with the dealer of vengeance and fury and founder of peace and love. The creator was not bound by books or teachings, not bound by corrupt hypocritical religions. The ultimate one was all these things and none of them, defying all mental constructs. He communed with the co-creator always close at hand, the one within every living thing.

The space ark was cruising now through deep space with surprisingly little trouble slipping past the proud system defenses of Earth. They had been blessed with smooth sailing so far and with the endless winds of ether at their backs they pressed on, looking ahead to a new beginning. They would reach ninety percent light speed soon with the help of the manmade spinning black holes, the dumpsites and graveyards of wasteful Earth. It was a dangerous maneuver but one which resulted in tremendous speeds when executed with precision. The congregation was aware of the risk of gravitational entrapment, but speed meant survival, greatly reducing the percentage of warships capable of giving chase. There were no other options for them if they were to attain the speed they needed; they must make use of the synthetic black holes.

The space ark rocketed for the first manmade black hole and dipped past the event horizon and into the flow of the swirling mass where no light escaped. The synthetic black holes of Earth were tornado pits of rubbish and scum but minuscule in mass compared to the sun swallowing giants created by nature, which gobbled galaxies. They were convenient garbage disposals but they could also be used to gain acceleration boosts by less advanced spacecraft such as the space ark. The acceleration gain from skimming the ergosphere of a synthetic black hole was not a maneuver for a bulky battle cruiser, but for the space ark it was no trouble at all.

They skimmed three synthetic black hole dumpsites in succession, and the flock of starry-eyed believers was soon hanging onto the throttle at ninety percent of the speed of light. The mass of the space ark was double at ninety percent light speed, but the mass of the space ark would increase exponentially if they pushed the ship any further past ninety percent. The thrusters could live with the doubled mass, but pushing the ship any faster would put them short on fuel. They held the space ark at ninety percent light speed with double their normal mass and pushed on, counting their blessings with each parsec put behind them.

Jenniper was there, remembering lost love. She kept to herself as she vowed, without uttering one word. She was alone again. She never felt so alone. She vowed to take it until she grew stronger, and only time could heal the wound. She vowed to let time heal the wound. She rolled over in her bed to discover again and again, she was alone. She made no plans. All plans were lost. She would grow strong in time. She knew that time was a friend of the wounded. She needed time, time to heal.

The congregation organized themselves and their duties. They worked well together. They worked hard and spirits were high. They left Jenniper to herself, the way she wanted it. They prayed for Jenniper and the lost souls of Earth. A long journey lay in front of the cult. They knew this and were prepared. They would eventually be missed on Earth but not before some delay. It had all been planned with surprisingly intricate detail. They had taken leave from normal duties for various reasons. They would be missed in time, but it would be too late. Most had called into their normal work locations for various fabricated reasons. The reasons people gave for not showing up were designed for delay and diversion. Many called in to report that they had contacted fictitious infectious diseases. The questions would arise, but not anytime soon, and not in time.

Many in the congregation were simply fugitives and outcasts from the system, running from the global police and living outside the protection of slavery. The homeless and forgotten did not last long in corporate society. They were periodically gathered up by the global police and sent to laboratories to be used in experiments or as organ donors, whichever was convenient or in demand. Prison overcrowding was no longer a problem on Earth; another problem solved with ruthless disregard for human life. The forgotten poets, worthless dreamers, hapless losers, and hopeless idealists hid out in the old cult building in preparation for this odyssey. They were the ones who carried no implants, no corporate serial number. Leaving was easy for them. They were accustomed to being ignored by corporate slaves and hunted by global police, and had nothing on Earth to lose.

The world that these hopeless dreamers left behind was known as the New World Order. It was a world owned and dominated by Shareholders, and directed by teracorporations. These pilgrims left behind a world of corporate slavery, mind numbing brainwashing, population reduction programs, complete loss of freedom and liberty, mandatory mass conformity, a global police state, and total global dehumanization. Earth was doomed and ruined, and there was nothing left to lose.

The Cult of What Is humbly believed that high minded opinions were shackles hindering perception. They believed what is simply is, without regard to the opinions held dear. History was riddled with those who proclaimed perception, whose opinions were sought after, who claimed enlightenment, and who claimed to speak wisdom. History was colored with those who justified their opinions for political reasons, for reasons of greed, vanity, or pure ignorance. Prized opinions were viewed as obstacles to insight.

It was a difficult path, to hold no opinion dear, and to perpetually strive for objective perception. The doctrine was ridiculed as hopelessly ambiguous, but it was a path they felt comfortable with. Every step was a risk in this way of thinking. Every decision was based upon deep skepticism of the past teachings. Each act was an act of faith. The ones who joined this cult felt comfortable acting on faith alone. Reverend H was the leader of the cult, knowing that everything he taught was viewed as simply words from a man. It was a burden he felt comfortable with. He realized humbly and thankfully that he was not the one in control.

Reverend H partook in his daily ritual of supplements as he prepared for a sermon as they traveled through the space-time continuum. The soft spoken Reverend H avoided free radicals like the plague, with the use of sophisticated antioxidants in order to greatly reduce damage to his DNA. He had followed the breakthrough developments in gerontology for more than a century. He did not have access to the exotic body cleansing operations of the wretched Shareholders, in order to maintain their self-proclaimed immortality, but this did not concern him. He was not fanatical when it came to the subject of life extension. He simply needed to stay alive long enough to accomplish this, his final goal.

He was in excellent condition after one hundred twenty years of living, and although he had been around the sun many times, he still had lessons to learn and things to do. He looked much younger so the herbal antioxidants had helped. He was amazed that he had lived so long, and naturally he wanted to live longer since he was healthy and sound. He realized long ago that aging rates were severely retarded by the prevention of damage to the DNA. He was not afraid of dying, and was at peace with leaving when the time was right to leave. He had resolved the issue of his own demise in his mind long ago. He was not vain or cowardly. He did not desire to depart this world until his final unfinished business here was completed. He saw no good reason to experience a rapidly debilitating aging process so he took his regimen of vitamins, nutrients, herbs, and supplements with strict discipline.

The Reverend H started his sermon on the observation deck of the space ark, surrounded by a sea of stars, traveling at ninety percent of the speed of light. The congregation gazed in wonder at the twinkling jewels of starlight around them as the sermon began.

"As we look deep into this eloquently crafted cosmos, we all agree it is a little nicer than the richly stained glass windows of the old building back home. This breathtaking view easily contains more beauty than sculptures, paintings, or artworks of any kind, and yet it is still a creation. Human creations often pale in comparison to creations from the ultimate potential. We are in wonder of the patient one, that one within us all. The illusion is that we are separate from that one and from each other. That one has witnessed the dawning of mankind, the birth of technology and industry, and the events leading to this point in time.

We found ourselves no longer able to live peacefully in our own solar system, no longer able to enjoy life, liberty, or the pursuit of happiness in the New World Order. Most suns have a limited lifespan and eventually destroy planetary satellites in final catastrophic death throes. We discovered that our sun was not destined to live a long life and it was not going to die a normal death. We discovered that our sun was targeted for destruction long ago as a result of an ancient religious conflict. This migration was destined to happen, and we were destined to be here now with the cosmos stretched out before us.

We do not know what lies in store for us, as no one can ever know what lies in store. Countless times leaders claimed to know the answers and claimed to know what the future held. When one has the courage to admit how little they really know, and how little they are in control, they have taken the first step to knowing more than anyone has ever known.

It is a blessing and we are thankful to have survived to reach this point in our journey. We share a past dominated by the shortsighted, the selfish, and the ignorant. We are the humble survivors of a world that did not ponder future consequences of present actions. A century ago people never asked what would happen if Earth became so overpopulated that people were forced to live like sardines stacked on top of one another, filling all land and sea. There were not many who stopped to consider that the world's population would one day double every fifty years as people acquired longer life spans.

The New World Order concocted a solution to curtail population growth with programs to destroy weak unproductive members in society. This was another inhuman solution to a human problem. In a thousand years, there may not be enough inhabitable planets in this galaxy to accommodate the human race. Migrations to new inhabitable worlds are the only answer.

We come from a world where we relied upon leaders for the answers and these leaders were filled with euphoria, pride, and power. They were awarded great rewards. They now have their rewards in full, but death removes all their glory. We were pacified and enslaved by these leaders, and forced to accept the lack of reason and the self-serving lies. We now have rewards that no one can take away, even in death. We were never ultimately in control of our own fate, and this is as it should be. Let us enjoy this ride."

26

Punishment

Deep in bombproof chambers sat the rulers of storm ravaged Earth. These were the Shareholders, the owners of everything, and they lustily placed bets on a teracorporate battle raging in space. The dimly lit room was stenched with the smoke from the finest opium, hashish, and tobacco. There was the clink from the wine glass, the bottle, and the jug as drinks were generously poured by the servants and guzzled by the Shareholders. There were no morals or ethics held in high regard, and there were no pretentious attempts to conceal this ugly truth.

"Enercorp does not have a chance and you will lose. They are investing too much in Centauri and Sirius mining operations to give this battle their full attention," snarled a Shareholder to another.

"Shut your trap," snapped the other. "I placed my bet. I do not care what the odds are. They will not invest so much in Centauri or Sirius, once they learn what is out there. You will see. This is a rich claim and they will fight hard to keep it. This claim will be more valuable than Pavonis. Does anyone realize how closely this new sun matches luminosity with Sol? No of course none of you do. Are you all so ignorant as to ignore this valuable claim? I will say again that I do not care what the odds are. I have placed my bet," announced the indignant Shareholder to the others.

"You will soon become very concerned if you lose all of your shares. Pavonis is nineteen light years away and valuable beyond measure. It is no doubt a precious treasure. In comparison, this new find is too far. We do not mind taking your bet but you know the rules. If you lose all your shares, you will be finished. We will see to it," threatened the first Shareholder.

"You have the nerve to remind me of the rules. I do not care about the rules," spit out the indignant Shareholder. "I got where I am today because I broke all the rules. I became a Shareholder the hard way. I ruined everyone on my way to the top of my corporation, and then I destroyed my competitors at the top of many other corporations. I take risks, and I came up the hard way," growled the Shareholder to the others. "I am not like you others who were bred into this role. You purebreds should enjoy this while it lasts, because I will eventually own every last one of you," threatened the Shareholder with darkening malice.

Some say the pyramids took mankind many generations to build, and others say it took an advanced race of aliens just one afternoon. The pyramids now crumbled in decay and it no longer matters who built them. The stock market also crumbled in decay. The Shareholders owned it all, the stock market and the pyramids. Mankind spent generations investing, speculating, and gambling to play the role of shareholders in building national and then global markets. In the end the masses were left with nothing except corporate slavery. The world embraced a global economy and global competition. Markets were globalized and centralized. A global currency was created. Once total globalization was complete, a global takeover was then feasible and even inviting. The New World Order was the culmination of the final global takeover. In the end these few, known as the Shareholders, owned everything.

"We have some business to attend to today," said one Shareholder after bets had been placed. "Some corporate slaves have escaped, and are currently in route to Eridani," the Shareholder informed the others.

"Who was responsible for this?" asked one smoking Shareholder.

"They are waiting outside," said the first.

"Then bring them in," said the smoking one with an evil grin.

"Bring in the guilty parties!" commanded a horrid Shareholder to the android standing at the door.

The android returned with two men. One was the system slug. He was placid and pretentious. He was unapologetic and stoic and stood without regret. In his eyes, he was simply doing his job and he felt that the religious cult was not serious and could not possibly leave Earth. They had talked about this migration for so long now. It was old news. The other man was the space traffic controller who let the religious cult pass through. He was sobbing.

"I swear that I thought they had proper clearance," cried the space traffic controller to the Shareholders sitting there in the dark room thick with choking smoke.

"We are sure you meant well," responded a pale skinned Shareholder as he exhaled a cloud of opium smoke that floated slowly in the direction of the two standing accused. The space traffic controller felt his stomach turn as the smoke hit him, and tried to maintain composure. The Shareholders must be reasonable people, he thought, or they would not be in such high positions of power. It was an honor to finally meet them here in person. They must be made to see that his was a human error, a mistake anyone could have made.

"You must understand your positions gentlemen. You have been terminated. We must now determine what knowledge you possess so that you might possibly be useful to us. We need to determine your salvage value. What do you have to say for yourselves?" asked a Shareholder to those standing accused.

"I can be of value to you," said the space traffic controller desperately and pathetically. "I understand astronomy and space travel," he babbled and sobbed. "I know that I can be of service to you." He did not yet fully realize the seriousness of his situation. He figured he was going to spend the rest of his life digging in a cave in a harsh world somewhere far away.

The system slug said nothing. He had previously volunteered to subject himself to brain surgery which had left him wondering what all this fuss was about. He was unquestioningly doing his job and whatever mistakes he made must be the fault of the surgeons. He did not realize the seriousness of his situation at all. He figured he would be reprogrammed to avoid future mistakes such as this one.

"We are sure that you both can be of service to us. Take them to the operating table and archive their knowledge, and then make peppered jerky out of these two. We love peppered jerky," proclaimed a Shareholder.

The android standing there shot them both with tranquilizer before they could react. They both fell hard and then the android removed the bodies without saying a word. They were placed neatly on operating tables that same hour. Their mental knowledge banks were archived, their organs were placed in cryonic suspension, and the meat that once clothed their bones was cut and cured into peppered jerky. They were given no chance.

27

The Hunter

Nighttime sleeps in the daytime.
But I'm usually awake at night.
People going home,
On the freeways they cuss and fight.
They don't need a reason,
Just that it is this way.
They pay no attention to seasons,
And take what they can from the day.

We're a part of the daytime.
We're all a part of the night.
Forced to play another man's game,
As if he's seen the lights.
You ask me for my reasons
As if you were never my way.
One day you'll want your freedom,
But it'll be given away.

I'm searching my brain
For something I lost today.

Something I wanted to keep
But I must have given away.
Given to some smiling face,
Or some long lost friend,
Or lost in some hiding place,
Like money I'll never spend.

Derek woke early as dawn was breaking across the wilderness. He packed a day's worth of provisions and set out to find the thing that had tried to have him for dinner. He had decided to go hunting but for reasons he could not rationally explain. If the crew were to survive they needed to find out what dangers threatened them, here in this uncharted region of the unknown, but that was no reason to go dinosaur hunting alone. The food rations and propulsion reserves onboard the Solarion were not endless, and they could not afford to spend fuel performing dramatic aerial surveys. They had enough to blast into the sun for the cyclotronic journey back to Sol with big plans of destroying the Shareholders. Derek did not desire to jeopardize that mission. These seemed like rational enough reasons, but there truly was no rational reason as to why he set out into the lonely wild.

He would make do with crude instruments of navigation and protection. He recovered the femur bone that he had used on the beast the day before and he carried this with him as he walked in the early morning mist. Thanks to the stout club, he was hunting for a one eyed beast with an empty aching eye socket.

The young long haired wanderer valued courage and he was out early this morning to test his own. He wanted to have courage, but he was not sure how much of it he truly possessed. He realized that those who value courage do not advertise it, but neither do those who do not. He pondered the qualities of courage as he walked through the jungle. The differences between courage and cowardice were clear to him, but it seemed the differences were not so clear to some, probably due to the discomfort involved with such inward examination. He knew courage was not a trait as unchanging as DNA, and courage could be acquired to replace cowardice. It was much like anything else in this life, if not exercised, courage will atrophy into cowardice. The difference between courage and cowardice is as simple as a decision in a crucial moment. Courage could not be the absence of fear, because he humbly admitted that he was afraid, but not a coward.

It was a dinosaur that bit him, but the episode occurred so fast that there was no time to closely look the thing over. He figured there must be plenty of available prey for the creature to hunt and feed upon since the thing gave up relatively quickly and stalked off, leaving the youth to grope his way back to the ship in the dark. The campfire saved him. It was such a basic thing, a campfire, and yet it was completely novel to this modern young man and stirred feelings of comfort and awe in him that he could not explain.

He figured that dinosaurs must not be as maniacal as fiction writers had depicted them in books and movies of centuries past. Early writers who wrote tales of dinosaurs gave them complicated human behaviors. Dinosaurs did not possess human brains so it must have been done to create suspense for human brains to enjoy. Stalking humans through offices and corridors of buildings and devising sophisticated ambushes made for good fictitious thrills. He figured that dinosaurs were simply creatures of the wild, both predator and prey, and humans were walking meals for carnivores of such magnitude and strength.

It now seemed clear. This world was simple yet powerful. He was not on a paleontology expedition. He was not out to classify species or separate them into known and unknown. He did not desire to study biological behavior or record any findings. He was hunting.

This was an insane idea. It almost made him laugh out loud when he thought about the strange desire he possessed. He felt a spirit swelling inside, a wild spirit. The spirit was all around and it crept into his soul. The spirit was in the gentle breeze and in the bald cypress conifers, in the spruce and in the oak. The spirit of this land was untamed and uncivilized. It was ruthless and delicate. It was roaring and peaceful. He walked quietly through the still morning, alert to his surroundings, looking for signs of life, staying hidden in the shadows.

Derek found the tumble of boulder and rock where he had been forced to lay on his belly and bleed while the creature drooled and howled over him. He picked up the trail of three claw tracks leading into the thick timber and stalked along, moving very slowly and quietly. He scanned the wild in all directions both far and near before making every move. He stayed in the early morning shadows, silently slipping from tree trunk to tree trunk, and crawling from bush to bush. The tracks were easy to trail but the animal moved swiftly with huge strides and covered lots of territory. There were occasional splashes of dried bloody goop along the way undoubtedly from the blow to the eye.

There was a gentle breeze in the face of the young stalker and he knew this was good and luck was with him in this respect. He knew instinctively that it was better to keep his scent out of his direction of travel. He also kept a sharp eye on his backside for predators that might be hunting him. The only weapon this young hunter carried was a bone club, and he was amazed with the beauty all around. He knew this beautiful world was filled with danger but continued on.

He had no hunting experience. Hunting on Earth was banned long ago before he was born. All personal weaponry of any kind was banned on Earth very long ago, as the global police state emerged. Weapons were banned in phases, with hunting and sporting weapons the last to go. The first weapons banned were assault weapons. It was then determined that there is little difference between assault weapons and weapons for self-defense. Law abiding citizen do turn to crime, so all guns were gathered up. Weapons for self-defense were banned with promises of a stronger global police state. The global police became a formidable force but as decades past, the definition of crime changed. Hunting and sporting weapons were finally banned since these were the only weapons left, and the only weapons criminals could acquire. Crime increased as criminals began to realize that all common citizens were unarmed. Crime also increased because the definition of crime was tremendously expanded. Both liberty and the pursuit of happiness were considered capital crimes in the New World Order.

The previously hunted animals of storm ravaged Earth ceased to be managed by the wildlife authorities, because the majority of game management and conservation funding came from the hunting communities and clubs. Hunting clubs were disbanded and made illegal. The wild animal populations rapidly decreased due to starvation and disease. With the lack of game management, overpopulation occurred in increasingly smaller habitats. The supportive habitats continually decreased as human population expanded. The remaining feral animals to hunt were eventually gone.

Derek wondered what hunting on Earth was once like. The final days of hunting must have been reserved for the elites, and was not really hunting at all. In the end, hunting was nothing more than the glorified shooting of exotic game in controlled areas. Here in this wild world, there were no high game fences, no game feeders, no hunting guides, and no high powered weapons. He was alone in a dangerous wilderness, and he snuck through the foliage with all of his senses on high alert.

He came to a quiet riverbed wash where the predator had stopped to take a drink. Derek paused at his reflection in the shady water's edge. He looked like a prehistoric wanderer himself, with a menacing frame of chiseled muscle, long hair past his shoulders, and large bone club at his side. He noticed there were other animal tracks in the mud. There were hoof tracks of prey and the clawed tracks of the hunter. The air was thick with flying insects buzzing above the water where he stood. He carefully scanned the underbrush on all sides and bent over and scooped handfuls of mud. The young hunter smeared the mud on his face and arms and legs. A turtle poked its head out of the water to warily watch. The young wanderer then resumed the trail of clawed tracks left by his prehistoric adversary.

Fiction sometimes painted pictures of predators as lovable cartoon creatures with charming personalities all for the sake of entertainment. He wondered why there were so many cutesy silly depictions of what should have been fearsome beasts in the volumes of fiction. Fictional encounters with wild creatures struck the brilliant dumb with awe, spurred the uninitiated into fearful flight, and filled the bellies of beasts with the bad guys. It was all too scripted and clean, too prearranged, and not a reflection of the natural world. The wild creature might have easily have been a hooded villain, a disease, or a bomb designed to kill only the deserving. In the natural world, the innocent and slow lost their lives to hungry impartial predators. The moral and the immoral all tasted the same. He felt as helpless as a baby in this world. He crept on with caution.

Derek moved quietly down the trail into the long grass still keeping in the shadows of the majestic fern draped forest. The water seemed to attract the biting insects and they continued to buzz around his head. Despite his careful efforts, he knew it was difficult to go slow and undetected in this jungle. He made a conscious effort to crush the biting bugs with slow quiet fingers, rather than resorting to furious swats. A raucous flapping came from the grass somewhere ahead and a large bird took to the air. Derek crouched with femur club in hand and watched in silence. The pterodactyl rose high above and circled like an old buzzard. Derek waited and watched with his eyelids low, silent and still. He knew instinctively that these prehistoric birds possessed keen eyes. There was squawking and rustling up ahead in the grass.

The big pterodactyl winged its way out of sight as Derek slid over a log and slowly crawled on his belly closer to the commotion. There in a matted clearing was a crumple of bone, antler, and hide. There were several pterodactyls at the kill scene fighting over the remains. The massive prehistoric buzzards squawked and tugged at the picked over carcass. They had long snouts filled with glimmering knife teeth. They stood on clawed feet with folded wings used as forearms. Their big eyes were bright and keen, and constantly on the lookout. Derek stayed low and still, carefully avoiding attention.

There was no wind at ground level in the tall grass. Derek decided he had seen enough and slowly crawled back to the fallen log and slid back over to the other side. He moved down the length of the broken timber and slowly circled wide around the kill scene to pick up the trail on the far side. He kept to the backs of the ancient conifers and soon found himself venturing further into the forbidding forest on the far side of the raucous feeding pterodactyls.

There was a jutting mountain up ahead within a kilometer and Derek decided to scale the peak for a better look around, leaving the tracks behind. The fresh tracks he had followed all morning led up the steep mountainside to a level shelf a hundred meters from the base of the peak. The creature had turned and followed the shelf around the mountainside. Derek took the short cut up and scaled the steep incline. He crossed several mountain brims all showing signs of frequent travel and reached the crest which was fairly flat and thickly wooded.

He sat on a rock at the crest gazing back across the land in which he had traveled. It was peaceful and enchanting and he was reminded of the gentle touch of his lost love. When he thought of Jenniper, he felt an unquenchable longing. The wind was cool and stronger up here. It was midday now and he felt sleepy on this mountainside. After some contemplation from the majestic view, he slid off the rock and decided to take a nap. He found a shady rock ledge hidden from the high mountain winds. The animals were not moving much in midday, so he curled up under the ledge and slept like a lazy cat keeping out of the noonday sun, and dreamed of Jenniper.

Love dreams, incredible schemes.
Hitching rides on twenty mule teams.
The flavor of honeysuckle love
In cumulus fluffs high and above

Mountain's dawn, a newborn fawn
Sleeping with the stars when the day is gone
The reasons why a white dove flies
And plays so high in wind filled skies

Sunlight beams, nature sings.
Swimming in pools of crystal springs
Worldly cares just aren't there
When compared to grizzly bears.

Sunset streaks, sparrows retreat.
The campfire warms something to eat
This day is through and thoughts of you
Have made my love dreams come true

28

The Hunted

He awoke in the new strange world and rolled out from under the mountain ledge. He stepped out and stretched and felt a little groggy but better for the rest, so he headed for the mountain crest and quietly into the thick timbers of the mountain top. Up here, the underbrush was sparse and the walking was easy and quiet. He ambled through the forest, not able to see very far into the distance through the thick trees. There were birch and pine here stretching straight and tall, growing close and thick and surrounding the young hunter on all sides. He used the sun to keep his direction true, and continued across the top for more than a kilometer, until he could see the rim of the far side in the near distance. He moved to the edge as slowly and quietly as he could manage. He was at the edge of a sheer canyon wall and crouched to study the terrain.

In the shadows of the dark canyon below he could make out shapes and muffled sounds. He could not see exactly what it was though, but something was hiding in the dark canyon. Out past the canyon, a river was running through the valley floor and in the open of the riverbank and meadows were the largest creatures he had ever set eyes upon. A herd of massive seismosaurus dinosaurs were grazing. They were the stupendous herbivorous sauropods of a lost prehistoric age. Many were fifty meters in length, with bodies five times the size of a large elephant, towering fifteen meters in height. Some dipped their long necks into the clear water for a cool afternoon drink while others scanned the horizons for signs of trouble. They were mud brown in color with long folds and wrinkles in their hides and they looked to be peaceful serene creatures. There were smaller ones playfully jostling one another. These young ones sometimes rose on hind legs and snorted and boxed with juvenile peers, front legs waving in the air.

The mysterious snarling shapes in the shadows of the canyon below were again moving and nearing the wooded edge of the clearing. He could see now that the figures hidden in the dark of the canyon had the striped fur of tigers. They moved on powerful hind legs with shortened upper limbs armed with dagger claws, as they swiftly covered ground. He could see them clearly now. They were a pack of vicious deinonychus, the smaller of the velociraptor species within the 70 kilogram class. They hopped over stumps and broken rotting timber of fallen trees and paused at the edge of the canyon cover, hungrily eyeing the herd of giant lumbering seismosaurs.

A lone deinonychus gave a low rumbling growl and charged the grazing seismosaur herd while the rest of the tiger striped pack remained hidden in cover. The long necks of the seismosaurs raised high in alarm and they began to snort deep bellows with sprays of mist shooting from their relatively small heads. The herd bull galloped out in front to greet the charge and went up on his hind legs and came down hard but the deinonychus front runner was quick and dodged the crushing front legs. The ground shook as the herd bull came down. With a broad jump leap, the deinonychus front runner cleared the deadly swishing tail of the herd bull. The front runner was past the herd bull and running through the frightened herd, scattering the cows and howling malevolently. The herd bull gave chase, leaving the cows unprotected and in the confusion, the rest of the deinonychus pack rushed in.

The herd of seismosaurs stampeded with the cows leading into the grassy plains in the distance rumbling the earth beneath them in their retreat. The ground shook so violently that Derek could feel the vibrations from where he crouched on the mountainside above. The bulls and the calves followed the lead of the cows.

There was an old bull that did not join the retreat. The wrinkled old bull was just as big as the younger herd bull but his muscles sagged and his pot belly hung low to the ground. He stood his ground. He made an attempt to rise up on his hind legs and groaned and it was just no good anymore. He could not get up in the air. He wheezed and snorted in disgust and somewhere in his small brain, he was the herd bull again. He would protect his cows and hold off the hungry pack hunters, and that would be that.

The striped deinonychus were quick, much quicker than they used to be in the old days. They did not scare as easy either, but neither did he. He stomped and swished his old tail but his bony tail never connected and the deinonychus were quicker than they used to be. The deinonychus were also smarter than they used to be. When he charged one group, another group of deinonychus jumped on his aching back and began climbing up his neck. They were all over him like fire ants on an unsuspecting leg. He tried to shake them off but lost his balance. He crushed some of them as he rolled on his back. They were on his belly now, and it was just no good anymore.

Derek got up from the rock ledge and walked the level mountaintop following the drop off, but staying far enough back to keep his profile off the ridge. The carnage was thunderous down below. Evening was rapidly approaching and the stillness of dusk grew near. He had a long walk back to the ship and he realized daylight was quickly running out. He held his bone club tight and his heart raced in his chest.

29

Lost

Darkness was closing in quick as Derek wandered through the jungle in what he believed to be the direction of his home ship. He was not feeling like the grand lone hunter anymore. He was feeling vulnerable and weak in the midst of wild beasts of lost prehistoric ages. Nothing looked the same in the growing darkness. He searched for familiar landmarks and could not make them out in the dim light of dusk. The cycad fronds blended with the angiosperm flowers and the forest closed in on him. He was no longer sure of his direction of travel at all, as he was only able to make out immediate shapes in front of him. He was lost and could not safely travel any further.

The inexperienced explorer had not carried a webpod with him and had no way of contacting the others back at the ship. He cursed his early morning optimism. It was his idea to leave such things behind, in order to travel light, but it was a big mistake now. There were howls and grunts in the gathering dusk, rasping groans and movements in the bush that came from places unseen. He surveyed the bleak twilight in all directions and could make out no raging campfires to guide his way in. He could hear no human sounds, only the sounds of a jungle coming alive with nocturnal activity.

Darkness was deep now and further travel was foolishly useless. He resigned to spending the night in the jungle, an event he had not prepared for. He remembered back when he had told his supervisor that he had earned enough credits to stay out of the jungles, yet here he was. It was ironic, but he never before felt so alive in this wild world. He could picture the production complex where he suited up each day and dove beneath the ocean floor to search for expendable resource. He was helplessly enslaved then, but now he was free from that corporate prison, never to return.

He was now a slave of an untamed darkened world but he was not worried. Mankind had always been enslaved, and had always sought to gain freedom through technology, which ultimately resulted in isolation then corporate slavery. Mankind traded freedom for security, the final nail in the coffin of personal liberty and dignity. He had come full cycle and was now at the beginning. Freedom was subjective. He was free from a subdued life of corporate slavery but now alone in a dangerous land, separated from a lost love that was now as distant as a star in the moonlit sky. Freedom pulsed through his veins, but he must take care in this dangerous place.

He came upon a vine covered bald cypress tree with branches that looked manageable and he used the vines to hoist himself to the branches and climbed high up into the tree in the dark of night. Up in the tree he felt a little safer as he wedged himself into place to avoid falling while asleep. He listened to the sounds of the night and counted stars until sleep finally took over. There was no sound sleep to be had in this dangerous place. He lightly dozed and abruptly woke with each new noise throughout the long night.

He awoke well before sunrise with water pellets splashing in his face. Dark clouds obscured the stars and rain was starting to come down. He sat up in the cypress trying to make out his surroundings but it was no use. The rain started coming down hard. He would have to wait until sunrise and until the rain let up.

Dr. Zeek was also awake back at the ship. Dr. Zeek was worried again. He wished that the youth had packed the webpod, but Derek insisted on traveling without it and had assured the scientist that he would return well before sundown. This did not happen, as sundown came and went with no young wanderer to be found. If Derek were in trouble there would be no helping him. Derek did not mention his plans to hunt, because the young hunter knew there were no rational reasons why.

The old scientist would not find it rational to wander through the wild, hunting as prehistoric hunters once did. The urge to hunt was not justifiable, so the modern old man would say. When the youth did not return by nightfall, Dr. Zeek blamed himself for not strongly insisting that he take the webpod. That jungle was no place to spend the night and it gave Dr. Zeek goose bumps thinking about it. He was an old scientist who lived in laboratories, with no experience in the field. He was scared silly for the young boy's safety. He was now busy working in the lab just as he had through the night, to make determinations about this planet. He did not know what else to do until daylight. If the boy did not return soon, they would have no choice but to search. He needed to gather the others to formulate a search plan.

Dr. Zeek reached the conclusion that Planet P was indeed well populated with herbivorous and carnivorous dinosaurs. Even more startling than this revelation was the additional discovery that this planet was also thickly populated with herbivorous and carnivorous mammals, which had achieved significant evolutionary levels. There was yet another enlightening conclusion to his studies. Global mass extinctions had not occurred on this planet as had periodically occurred every 26 million or so years on planet Earth. This explained why mammals and dinosaurs were evolving side by side here on Planet P.

The lack of mass extinctions was not difficult to believe, but it was a notable difference from Earth. It was a fact that not every sun possessed a dim red dwarf companion traveling in a large elliptical orbit, bringing it close enough every 26 million or so years to disturb the frozen asteroids and comets and other remnants of the solar system origins of the Oort cloud. This periodic disturbance showered sun, Earth, and the complete solar system with massive asteroids and crushing comets. These boulders were of daunting size and struck with devastating impact and periodically extinguished most life on Earth. Terrestrial tidal waves and clouds of dust blocked out the sun and eventually killed off all photo-dependent plant life. The plant dependent herbivores and herbivore dependent carnivores then died off to complete the cycle of mass extinction on Earth. This periodic cycle of global cleansing was sometimes preempted by the rogue comet of planetary magnitude crashing into Earth such as the events which destroyed the mythical city of Atlantis, some 12,000 years ago.

Dr. Zeek had not yet determined to what extent the apparent lack of mass extinctions influenced evolution here in this new world. Mankind owed its very existence to the six most recent major global planetary mass extinctions, and mammals were thought incapable of challenging the terrible reign of the dinosaur. The evolution of species in this strange world called Planet P did not appear to have suffered disruptions such as mass extinction. There was sign of large mammals carrying and giving birth to younglings, in coexistence with egg laying turtles, reptiles, lizards, crocodiles, winged birds, beasts, and dinosaurs.

Dr. Zeek was intently studying a projection screen sphere from images produced by the gamma ray scanner when Ami emerged in the laboratory door. She yawned and sipped her morning cup of coffee. "There is no sign of Derek?" she asked.

"No. He should have taken the webpod with him," said Dr. Zeek through bleary eyes.

"It is really raining really hard out there," Ami commented after she opened the hatch of the ship to peek out.

"That is what we used to call a gulley washer," said Dr. Zeek, not looking up from the projections as the database search displayed several possible matches to the bone fragment currently under analysis. There were too many matches. He narrowed the search by adding additional characteristics, and added a genetic identity range from the DNA detected with the neutrino microscope. He launched the search again and looked up at Ami. "It seems that Derek wants to experience nature on nature's terms, rather than his own. What has gotten into him? Doesn't he realize that nature is a very harsh teacher?" asked Dr. Zeek.

"I believe he is very wild at heart. There is no other reason. Let us just hope he is all right," said Ami, between yawns, still not completely awake.

The sun was rising and Derek sat in his tree and watched patiently as his surroundings slowly came into view through the pouring rain. He finally inched his way down from the vine covered cypress and picked up his bone club. He felt wholly drenched and looked up at the dark clouds hanging low overhead and made his way into the pelting forest. There was no reason to keep quiet in the deafening downpour, so he sloshed along and took the easiest path in what he figured was the direction of the home ship.

The attack came fast and hard, knocking Derek on his back and into the mud and fronds and slamming his head to the ground with the force of an explosion. He opened his eyes and blinked only to see blackness and twinkling bits of light. He coughed and tried to rise but could not and as his vision cleared he saw that he was pinned to the mud by sharp claws extending from a hulking tree-trunk sized leg. He helplessly winced as the rain beat down. Above him surrounded by dark clouds, lightning, and drenching rain was a towering creature of unspeakable horror. It was a red rimmed allosaurus.

He had intently studied the dinosaur database back at the ship night before last and there was no mistaking this one. Its hind leg claws gripped and dug deep into his chest but without full crushing body weight. The creature holding him down could have already killed him. It looked him over. It leaned its head low and there was an empty dirt filled socket where a large green eye once was. The allosaurus stuck its muzzle into Derek's rain soaked face and sniffed curiously with sharp rows of teeth cutting into his throat and chin. He was blasted by the smell of hot rotten garbage breath as the thing sucked in the young hunter's scent.

The allosaurus raised its head sharply and scanned the drenching forest, hearing something that Derek did not hear. The allosaurus sniffed the air above furiously for a moment. It then looked down again with its one good eye curiously studying its pinned prey choking in the mud. It wagged its clawed forearms, almost gleefully. The allosaurus heard something again and cocked its one good eye toward its backside. It let out a hideous deafening roar and instantly shifted more weight onto its claws cutting into his chest now streaming with blood. He was having great difficulty breathing as he lay trapped in the mud. He wondered for a frightful moment if the roar were a call to others, but there was no time to ponder.

The bone club was on the ground beside him and he reached and grabbed it and slid it above his head where he could hold it tightly in both hands while laying in the mud. The allosaurus watched from its good side but did not stop him. The allosaurus dipped low again with its head cocked to admire its prize again with its one good eye. Derek's body tensed and recoiled and smashed the bone club with all his might on the one good avocado eye and was rewarded with gushing goop.

The creature snarled and screamed and for a heartbeat raised its gripping hind leg in a forward stroke intended to rip from head to toe. In that same heartbeat, the youth quickly rolled out of the way of the deadly claw stroke and pounced to his feet. The claw struck empty splashing mud. With bone club still in his hand and terror peppered with unleashed rage, the youth gave a guttural growl as he swung the club with all his strength. He buried it deep across the front teeth of the blinded monster and he heard and felt the crunch of a solid strike.

The allosaurus blindly rushed and the youth sidestepped and struck hard across a pitted ear on the side of the big head of the creature. The allosaurus shook its huge head violently and wobbled and then wailed a deafening moan. Its forearms clawed at the rain and its bloody head dipped low to the ground in the direction of the blow and sniffed angrily for its escaped prey.

Derek was already running around behind the thing in a circle and crawling under its tail on the other side, of the allosaurus. Without losing momentum, he unmercifully smashed the other ear. The prehistoric beast wobbled again and turned to face him with its forearm claws wickedly thrashing and groping. Blood ran freely from the broken toothed snout.

Derek reached back and unleashed the club once again dead center of the empty sockets of the big dinosaur. He struck again and again, and the unseeing beast stood growling and gurgling blood with its head now hanging down and its clawed feet staggering forward. The dinosaur opened its jaws wide and bellowed and Derek thrust the bone club down the throat of the allosaurus, burying it deep inside. The snaggle-toothed jaw clamped down and crunched the lodged bone and choked. The creature gagged, wheezed, coughed, and struggled for air. It rocked from leg to leg, splashing in the puddles, madly trying to get to the pieces of bone lodged down its throat with its shortened fore-claws.

The massive red rimmed allosaurus was out of air and life and fell forward, sprawling in the mud. The hulking youth stood heaving over the prehistoric creature with rain still pouring down.

30

Found But Not Alone

Derek walked through the wild jungle now with no weapon in hand. He truly felt alone and did not have a clue where the home ship lay hidden through the deep forests. The violent episode with the red rimmed allosaurus left him weak and sick to his stomach. There were thousands of grassy plains that could be the one he searched for. There were thousands of peaks and valleys. He desperately scanned the terrain for a welcome landmark, but he saw nothing familiar. He wearily scaled a sharp incline and ascended higher and higher to reach the top of the peak for a better view. He crossed several shady brims on the way to the crest above. The sun beat through the departing rain clouds, as he moved higher, and steamy mist drifted up from the lowlands. He felt completely exhausted when he finally reached the top.

At the top, he thought he saw the river in the distance where the seismosaurus herd had come to water. He studied the vast terrain intently and thought he recognized where he had watched the deinonychus attack the herd of seismosaurus on the previous day. He visually retraced his path from the mountain since yesterday evening. He had left the Solarion the previous morning heading due south, but he was no longer sure of his northerly return direction. He had not covered a vast amount of ground since the night before, so there was no chance to have accidentally walked past the ship.

He rested for awhile to regain strength and wits. He drifted off then came back around. He found a straight stick and stuck it in the ground and noted the position of the sun. It would eventually be high noon. He marked the line in the dirt cast by the shadow of the sun and waited. The ship was aground in a northern continent, and the planet revolved counter-clockwise in orbit of Epsilon Eridani, and the sun moved across the southern sky east to west. He gazed at Epsilon Eridani and realized it did not burn as bright as Sol. The climate was mild in this region. The mean distance from Earth to Sol was an astronomical unit so the distance between Planet P and Epsilon Eridani was probably somewhat greater than an astronomical unit. The astronomical unit was an arbitrary provincial measurement, and an example of the narrow minded thinking of mankind. The frustrated youth waited for the shadow cast from the stick to change.

He studied the terrain between the distant peaks to his current position until he was fairly sure of the path that he had taken. He took a deep breath of cool mountain air and suddenly realized how hungry he was. His stomach rumbled in reply to his thoughts. His shoulder pack lay somewhere in the mud ripped to shreds with the crushed ginger protein loaf it had carried. He was covered in caked splashes of blood and muck, and his chest was streaked in coagulated claw marks but the cuts were not life threatening. The rain had washed his wounds. His body reeked from sweat and blood which bothered him the most, because his scent would be strong now.

He did not want to stay in one place too long smelling like he did, but he had to confirm his direction. He checked the position of the sun and it was now close to high noon. He leaned against a birch tree remaining motionless and quiet. He had learned this much that unseen and unheard were desirable traits to possess in a world where hunter soon became the hunted.

The red rimmed allosaurus had played with him like a cat toys with a helpless mouse. He felt sick from the violent encounter. The vicious carnivorous beast obviously killed routinely without hesitation, but it had grown curious which gave the young hunter with the bone club the advantage. He wondered what levels of intelligence such predatory dinosaurs possess, and was thankful it had spared his life in those first few moments. The beast was well fed or it would have ended quickly. Curious predator and horrified prey lived in nature on nature's terms. He humbly admitted he was not ready for this. He realized that he had no understanding of the natural world at all. Dinosaurs had more sophisticated brains than he had ever imagined. He had never killed before. He had much to learn.

Humans progressively distanced themselves from nature, as technology and automation became more pervasive. The human spirit was apparently at war with nature, and most believed that nature was to be conquered and controlled. History was essentially a struggle for humanity to subdue the power of nature. True understanding of nature was distorted through misinformation. In an effort to defeat the fickled whims of nature, climate and weather were soon viewed as inconvenient aspects of an environment to be controlled. Grandiose attempts to control the weather eventually backfired, as Earth became ripped and riddled with superstorms of continental proportions. The merciless storms were unending. The lesson eventually learned was that nature could not be conquered, controlled, or subdued.

Nature had survived all that mankind could imagine or conjure, and was never really in trouble at all, but humanity was in deep trouble. The industrial age heralded the information age, a beginning to the end. Complete countries became nothing more than factories, as transnational corporations exploited cheap labor around the globe. There was a corporate gold rush to discover and lay claim to the cheapest labor possible, creating working conditions worse than slavery. In the end, global corporate slavery was the new answer to cheap labor.

Hopeless generations no longer appreciated the beauty of the natural world. They became indifferent and inconvenienced by the whims of atmospheric climates. The overwhelming obsessions were jobs, houses, vehicles, entertainment, and unquenchable unsustainable material consumption. Sanctuaries and habitats were built for animals near extinction in hopes of saving nature. This was all vanity because nature was never in trouble.

In the final world war, deep space rocked and shook with nuclear detonations as all national superpowers were destroyed. All governments and countries dissolved into chaos and confusion. National boundaries, laws, and governments were no more. There became only one global language, one global currency, and one world council appointed to govern. The final war destroyed all governments and nationalities because it was a global corporate takeover in disguise. The New World Order was heralded into power. Earth was run by terascale corporations, and these teracorporations were owned by the Shareholders.

Derek realized nature had not been affected by any of this, as he gazed across the fern draped ancient trees and into the valley below. The sight dazzled his eyes, but he needed to focus upon the immediate problem at hand. He was lost in a dangerous and unknown world.

He checked the position of the sun again and it was past high noon, enough to get a measurement. He marked the shadow projected from the stick in the dirt and he then had a line drawn from each shadow mark forming an angle in the dirt. He drew a line bisecting that angle. The line bisecting the angle and pointing away from the stick was what he took to be north. He picked out a landmark of distinct rock formations in the distance and once again embarked into the deep woods towards the next leg in his journey.

Derek made it to the rocky landmark and lined up his starting point at the birch on the distant peak with the rocky ledge from where he stood before. He picked out another landmark across an unfamiliar canyon and started down into the shadowy terrain and realized he was either too far east or west of the ship. His only hope was to spot something familiar in the peaks through which he slowly and quietly traversed. He had seen many animals in his long journey and he stayed out of sight from them as best as he could.

He hiked throughout the day and into early evening. He knew now he had walked far enough to the north and he scanned the country intently to the east and to the west. To the west, more peaks and valleys, and to the east less prevalent peaks with stretches of high grass lined with thick jungle and dark lowland swamps. Neither direction was inviting. In the late afternoon of the forbidden world, he suddenly heard something strange and unearthly, howling and wailing, screaming and shrieking. He crouched and listened and recognized. It was a melody from the laser axe. His heart skipped for joy.

Benny 42 stood on top of the ship with laser axe cranked to full soul piercing volume. He fingered and banged, belting out unbelievable sounds putting all wild animals within range on alert. Benny cut loose with much musical mojo and he was oozing with it. A long horned carnotaurus looked up and sniffed the humid tropical air for signs of trouble. The monster predator had never heard such foreign sounds before, and the creature experienced a rare twinge of fear, an uncommon emotion for such a natural born killer. The carnotaurus feared the raucous eruptions of sound were coming from a larger more formidable foe, and the carnotaurus ran for its life.

Derek followed the unearthly sound of the laser axe as the sun began sinking into the tree tops. He could not take a chance on losing the sound, so he jogged through thick foliage toward the welcomed high pitched searing of musical bombast.

The young wanderer was well on his way when he stopped dead in his tracks to gaze at an object lying there in the grass in front of his path. He scanned the jungled surroundings but all was clear. He crouched, bending his knees, and dug at the overgrown grass and gently unearthed a strange object from the ground. He examined the object closely from one end to another. It was a wooden arrow. At one end, there was a notch with fletching made of feather. At the other end was a razor sharp broadhead of hammered flint.

31

The Gift

He clutched the arrow and continued jogging toward the sounds pouring from the laser axe. His pace was measured because he wanted to avoid getting too winded in order to be able to deal with surprise threats arising from the surrounding swamps. The possibility of human inhabitants in this land caused his mind to race. Darkness was falling, but he saw the glow from the raging fire beside the home ship in the distance. The sparks raced upward and mingled with the stars before fading. The sight brought a welcome relief.

He could make out Benny on top of the ship in the distance with the searing laser axe strapped to his shoulder. The wiry minstrel strummed, banged, belted, and fingered the unique instrument with detached delight and emotional fury. It looked like a scorching scene from hell itself, but Derek only smiled the weary smile of a lonely wanderer, the smile of a lost and hungry hunter returning home.

He finally made it safely to camp and walked in and waved to Dr. Zeek and Ami, who sat by the fire. They were surprised and happy to see him. Cookie who stood in the doorway of the ship went off to make the young pilgrim a spicy vegetable juice. Benny snuffed the raging laser axe and slid into the top hatch and came down to the camp fire with the axe still slung across his back. They gathered around and gazed in wonder at the arrow.

"This is an amazing discovery," exclaimed Dr. Zeek. "Sentient life exists on this planet and not just sentient life, but human sentient life. I must take this into the laboratory to perform further analysis," said Dr. Zeek excitedly.

"It is all yours, Doc," replied Derek. "I just have one request." Dr. Zeek looked up and eyed the hunter inquisitively.

"Yes?" asked Dr. Zeek.

"When you are finished, I want to construct a dozen just like that one, and I want to carve a bow with which to accurately propel them," said Derek. His yellow eyes blazed. Derek had experienced a wild spirit which he could not explain, and he wanted more. He wanted to wander and hunt in this untamed wilderness.

There is a big difference between the psychophysics of neuroton projection and the physical aerodynamic properties of a wooden arrow found in the forest, and Dr. Zeek was challenged. They never dreamed that they would be designing such a primitive weapon of stick and string. This was beyond the scope of the original plan, which was to hide out on a forgotten planet while formulating a plan of attack upon the small powerful group of corrupt world leaders. This crazy business of hunting and wild adventure was not something Dr. Zeek fully appreciated, but he was intrigued by the presence of planetary natives. There were mysteries waiting to be uncovered in this melting pot of prehistoric evolution.

Later that evening, Derek sat by the campfire along with Dr. Zeek after the others had retired for the night. Derek gazed into the embers and nursed a vegetable juice and brooded. Dr. Zeek leaned back in his chair. The flame was reduced to peaceful glowing coals that occasionally popped. Dr. Zeek stared into the starry night sky. "It is nice by the fire. I have been counting shooting stars. It is amazing the number of meteors that pelt the atmosphere of a planet on any given night. Most people live their whole lives without enjoying one clear night sky like this one," said Dr. Zeek. They quietly admired the panoramic view of the stars in silence for awhile. "I suppose you never knew your parents," said Dr. Zeek to the youth.

Derek never looked up from the dying embers but answered, "Of course not. No, I never did. That was not part of the deal," he replied.

"Incredible as it may sound to you, I got to know mine," replied Dr. Zeek. "They were good people, very honest and loving. They were taken away when they were too old and could no longer work, during the first phase of global population reduction," said old Dr. Zeek.

"Sorry to hear it," replied Derek distantly.

"I was blessed to have known them," said Dr. Zeek, smiling at the memory, but then his smile turned to a frown. "There was nothing anyone could do. It was a sad time, but no different for me than the billions of other people in my age group who lost their parents. They avoided the emotional scars that we suffered in future generations by complete laboratory conception," said Dr. Zeek.

"Yes, I was a test tube baby, just like Ami and Benny, and the billions of others." Derek sighed. "I am the product of human embryonic genetic factories," he muttered, but it was obvious that he did not care to elaborate.

"One of my earliest memories was when my father was young and strong, and it was snowing outside. I stood inside the screen door and he made a snowball in the yard and threw it at me. The snow pelted the screen and he grinned. That picture of him when he was young and strong standing there in the snow grinning back at me is frozen in my mind. I also remember holding my father's hand in church. To me, his was the biggest strongest hand in the world," said Dr. Zeek.

"I do not have such memories," said Derek. "You are a fortunate man," he added dreamily.

"My father left me something," said Dr. Zeek. "It was in the box sent to me after my parents were both gone. I have smuggled it around with me all these years. I lent it to Benny and Ami when they were collecting samples," he said as he produced an object sheathed in leather. "It hasn't been easy keeping this thing hidden. It should have been confiscated long ago. I would like for you to have this," he said and he handed it to Derek.

Derek unsheathed the knife. It was solidly made of fine stainless surgical steel with an antler bone handle. The grip was comfortable in his hand. Etched at the base of the blade was an inscription no longer legible from wear. He did not know what to say. On Earth, gifts were illegal so this was the first he had ever received. The shiny steel glistened by the firelight. He tested the edge and it was razor sharp. It was a solid hunting knife, forged more than a century ago. "Thank you," were the only humble words he managed.

"You needed a tool both to protect yourself and to carve a bow with, and now you have one," smiled Dr. Zeek. "I am off to get some sleep," he said and yawned, as he got up to head to the ship. He left Derek sitting there by the dying embers admiring the magnificent blade.

32

New Home in a New Sun

The days and weeks passed, but they were days and weeks measured by the risings and settings of Epsilon Eridani. The solar survivors settled into life in the wild. Derek began the work of fashioning a long bow of maple and arrows of cedar. He whittled and carved, cursed, and carved again. He was determined to create his very own primitive weapon of old. There were some power tools for ship maintenance that proved helpful in the construction. He made use of the knife, whittling and sculpting until he was beginning to have the makings of a bow and arrows. Dr. Zeek continued his studies and data collection in the laboratory. Benny and Ami worked on a makeshift early warning system to scan the perimeter of the camp for intruders. The solar pilgrims began to call Eridani their sun, and Planet P their new home.

There were many passing herds of dinosaurs keeping the pilgrims constantly wary and watchful. Herbivorous herds in large numbers ambled by daily. The vicious nomadic predator packs were always tracking close behind the herbivorous prey, lurking and stalking in the shadows, nabbing the slower and weaker members from the herd. The crew devised search and rescue plans for worst case scenarios and unforeseen disasters. They felt very alone and vulnerable. They came to greatly depend upon each other. They hoped they would soon find the humans sharing their new world.

Deep in interstellar space, Reverend H and his followers traveled at the ninety percent the speed of light in a space ark bound for Epsilon Eridani. They were destined for a planet in the solar system of Eridani that they believed to be a paradise. The refugees were bound for the same Planet P, the place the Solarion crew now called home.

These cult refugees were not experienced space travelers, but they were organized, and the trip had been planned for decades. The space odyssey would take 13 Earth years at 90 percent the speed of light, but the trip would be completed in less than a year for those on board the space ark, due to the tricks of traveling high speed through the space-time continuum. Earth clocks would register 13 years but clocks inside the ship would move much slower relative to Earth, appearing completely normal to the refugees.

Ten months was a long time to be cooped up in an ark, but there were no more options. Living a life of slavery was no longer acceptable, and Reverend H was convinced that Earth had indeed been targeted for nullification by alien religious crusaders from another galaxy. He was not entirely sure of the method or means of the earthly nullification, but he was convinced that it was going to happen. The proof was unearthed from natural receiving elements long ago, and nature had archived the encrypted transmissions demanding religious conversion.

Reverend H believed this inevitable destruction had been kept a secret by those who tell the Shareholders what they want to hear. The Shareholders would learn very soon if they did not know already. When they discovered the truth, they would undoubtedly flee their world for another, because their world was doomed. One thing was for certain, the general population was going to be the very last to know of this catastrophe.

33

Only One Shot

Derek worked on his maple longbow with slow deliberate and delicate finishing strokes carving the final touches with his knife. He always carried the blade with him now, either strapped to his boot or at work in his hands, and he thanked Dr. Zeek often for the fine blade. Derek enjoyed thanking him, as much as Dr. Zeek enjoyed being thanked. The knife was indeed a weapon and a tool for the modern young man. It was a mystical forge of steel and bone, conjuring up images of a lost time and place, precisely the world that he found himself part of now. He labored for a month, judging by the moons of Planet P, and the bow and arrows were near completion.

His arrows were duplicates of the one he had found in the wilderness. They were cedar shafts, feather fletched, with broadheads of hammered flint. He scrounged up threading that he braided and used for the bowstring. He worked on the double grooves at each end of the longbow until they were just right. Final adjustments were made to the threading, the bow-grip, and the arrow rest. He was finally finished and ready to shoot. He constructed a grass target, and nocked an arrow as the crew gathered around.

Derek drew back and pointed his carved creation at the target some forty meters away. The arrow was poised and ready to fly. The moment of truth after so much work had arrived. He breathed easy at full draw and faced the target with both eyes opened and released the arrow from his steady relaxed grip. The arrow whispered through the air with surprising velocity, homing in on the distant target. The arrow then flew on past its destination, high and wild and buried into the grass twenty meters beyond the other side.

Benny chuckled. "You still have the knife if all else fails."

Derek only grimaced. He could not risk losing a precious arrow, so he was off immediately to retrieve the shaft. The young man was seriously determined. He understood that when hunting with stick and string he would be granted only one shot, and if he missed, either his prey would escape, or attack. He needed lots of practice.

"Should we give it to him now?" asked Ami to the others. "Maybe we should wait to see if he gets any better," she added while Derek was off searching for his arrow in the grass.

"He will get better," said Dr. Zeek, with a touch of fatherly pride.

"Give it to him now, Ami. He will love it," replied Benny.

Derek walked back with the arrow in hand, surveying the damage. It was a sturdy shaft, but the broadhead would need to be sharpened after more trips into the dirt like that. The crew waited back at the shooting line. They were smiling as he approached. They seemed to be amused with his shooting.

"This is a little tougher than it looks," announced Derek to them, grinning sheepishly.

"We have something for you," Ami said. "We hope you will find it useful." She took her hand from behind her back and handed the gift to him.

"What do you have for me, another present?" asked Derek incredulously. He was not sure what to think. This was the second gift he had ever received.

It was a stitched wolf hide quiver attached to the shoulder straps from his salvaged but shredded daypack. He put his cedar arrows into the quiver and strapped it across his back.

"We found a timber wolf hide and we tanned the hide and stitched it into an arrow quiver for you. We also thought you might need all the help you can get," said Benny smirking.

"It is perfect," replied Derek sincerely. He reached back for a shaft, nocked, and drew. His stance was solid as rock. His muscled limbs held the big longbow without a twitch. His eyes focused down the shaft, the razor sharp broadhead, and through to the target, and he released. The arrow went wild and high again and buried in the grass, but this time a little closer to the target. He turned to them and smiled. "Thank you all so much," he said.

"You must judge ground distance precisely with your eyes," offered Ami, trying to be helpful.

"You will probably be getting better at finding arrows as time goes by," joked Benny.

"Some fine tuning of your nock point position, arrow rest, and fletching will reduce porpoising and fishtailing in your arrow flight," commented Dr. Zeek. "After a little fine tuning, all you really need is a little practice," he said. Derek let another fly and it was again closer to the grass target. "When you release, hold the bow steady during the follow through until the shaft fully clears," observed Dr. Zeek, and the youth listened reverently.

Derek let another one fly and it was again another miss over the top of the stuffed grass target, but this time the arrow stuck much closer near to the intended destination. He practiced shooting the bow and made fine adjustments to the arrow rest and nock point, until the sun sank low and he could no longer see to shoot. He soon realized that he was using a new combination of muscles to fling the shafts and the arrow shooting left him aching that evening and stiff and sore for days afterwards. He continued shooting day after day, sunup to sundown, and sharpened his broadheads in the evenings by the fire. He took comfort and solace beside the firelight but still found himself brooding over his lost love.

34

Dinometers

Ami developed an early warning system to better alert the crew when dinosaurs were dangerously close to base camp. She called the early warning sensors, dinometers. She used modular ship components designed for easy replacement and repair, but only after convincing Dr. Zeek that the modules would be carefully preserved. They had carried aboard the ship a supply of replacement solar panels and upgraded thermographs for intended studies on Mercury. There was a load of seismometers, part of the assignment to measure Mercury quakes. Each dinometer module was built from radar and optic modules pulled from the ship, a thermograph, a seismometer, a webphone, a webcam, an audible alarm loudspeaker, and a solar panel power supply module. There were also fusion generator modules on the ship but Dr. Zeek refused to let those be taken. It was all they could do to talk him out of the ship's radar and optic modules, because this meant the ship could not take off until it was put back together.

Sensitivity levels for the dinometer modules were adjusted to relay real time movement data back to the ship's communication processors. The dinometer modules were installed in trees. A seismometer was buried near the base and up in the tree they mounted a radar and optic module, thermograph, solar panel module, audible loudspeaker, webphone, and webcam. There were power supply feeds running down from the solar panel module and data feeds from each module to the webphone. The dinometers were strategically placed to monitor the surrounding perimeter of the base camp.

Benny helped Ami with the dinometer installations, as Dr. Zeek worked on the array of parallel communication processors which uniquely identified each dinometer and split the load of the incoming transmissions evenly across arrays of processors. He adjusted startup and shutdown scripts for the communication subsystem; testing until he was satisfied the data was being properly fed into the real time distributed object database. The alarm and display subsystems were tested and configured until the dinosaur detection system was fully operational.

Dr. Zeek was satisfied that the data was being properly read into the database, so he set about creating a set of known objects allowed through the dinosaur early warning system. The first object he created was a human object with a list of human properties. The properties were defined with allowable ranges. He created instances of human objects by assigning attributes to describe each member of the crew. A special android object was created for Cookie, but allowing a wider range of values for attributes. He assigned attributes to describe Cookie, so that the android would not set off alarms. He granted permission into base camp to all instances who were members of the crew, but the guest list only included the crew of the Solarion. No one else was invited into the base camp perimeter.

Dr. Zeek then generated a historical database structure, in which he performed a snapshot of the real time database at specified intervals, to collect data to create other objects detected and identified by the early warning system. Any object not on the carefully crafted guest list would set off alarms. The alarm subsystem could be configured to perform a variety of tasks in the event of an alarm, depending upon the severity level and the filtering mechanisms. He configured the alarm subsystem to set off audible alarms for all intruders, but alarms could be suppressed when an event was acknowledged. Events were tracked and precisely recorded. They monitored anything that entered the dinosaur detection perimeter. While they were out and about, they set the dinometers to audibly alert at the loudspeakers in the trees, so as to give the crew time to make it back to the ship in advance of uninvited guests.

Dr. Zeek planned to configure various detection filters so the alarm subsystem took specified actions depending on severity levels. He realized the system could eventually evolve from an early warning system into an early defense system.

Ami was talented with creative practical ideas, and she and Benny worked hard to get the dinometers in place. Dr. Zeek labored at the consoles of the powerful ship supercomputer to build and test the database platform and communication processor subsystem. The crew came up with a rewarding project to occupy their time with. They worked well together.

Derek was not involved in building the dinometers or the early warning dinosaur detection system. The project gave the others something constructive to do with their time, but he relentlessly continued flinging arrows at grass targets. He did not plan to live at the base camp forever but he kept that to himself. The spirit of the wild had infected his soul. He longed to roam the badlands of this lost world. This crew had become his very good friends, but he could not drag them along. Derek nocked, drew, and released another shaft. His fingers had grown so bloody and sore that he now used a strip of slotted hide for gripping and releasing the string which flung the arrow.

He practiced shooting arrows at various distances and discovered he was developing instinctively keen senses, and a distance of one meter made a difference in the desired arrow placement. He practiced kneeling and shooting then drawing and releasing in rapid succession. He practiced shooting in various hunting situations, shooting through ground cover, and shooting over obstructions where the arc of the arrow cleared the obstruction to settle into the intended target. He practiced shooting at moving targets, remotely releasing a target that dangled or slid down a rail, hitting the target as it passed across his shooting lane. He was becoming a more proficient archer with each passing day.

The dinosaur detection system had been online for some time now. The initial glitches were mostly worked out. The little crew retreated several times into the ship when audible alarms sounded as they watched in fascination at various creatures passing through the perimeter detection zone, sometimes venturing very close to the ship. Carnivorous predators who hunted down their food proved to possess a dangerously healthy curiosity. There were close calls with the tiger striped deinonychus. These vicious predators always traveled in packs, and had explored in detail the exterior of the Solarion, as the crew watched from dinometer viewing consoles inside.

Dr. Zeek used the dinometer inputs to build object profiles of the various creatures detected. His initial observations proved to be strikingly accurate, and this was a planet without mass extinctions and one that was indeed crawling with wild things. The Cenozoic Era was fully represented along with Mesozoic and Paleozoic Eras. The Cretaceous, Jurassic, and Triassic Periods of dinosaurs were all intermingled and represented here. Mammals emerged and evolved to roam among dinosaurs here, creating a vast evolutionary melting pot.

Food and water were not in infinite supply upon the maiden voyager Solarion. This became a growing concern to the hidden solar survivors. As wild and dangerous as Planet P had proved to be, it was now their new home and they began to talk in terms of making it permanent. They began to talk in terms of returning to Planet P to live, after the Shareholders were put out of commission. They knew Earth was ruined. This was more evident than ever, the more they came to know the pristine wilderness where they camped and lived. They realized in contrast how irreversible the damage truly was.

Dr. Zeek peered through the viewing lens of his neutrino microscope at multitudes of insects captured from solar powered bug-zappers which Ami had designed. The dinometer project wound down, so Ami rigged up the bug-zappers to provide Dr. Zeek with an endless supply of specimens to investigate. He was a theoretical laboratory scientist, so he was amazed at the practical applications she had concocted with such limited resources. He was not accustomed to seeing scientific ideas applied so quickly to anything other than research papers.

Dr. Zeek isolated various strains of dangerous looking viruses taken from the insects captured in the solar powered bug-zappers realizing the crew was in need of vaccinations. They needed protective antibodies against alien microorganisms which he soon began to uncover. He ran comparisons with known viruses and discovered correlations with disease causing strains. He believed the viruses he observed were cause for concern. He began preparations to kill the disturbing viruses to create injectable vaccines. Some viruses contained inactivated forms of toxins known as toxoids, which could also be used to create vaccines to produce the protective antibodies. Other vaccines could not be created with dead viruses or inactive toxins, so he had to use live attenuated versions of the microorganisms.

He adjusted the proton and antiproton levels and ran the isolated strains through the gamma ray scanner. This was one area of medicine to survive through the ages, after drug, radiation, chemical, and surgical therapies had all eventually become obsolete. Properly formulated, immunizations worked as well as preventative medicine. In the former days of drug companies, most immunizations were concocted from dangerously deadly mixtures. Most people were better off not taking the immunization or risking exposure, because immunizations were hastily concocted for quick profits, and disease prevention was not always the top priority or primary motivation. Eventually, preventative medicine was the only medicine because curative medicine became too expensive for anyone to afford. Only the Shareholders could afford to have diseases cured.

Lunch was served this day outside on a picnic table, built by Ami. The wooden table was a simple and functional product of the trees nearby. Cookie spread out platters of ginger protein cakes, condensed fruit, and tall mugs of vitamin shakes. The crew ate and talked of the happenings of the day and future plans.

"I wish we could find whoever that arrow belonged to," started Benny. He was beginning to suffer from their prolonged isolation. "I would like find out if there is music here. If there are natives, I would love to hear their music. All people of the universe enjoy making music. There must be musicians."

Dr. Zeek smacked on a protein cake. "We are running low on supplies, but I prefer for everyone to hold off on drinking or eating anything from this planet until I have vaccinations ready," he said. "They should be ready soon. I should have a broad enough sampling this week. After the vaccinations are administered we can feel more comfortable drinking the natural spring water and searching for food sources."

"We'll find whoever that arrow belonged to," said Derek, "Or they will find us."

"Have you given any more thought to our vehicle, Ami?" asked Benny. There was a hovercraft vehicle aboard the ship, but it was built for Mercury, a planet with less gravity and void of an atmosphere.

"We need to perform conversions on the levitation system and make modifications to the suspension system, but I think it can be done without too much trouble," replied Ami.

"There will be nothing left of this ship if we keep scavenging modules, the rate we are going," lamented Dr. Zeek.

Just then the audible alarms sounded and Cookie appeared in the front door of the ship. "We have company!" stammered the android.

35

Picnic Pests

"Button down the hatches!" yelled Dr. Zeek to the android, and the crew hastily scrambled into the ship. The crew was inside but Derek stood at the door and watched as the giants came through the woods from the far side of the grassy plain. They were huge. They were grazing on the wild berries at the edge of the grassy park, with the green mountains in the distance. He could see cubs tagging along. The mountains of fur occasionally rose up on their haunches and sniffed the air. They were headed right for camp. The creatures were following their noses and undoubtedly smelled the meager lunch of the small crew.

Derek ran to the picnic table and gathered up the mugs and pitcher of vitamin shake and quickly wiped the table. He looked back and realized he had been noticed. They gazed at him in the distance. They stood disturbingly still. He wondered what they would do next. They appeared to be herbivorous but he did not know for sure, and they could easily enjoy meat also. They studied him intently from the far side of the grassy park. A low growl rumbled across the field and they charged. Derek scrambled for the door of the ship and slammed it shut, as they came in fast.

The crew watched from dinosaur detection consoles inside the ship. "What are they?" asked Derek.

"Iguanodons," replied Dr. Zeek. "They are herbivores according to ship database. Real time data is still coming in, but initial profile readings match up. My god, they are huge."

"Uninvited guests," sighed Benny.

"They are going for the smell of the food on the table," said Ami remorsefully. The iguanodons licked the table and crushed it in the process. Anything they put their front paws on crumpled like cardboard. The iguanodons possessed peculiar looking thumb spikes on their front paws, long snouts, and turtle beak mouths. One iguanodon put its nose to the ground and followed the path to the door of the ship. A faint crunching and creaking could be heard. "Let's see how the ship holds up to this," said Ami, with deadpan humor.

The cubs bounded up. They were huge balls of frivolity, four of them. They rolled and dove and climbed. The rode on each other's backs and ran in circles. They played chase and wrestled. It was all fun and games for the cubs. The iguanodon adults in contrast were somber and alert, constantly scanning the surroundings. One iguanodon circled around to the port side of the ship steadily sniffing looking for the little human that got away. Scent was faint on the other side, and the iguanodon returned to the door where the scent was stronger. Faint scraping sounds were heard outside the door.

The iguanodons rooted in the dirt and sniffed the chairs sitting around last night's smoldering camp fire. They crushed and ripped off bits of cloth from the chairs and munched on the material. They sampled the different materials and exchanged comparative glances, as if they were taste testing judges. The lumbering dinosaurs finally moved off toward the swampy lowlands with the cubs tagging along behind.

The crew climbed out of the ship to survey the damage. Everything outside was crushed, broken, or eaten. It could have been worse, but luckily the iguanodons moved on quickly and this time there was only relatively minor damage. History has it that picnics were traditionally ruined by ants, but in this world the picnic pests came in jumbo sizes.

36

The Dream

Reverend H was in his rocketing space ark packed with people and provisions and speeding along the warped tracks of the space-time continuum. They had been in flight for months now. Reverend H lounged in his study and tweaked his next sermon. He set about describing the wonderful paradise nestled in the solar system of Epsilon Eridani. With masterful words, he painted a beautiful picture of lush tropical gardens, peaceful lakes, and majestic sunsets. He artistically chose his words like a skilled craftsman. He likened the planet to the mythical Garden of Eden, and presented their voyage as a second chance for mankind to make good intentions come true. He was truly excited about this migration to a new world, and he firmly believed that they were on a mission to save the best of what was left. All these gentle thoughts filled the ancient Reverend H with a feeling of peaceful tranquility and he nodded off and napped for a time.

Reverend H dreamed and in the dream he was young again and in love. He was a carpenter again, framing apartments and high-rises for a living, working from sunup to sundown. He was hard and strong and worked with a tool belt strapped to his waist all day long. It was a time when they never had enough money and never really cared. He enjoyed the hard work and he moved with graceful easy efficiency. At the end of the day, he enjoyed his weariness as the dirt and sweat washed off in the shower. There was the pleasant aroma of cooking coming from the kitchen where his young bride prepared the evening meal.

They married young, and maybe too young, but they were in love as deeply as two people could be. They had big plans for the weekend. When the weekend came, they drove into the hill country and got a room at a hidden Bed and Breakfast Inn nestled in a quaint cozy old town. They went from shop to shop holding hands, with the hills in the background, checking out the antiques, arts, and crafts. She tried on a dress that caught her eye. He loved the way she looked, but he could not afford to buy the dress for her. They fell asleep in each other's arms that night.

It was a dream Reverend H had over and over again. He awoke from the dream and his eyes swelled with tears. That was another time and there was no turning back time in the path of one's life. His young bride was gone forever, but the old lover remembered her well.

37

Vanity Fair

Insulated from the stench of the ruined environment below, high in the heavily guarded and pillowed quarters, were the meanest ugliest most powerful people this world has ever known.

Some had ruthlessly risen to the top positions of the corporations of the old world. These were the ones who guiltlessly took credit for the achievements and the ideas of others. They were the ones who thought it good to exploit third world countries for cheap labor by setting up dispirited sweatshops to work poor children into early graves. There was a global economy, a global currency, but no global laws. Corporate policy became global law. Cheap labor was ubiquitous in the backward countries where protest against the exploitation of people and environment was easily squashed. Profit was all that mattered. It became more and more expensive and impossible to become rich and the gap between the haves and have-nots grew vast.

These early corporate executives cared only for themselves, not for quality, ethics, or morals. They were the ones who used every advantage to get ahead no matter how unethical. They were two-faced chameleons of the corporate world, willing to be whoever they needed to be for the sake of power and wealth. They were the information thieves who engaged in insider trading while disenfranchised workers lost a life's savings. This was the corporate fast track crowd, ones who gave no thought to the future, only to self-centered self-promotion.

There was no more room at the top of the hill, so the greedy and powerful wallowed in stupendous success. Those on the hill dealt out gleeful knee-jerk reactions to fabricated news in order to create wildly volatile stock markets. Honest hardworking laborers lived paycheck to paycheck, struggling to save, and lost it all in wave after wave of stock market crashes. The markets became too risky for any sane investor. All possible avenues for personal savings were eliminated. A generation was bankrupted. Physical environmental constraints and real world realities were not factored into these monetary models. The pursuit of ceaseless earnings growth was the corporate mantra. National markets became global markets. The global market crashed again and again. There were billions of people left too broken, sick, and old to continue. The world was bankrupt. The Shareholders foreclosed upon all real estate property and grabbed all shares of the teracorps. They possessed everything in the end.

The ravenous hunger for short term profit continually diminished product quality until consumers and laborers were merely disgruntled participants. Smaller corporations occasionally arose to challenge monopolistic multi-national corporations in the early days. These upstarts were generally bought out and decimated. Successful upstart corporations adopted the same ruthless characteristics as the others once they were also on the top. There was fierce competition between corporations, sometimes resulting in technological breakthroughs, but mostly resulting in mergers and monopolies. Corporations grew to terascale proportions and corporate policy became the only law of the land. In the midst of more labor-saving devices in history, people worked longer than ever for less than ever.

The final world war then came, a war fought between the old weakened world governments and the powerful multinational terascale corporations. The world governments lost and all nations were destroyed. The previous environmental regulations, sweat shop restrictions, trade barriers, national borders, and government taxation were all eliminated. When all governments were defeated, a one world council was given supreme authority. Teracorporations ushered in the New World Order and a small one world council was awarded ultimate power. This initial one world council was soon owned by the Shareholders. It was the beginning of the dark age of slavery, population control, and life without hope. There was no more freedom, democracy, rights, or constitutions. There was only corporate policy. Stock markets were not as they existed before, and stock trading was reduced to bets waged among the Shareholders. Battles were fought in deep space between the teracorps over the acquisition of resource.

Not many Shareholders had risen up through the corporate ranks the old hard way. Many people had desperately tried to become Shareholders but instead had become slaves themselves. Even in the early years, most Shareholders were born rich and had bribed their way into the evil clan, never knowing a day of work in their lives. In the old days, a few had been sports celebrities and entertainment idols amassing great wealth during their careers. A few had even been successful entrepreneurs in the early days. These were exceptions even when the New World Order was in its infancy. Most were born with more money than they could ever spend. Shareholders were very different indeed, because only the ruthless and evil became Shareholders and stayed that way. Those who attempted to introduce ethics or morals were destroyed, because that was not good sport, and the Shareholders enjoyed good sport.

The newest Shareholders were bred for the position. They were appointed in mock elections. They were called gods in mockery of all established religion. They were schooled, brainwashed, and tutored in evil arts from early childhood. These gifted young telepathic channels and seers were trained to become experts in remote viewing, but their training was warped and tainted to dark wishes. These new additions added spice to the small powerful clan, which pleased the supreme rulers, and pleasing Shareholders was the order of the modern age.

The new god of all worlds was there. She was wickedly beautiful, and wore a revealingly shear gown which might as well have been nothing at all. Tiny naked android servants were also there carrying goblets of wine, platters of fine cuisine, and bowls of opium. The small droids dutifully fulfilled the requests of the barking Shareholders. It was a wretched scene of perverted lust and eroticism. The narcotics burned thick choking smoke and the gut wrenching stench floated and hung in clouds. The new god of all sentient beings was stoned out of her mind and she sat in the middle of the gathering, swaying back and forth, moaning and putting on an evil show.

The old school Shareholder was also there. He had previously placed the big risky bet and he had lost but he did not care. He had lost all his shares but he was not concerned at all. He had taken risks all his life and he was lucky in risk. He had always been richly rewarded for taking big risks and he always came out on top in the long run. He was a Shareholder because he took risks. He pushed his way to the top of his first corporation by taking risks and by breaking all the rules. He knew of no other way to get ahead. He had lost all his shares in the bet but he would come out on top in the long run. He had been down before and he always came out on top in the long run, by taking even bigger risks. He was a lucky man and he was a Shareholder, one of the most powerful men the world has ever known.

He sat there enjoying the lurid show put on by the wickedly seductive girl, this new god. He sat at ease in the smoke and haze, and lazily puffed fine tobacco. He smoked the finest tobacco in all the world, and left the opium and hashish for the others. He needed to raise capital. There were people he needed to call to put himself back in business. He was a powerful man, with wealth and influence, but this was not the old world anymore. The global credit system was very different now from the old global market. He suddenly felt old, but he had no regrets. He was a winner and a risk-taker. His wife and children were long gone but he had no regrets. They had always held him back. He cursed his wife for not swallowing her beliefs and morals and getting with the program. He was an ambitious man and saw to it that nothing got in his way.

He eyed the moaning new god and worried about nothing. He would make some calls and be back in business. It would be risky but he would come out ahead in the long run. He did not care about the rules. He broke all the rules. He called for a dry martini and studied the sexy new god while a naked little android servant scurried off to fill his order. He puffed his fine tobacco and let the smoke roll up his nose. It was the finest tobacco in the world. He was not worried at all. The bet was a minor miscalculation. They knew that. It could happen to anyone. He was a wealthy and powerful man. He demanded respect. The androids respected him. They were programmed to. He did not care about the others. They knew nothing of ruthless desperate ambition. Everything had been handed to them on a silver platter.

He wondered what his children looked like now. They had held him back and slowed him down, them and their mother. They were grown and on their own now. It was no use thinking about their miserable lives as slaves. He had not seen his family in fifty years. He was better off without them.

A large hulking bodybuilder android appeared in the doorway of the luxurious quarters with what looked like his dry martini order, held conspicuously in one hand. The old school Shareholder eyes widened at the sight of the android through the smoke and haze. The android stood and slowly scanned the scene. The android took it all in with cold unemotional eyes without the trace of a soul. The laughter and talk died to stony silence. The moaning new god became quiet as she turned her stoned and glazed eyes to the doorway where the menacing android unflinchingly surveyed the gathering in search of his target.

The android eyes rested on the old school Shareholder. The Shareholder from the old school suddenly felt weak. He felt too weak to get up, too weak to take another breath. He tried to say something, but he was too weak. The android coldly yet vacantly stared at the old school Shareholder and crushed the martini glass. The dry martini ran off his hand and dripped to the floor along with pieces of wet glass. The android walked slowly up to the old school Shareholder and clutched the throat of the old school Shareholder with the same hand that crushed the martini. In a gasp, the Shareholder smelled the faint aroma of a dry martini. It would have been a good martini. The android grabbed the weakened Shareholder by the crotch and the throat, and lifted the old school Shareholder high.

The old school Shareholder looked down at the android. The

android was amazingly strong. He also caught a glimpse of the new god. She was grinning up at him and looking very wasted. She was an evil new god. The android gripped hard and the Shareholder felt a deep pain as his privates were crushed and then he could not breathe even if he tried. The android flexed his strong triceps and gave the Shareholder's body a light upward push then flicked his agile wrists and hands, spinning the Shareholder in mid-air. The Shareholder saw the ceiling only for a second and had never looked closely at it before and for this mere second, he was drawn to the twinkling lights above. The android kneeled and brought the old school Shareholder down full force onto his one forward bending knee. There was a loud crack as the backbone of the old school Shareholder snapped. The android was indeed graceful in execution.

The old school Shareholder lay on the floor twitching and blankly staring at the ceiling. That android was amazingly strong and had put on a good show. He would make a few calls and be back in business again. It was a risky business, but he did not care about the rules. He pictured his wife and kids again and wondered what they looked like now. He was glad they never got in his way.

The bodybuilder android curiously studied the twitching human with the severed spine lying on the floor. His job had been completed quickly and efficiently as promised. The android then scanned the others with his soulless searching eyes. Then from deep within came a strange feeling and he suddenly wanted to kill them all. He was trained to kill without compassion but also trained to do what he was told and nothing more. The Shareholders had clearly enjoyed this spectacle and were clapping joyously. The android turned and left the room and tried to feel something more but once again he felt nothing at all.

We're all there at the Vanity Fair.
With skin so fair and full heads of hair.
What will we wear to the Vanity Fair?
We breathe bottled air at the Vanity Fair.

It costs lots of money looking half your age.
I want my youth; don't want to be a sage.
I am going to see my doctor,
And I am really going to pay.
But I'll really look fine,
And I'll really look great.

At the Vanity Fair we'll never cry.
At the Vanity Fair we'll never die.
At the Vanity Fair we don't look inside,
'Cause at the Vanity Fair,
It's just foolish pride.

There was an old woman, living on a farm.
Her skin was parched and her hands were hard.
She wore dirt and sweat in the sun so warm,
But she touched my soul with her own charm.

At the Vanity Fair we'll never cry.
At the Vanity Fair we'll never die.
At the Vanity Fair we don't look inside,
'Cause at the Vanity Fair,
It's just foolish pride.

38

Eridani Rain

The rain poured down in sheets for days. Derek shot his bow in the rain. He was slowly beginning to master his crude weapon, this maple longbow. There was a wild spirit in this new world and it was burning strong in this young man's heart. Shooting in the rain was a radically different experience than dry weather. The wet feather fletching was not as effective in creating arrow spin and waterlogged arrows dropped lower on the targets. He stood sopping wet and experimented at different distances. There was not much difference in arrow flight at close ranges as is on a dry day, but the rain became a greater factor at longer distances.

He was learning to shoot instinctively, and as naturally as throwing a rock. The arrows were beginning to go where he wanted them to strike at various distances, with a naturally instinctive style of shooting common among early hunters. This was instinctive archery as discussed in writings of Zen Archery. Zen was something to be experienced rather than described. This involved quieting the critical conscious mind so that the subconscious could perform such a surprisingly complicated act. The trick was launching an arrow accurately but also as naturally as breathing.

He came out of the rain and into the comfortable ship. Cookie brought the youth an icy vegetable juice with extra spice. Derek sipped his favorite drink and listened to Benny practicing his laser axe. Benny was bent over studying a new scale pattern he must have just happened upon because it drew the wiry musician's full attention. Dr. Zeek and Ami were working with the ship supercomputer on the redesign details of the excursion vehicle.

Dr. Zeek looked up from the console. "Now that we are all here, I have something for everyone," he announced. He went to the laboratory and returned with the vaccinations. They were in the form of skin patches. He opened a containment vessel and applied the patches to their arms. "Just leave it on and it will completely dissolve into the outer layers of your skin, and it will be gone in a few hours," said Dr. Zeek. "These patches will produce antibodies for the dangerous viruses that I have isolated so far. The bug-zappers produced quite a sampling from this region."

"What's for supper, Cookie?" asked Benny.

"Ginger protein cakes, condensed fruit, and vitamin shakes," replied Cookie dutifully.

Benny let out a groan. "I'm getting tired of the same old thing day after day, Cookie. Is that the extent of your culinary skill?" he asked.

Cookie became defensive. "That is all that I have supplies for. I do know how to prepare other dishes, but not with these limited supplies," replied the android in a hurt tone.

"Don't worry about it, Cookie. You are doing great with what you have to work with," said Benny, not wanting to offend the dutiful droid.

"I think we can begin to sample the planetary cuisine now that we have been immunized," said Dr. Zeek to them, as he admired Ami's design work at the supercomputer console. "But don't start eating things without first letting me test them."

"I am going hunting," announced Derek. He paused for the reaction. "It may be a few days, but I will bring back some meat for us to cook." There was silence as his announcement was processed.

"You are now a predator?" asked Benny in disbelief, but he quickly added, "The meat would be a nice change from protein cakes. I have never tasted cooked meat. I hope you are successful."

Dr. Zeek cast a disapproving glare upon Derek. He could not order the boy to stay in camp but he did not like the sound of hunting at all.

"A predator isn't just the one who kills," replied Derek. "The hunter is no doubt a predator, but so is any meat eater. They acquire the fruits of predation and stick it in the nanowave oven, so they are also predators just the same."

"What about vegetarians, such as we?" asked Dr. Zeek provokingly, while watching Ami's graphic design of the hovercraft modifications, but still listening to the conversation. "How do we vegetarians fit into your predation philosophy?" queried the old scientist.

This was a debate which had died generations ago because people from Earth had no choice in the matter. All meat and dairy products were eliminated from the human diet long ago. "Humans are omnivores, both carnivorous and herbivorous. Just because someone swears off meat either by choice or mandate, it does not necessarily mean that they are suddenly biologically transformed into an herbivore. We vegetarians are still carnivorous due to our ability to process meat, and we may need to eat it to survive. Anyone who has tasted meat and enjoyed the taste, and has a normal human digestive tract, is also a carnivore. I believe we vegetarians are still predators but are only filled with enough protein cakes and vitamin shakes to keep from violating either our vows or our mandates."

"Sounds as if you have wrapped your theories neatly in butcher paper," smirked Dr. Zeek.

"What about people who are revolted by the thought of eating meat because it is from another animal?" Benny then asked, as he looked up from his musical twiddling and doodling.

"That is why I threw in the part about the digestive tract," chuckled Derek. "We are all predators, and we will all soon be hungry predators if we run out of rations," he said seriously.

"Many may disagree with your theories," replied Benny. "But I for one would like to try cooked meat. Do you really think you are good enough with that bow?" asked Benny.

"I am going to give it a try. I am leaving tomorrow, even if it is raining," the yellow eyed youth replied, and the Eridani rain continued to pound away outside.

"I want you to take a beacon with you, Derek," said Dr. Zeek. "If you get lost or in trouble, you can set off the beacon so that we can try to find you. There will be nothing left of this ship if we keep using the modules but I do not want to lose you to the wild. We need you. We once had big plans to destroy the Shareholders. I hope you are still part of this crew," said Dr. Zeek.

"Our original plans do not seem so urgent anymore," replied Derek moodily. "I am still part of this crew. You know that. We are free for the first time in our lives, and we have time on our hands. I want to hunt as early humans once hunted, with stick and string, the way the natives hunt in this world."

Dr. Zeek smiled, "How is the knife treating you?"

"It is treating me well, and it has become invaluable to me, and I thank you for the gift," said Derek genuinely, also knowing Dr. Zeek enjoyed being thanked.

"I would like to walk part of the way out with you in the morning, Derek, down by the river," said Benny.

"That sounds good to me," said Derek, "But what is going on at the river?" he asked.

"You are not the only outdoor adventurer among us. I have put together a fishing rig," announced Benny proudly. "I have made some hooks and I have some strong thread. I bet that river is full of fish," said Benny excitedly.

"Let me see what you have," said Derek. The pointed barbed hooks were made of carbon steel with wire loops tied to a very strong thread. "They look like they will do the trick," admired Derek. "I bet you are right about that river." Derek mused.

"Take a couple of hooks," offered Benny. "I have plenty of them. I plan on sitting out near a dinometer and fishing until I snag something with more flavor than a protein cake. Doc, have you ever tasted fish?" asked Benny.

"Yes indeed I have tasted fish, and it is quite good," replied Dr. Zeek. "I have sampled flounder, trout, and salmon to name a few. Fish was once a big favorite back on Earth," said Dr. Zeek.

"What do you think is out there in that river, Doc? Do you think there is anything worth catching in those waters?" asked Benny.

"If you get lucky you will hook something, and then we can find out how it tastes. It may be really tasty. Just be careful out there. There is no telling what you might pull out of that water," warned Dr. Zeek. "Cookie, do we have any cooking grease?" asked Dr. Zeek. "We may want to fry these fish," he said.

"Cooking grease?" asked Cookie incredulously. "I was not aware of any cooking grease. Is there such a thing?" asked the android in amazement.

"It was before your time," replied Dr. Zeek. "People used to fry fish in grease. I know it sounds pretty crazy. Cookie, you can just bake the fish for us in the nanowave oven," said Dr. Zeek.

Benny continued experimenting with his new musical scale. His long multicolored hair hung down below his right picking hand as his fingers delicately explored the soft tones gently flowing from the laser axe. Music seemed to ripple from the instrument like water droplets falling into a soothing water garden wishing well.

"The levitation mechanism retrofit is starting to shape up," said Dr. Zeek, as he watched Ami at work. "The redesign of the hovercraft excursion vehicle is almost complete. A practical application of Stick and String Theory will allow us to be able to configure a graviton levitation system with very little structural changes to the main framework. We can start tomorrow in getting our hovercraft rover geared up properly for this planet."

39

Gone Fishing

Morning came and a mist hung heavy after the rains. Derek and Benny left before daylight. Benny carried his fishing pole rig in one hand and his laser axe slung over his shoulder. He seldom went anywhere without his laser axe. In the other hand Benny carried a flashlight but it was not much use in the heavy mist. Derek carried his long bow and the quiver filled with arrows strapped to his shoulder. A pack of provisions was strapped to his waist.

The night sky was fading and day was breaking as they made their way down to the river. Dr. Zeek was awake back at the ship and he apprehensively studied the dinometer inputs. The coast was clear as far as he could tell. All was quiet in the wild. They had noticed that animal movement was very slow during rains. It was understandable, with keen senses of sight, hearing, and smell rendered ineffective during such downpours. With the subsiding of the showers, the hungry animals would begin to move again. This worried Dr. Zeek as he studied the dinometer communication consoles. Benny wanted to do some fishing, and this was understandable. Benny had been feeling cooped up in the ship and he was becoming frustrated with feelings of isolation. He needed to get outdoors. It would do him good.

"What are you hunting for?" asked Benny softly as they quietly made their way to the river.

"I am not sure," whispered Derek. "I am going to take it slow and easy, but I will probably pass on those seismosaurs," he said with a wink.

"Do you know what the killing power of your bow is?" asked Benny curiously.

"I am not sure. The meat will need to be packed back in to camp so it must be manageable," said Derek.

They made their way through the mist and undergrowth toward the river. They walked past the dinometers and Dr. Zeek observed the progression at the webterm consoles. The two young men appeared as shadowy figures walking through a spherical projection.

"What are you using for bait?" asked Derek.

"I have some of the insects from the lab, collected from the bug-zappers. I will just hook them and flick them around or let them drift with the current. Maybe I will get lucky," said Benny.

"You will do well," said Derek "I bet this river is teaming with big fish, and let us hope they are good to eat," added Derek. "Today we both try our luck with infamous Stick and String Theory, you with your pole and line and me with my bow and arrow. I wish you lots of strikes."

The river was close now and they could hear water bubbling and the rushing of the current. The banks were high from the rains. They located a dinometer installed near the edge of the river and Benny sat down nearby so that he was conspicuously seen by the webcam. He was not comfortable being alone in the woods, but he needed to get out. It would be good for him to be out in the wild for awhile, and maybe he would get lucky and catch some fish.

"I am going to follow the river off to where it empties past the canyon near the timber bottom," whispered Derek. "From there I am not sure where I will go. Good luck with your fishing," and with that, Derek disappeared into the mist that was still hanging thick in the early morning light.

Benny was alone with his fishing pole and line. He found himself automatically trying to keep as quiet and still as possible. He was not at ease in the wild wilderness at all, but the dinometer modules hanging above were comforting. He studied the tree where the dinometer was installed. It was a climbable tree, and this was also good to know. He could be up that tree in a flash. He just needed to stay alert. He would catch some fish and get some fresh air and head back to the ship after awhile. He would soon feel a lot better. He kept telling himself this but he was still uneasy.

He hooked a large dragonfly from the bug-zappers. He flicked the pole and line and the bug floated out above the rushing water. The dragonfly gently landed on the surface of the rain swollen river. The rushing current took the bait out to the full length of his line. The bait bubbled on top of the water at the end of the line. Benny leaned his laser axe against the tree and again looked apprehensively into the dinometer above. He felt wholly helpless by this riverbank. It was some consolation that he did feel somewhat hidden since he was blanketed in a low hanging mist. He thought it was ironic that he was now taking comfort in being monitored by a webcam. He would have a hard time running in this mist. He would not know where to go and he would quickly be lost. It would be safer to climb the tree, unless whatever giving chase was something big enough to get to him up in the tree, or something that could climb a tree and move faster than he. Running through the mist was no good. That would be sure disaster. He would end up playing the role of the helpless fleeing prey if he tried to run. He would get lost in no time at all, and he knew he could not outrun a velociraptor. Running was no good.

Some time passed and Benny was starting to think that his idea of fishing was pure insanity. He started to think that only a fool would be caught in these woods alone. He could not run through the mist. He could not even see the trail that he had come in on. Trails were easier to walk with two people. Two people were more decisive than one on a trail. Two people were less patient with side trails. Someone walking alone on a trail can get off the trail, onto a smaller side trail, and pretty soon they are lost. Those trails were not even made by humans. It was not that far back to the ship, only a couple kilometers. It might as well have been a million kilometers. What had he been thinking? Leaving the ship was crazy, pure insanity. He could still be sleeping safely if he had never left the ship. This was nuts.

Suddenly he felt a tug. There was something nibbling on the end of his line. He sat up straight. There were several successive jerks as the pole bent and the end of the line went swimming. Benny excitedly set the hook. The fish was hooked well and dove deep and cut wild across the river. Benny stood up and held his fishing pole tightly. This fish felt huge. He tried to raise the pole higher but the fish fought him hard and bent the tip of the pole down low. Benny's heart raced and his breath quickened. This was a fighting fish. He held onto the pole as the tip dipped and jerked and the line raced back and forth cutting through the river currents. He felt the fighting fish rising to the top of the water and in a splash of fury it broke the surface and jumped and thrashed in midair to free itself from the hook and then dove deep again. He excitedly caught a fleeting glimpse of the big fish as the splash broke the silence of the morning. Benny held the pole tight and reached for the line at the tip of the pole and tried to grip the line but the pull was too furious and it cut into his hands. He grabbed the pole again with both hands and let the line run. The fish had too much fight left.

Benny straddled the bank of the river now and he held the pole tighter than ever. The pull slackened as the fish tried swimming towards the bank to loosen the hook. Benny thought he had lost the fish. The fish swam right for him and the line was full of slack. Benny could see a shadow streaking as the hooked fish traveled like a missile toward him. Under the surface from the bank of the river the fish turned and went out for another run against the hook. This was a big fish and Benny struggled to grip the sturdy pole. The fish put up another struggle against the hook, but this time the swimming was slower and weaker against the current of the river. Benny reached for the line again and was able to pull in the line with his hands this time. He brought the fish to the edge and lifted it out of the cool water and onto the sandy bank. The fish flipped in the sand. It was a whopper. He did not know what it was, but it was a big fish. It had blue spots and pink and yellow stripes down both sides.

Benny brought along a thick cord to use as a fish stringer. He ran the stringer through the fish mouth lined with tiny teeth, and threaded the cord through the gill and tied it in a good knot. He fastened the cord to a log and let the fish back into the water and it swam to the length of the cord. The log did not budge as the large fish tested it with several fierce tugs.

Benny quickly hooked up another dragonfly and cast the line out again. He had forgotten all of his previous anxieties. His cabin fever was cured. He felt refreshed, alert, and alive. He suddenly realized when he was fighting fish, his worldly cares were erased. All troubles faded. At that moment, he could feel life at the end of the line. It felt like he and the fish were linked in a shared struggle. It was pure renewal and rejuvenation. There was nothing else in the moment when he was bringing that fish in. He experienced the release and exhilaration that comes with bringing in a fighting fish. He watched the bubbling new dragonfly at the end of the line and held his pole in the anticipation of another strike.

40

The Second Coming

Deep in space, a loaded vessel was destined for Planet P and the solar system of Epsilon Eridani. It was a space ark filled with the cult followers of Reverend H. They traveled at 90% light speed but dared not go any faster due to the exponential increase in mass, and because their ship would not hold together. There were limited by an outdated propulsion system based upon Newton's Third Law of Motion, so they had to live with double mass at 90% light speed but they could do no more. They dare not if they hoped to arrive at their dream destination. They would have preferred to travel at light speed, once believed to be the natural speed limit of the universe, according to the theories of relativity. It was discovered that the 300,000 kilometer per second speed limit of the universe could be broken. Theories of quantum mechanics described the subatomic world and integrated with theories of relativity describing the space-time relationship, warped tracks of gravity, and energy. These theories evolved into unified field theories then superstring theory, and finally Stick and String Theory. There was a new understanding of the fabric of the universe, and faraway unreachable realms were suddenly more accessible as practical manifestations of Stick and String Theory unfolded.

When the light speed barrier was finally broken, it was the herald of a new age, the fabulous New World Order. Breaking the barrier was considered a giant leap for mankind, much like the first moon walk. To go faster than light speed was expensive and there were obstacles. Whenever the barrier was broken, a time shock wave emitted, experienced in the form of the deja vu effect. Only the finest ships were capable of faster than light speeds and FTL maneuvers were keenly executed when the stakes were high. The presence of pricelessly valuable goods was often enough to warrant such expensive hops through space. This travel still produced perplexing mysteries. In contrast, near light speed travel was commonplace with the primary side effect being that travelers upon return had aged a little less than those back home.

Reverend H approached the podium and began easily, because it was a sermon he had given a thousand times if he had given it once. It was a story of the wide pride of humanity, the depth of ignorance, and the height of unquestioning belief. It was a story of dark ages. It was a tale of idiocy, pomp, and death to unbelievers.

"From the beginning, certain men have taken it upon themselves to speak for the creator. They taught us that the opinions they possessed were equivalent to words from the maker of the universe, thanks to divine inspiration. Some leaders found this endeavor rewarding and some were crucified. Claiming to be possessed by the almighty, these writers and teachers denied ulterior motives or any personal motivation whatsoever. Many truly believed divine inspiration set in motion drove their fingers to write and their mouths to speak. They claimed to be unique and divine channels, with a distant unreachable creator speaking directly through only them. These teachings were misleading and ultimately selfish, because there are no middlemen to get to the creator, but let us forgive and dwell in thankfulness. Our souls may all commune with the ultimate creator of the universe, within each of us, and we all possess an equal level of access.

The leaders of the established religions of all generations have been involved in government, politics, personal wealth, and subjugation of the masses. They have actively engaged in ruthless personal gain. They have instigated lethal religious wars solely for the sake of power. They have carried out shady deals to benefit their social political position. These religious leaders cared more for impressive church buildings, tax exemptions, perks and pride, than for helping the needy. The beatitudes of compassion were largely ignored, simple words that may have united all beliefs. Instead, countless deaths resulted from the constant religious wars of history. We now realize that there is a difference between the words of religious leaders and words that come from the creator. Distrust the opinions of any leader, as I hope you will distrust my own humble opinions.

They once espoused the belief that the sun and stars revolved around Earth, as Earth stood still, the static center of all creation. It was surprising to discover Earth orbiting Sol, Sol orbiting the Milky Way, the Milky Way orbiting the universe. Our sun turned out to be another star. Giordano Bruno, the forgotten philosopher, was put to death for making such a claim. He dared to imagine a universe of inhabitable worlds, and remains a martyr for liberty. Sol travels at relative speeds of hundreds of kilometers per second and there is nothing static about our universe. The universe is growing, evolving, and alive. Sol is one star among a hundred billion in this galaxy, and the Milky Way is one galaxy among a hundred billion in the universe. The foundations of religious belief were rocked when life was discovered in the far reaches of the universe. Evidently our universe is teaming with life. We often find life similar to that once found on Earth. There is an underlying cosmos within the chaotic madness of the evolution of life as we have learned.

They told us the universe was created in six days and that the creator rested on the seventh. This seemed incomprehensible to us, but persuasive propaganda is often crafted by telling a little truth to hide a big lie. They wanted us to accept that the works of the creator are impossible to comprehend. This has always been what they have wanted us to believe. They hoped we would feel apart from this distant creator but this separateness is an illusion. The creator is in everyone. We were taught that we were too pitifully equipped to understand the mysteries of nature. They taught that the creator only speaks through enlightened prophets. Divinely delivered messages only come through chosen channels so they said. They taught us we could never hope to fathom this infinite power at work. The stars are only there to provide light by night and nothing more. The big lie they wanted us to believe was that we were never built to understand.

We now embrace understanding. The days it took for the universe to unfold are not measured in provincial Earth days and they measure close to three billion Earth years each. On the seventh day the creator rested and is still resting inside each of us. Let us awaken to the creator inside. The seventh day of rest has been estimated to be one billion more Earth years but sadly our world does not have long. The barely living world we flee has been ripped apart and eaten alive by ravenous corporations which exist forever, possessing what once were human rights, and yet corporations are neither human nor alive. The only thing living about a corporation is the people who give their life in service.

New forms of life are often the products of evolution but we are co-creators in our lives. Each new creation is not necessarily new work from divinity; but part of a divine program. They lobbied a political stance based upon the belief that a lack of understanding is inevitable, to be accepted without question. There was no compassionate solution for the eventual population explosion, poverty, and slavery. They labeled those critical of accepted beliefs. They ridiculed and blocked the striving to understand the inner workings of life. Programmed with evolutionary properties, life is a continual struggle to adapt, and those adaptations are passed to ancestors. The longer we remain awakened the more we realize the impermanence of this physical world. There is cosmos hidden in chaos and hope of understanding.

The lie was to protect power and conceal our gifts. Our ability to clearly reason and critically think has grown stale because our ancestors believed the lie. The adaptive behavior passed onto us is conformity to prevailing beliefs, but any belief based upon ignorant submission to a higher authority is doomed. To do worthwhile things, we need a relentless searching for answers and full usage of our mental faculties, not vacant submission to authority. Living beings grow and evolve and things that do not are static and dying. As our own personal understanding improves, we grow and evolve. Personal beliefs often distort our vision and evoke pride and self righteous indignity, instead of continued growth and evolution. Our greatest tragedy is that we once traded freedom for the emptiness of security, the emptiness of not understanding, in deference to corrupt leadership.

Our gifts have been used so little and are almost lost. Everyone has gifts of healing, understanding, love, reasoning, instinct, intuition, vision, courage, compassion, imagination, and creativity. Everyone possesses the power of attraction to manifest what they focus upon. Let us pursue a better understanding of our world with the courage to manifest a brighter future. Laws of nature were discovered because people used their gifts and let their light shine. They questioned authority and prevailing beliefs. These enlightened discoveries were not for the sole benefit of the Shareholders.

Messages from lost ancestors who slept in trees come to us in dreams of falling, sent upon the genetic network. The blind can dream in beautiful colors. The deaf compose magnificent symphonies. The conscious mind is our watchful guardian and the subconscious is the most powerful supercomputer ever known, but these are not truly who we are. Our bodies and the souls they contain are not loathsome in the eyes of our creator as past religions taught. When we surrender to vacant inadequacy, we are rendered dysfunctional. This is an ungrateful insult in response to the gift of our creation. There is no thankfulness in feeling ashamed and guilty of our existence. Let us dwell in thankfulness for the gifts we have been given.

They taught us to live for a better afterlife, but this belief became the opiate of the disenfranchised as generations lived unconsciously. Let us awaken from this sleep and give this life and the lessons we face our full attention, and anything less is to repress basic instinct. Animals fiercely struggle to survive, instinctually fighting to live without question. Our greatest gift is here and now, appropriately called the present. There are no ordinary moments in this experience.

The creator rests within each person, anxious for our awakening. It has been less than a week for the one responsible for everything. Our consciousness evolves as our understanding improves and our lessons are recognized. We were built to comprehend the mysteries of the universe. The creator within accompanies us as we grow and evolve. We are spiritually one with the creator and each other and yet we confront and contemplate the illusion of separateness.

We are in a desperate migration. We travel from Sol to Epsilon Eridani. There is a planet in the solar system of Eridani where we hope to make our new home. It would have been better if this migration were part of a unified effort to save the human race, but there was no courage or foresight to put away petty agendas and protect the human race against global disaster. Self-righteous leaders scoffed at impending destruction and assured themselves that problems were going to be solved through better technology or in the next life. Planned migrations may have taken generations to complete but sadly each generation lived only for itself.

There are at least one hundred stars within a radius of 25 astronomical units from our sun. Epsilon Eridani is only about eleven light years away and it has given birth to an inhabitable planet. At 90% light speed, we are getting there as quickly as we can. We stole away in the dead of the night and left many behind. Many were not convinced of the impending catastrophe from ancient religious origins, and are now among the doomed. Our prayers are with them."

41

Fishing Blues

Benny now had several fish on his stringer. He proudly looked them over then he set another dragonfly out to float and gazed at his reflection in the pool of water. It was calm near the shore out from the main current. His multicolored hair was long down past his shoulders, and hid the sun from his eyes. He wondered why it was the norm for men to wear their hair longer and women to wear theirs closer cropped. Many positions of authority within the teracorps were held by women. Women had become the supervisors and managers of the modern age. Men found themselves mostly in technical roles or as physical laborers. Ami was an exception to the norm, but then the Solarion crew members were all exceptions. Shorter hair seemed to have something to do with authority, but corporate dress codes were written so long ago that the origins were unclear. His multicolored hair was the result of a genetic designer drug that he had ingested when he was younger, one that permanently turned the strands of his hair different colors. His wildly colored hair was much like a tattoo, and something he could not reverse. As with tattoo ink, it was forever colored and the reasons why were forgotten.

Benny was no longer a boy and his rebellious youth was behind him. He remembered the woman he once called his mother. She was not really his mother. She was the woman in charge of his early training along with the other children in the group. Benny was conceived in a test tube just like the others of his generation. He belonged to a generation that never knew their parents. Parental bonds were avoided, because parents eventually grew old and could no longer work, and this was a burden on the system. Without the parental bonds, taking care of senior citizens was cheaper but dirtier business.

Benny formed a bond with the woman he once called mother. She was a good woman and wanted the best for the boy, but he became a very rebellious lad. He took the drug to permanently color his hair, like other rebellious young boys also had done. She loved him as a mother loves her child no matter what trouble he found himself in, but he also made her sad many times. Those troubled days seemed so long ago now. He was a man now but his boyish nature lingered into adulthood. He wondered what had happened to the woman he once called his mother.

The fish strikes were slower as the sun came up. He leaned against a tree and finger picked his laser axe, and realized that in some way his laser axe was also a form of stick and string. It was good to get out of the ship for awhile to catch some of those speckled striped fish. This was truly a wonderful world, so wild and untamed. It felt more like his home now after he had caught some fish and overcome some of his fear. He felt much more like an artist, more like an artist than ever before. He wanted to paint this world on a canvas with oil based paint, but he had no oil based paint. He would be an artist in this world he told himself. He could do whatever he wanted to do in this world. He did not care anything about vengeance and no longer desired to destroy the Shareholders. He knew that Derek was no longer obsessed with or wasting energy on the Shareholders either. The little crew could not take on the Shareholders. They should and would make this planet their permanent home. He finger picked the laser axe by the river bank and sang a tune that came to him and fit the mood he was in.

I am tired of running round. I am going to settle down.
Put my feet on the ground, and take a good look around.

Don't want to be on my own. I want to build a home,
With someone who cares, in my dark despair.

I've been an angry young man, and things got out of hand.
I broke my mother's heart, and tore her world apart.
But momma you'll soon find out, I don't want to scream or shout.
We'll never be the same, but neither one's to blame.

Crowded streets and crowded lanes, towers of steel, concrete plains,
Booming progress a whirlwind spin, the sky's the limit, will it end?
A child is born and makes a start. Quick to think and will go far.
But soon we slow and pass away. We leave this world another day.

Benny gathered up his catch and headed back to the ship. He walked lightly down the trail with the stringer of fish over his shoulder and his laser axe at his side. It was a wonderful planet, and a perfect place to call home. He had made up his mind and he wanted to convince the others. This should be their home because they had no hope of destroying the Shareholders. They should make themselves comfortable on this planet and live their lives here. They should be happy to have escaped the Shareholders and leave it at that. Benny enjoyed fishing and he was anxious to get back to the ship. Cookie would go to work at the nanowave oven so that he could have a taste of warm baked fish.

In the distance back down the trail near the river, a dinometer alarm sounded. The alarm cut through the quiet wilderness and he gripped his laser axe and stringer of speckled striped fish and ran without looking back. He did not want to know what it was; he just wanted to make it safely back to the ship. The fish flapped and dangled from the stringer as he ran. He heard an eerie howl above the wailing dinometer alarms. He let go of the fish and gripped his laser axe with both hands and ran for all he was worth. He could hear thrashing through the underbrush getting closer. He could see the ship in the distance and he could make out the figure of Dr. Zeek at the open door, frantically waving him in.

"Hurry up, man! Run hard! Run hard, man!" Dr. Zeek shouted but

Benny could not make out what he was shouting but he knew it was not good. Benny was gripped with fear and he ran hard, as his lungs sucked and heaved. This was a forsaken world. It must be bad or they would not be shouting at the door. "Come on, Benny! You can make it!" hollered Dr. Zeek, but he could not make out the words clearly. He was running now for all he was worth and thrashing was close behind. He clutched his laser axe fiercely and charged through the brush. This was a lonely forsaken place. This was not a place to call home. This was no way to spend a life. He had been unrealistic. He had underestimated the dangers. There was so much risk. He could not paint with oils here. He could not capture the beauty of a world, while running for his life. No one was free from peril. How could anyone survive for long in a world such as this one? There is no time for art when survival is so tenuous.

Benny heard distant chomping. He involuntarily paused for a moment behind a tree to gasp for air. He struggled to quiet his pounding heart and heaving chest. The beasts were devouring the fish that he left dumped on the trail. The creatures huddled and fought over his catch. One looked up and directly at him. They were so keen. They saw he had paused. Dr. Zeek was jumping up and down and waving his arms wildly in the doorway. It was bad. They were large fast-moving predators. The fish would be gone in another second. Benny cursed and gasped for air and ran hard. His legs were getting weaker and heavier and the harder he pushed the more his lack of conditioning became revealed. He could not go any faster. He ran with all his might but he was slowing, and he could not make his body go any faster. He was out of steam. He tried to push himself beyond all limits, groaned, gasped, and heaved. He should have paced himself, but then it would have ended even sooner. It was a mere hundred meters to the ship, but the predators were now finished with their meal, and would easily overtake him.

42

Utahraptors

They chased the scent of a tasty meal and leapt through the underbrush, quickly getting closer. They were large striped predators. Benny stopped. He could run no more. He shouldered his laser axe and cranked it to full volume. The axe came alive and howled. It rocked the beasts with screams from hell. The terrible menacing creatures halted and shook their heads. They tried to cover their pinhole ears but it was no use. The axe was too much, and Benny wildly banged and abused the musical instrument to his advantage. He shakily walked the rest of the way back to the ship, gradually gaining control of his breath, careful not to stumble or stop the music. The disoriented beasts rolled on the ground, kicking their hind legs in the air, and reacting in strange ways to the sensory overload. The creatures struggled to their feet against the raging laser axe and groggily began to move forward again, but Benny was back at the door of the ship. The searing laser axe had disarmed the towering carnivores long enough to get to safety, and this was good to know.

"Thank god you made it," shuddered Ami, who was standing with Dr. Zeek at the doorway. She took his hand and helped him in and he collapsed inside the ship. She had been busy monitoring the dinometer consoles from within the ship while Dr. Zeek yelled himself hoarse at the door.

"That was very close," croaked Dr. Zeek, looking as exhausted as Benny. "That was too close. We need to think about implementing a defense system against these things. Look at them! Here they come now after the laser axe has gone quiet."

"What are they?" panted Benny as he struggled to his knees inside the ship. He peered up at the screen sphere.

"Utahraptors, according to our database of dinosaurs from young Earth," said Dr. Zeek. "They are big, mean, fast, and smart according to paleontology theories." With that they slammed the doorway hatch of the maiden voyager Solarion shut and watched from inside.

"They are very curious, and in no hurry to leave," said Benny.

"Those nasty raptors are not accustomed to being afraid of anything, and they do not appear to be overly cautious," said Dr. Zeek. They watched intently from inside as the big raptors studied the ship.

"They are intelligent, aware, and inquisitive," commented Ami incredulously. "They realize this ship is not part of the natural world. You can tell by the way they are searching for weaknesses in the ship's outer shell," she said.

The utahraptors made loud calls and others came up from the river. Soon there was a huge pack there at the ship. The pack was a nasty group of towering snarling vicious striped carnivores. They were fearsome and fearless, drooling and hungry, provoked and curious, all bad combinations in such large predators. They dug and hammered at the ship as if it were a large egg to crack open. They clawed and scraped and screamed outside. Merciless fights broke out as the ruthless raptors competed for spots to scratch and sniff upon the hard shell of the ship.

"What are we doing here? How can we ever live in this place with those things roaming around?" asked Benny to no one in particular, as he cringed at the mayhem rising from the creatures outside.

43

Jenniper

Reverend H was in his apartment module studying fuel consumption and flight reports. The trip had been smooth sailing so far, and their long awaited getaway had been pulled off without a hitch. He had planned this trip for decades, but there was always an endless flood of tasks, problems, risks, and curiosities, all requiring decisions. There was always the element of the unknown when chaotic humans ventured into the wild frontier of space.

He realized that the universe moved from an ordered state to one of disorder. This entropy could be measured and studied in nature. He managed the natural disorder, rather than believing that order was achievable. He knew disorder was the reason why things did not fix themselves in the forward progression of time. Broken pieces did not fall onto the table to become beautiful objects. This was the natural tragic fate of all things physical. The longer one remains awake and in the moment, the more one realizes such ubiquitous impermanence. He loved chaotic humans though and was not deeply disturbed by the unpredictable. His plan was dynamic and there were built-in contingencies, alternatives, and backups.

Someone buzzed his apartment module. He looked up from the flight reports. He snapped his fingers and the three dimensional sphere and vivid graphics faded and the paper thin console on the coffee table before him was replaced by a placemat design. He used the console for that very purpose, a placemat. He rubbed his tired eyes and realized in all his years that he had never become fully accustomed to staring into computer projections for hours upon end, although he spent many hours doing so each day. He longed to sit and read an old fashioned paperback novel. He still preferred paper, although it was nonexistent today, and not many people were left to recall back when books were a primary source of information and entertainment. Reverend H was feeling ancient, and indeed he was.

It was Jenniper, looking as sad and beautiful as ever. Reverend H did not wish to erase the sadness nor try to cheer her up by taking her mind off the sadness. He knew it would be better for her to face the sadness, and accept the loss. He looked at her stunning blue eyes and smiled. "Come in, Jenniper. It is good to see you. Have a seat so that we can talk," he said. She moved with physical grace and possessed a natural beauty. She had been very close to the young corporate slave named Derek, who was destroyed with the others who were labeled nonprogrammable nonconformists. "You are on time but I have been running behind all day," he said.

"I hope that I have given you enough notice. I really needed to talk to you," started Jenniper.

"You gave me plenty notice. This is exactly what my counseling time is set aside for. I try to be prepared for walk-ins but lately I have been stretched a little thin. It gives me pleasure to help out whenever I can. There has been so much going on lately though but I will make time for you," said Reverend H.

"I will try to get to the point. I have been having problems with some of your teachings. They are mostly in the area concerning the afterlife. Most of us think of the afterlife as an unknown, but other religions do have some opinions about what they believe the afterlife to be, as nebulous as some of those explanations are," said Jenniper.

"I appreciate your direct, to the point, nature," said Reverend H with a broad smile. "Hopefully I will try to return the same favor. I do not claim to hold in my hands a detailed description of what the afterlife will be like simply because I am still alive and still formed in this physical body," he replied humbly. "I have not yet died and have not let go of this form but when I do finally die you will be the first to know," he smiled and chuckled hoping to lighten the mood, but she did not smile. "I do not wish to presume, frighten, or manipulate anyone with my wild imaginative view of what I might picture the afterlife to be. The most important decisions are those of the here and now. This is one of the primary tenets of our cult. We try to clearly look at what is and only what is, in the present moment here and now," said Reverend H.

"The Shareholders tell us that there is no afterlife. They tell us the belief in an afterlife was largely promoted by overthrown faith based governments in order to keep the working class from rebelling, giving workers something better to hope for in the next life," said Jenniper. "Are we really to believe the Shareholders?" asked Jenniper.

"It is partially true," admitted Reverend H. "The Shareholders often use a little truth to make their propaganda more persuasive. These little truths distract from big lies. In the past, national governments did rely upon faith based governing to placate the masses. Hard working people never openly questioned authority and held onto the hope of a better afterlife, and these pacified hopeful believers rarely criticized corrupt religious and corporate leaders they sometimes grudgingly served. If people did not believe a happy home in heaven waited they may have confronted the issues of this life much differently. That part is partially true, but no one lives or dies in vain. I strongly believe there is an afterlife and it will be bliss to finally leave this tired old body," continued old Reverend H. "The Shareholders say such things to break what spirit the slave class has left. To tell us there is no afterlife is not a message of hope or victory for mankind. It is true we live longer, but this is no great victory. I am at least a century old, at which point I quit counting. I know I will die soon. I am not physically immortal and no one is, not even the Shareholders. Dying is only natural but my work is not complete. I still have things to accomplish. This migration is one of them. It was my destiny to be here guiding this ark," finished Reverend H.

"You teach that the here and now is of greater importance than the afterlife, correct?" asked Jenniper. "So are you also saying that we should never concern ourselves in any way with the afterlife?" she asked.

"The afterlife is somewhere in the future, not in the now. To live in the future or in the past is to live unconsciously. I prepare for the afterlife by living each day as if it were special and my last, humbly striving to be sane and awake, and not cluttering my mind with things that were or things that may never be. Life is our school and about learning the lessons we were put here to learn. An education in theology is not required to understand the truth, as children teach us. We once dwelled in the truth as children and then we forgot as we grew older. Life is remembering forgotten truths. Life is lived either consciously or unconsciously; it is our choice. We eventually become who we really are, fully realized, and discover our gift, our purpose for being here. This is a strong channel; the pipeline to the ultimate universal potential. Uniqueness is in everyone and perceptions will never be equal therefore compassion is our center, because we all depend upon one another. Personal visions cannot be forced into the same mold, and the beauty is that everyone contributes to this experience and to this vision. There is an eventual letting go and waking up into the present moment, and it is as if our life was previously spent sleepwalking and daydreaming, unconsciously guided by ego and pride. We awaken and live with consciousness and compassion and become thankful for each moment. It is always better to be happy than to win. Life is not only a quest for understanding but a compassion for others and the urgency to fight injustice. There is an urgency to clearly see through the many distractions and illusions before us," said Reverend H.

Jenniper persisted. "So we should not concern ourselves with what the afterlife may be like?" she asked again. "Are you saying that we should not worry as to whether or not our souls are saved?" asked Jenniper.

"Many are misguided when someone playing god decides who is saved or damned. These self-proclaimed judges are always among the saved. There is no need to worry about how we will be provided for in the future because we are thankful that there is universal abundance. Many have the goal of everlasting life and are motivated more by sacrifices they consider to be good deeds rather than by compassion. They picture a piece of paradise waiting for them. purchased for what they consider to be the cost. They have faith that they are among the saved, but this can be a selfish emotion instead of a title to real estate in heaven. My sincere hope is that people will soon see that faith is the belief in the good within everyone, a good stronger than all worry, a good that awakens the living to an abundant universe. This universal good removes all fear. doubt, violence. and aggression," said Reverend H. As he spoke, his intuition told him why she asked these questions and why she was here before him. He began to realize what this session was all about. He suddenly felt like a rambling old fool once again.

"There is an afterlife, even though we are not worried about the details," said Jenniper.

"The word is ambiguous and refers only to the life of the physical body because only the physical body dies but the soul remains alive. I believe we have lived many lives in many bodies until finally our lessons are learned and we choose whether or not to come back again. I hope I am helping you to find answers to your questions. I truly believe there is an afterlife and our souls live on without fear or worry," finished Reverend H.

"What if I have given up on this life?" she asked. "What if I need to cling to the hope of a better afterlife? Can I not live for the day when I will be with Derek again in the next life?" she sincerely asked.

"Consciousness does not awaken by living sometime in the distant future. in expectation of something that may never actualize. It would not be truthful for me to claim to possess the details of where he is now within the spiritual realm. I am sure you have not seen the last of Derek. I could go on but my imagination has been known to run wild with speculation." he replied. "We are spiritual beings within these physical dimensions. You are here for a purpose just as he was. Nothing happens without a reason, and no one lives or dies without a purpose. There is a spirit alive in all dimensions, just as there is unlimited potential within everyone," he said.

"What about Derek?" she asked. "Where is he now and what is his role in the spiritual world?" asked Jenniper, now with tears.

"His death was proof of the indescribable evil conjured up in the minds of those in power, the Shareholders. This is an evil we must fiercely deny. He is on our minds and in our prayers. His soul is one of a spiritual warrior, never to surrender," said Reverend H.

"Will I see him again?" sobbed Jenniper.

"You will know the answer before I will," he replied. "I cannot prophesy this because I truthfully do not know the details. Please do not ignore the issues of this life or cease to grow or live your own personal purpose. Please do not live only in hopes of a better life somewhere in the hazy future," said Reverend H kindly.

"Will I see him again?" asked Jenniper again. "That is all that I am asking you," she said fiercely.

Reverend H looked into her tear reddened blue eyes. He felt like the rambling old fool once again and he had no good answer for this beautiful young girl, but one. "Yes, you will. You will both be together again, just as you never were apart. I am sure of it," he replied. He suddenly intuitively realized that he had just spoken the truth, and was not merely telling a grieving girl what she wanted to hear.

44

The Hunt

Derek crawled to the top of the mountain in the gathering dusk. The former slave was looking for a place to sleep for the night. He preferred higher ground, the higher the better. He also preferred rocky ground, the rockier the better. He preferred lots of slippery rocks scattered around whatever place he chose to fall asleep for the night. There was no outrunning a dinosaur. He was reminded of the old joke of the hunter told he could not outrun a bear, to which the hunter replied he only needed to outrun his partner. It was better to find a place with treacherous footing and forbidding drop-offs. Derek found such a place, an old weathered oak tree overhanging and halfway up a canyon rim. It was a sixty meter drop to the valley floor with sliding slipping rocks piled on the incline leading to the base of the ancient tree and continuing to the mountain top. The rocks had poured over the mountainside and were waiting for the day they might someday reach the valley floor.

He walked the mountain brim to the rock incline and began to fight his way up to the big oak tree. The oak looked thick and strong. His bowstring was tight across his chest and his bow across his back, and his quiver was strapped to his shoulder. He was vulnerable against the sliding rock, as he inched his way up to the lonely oak. His quiver was still full after his first day hunting. He was tired and needed sound sleep after covering many kilometers on foot. He was many kilometers from the nearest dinometer and far from safety or another human being. He reached for the base of the oak tree and grabbed hairy old strands of bark. He scratched the sliding rock ground and pushed himself closer. He was at the base now, and he hugged the old tree and pulled out a coil of rope from his pack with a magnetized ball at the end separated by a magnetized socket. He pulled the ball out of the socket and slung the coil high and it unwound as it flew and wrapped around a thick limb above and found the socket and locked solidly in place. Clinging to knots and using them for footing, he began to climb the rope dangling out above the darkening canyon below.

He was up in the tree now and tested the thick live oak that had picked a lonely and peculiar place to grow old. The old live oak held strong and was solid as granite and Derek climbed higher and found a place where he could sit and lean back and rest. He pulled out some twine from his waist pack and tied himself to the tree for he was extremely tired and needed some good rest. He knew it was better to sleep tied to the tree than to worry all night about falling. It was an awful drop to the bottom, and he did not want to take that fall fully alert much less sleeping like a baby. Once he was comfortably secure, he hung his quiver, waist pack, and longbow in the branches and left his knife strapped to his boot. Night was settling in, and Derek was soon to be sound asleep.

The moons of Planet P were out and they shone brightly. Animals moved in the twilight, and rustling was heard in the depths of the shadows. Derek listened for awhile but finally drifted off and slept. He was exhausted and needed some good rest. Herds moved in the shadows and fed on plant life. Predators stalked the herds, and the same old act was played out again. The unwittingly slow of the herds were taken down. When predators had their fill of the kill, the pterodactyls swooped in and picked the bones clean. There was no shortage of food in this world of prehistoric pillage. Mammals and dinosaurs intermingled in a mix of unbridled evolution. This was a true melting pot, never having experienced the disruptions of mass extinction.

He awoke in the early morning shadows of misty dawn. The former corporate slave with yellow eyes came to life and stretched his stiffened limbs and breathed deep the rich oxygen of this mild tropical climate. He unstrapped himself from the trunk and leaned out to look across the valley below. He wanted to get out of the tree and into a better position to possibly get a shot. The animals were moving from their nightly feeding grounds to the places where they played hide and seek from the sun and heat all day. He could smell the herds of moving prey in the humid air. He quietly crawled down the rope from the tree and inched his way over the rocks to the mountain brim below. When he finally stood on level ground he moved quietly along the well traveled brim littered with the spore of passing wild critters.

Derek rambled on down the traveled trail. He knew not what he hunted only that he hunted with stick and string, but he was not an experienced hunter. He was touched with the spirit of the wild, and wanted to experience the ancient ways of living in the badlands of an untamed wilderness. He knew that he would surely get a shot because there was no shortage of wild animals, but he must get into position. He planned to use his blade to quarter the meat and bring the food back to camp. He slowly and quietly followed the trail and was alert to any movement in the early morning shadows. He had eaten his fill of bland foods processed by condensers and cooked up in nanowave ovens. He longed to sample the succulent local cuisine over a roasting fire.

The peaceful early morning erupted in a deep-chested bellow echoing up from the dark canyon below. Derek moved off the trail and crouched among a patch of flowering angiosperm. He pulled an arrow from his quiver and nocked it. He held the longbow and nocked arrow in one hand and waited. He fitted the piece of hide for gripping the bowstring to the three shooting fingers of his release hand. He heard movement down below but he could not see what it was. He heard rocks tumbling, and the sounds were coming closer, aggressively scaling up the mountain incline. His heart was racing. Suddenly he saw a shape scramble over the rim, and it was coming for him in a dead run. Derek crouched not knowing what to do. He could see it clearly now.

It was a calf running blind. Something had spooked the yearling, and the hoofed mammal looked to be all legs and big eyes. The calf galloped up within a few meters from where Derek was crouched. The calf shot the crouching young man a lost and frightened look with its big round eyes, but Derek stayed put. The calf then veered and galloped off, disappearing down the well traveled trail. He listened but did not hear anything else chasing up the ridge in pursuit. He then heard the distant calls of the lost calf further down the trail. He caught the faint smell of the herd and wondered what had spooked the yearling calf. He decided to get a closer look.

45

Debriefing

The Shareholders gathered in luxurious secret chambers around the world and chatted while waiting for the videoconference debriefing. They occasionally jeered at one another in braggadocios barbs. They were all overly confident that whatever the news may be, the support staff had everything completely under control. Military armaments had been tremendously increased after the new god experienced a vision of an impending space-side attack. They were prepared to subjugate all unknowns. They were confident that they controlled the most powerful weapons in the physical universe.

A member of the support staff entered the room. He was an astrophysicist, and he looked frightened and nervous. He was about to reveal information that had been kept from the Shareholders. He was not sure how they would react. He was not sure if he would ever leave the room alive. He had heard wild stories of the ruthless ways in which many unfortunate ones had been sadistically dealt with. He was a smart man and did not intend to be destroyed for entertainment. He was fearful, but he hoped that he might be able to scare them as well.

"Let us hear this terrible news, you scientific swine, and make it quick," barked one Shareholder.

"As you wish, I will be direct. It does not look good," said the astrophysicist tersely.

"What do you mean, it does not look good?" questioned another Shareholder with thick sarcasm. "Did the oceans heat up another couple of degrees due to global warming?" Loud laughter broke out with hooting and stomping. The Shareholders were in a jovial mood today. The astrophysicist nervously waited until the raucous bellows subsided.

"This planet is going to be destroyed," said the astrophysicist amid the final chuckles. There was then total silence.

"We are prepared to subjugate any space-side unknown!" shouted one Shareholder suddenly breaking the stony silence. "We beefed up armaments," added the Shareholder. "What the hell are you babbling about?" he fiercely demanded of the astrophysicist. "We have the most formidable military force at our fingertips and a battle is obviously brewing as the new god has foreseen," the Shareholder concluded.

"This planet is going to be destroyed, and there is nothing we can do about it," replied the astrophysicist. "Our sun is going to be wiped out and when this occurs, the immediate demise of this planet will follow," he said. He had finally told them, and he figured the most difficult part was done. It was up to these nasty leaders to decide what to do now.

"How can this be? Have you lost your mind?" asked one Shareholder in a threatening tone.

"To the best of our knowledge, we were targeted for annihilation thousands of millennia ago for reasons that are currently unclear to us. Unfortunately, we do not know of any way to neutralize the destructive mechanism which rapidly approaches," replied the astrophysicist wearily with a sigh of resignation in his voice. He noted the bewilderment and concern in their faces. This was going better than he thought it would. These ruthless rulers might actually be able to still feel fear and he figured this would be good for him. "We do not know the original source of this attack, because it was initiated so far in the past, before we possessed even the crudest technology," concluded the astrophysicist.

"How long have you known about this coming catastrophe?" asked one Shareholder bitterly menacing.

"We have not known about this impending disaster for very long," he lied. The cunning astrophysicist quickly shifted gears to even scarier details for them to absorb. "The approaching destructive mechanism was built from technology more advanced than our best," he said with theatrical exasperation. "There is nothing we can do to stop it," he assuredly concluded.

"Give us the details please," said another Shareholder smoothly with a new found patience.

"We are about to witness the premeditated cataclysmic death of our sun," replied the astrophysicist. He knew the reputation of the Shareholders and knew how they disdained technical details and intricate explanations. They turned up their noses at technicians and scientists. Technical details usually amounted to pathetic excuses to these ultimate rulers but the news this scientist brought on this day was not typical techie drivel. This news was deadlier than the murderous political games they so enjoyed. The astrophysicist knew this was to his advantage.

"What do you mean when you say the death of our sun?" asked a Shareholder quietly with much reserve. All sarcasm had fled from the videoconference rooms and foolish pride followed close behind. "Please explain it so that we may understand," said the Shareholder with halting patience.

The scientist now had their attention. "Our sun will acquire an auto-immune disease and will die very soon, long before its time. This sun of ours will not live to a ripe old age but will die violently in a midlife crisis, vengefully taking the solar system with it. Earth is not truly separate from the sun as we all know. If the sun goes, we all go. This approaching mechanism is an antiquark implosion bomb. It is unstoppable with our current technology. This device is not something that could have naturally occurred. It was built. Our modern technology is ridiculous and inane compared to this thing. The thermonuclear reactions that fuse hydrogen inside the solar core of our sun will be altered. Our bright yellow sun will go through a much different dying phase and in an accelerated manner. We believe our sun will not collapse into a white dwarf as normal yellow suns do. It will not form a red giant before becoming a white dwarf, as do little yellow suns such as ours do in normal dying cycles. Left undisturbed, our little yellow sun would have gone on another five billion years, but this will not be the fate of our little yellow sun nor ours," said the astrophysicist. He had their attention now and it felt good.

A Shareholder suddenly roared, "Stop saying 'little yellow sun' you little yellow man!" The astrophysicist felt sweat break out across his forehead. There was grumbling among the Shareholders from across the videoconference rooms.

"Do not get cute with us!" another Shareholder shouted.

"Continue with the details," growled a Shareholder.

"As I was saying," said the astrophysicist shakily. "The sun that we call ours will instead grow much greater in mass and will become a super-giant as the hydrogen core is rapidly consumed. The byproduct of this antiquark implosion bomb will leave much heavier material but quickly collapsing, and giving birth to a synthetic neutron star. This will all occur in an accelerated manner. The outer gases will violently explode in bursts of supernova energy. Anyone this side of Pluto will quickly die from the tremendous radiation energy emitted by this solar upheaval," concluded the staff astrophysicist. He was relieved. His difficult task of explaining the details of this mess was finally over.

"Why is this thing so tough to stop? Tell me that, you sorry excuse for a scientist," snarled a Shareholder.

The astrophysicist had the feeling that he had somehow managed to spoil the longest running party in history. There was a sinking in his courage and his face drained of all color. He now spoke with great effort as one speaks who has given it their best and still failed and is finally beaten, and now must explain why. He slowly spoke. "We know not how it moves. We know not how to stop it. We know not how it was constructed, nor how to disarm it. We know not how to destroy it. All we have to go on is an encrypted transmission which took our parallel supercomputers months to crack. We finally deciphered that transmission. It describes the dramatic effects that I have already detailed today. This is all we know for now," he finished.

"What are our options?" asked a Shareholder. The Shareholders were gravely concerned and demanded options.

"There are always options," said one Shareholder.

"If you do not present us with options, you will never return to your position," threatened another.

"What good is a debriefing without options?" asked yet another.

"Flee the solar system," replied the astrophysicist. "There is no other option. This solar system will be destroyed very soon. Our best minds cannot stop this antiquark implosion bomb. Our best technology is lacking. We have brought in the brightest minds of this world to help with this crisis and we are out of ideas and time. The human race is evolving technologically and this may have been viewed as a threat by an alien race. We are not sure of the reasons. The only thing we know for certain is the technology that constructed this antiquark implosion device is thousands of years more advanced than our present capabilities. It is as much a mystery to us now as when it was first detected. We call it an antiquark implosion bomb for lack of a better term and because of the implications of the chain reaction which we are convinced will occur upon entry into the sun," said the astrophysicist.

The Shareholders were stunned. There were many questions and deep concerns from the Shareholders now. "What about our teracorps? We need slaves. We need subjugates. Without the masses we are ruined. We need to sustain our lifestyles. We need luxury and wealth. Without this system we are going to suffer. We will not stand for this. Is a migration possible? Do we have time for a calculated migration to another inhabitable world?" asked the Shareholders.

"We have known about this for such a short time," the scientist lied. "And now we have no time left at all," he added truthfully. "There is only time to save ourselves. I am no expert in the logistics of the next steps to take, so we have brought in a consultant to advise you in this matter," finished the astrophysicist. The consultant entered the videoconference room.

The consultant began without introduction. "We have the peoplemill breeding facilities to clone a significant slave population. We do not need the masses, because we can rebuild them. We can carry the best products of our technology to sustain our lifestyles, and migrate to another world. The teracorps will worry about their own survival. We only have time to stock an FTL luxury cruiser and an elite military defense unit and flee. At faster than light speed, we can manage an escape to another inhabitable world in time to save ourselves. We can rebuild this system again in another world. This is our only option." finished the consultant with authority.

The intelligent astrophysicist felt things were going better now. He had gotten through the worst part and had presented them with the details of the impending destruction. The consultant had given them the only option. He was afraid they would ask again how long they had known of this inevitable catastrophe. If they knew how long this predicament was kept from them, he would be dead before he left the room. These sadistic rulers were now bewildered and terrified and asked no such questions. They were frightened into stupidity. They also needed the support staff and again that was good for him. The Shareholders would need slaves faster than the breeding facilities could produce them which worried him. The astrophysicist was not looking forward to this trip, or to the prospect of babysitting these decadent leaders.

46

The Kill

Derek crouched and watched the moving herd through an opening in the underbrush. He wanted to take a shot at one of the big bulls, but the herd would not stay still. They were antlered mammals. He had never seen anything like them and the herd bull stood out from them all. They were agitated, but the wind was in his favor and they had not winded him. He checked the small feather that hung by a thread on his bow. The gentle wind was in his favor so he pushed on from behind them. The herd bull moved and worked the cows with purpose and precision, and there were other bulls following on the perimeter, bulls that would someday successfully challenge the herd bull but not thus far. Derek sometimes ran to keep up, but he could not get any closer than 80 meters which was out of the range of his arrows.

The sun was coming up fast, and the antlered beasts were still on the move, quietly heading for shade and cover. His only hope of getting a shot would be at their destination, but he had no map and no idea of where he was or where they were going. He realized it did not matter because he could circle around, if he wanted to get a shot at one of the big bulls. He ran straight for the herd. He wanted to scatter them into confusion as he had seen the deinonychus do to the herd of seismosaurs. Regrettably, the herd did not scatter into confusion as he planned. They saw him coming well before he was near, and they ran from him departing in an orderly group, and he was quickly alone again. He cursed and realized he let his excitement cloud his judgment.

The antlered critters disappeared into a narrow divide. It was the only place they could have gone. Derek proceeded to circle wide. He figured the big beasts would need a drink of water soon after running but before they found a place to hide for the day. He ran off and up a steep crevice bordering the divide. He scaled the steep mountainside and at the top of the ridge he ran along the edge but far enough back to not be silhouetted. Down the far side he saw water in the distance and decided to take a chance. He slid and stumbled down the mountain and made for the water hole. When he arrived, he noticed that the mud was covered in hoof tracks, a good sign. He got into position and waited. He crouched in a bush, some forty meters from the edge of the water hole. The herd came in.

The cows came in first. They were cautious and alert. Derek stayed perfectly still and they did not notice him. They stalked in and drank from the water. The bulls stayed back letting the cows check out the watering hole first. Derek could see antlers out above the tall grass. These creatures were out of place in this land of lizard monsters. He wondered how they survived day to day in this world of large predators. He knew that antlered mammals were once hunted on Earth and that they were good to eat, and he hungrily desired to find out.

Derek realized that he did not know what life cycle these animals currently were in or much about their habits at all. He did not know if there was a mating season, if these animals battled for dominance of the herd, or if they simply survived. He wished to know more. He wanted to find out more about the wild animals here in this untamed exciting place. He wanted to learn, but he would need patience. There were many mysteries in this world and he was a newcomer. He wanted to learn how to hunt and survive in the wild, to experience the lost ways of hunting with stick and string.

The cows were drinking more confidently now. Derek was hidden well and remained perfectly still. There was an opening through the underbrush large enough to put an arrow through. Behind him were colors close to what he wore so when he drew his bow this would not be easily detected. The air was still, down in the high grass of the lowlands, which was good. The cows were comfortable and milling around now but cautiously looking back at the bulls. Some of the younger bulls came in to have a drink. Derek still waited. There was a grunt and the younger bulls scattered and the big herd bull came in. The large bull possessed a massive rack. The heart of the young hunter pounded furiously, and he was excited beyond words.

The big bull commanded the respect of the others as they let him have the water hole all to himself. The bull emerged broadside of the crouching hunter. The bull walked out into the water and stood there with the water lapping against its underside. Crouching so close, to him the bull looked very old, with gray fur and a big pot belly. The bull drank from the water hole warily, checking surroundings between sips. The massive antlered mammal grew more comfortable with its surroundings and then began to lustily gulp the water. Derek had an arrow nocked, and drew back. The old bull blinked and Derek released the arrow. The arrow flew forty meters and swallowed into the big breast of the old gray bull.

The bull splashed and bolted from the water hole and disappeared into the high grass. Others from the herd followed in confusion. Derek waited and kept still, giving the huge animal time to lie down and die. He waited for what seemed like an hour then he quietly walked over to the edge of the water hole where the bull had disappeared. The hoofed mammals had all fled. There was blood on the ground. He found his blood covered arrow stuck in the mud past where the big bull was hit. His arrow had traveled cleanly through the chest of the large animal. He retrieved the bloody arrow and slowly and quietly followed the trail of splattered blood into the high grass.

47

Final Hour

Reverend H prepared for a short talk at 90% light speed. He listened to classical music composed in previous centuries while preparing. The classical music soothed and inspired and he really needed a little soothing and inspiration. He took his daily supplements and scribbled down his thoughts on his paper thin console in preparation. The space ark had embarked upon a monumental cosmic migration many months ago. There were many of the congregation harboring old vengeful thoughts and feelings of regret. They all had left hopeless situations behind, and they all had chosen to flee the only world they knew. They were all justified by vanishing in the dead of the night, and yet many harbored ill feelings.

"In life we encounter enemies and obstacles, especially when we attempt to accomplish worthwhile things, and we should pray for our foes if only because it will do your heart good. Try not to succumb to lower emotions such as worry, regret, hatred, anger, or vengeance. These are different aspects of fear, and nothing is accomplished through fear. We once lived a suppressed life without hope and many feel their life and those years have been wasted. Everything has a reason, everyone has a purpose, and there are no ordinary moments. No one lives or dies without a reason. The power of now is our greatest gift and appropriately called the present. We are priceless with unlimited potential, networked with each other, and here to help one another. Separateness and isolation are no longer unfathomable illusions. We are all one with each other, and one with the ultimate creator. We were once trapped in useless mediocrity. We thankfully and handily left our captors behind so this is a time to hope and dream.

There was the supervisor who devalued our worth and unquestioning servants ambitiously seeking the favor of superiors. There were the rules to a game we could not play. There were those who took credit for the ideas and work of others. There are the teracorps pursuing unsustainable growth to no end without regard to the finite environment once called our home. There were the people packed on top of people and forced to live in that finite environment. There were the Shareholders who claimed to be gods, making a mockery out of all that we cherish.

Many consider the opposite of fear to be love and compassion. Truly love and compassion are without fear. Once we let go of vengeful thoughts and feelings, we can continue to grow and learn and humbly become a little more enlightened. The truth is that we are now light years above those problems, so let us dwell in thankfulness, with optimism and confidence. Faith is the realization that the universe is abundant, supportive, and nourishing, and then taking courageous action. There is a design for good at work in our lives as the master programmer within us planned it to be. We possess infinite potential and infinite worth. Let us create a new definition for revenge. If there is to be any revenge then let it be healthy living centered upon thankfulness, for this is the most rewarding revenge of all," said Reverend H as he gazed upon his cult.

As Reverend H looked out over the gathered congregation, he had a feeling that he had been there before. He suddenly had the feeling that he had just completed this sermon in the endless warped space-time continuum countless times before. The cult who sat and listened to Reverend H also felt they had heard this sermon many times before. They felt they had listened to this sermon at 90% light speed thousands of times now. It was the deja vu effect. It was a time shock wave.

Reverend H stood speechless before his congregation and he felt he had stood speechless before his congregation as he did now many other times before. He floated through multitudes of vivid mental images of himself standing before his congregation speechless.

They were all lashed by the deja vu effect of the time shock wave. They all experienced the sensation that they were doing what they had just done over and over again. It was the deja vu effect of breaking the light speed barrier. The cult was lost and locked in a loop of time, experiencing over and over what had just been experienced.

Reverend H tried to gather his composure and stumbled down from the podium. He sat down in the bench at the front of the congregation. A member of the navigational crew emerged in the doorway and made his way to the front. Reverend H was stunned by the deja vu effect and the whole cult congregation was also stunned by the same deja vu effect. The navigator came to Reverend H and told him urgently, "We have been hijacked. An FTL ship has a lock on the space ark and we are being towed through space at faster than light speed," announced the fearful navigator.

"Have we made contact with them?" asked the shocked Reverend H.

"No, we do not know what this is about," replied the navigator. "They have full control of the ship including control of the computer system. They have shut us out completely," said the navigator.

Reverend H looked up at his cult congregation. They were all dumbfounded from the intense time shock wave. He was at a loss for immediate words. He paused and gathered his composure and managed a smile. "It seems that we have company," he said to the congregation. "I will get back to you when I know more." He then followed the navigator back to the space ark consoles.

The space ark consoles betrayed the presence of the unknown visitor. The cult's normal access was blocked and Reverend H and company could only helplessly watch the activity. "They are scanning our databases," said the navigator. "It appears they are interested in the passenger list," he added.

"They are examining the passenger profiles," said Reverend H in disbelief. The unknown visitors methodically picked through the database containing the personal profiles of every cult member. "They are downloading our databases," said Reverend H in dismay, as they watched helplessly when the file transfer protocol initiated then completed.

They watched as the unknown visitors examined the event logs and the flight scheduler database. "They have determined when and where we left and where we are going. Our destination is now known," sighed the navigator. The webscreen sphere flickered on. Reverend H and his flight crew listened and watched as the unknown visitors spoke.

"So we are off to Eridani, are we?" crackled the webscreen sphere as a grainy image appeared before them. It was the recently elected god of Earth and she laughed wickedly. "You have quite an impressive passenger list," purred the new leader. "My slaves should not be subjected to such horrendous lengths of time in space, so we are going to give you a lift. We are headed your way and so we will tremendously shorten your time in space. This rowboat you call a space ark would never have made the long trip. We will be arriving soon. Your little so-called freedom migration was doomed from the start. Our heroic rescue of your rickety ship requires no thanks, but you soon will have the pleasure of serving us. We will all make Eridani our new home," she finished.

With that the webscreen projection faded. The space ark was now sailing through space-time at faster than the speed of light, but not by its own power or propulsion. The hardy little space ark was now being towed by an elite Shareholder FTL cruiser. They were off to see Eridani.

48

Hot Blooded

The utahraptors at the maiden voyager Solarion were patiently waiting outside like a cat waits by a small hole for a mouse to peep out. Dr. Zeek, Ami, and Benny watched from the consoles inside. Utahraptors were the largest known velociraptors according to the dinosaur database. The curious utahraptors studied the exterior of the ship and sniffed outside the doorway where the humans had last been. They became still and quiet and waited for the fish toting humans to emerge from their nest. When the humans did not emerge, the creepy predators stalked off and hid in the shadows of the grassy perimeter and staked out the human nest from a distance. If not for the dinometers, the crew would have ventured outside and been quickly eaten alive.

The utahraptors were large striped and spotted versions of the smaller deinonychus. The snarling deinonychus had come through several times before in large packs. The utahraptors had huge heads and bodies but were shaped proportionately the same as deinonychus. They had the same shortened forearms relative to their huge bodies. They possessed powerful legs for jumping and running at high speeds. The utahraptors had huge birdlike claws. There was one curved claw used for gripping and ripping flesh. The crew hoped to not become eaten on this day. These were the smartest predators the crew of the Solarion had yet to encounter.

The little crew busied themselves by working on the excursion vehicle as best they could from the inside. The graviton hovercraft was designed for Mercury excursions, planets with no atmosphere and a weaker gravitational influence. The redesign was almost complete, but there was only so much they could do from inside the ship. They needed the hovercraft to be able to travel quickly and safely across this planet of lurking monsters. The hovercraft rover was crucial for their survival. Food supplies were extremely low. They would soon be forced to live off the land.

Dr. Zeek decided the utahraptors were more curious than hungry and assured the others that these fierce predators would eventually move on. They needed a defense system in conjunction with the dinometers. Their creative use of Solarion components had left the ship stripped and dysfunctional. He worried that they would not be able to put the ship back together fast enough in order to make a hasty getaway. The necessity for a quick launch from this isolated prehistoric world seemed an unlikely possibility. The rebuild of the graviton hovercraft was critical because they were so low on rations. They had not heard from young Derek for days now. Derek had carried a beacon this time with him to use in the event that he became lost or in trouble. Dr. Zeek hoped to have the hovercraft operational by the time the adventurous boy decided to set off the distress beacon. Otherwise, there would be no way to get there in time.

The utahraptors were warm-blooded creatures without a doubt. This was once debated in the science of paleontology. Once upon a time dinosaurs were thought to have been cold-blooded, much like snakes and lizards, relying upon external heat for internal metabolism. This accepted theory was challenged by scientific heretics who proposed that carnivorous predatory dinosaurs were instead warm-blooded, and were more like birds than snakes. The utahraptors were obviously warm-blooded, fast-moving, and excitable. These hot-blooded uninvited guests would not go away and they remained lurking in the shadows of the perimeter of the camp. The bird-like beasts hovered around the centerpiece of the inviting scent pool, and sniffed something delicious that only they could smell. It was not safe to go outside with those people-eaters lying in wait. Much as a crowd draws an even larger crowd, the pack of utahraptors grew sizeable in a short period of time. The crew figured these predators would get hungry enough to venture off eventually. They would move on soon or so the crew inside the Solarion hoped.

"I am getting another alarm," said Ami, looking up from the ship computer console sphere. "What do you make of it?" asked Ami, as Dr. Zeek walked up and examined the alarm entries.

"Real time inputs are linked to the dinosaur database. We should find out shortly," said Dr. Zeek. "It is big and fast," he added.

"There are more of them," said Ami. The shapes were coming into the perimeter zone of the dinosaur detection system. The console projection sphere displayed the shapes, estimated to be 2700 kilograms in size by the ship supercomputer. They were also predators by the looks of them but much larger than even the utahraptors. They were as large as adult iguanodons but were the shape of vicious predators. They were too large to be members of the vicious velociraptor species.

"The dinosaur database search is complete," said Dr. Zeek. "The input search matches on acrocanthosaurus. I will bring up a description," he said as he manually scanned the database and brought up the paleontological description of acrocanthosaurus. "They were called acros for short. They were from the same habitats as utahraptor although much larger and were enemies of the utahraptor," said Dr. Zeek.

"Looks like they still are enemies here in another world," said Ami. "They are following the path of the utahraptors. They are trailing them," she said.

"The acros should have no trouble finding what they are looking for. The utahraptors have been hanging around leaving plenty of their own scent. There is going to be a fight," said Dr. Zeek. "I do not like the looks of this. Let me bring this up on the big screen," he said and focused the big screen optics on the utahraptor camp.

"Benny, you have got to see this," called Ami, across the ship webphone mike.

"I will check it out on the observatory deck," he replied. Benny put down his laser axe and made his way to the observatory deck of the Solarion.

"I will join you there," said Ami.

"I will pipe the sound to the observatory deck to create a full theater effect," said Dr. Zeek. Ami made her way to the prow of the Solarion to the observatory deck.

The acros were moving slower now, as the scent of their natural enemy strengthened. They were creeping closer to the utahraptor pack. The utahraptors were together and appeared to be mostly sleeping except for those perched on the perimeters of the pack. The sentry utahraptors kept watch with their backs to the gentle breezes so that they could smell movement to the rear and see movement out in front. The acros crawled closer and closer to the ground keeping their scent and their huge bodies low. The gentle breeze sometimes shifted directions. The sentry utahraptors adjusted their positions with any subtle changes in the wind.

One lone sentry utahraptor snorted and stood up. He stretched his snout high in the air and sniffed intensely. There was a rumbling growl and the lead acro charged. The sentry utahraptor shrieked and squawked and ran into the middle of the sleeping pack. The utahraptors stirred. The acros were coming in fast. The lead acro roared and lunged upon the back of the fleeing sentry utahraptor. The sentry utahraptor crumpled under the weight. The acro crunched down upon the head of the sentry. The acro ripped the sentry head from its spine, leaving a clawing blood spurting torso. The acros circled in on the snarling shocked but awakened utahraptors.

One utahraptor rushed the acros with a mock charge then tried to dodge through them and flee and the closest acro clamped down on the leg of the utahraptor as it leapt past. The snagged utahraptor kicked desperately with its one free leg. The kicking utahraptor ripped huge slashes across the eyes and snout of the larger acro, as the acro desperately tried to get hold of and subdue the deadly kicking leg. They rolled, snarled, and howled. The desperate utahraptor mutilated the head of the acro until another acro pounced in and crunched down upon the wild leg of the snagged utahraptor. Both acros tugged in opposite directions and ripped the utahraptor in two as the utahraptor screamed final screams of agony.

The one acro had been mauled, now with a ripped up snout, and dripped blood and roared furiously. He suffered from a deep gash exposing its top row of teeth. The tough flesh once covering its teeth hung down from a huge gash. He tore into the carcass of the utahraptor but unwittingly bit into its own hanging flesh, roaring pitifully each time this happened.

Unleashed mayhem erupted. The cornered raptor pack ran wildly in all directions, with acros chasing down and killing any utahraptors they could catch. The acros fed on and fought over the raptor carcasses. It was a horrible scene, displayed in full color and sound on the big spherical projection screens both in the control room and on the observatory deck of the Solarion. The crew safe inside the ship watched with jaw-dropped awe.

The acros eventually left the gnawed carcasses and started down the trail of the fleeing utahraptors. The big acro with the mutilated snout followed the others but not as anxiously. The others quickly left him behind, and he slowly followed the scent trail left by his brothers and sisters, but they were gone. He left a river of blood in his wake and finally came to rest and did not move again.

The pterodactyls were circling in the sky and landing on the remains of the bloody encounter. The pterodactyls swooped down and walked on folded wings. They picked at the bones and screeched and fought over the leftovers. Again a small crowd attracted a larger crowd and soon there were hundreds. After a time, when there was not much left to pick or fight over, pterodactyls began to ascend in search of the next kill scene further down the trail. The camp was finally clear except for what remained of the vicious bloody battle between the acros and utahraptors.

"These recordings were just what we needed to enhance our dinosaur detection system with defense modules," announced Dr. Zeek across the webphone mike. "We will need to get blood samples from what is left out there," he added as he hastily gathered containers from the lab. He was ever the scientist, and was always eager to analyze new data.

It was Ami who asked that same familiar question this time, "What are we doing here?"

"One thing is for certain," replied Benny, "We have discovered the land of the free and the brave."

49

The Local Cuisine

Derek stood over the old bull. If any kill could be considered clean, this kill was clean. His arrow had drilled through both lungs. The bull had run a mere eighty meters and died quickly. It had taken the herd bull just a few seconds to run the small distance after the arrow stung its chest. Derek stood there, knowing he needed to act soon, determining how to get this meat back to camp. He did not want to waste one morsel of the meat.

Derek suddenly realized it was honorable for the bull to go this way because it would soon be too weak and old to flee the vicious predators. The big bull lived with courage, roaming freely in this wild country, and died quickly. This was far better than the way domestic cattle were once handled upon Earth long ago. The hunter saw the magnificent beauty of the wonderful creature.

Domestic cattle were once raised for their meat but that was before his time. There were no meat-eaters on Earth now. The cattle once raised for beef were stuffed into cramped corrals and spent their lives wallowing in their own excrement, pumped up with steroids and antibiotics, and in a final abomination were fed meat from their own kind. They were fattened and sent to the slaughterhouses as cheaply and as quickly as possible. Brain wasting diseases were widespread among all domestic animals raised for their meat in those days, and the diseases soon became common in the free ranging animals and even in fish as well. This was all covered up by meat and dairy industries for as long as possible. It would have been prudent to cleanly destroy the diseased, and reform horrid methods of meat and dairy production. Instead, diseased animals were ground into cheaper meats, or fed back to the healthy of their own kind. Brain wasting diseases spread from animals to humans and millions died from the horrible epidemic. The brain wasting epidemic manifested in all species of deer, elk, goat, fish, pig, and cattle. Birds became the spreaders of deadly flu viruses. All animals eventually needed to be destroyed. Everyone on Earth was forced to become a vegetarian.

The big bull lived not knowing one day of confinement and only a few seconds of pain. Derek felt sadness and at the same time happiness that he and his crew now had something to eat. He needed to get his first kill with hand-carved longbow and whittled arrows back to his home camp. He examined the scars on the bull hide from the past battles, the pot belly from having plenty to eat, and the rack spread wide and long. He bent over and opened the mouth to look at the teeth of this antlered animal. The teeth were in bad shape from decay. The bull was past his prime.

Derek looked out across the high grassy plains and the distant tree covered mountain peaks with dark canyon divides. There was a gentle breeze whistling through his hair. There were long seismosaur necks poking above the grass at the edge of the grassy plain several kilometers away. He took a long deep breath of unspoiled wilderness air. He suddenly realized that he did not know how many days made up a year on this planet but it did not bother him so much. He felt an inner peace flood his senses unlike anything he had ever known. In this dangerous lost world he suddenly felt more alive than he had ever felt before. He was going to survive and bring this food home.

He knew he had to get out of the area quickly. The scent of blood drew a crowd and the blood trail would not go undetected for long. He tied the antlers of the bull with thick twine and struggled to drag the carcass over to a large oak with low strong branches. He threw the other end of the twine over a sturdy branch and used brute strength to hoist the bull up high enough to cut out the good meat. He removed the guts and skinned the bull where it hung. He stopped to sharpen his blade and raise the animal higher as the load was lightened. He came prepared and laboriously boned out the meat to salvage the best parts.

He brought with him several collapsible containment vessels which he soon filled with soft heavy portions of lean meat. When all salvageable meat was packed into containment vessels, he unrolled a lightweight sled, the same improvised sled Benny and Ami had used to gather piles of samples for the lab. He tied the bags to the sled then he tied them all together, and then wrapped the containment vessels in a heat reflecting sheet and made sure everything was snug to the sled. He then attached a shoulder harness to the sled.

He ran back to the water hole and cleaned up, hurrying to be on his way. He then rubbed the outside of the bundle down with strong smelling sage growing wild nearby in order to avoid any unnecessary spread of scent. He also rubbed the smelly sage into his skin and clothes. It was a long journey back to base camp and he did not want be detected. The sun-blocking sheet would keep the meat cool during the heat of the day. He fitted the shoulder harness to his upper body so that his bow and quiver would not make noise. He began to pull the sled and his thighs bulged but it slid easily and quietly along the ground. He needed to put some distance between himself and the pungent gut pile left behind.

The sled was the only way to get the meat back to camp. It was impossible to carry that load on his back. He needed to be able to drop the load quickly in an emergency and he could quietly unclip the harness for this purpose. He also planned to unclip the sled to scout ahead through the thick areas where he wanted to avoid unwittingly surprising whatever lurked in the shadows. He needed to avoid those surprises. The load was secure so he pushed ahead for the long trek back to the ship. It was midmorning so he figured if all went well he would make camp by nightfall. The sled was surprisingly quiet as it slid pliantly across the rocks and grass. Derek felt good about this. He wanted to make as little noise as possible but still make time in getting this meal back to camp. The wild predators in this land were not the type to run from sounds. He had already discovered that the fearless beasts of this world rushed to sounds.

Derek pulled his sled loaded with succulent meat across the plains as seismosaurs grazed in the backdrop. He made his way toward the mountain divide to where the antlered herd had ventured out to drink earlier in the morning. Thunder clouds were forming in the distance, and he felt cool winds swirling through the canyon. He hoped the rains would soon come to slow down animal movement and to shield the sounds he made as he pulled the heavy load. Lightning cracked the midday sky in the growing darkness of an approaching storm. In spite of his powerful leg muscles, and in spite of the slick sled, he was realizing that this was a very heavy pull and it would be tough going.

He recalled some words he had written a time ago, as the sky darkened and thunder booms echoed across the canyon. He wondered where Jenniper was now. He hoped that she had made it out with the cult. He knew he would never be back to Earth so if she had stayed there, then he would never see her again.

Life is bitter. Life is hard.
Crawling on my knees for another yard.
I know I'm down and I can't win
This game of chaos and sin.

Look at my life in the streets.
Working for the fool's gold I see.
Running for the president
Of believers left broken and bent.

But this is what we all do.
We don't give a damn about the truth.
And this is where we all live.
A generation of takers, who never learned to give.

50

On Top of the World

Deep in the maddening silence of interstellar space, void of medium to carry the raging sounds, approached the wicked laughing Shareholders. They traveled in luxury with the best of modern technology packed into the largest Stick and String graviton FTL battleship cruiser in existence. Once the sadistic rulers of the world learned of the eminent tragic disaster bound for their solar system, they flew like frightened ducks to safety. They did not care if billions died. It was not their concern. Those left behind were worthless slaves and not smart enough nor ambitious enough to have ever joined their ranks. Those left were not coveted immortal Shareholders.

They carried a payload that consisted of none other than the grandest known technological accomplishments and priceless treasures of mankind, an elite military defense unit, and a willing and competent support staff. They touted and glorified their cowardly flight, calling it a rescue mission to save mankind. They then happened upon a pitiful space ark stocked with renegade corporate slaves who were all members of a strange cult and they immediately confiscated the craft and all its cult cargo. They were in a rescuing mood. They drank and smoked and partied and toasted their good fortune. The teracorps were left to save themselves, and the Shareholders placed their bets in their stock market on which teracorps would survive.

It was a high time for the Shareholders and they celebrated without moderation, consuming their favorite poisons, feeding their favorite addictions, and relishing their personal vices of choice. They indulged in anything and everything that their hardened hearts desired. They had known for awhile of a quaint little inhabitable planet located in the solar system of Epsilon Eridani. They had kept the teracorps out by declaring it off limits. It was a privilege and a joy to possess such juicy bits of secret knowledge, and now this delightful planet would be their paradise retreat. They laughed long and hard when they learned of the silly migration led by the babbling old fool who called himself Reverend H, and of his ship of foolish followers. The joke was upon the starry-eyed believers who were duped into the crazy cult crusade dreamed up by such a senile old man. This was such a delightful cruise and the raucous party ensued and escalated into high gear.

The Shareholders decided in their revelry that it would be good fun to crucify the wise and venerable Reverend H for the purpose of after-dinner entertainment. They decided to do away with the old man in grand fashion. The old man needed to top off his wildly successful religious career by becoming a martyr. This joke was intoxicatingly good fun for the self-proclaimed gods. They heartily agreed the crucifixion of the religious nut would make for spectacular entertainment. They planned a feast and celebration, topped off with a crucifixion. They sent a transport module hurtling through the ionic cloud to shuttle the prisoners of the space ark back to the luxurious FTL battle cruiser. They wanted them all to be onboard to witness the crucifixion of their glorious cult leader.

The religious followers were shuttled back to the stupendous battle cruiser and placed in the brig. There was no means of resistance for the cult followers. They possessed no handheld weapons and knew nothing of hand to hand combat. They were not prepared to fight. They were not trained to defend themselves so they complied. They were helpless slaves once again. The bars of the brig were slammed shut and locked, and Reverend H hung his head and prayed. For this latest development he had no answer, and he felt that he had failed them all.

He did not have the words to comfort his poor bewildered congregation. He blamed himself and knew that he alone was responsible for this tragedy.

He prayed for the wretched slaves left on dying Earth, who knew nothing of the approaching annihilation. He prayed for his faithful cult congregation who had followed him willingly and now had fallen into this trap along with him. He asked for forgiveness for his somewhat naive vision of how events were to unfold. He wished that he was as smart and as wise as his followers believed he was, but he was not smart enough. He was an old fool, and he was so weary of fighting a system that could not be beaten. He finally prayed for his enemies, the Shareholders. He gave thanks that no one had been harmed yet and he asked that the greater will be done, in Eridani as well as in the heavens.

After awhile, three military men came to the brig. They eyed the prisoners with contempt. Reverend H did not look up, but continued his silent meditation and prayer. They walked from one end of the long brig to the other and studied the cult members through the bars. Finally one of them spoke. He was the captain in charge. He shouted so that all could hear.

"Listen up, I have some good news. We do not intend to keep you here long. I do not know what you have heard about our prison system, but the truth is that no one is held for long. We do not have an expensive prison system, and people behind bars are expensive. We will not tolerate extended stays especially for so-called religious or political prisoners. You have no rights. You do not exist as far as we are concerned. It is simple. Either pledge allegiance to the system and to the Shareholders or you will die," said the captain. He spoke rapidly as if he had given the same short memorized speech many times before in the past.

"We meant no one any harm," said one woman among the cult congregation behind bars. "We just wanted to live our lives in peace," she said tenderly. The first lieutenant standing by the captain pulled a chemical injection gun from his belt and fired two doses into the breast of the woman who spoke. She screamed, standing for a moment in shocked paralysis, as the poisonous chemicals streamed in. She began to convulse. The other members rushed to her aid but it was no use. She fell back to the floor in a full seizure, and died in a matter of seconds, as blood trickled from her nostrils.

"I do not recall asking for opinions, or commentaries," announced the captain flippantly. "Let us get down to business, shall we?" he started. "Which one of you happens to be the infamous Reverend H, leader of this ragtag group?" asked the captain impatiently, his loud voice echoing down the long hall.

"I am. There is no need to kill anyone else," replied Reverend H fiercely. The eyes of the old Reverend H were dark with fury. He gripped the bars in grief.

"Good," said the captain. "You are a lucky man because you are going to become a martyr today. You get to die good and slow," said the captain sadistically.

Reverend H was pulled from the brig, by the first and second lieutenants, and then crucified. They drilled holes through the flesh and bones of his hands and feet and then bolted them to a golden cross. They created a crown made of barbed metal and pushed it down snugly upon the old man's head. The blood was flowing thickly through his white dreadlocks. His ebony skin soon washed red with blood. They rushed him to the raucous celebration for the Shareholders to enjoy. They hurried so that he would not die before the wicked leaders got a chance to have their fun. They drug the gruesome spectacle to them. The Shareholders were presented with the evening's entertainment, a martyr dying on a golden cross.

Reverend H faded in and out of consciousness. He looked up through bloody eyes and a foggy haze of agony. The room was dimly lit and smoky. He could barely make out the horrid rulers. They slurped drinks, puffed smoke, and snacked on fine desserts. They had just finished an elaborate feast, and now were enjoying a unique spectacle. This was real entertainment for a change. It was not every day that one witnessed a cult martyr dying on a golden cross.

"You are much too quiet, good Reverend H," said one Shareholder with smacking lips. "You are boring us silly. Aren't you hurting at all? Find out if the righteous Reverend H is in pain!" boomed the

Shareholder. An obedient android walked over to Reverend H and grabbed the old man's waist and shook his hanging body viciously. Reverend H weakly wailed and coughed, as fresh blood poured down.

"The least you can do is to deliver us a persuasive sermon. Do you have any sermons prepared for us?" asked another mocking Shareholder. "This is a prime opportunity for you to save us, my good Reverend H. This is your big chance to make converts of us all," chuckled the Shareholder.

Reverend H muttered something but they could not hear his words. He did not have the strength to speak as he wished to speak. His once white locks of hair were red and thick with blood, and blood drained steadily from his hands and feet. He was losing blood fast and was not long for this world.

The Shareholders continued their mocking. "We did not hear you, Reverend H! You must speak with authority if you hope to convert anyone. We are waiting to be persuaded to join your faithful cult. We are waiting for that special moment when we will see the truth and feel the enlightenment take hold to change our lives forever. Speak up, damn you!" shouted a Shareholder, truly enjoying his after-dinner entertainment.

Reverend H struggled to find his voice. In a moment of silence, he said clearly, "You have your rewards," sputtered Reverend H feebly through blood covered eyes and blood covered teeth. He let his head hang down limply.

A Shareholder felt the urge to respond. "Of course we have our rewards. We all have our rewards. We have the rewards that come with success and we enjoy our rewards. We are on top of the world. You are not a very persuasive speaker, Reverend H," said a Shareholder.

"You have your rewards in full," muttered Reverend H without raising his head. Reverend H died then and there. At that very moment, Jenniper was sitting in the brig and clearly heard Reverend H whisper in her ear. She was stunned when his familiar voice whispered strongly and clearly, "Jenniper, it is true bliss."

They then took his body back to the brig where the captive congregation was held, his lifeless form still bolted to the golden cross.

They stood the golden cross in front of the cult prisoners so that they could weep and wail at the sight of their crucified martyr.

There was nothing anyone could do there behind the bars. The cult members did only what they knew how to do. They mourned, meditated, and prayed.

51

Vicious Encounter

Derek pulled his sled loaded with meat through the badlands of crawling howling monsters and keenly surveyed surrounding jungles for unwelcome signs of movement. There were large pterodactyls lazily drifting up above, scanning the terrain in search of their next meal. The pterodactyls were mostly scavengers, as far as he could tell, and as long as he was moving he was reasonably safe from them. There were more of them in the sky than usual probably due to the approaching storm. They hungrily and frantically scouted another meal before the rain hit. He heard their distant squawks at ground level back behind where no doubt some had discovered the gut pile left at the oak tree. Derek walked at the edge of an open grassy park, taking the easiest way while still staying in the shadows. He watched the dark rolling clouds approach. Lightning was streaking across the sky and striking the ground in sudden explosive bolts. A cool swirling wind pushed ahead of the storm. The winds were beginning to gust with growing strength.

Derek had never tasted meat before in his life. He wanted to discover the taste of a broiled steak. He only knew of meat dishes from what he had seen on the web, the video and sound bites salvaged from the past. His stomach ached at images of roasting venison. He was anxious to sample the local cuisine. He pushed on and watched for any dangerous signs of movement along the canyon rim. He was exposed and vulnerable walking through this area. There were so many places for hungry eyes to hide.

When he was around the furthest peak, he planned to raise the home ship on his webpod to get a bearing. It was too arduous to return the way he came, pulling the heavy load. He would have to take the easiest path to minimize risk of exhaustion or injury. A bolt of lightning struck a nearby cypress and the ground began to shake. Derek lost his footing and fell as the shaking became more intense. The thunder clouds were close now and the sky darkened directly overhead. The ground was shaking harder and harder. Derek lay flat on the ground and he struggled to rise. He rose to his feet and scanned the edge of the rim looking for falling boulders and almost in answer a massive boulder landed nearby. He thought this must be an earthquake. He looked away from the storm and back behind where he had walked, toward the remaining blue sky, and saw them coming fast.

The seismosaurs were stampeding directly for him charging blindly into the storm. Derek did not have time to unsnap the sled harness. He ran for the cover at the base of the rim to try to get out of their path. The ground jostled his feet as he struggled to run but everything around him was shaking violently as the herd of prehistoric giants rapidly approached. The earth rocked like waves as they neared, and he was pitched and thrown and rolled. A leg the size of a red oak tree trunk slammed down near his sled and the young hunter stumbled and crawled, clawing his way to safer cover. He dove into the thick cover just out of the canyon at the base of the rim as the herd pounded and thundered past. The sound was deafening, and above the deafening stampeding and whipping wind from the thunderstorm, he could hear a roar. The raging sound sent a chill to the core of this brave hunter. He crouched and held his breath.

He watched in mind numbing awe as three tyrannosaurs chased and lunged into the stampeding herd of colossal seismosaurs. The tyrannosaurs looked to be adults, 5000 kilograms in size, and at least fifteen meters in height. They easily gained on the herd and the lead tyrannosaur leapt and sailed and connected across the back of a trailing seismosaur. The wind, rain, thunder, and lightning were now backdrop for an unearthly spectacle. The trailing seismosaur was brought to a halt and lifted up on its hind legs and the tyrannosaur hung on and crawled forward onto the back of the victim and clamped into the long neck of its massive prey. The predator dug long dagger teeth deep into the thick seismosaur neck and shook violently and both creatures slammed hard to the ground. They tumbled onto their backs with a quaking explosive crash.

Derek struggled to get out quickly while he had a chance during the storming confusion and he began to crawl up the ridge inching his way along while witnessing the vicious encounter below. On his belly as low as possible, he tugged the stubborn sled further up the rim. He scraped and pawed his way into the mountain, amidst loud bellows of carnage echoing below. Up into the thunder clouds he ventured deeper into the heart of the storm. He was covered in mud and his clothes were in rags. His knee was twisted and slashed and bleeding heavily. His plan to make it back to his home ship by the twilight's last gleaming was not going to happen.

52

The Shareholders Arrive

Back at the Solarion, the crew worked on the graviton hovercraft which would serve as their land rover. They were putting the finishing touches on the levitation system and had moved the hovercraft outside. The vehicle would give them much greater freedom, and they needed desperately to complete the project. Their survival depended upon having the all terrain vehicle operational as soon as possible. They paged Derek on his webpod several times, but no answer. They were concerned, but they knew the youth was prone to wander and had probably left the pager muted while hunting, and would eventually check his pages. If he were in real trouble, he would surely set off the beacon. They wanted the hovercraft ready to get him out of trouble if he ended up wounded or lost. They were also running out of food and water, but they tried not to worry too much. They had traveled light years, met daunting challenges, and had endured greater obstacles.

"I think that will do it," announced Dr. Zeek, as he slid out from underneath the rover with a speed ratchet in his hand. "Fire it up, Benny," he said, and Benny jumped into the driver's seat and entered a code sequence and squeezed the levitate button on the right handlebar. Ami and Dr. Zeek stood watching in anticipation. There was a low humming and the hovercraft levitated a few centimeters off the work frame. "Bring it on up, Benny, and don't be shy," said Dr. Zeek. Benny squeezed the antigravity clutch grip located on the left handlebar. He clicked the up direction using the directional shifter located at his left foot. He twisted back on the accelerator throttle using the twist knob on the right handlebar. The land rover levitated a meter in the air. He clicked the forward direction using the directional shifter again located at his left foot. Benny clamped in the seat straps and twisted back on the accelerator control throttle in his right hand as he eased off on the antigravity clutch. He tested the brake grip located on the right handlebar, and it was working fine. He let off the antigravity clutch again as he twisted back on the accelerator throttle for real. The hovercraft took off in a blur of speed.

Benny accelerated to 300 kilometers per hour across the grassy field, parallel to the ground. He slowed and banked the vehicle at the far side in a tight 180 degree reversal while he straddled the rover. He accelerated again from the far side of the field and was back at the ship in an instant. He squeezed the clutch and brake as he twisted forward on the throttle to decelerate and the vehicle floated to a gentle stop in front of Dr. Zeek and Ami, hovering a meter off the ground. He touched the levitation lock, leaving the rover hovering in mid-air. "Good work, this hovercraft is running like a top," said Benny, as the low humming land rover idled. He hopped off the hovercraft as he gave them the thumbs up.

Dr. Zeek gave the hovercraft a quick once over to make sure nothing was leaking or spinning loose from the first short trip. When he was satisfied, he said, "Ami, take it for a spin," after Benny had pulled off his helmet and was out of the driver seat.

"Sure, why not," said Ami, and she climbed into the driver seat and strapped herself in and slipped on her helmet and twisted back on the throttle and punched the levitate button with her left thumb and the land rover started climbing and accelerating. She zigzagged through the trees and performed a banked 360 degree maneuver several times around a tall pine tree as the rover climbed higher and higher circling the thin tall tree. She brought it around and over the top of the tree and back down, gliding into camp, smoothly to a stop beside Dr. Zeek and

Benny. She made it look easy. "This is really going to help out," said Ami. "This will add a new perspective to our life here now that we can get around," she said.

"I would like to take a ride down to the river and try some more fishing this evening," said Benny to the others.

"I do not see why not," replied Dr. Zeek. "It looks like that thunderstorm missed us completely. It's starting to clear off," he said looking off toward the dark mountaintops. "I'll take a ride with you. I need to get out," he said. He hit the kill switch and four wheels came down to support the excursion vehicle and the low humming gradually died out.

Benny and Dr. Zeek loaded up the land rover and took off for the river, leaving Ami to monitor the dinosaur detection consoles. They found a spot along the river that was shady and looked promising and Benny cast out a dragonfly and let it float with the current. It was late evening and peaceful on the riverbank. Dr. Zeek took a deep breath and lay back on the fern covered slope. "This is amazing, just amazing," said Dr. Zeek.

"What is that, Doc?"

"I can look right into the setting sun. No manmade filters, just good old fashioned ozone. What do you think about it all, Benny?" asked Dr. Zeek lazily.

"I do not want to leave," replied Benny. "We do not stand a chance against the Shareholders. I would rather live with dinosaurs than slavery. We are better off out here in this wild world," said Benny and he jiggled his pole to give the dragonfly a little life in the water. He looked over at Dr. Zeek, "Well, you asked my opinion," said Benny.

"I think we are all feeling the same way, Benny. If we leave this planet we may never return. It is as simple as that," said Dr. Zeek. Just then the dragonfly disappeared and the water rolled and sprayed. Benny set the hook and the line danced and dove deep into the current. Dr. Zeek jumped up and Benny was already on his knees trying to get to his feet with his fishing pole sharply bent. "Hang on, Benny!" coached Dr. Zeek. "You've got him. Just hold on," said Dr. Zeek.

The line cut across the river current and Benny stumbled closer to the bank hanging onto the fighting fish. "This is a big one!" exclaimed Benny.

"Don't fight him too hard, Benny," said Dr. Zeek. "Let him wear down. You have him. Just take your time." The fish rocketed to the surface and tried to shake the hook. "It's a rainbow, Benny. You've got a big rainbow. Take your time with him. You've hooked him good." Dr. Zeek was just as wide-eyed as Benny. The big rainbow swam with the current to loosen the hook. "Just let him run, Benny," coached Dr. Zeek. "He'll wear down. He's a nice one," admired Dr. Zeek.

The fish swam shallow and Benny reached for the line and started gently bringing it in. He waded out into the river and brought the big rainbow close to the shore, and Dr. Zeek took in line while Benny grabbed the flipping fish. Benny carried the fish up the river bank. "So this is a rainbow. Are they good to eat?" asked Benny.

"You bet they are," said Dr. Zeek. "We are in for a real treat. This rainbow will be better than anything you have tasted before. Good job, Benny. You did good, son," said Dr. Zeek and heartily slapped the wiry musician on the back.

"Thanks, Doc," replied Benny. "I'll catch us another one. This river is loaded with these rainbows. We will be eating fish tonight," said Benny proudly.

Dr. Zeek's webpager went off. He walked over to the land rover and picked up the webphone.

"Tell Cookie to fire up the nanowave oven!" called Benny excitedly.

Dr. Zeek chuckled. "What is going on, Ami?" he asked.

"We have company," replied Ami urgently. Her voice was shaky.

"Where are they?" asked Dr. Zeek alarmed. Benny ran up with his big fish and placed it in the storage compartment in the land rover. Ami did not respond immediately.

"I am not losing this one to those hungry dinosaurs," said Benny. "Which direction are they coming from?" asked Benny.

Dr. Zeek pressed her for an answer. "Ami, I repeat, which direction are they coming from?" Dr. Zeek asked impatiently.

"They are coming from above," replied Ami, shakily. Benny and

Dr. Zeek both looked up to the clouds but did not see anything.

"Ami, what are you talking about?" asked Dr. Zeek with concern. There was another silent delay. "What sort of creatures do you see?" he asked again, and was very agitated now.

"It is a ship," she said. "They know where we are," added Ami. "They appear to be close to entering the atmosphere and are directly above where we are hiding," finished Ami.

Benny jumped into the driver seat of the hovercraft and entered the code sequence and pressed the antigravity ignition and the rover hummed to life.

Dr. Zeek jumped into the passenger side, as he replied to her into his webphone. "Button down the hatches, Ami" Dr. Zeek told her. "We are on our way."

53

Stripped and Exposed

In the central control room of the warship battle cruiser, the elite military command crew surveyed the situation. This planet had appeared void of sentient life in surrounding deep space and the magnetosphere also revealed nothing intelligent to contend with, and yet as the battle cruiser drew near, the onboard warship radar detectors soon depicted a tight cluster of ship radars in a concentrated area on the surface of the planet.

They now entered the near-orbit region of the only inhabitable planet within the solar system of Epsilon Eridani. The cluster of ship radars down on the planet surface below baffled the commandant. His general and lieutenant general were also there and they were all stunned at this surprising development. They gathered in the war room to investigate and discuss this aggravating predicament. The commandant was not in any mood for trouble.

They had traveled lean, leaner than the commandant preferred, with only one regiment but it was the best. He had demanded a brigade consisting of two regiments, and had even requested a division of three brigades, but he was overruled by the stinking Shareholders. The trip, at faster than light speed, had given him a throbbing headache, a condition commonly known as superluminal lag. They were at the helm of the most formidable Stick and String graviton FTL ship in the modern world. He was not terribly concerned over any possible threat from the planet below. The cluster of ships parked on this planet was merely an inconvenience. He would dispatch with these early planetary arrivals without talk or negotiation, and go to bed early.

Traveling faster than light was their only chance to survive. Their sun was going to die in an explosive gasp, engulfing all life in the solar system. The best minds of the modern world were not able to stop the antiquark implosion bomb targeted for Sol, so here they were. They had anticipated no resistance whatsoever, and yet when they arrived there was a fleet of spaceships boldly lying in wait on the surface of what they had believed to be a virgin planet. The commandant had superluminal lag, and this condition produced headaches far worse than the ill side-effects of mere spaceflight, or jet lag from atmospheric flight, and he was not in the mood for any of it.

"What do you make of it?" asked the commandant impatiently. He eyed his loyal general who knew the old commandant well. These were not men who backed down from a fight.

"We cannot make them out but we know they are there," replied the general. "Our radar detectors have pinpointed a concentration of spacecraft radars within a radius of several kilometers," he said. "There is a tight cluster of ships on the surface of this planet, I can tell you that much," replied the general to the commandant. The lieutenant general and major generals sat quietly wearing stern faces.

"How do we know these are spaceship radars?" asked the commandant as he massaged the temples of his throbbing forehead.

"We have indisputable proof that these are spaceship radars. They are ours," replied one of the major generals.

"Tell us again so we really get it. How do we know they are ours?" asked the lieutenant general, sitting beside his general.

"We know without a doubt because they are using our own encryption codes," replied the major general. "They were manufactured by us, and we are sure of it because we had no trouble at all decrypting their transmissions," replied the major general.

"So they are using webphones too?" asked the lieutenant general.

"Yes they are," replied another major general. "We captured and decrypted the tail end of one transmission," he added.

"And what did this transmission say?" asked the commandant impatiently.

"The transmission that we intercepted stated: we have spotted an incoming battle cruiser so keep it terse from now on," replied the other major general. "That is all of the transmission that we were able to capture but we will not miss anything from them anymore. They know we have arrived, and obviously we know they are down there waiting," said the other major general.

"I'll be damned!" fumed the top general. He was quickly losing his temper. He knew the commandant was in no mood for this complication.

"Why don't we just bomb the hell out of them," suggested the lieutenant general. "We can just blow them away and move on," he added.

"Are you so sure that bombing them is the best approach to this little annoying complication?" asked the general. "We do not have any idea what grade of weaponry they are equipped with," added the general.

The commandant tried to think but his head pounded and throbbed and thinking was difficult. "What about decoys?" the commandant queried. "Could they possibly be using decoys?" he asked the officers gathered in the war room.

"There is no way of telling at this point," said a major general. "They are well camouflaged down there. That's for sure. There could be more of them besides what the radar detectors have picked up," he added.

"As you all know, we prefer the space theatre rather than doing battle within the atmosphere," said the top general. "Battle within an atmosphere can have lingering effects and may get messy. A confrontation within this atmosphere will be tricky, since we do plan to live here. Damn it! How could they be ours? Could a teracorp have beaten us here?" asked the general. The general looked worried and his lieutenant general and major generals mentally struggled for an answer. The war room was drenched in silent labored thought.

"It is possible, in fact extremely likely, that they are renegade teracorps," said one major general, breaking the tense silence. "After all, we purchased this battle cruiser from a teracorp. They may have held out on us as they have done before in the past, and might possibly possess superior technology. Since we were beaten to this planet, it is obvious that we are dealing with FTL ships, and you can bet they are not going give up without a fight. It does not look good. They are down there, that is for sure," stated the major general.

"I know they are down there!" shouted the commandant. His headache was getting worse by the minute. A colonel sat in the back of the war room brooding over this whole affair. He was once the one in charge of this elite regiment but now he commanded only one squadron.

54

The Defense

The hovercraft glided up to the Solarion and Benny and Dr. Zeek jumped out and ran into the ship. Ami was in the control room monitoring the approaching battle cruiser. Dr. Zeek's webpager went off again. He pressed the acknowledge button and waited for a response. It was Derek.

"Doc, I need a position fix," said Derek. "I am almost ten kilometers from camp. I am going to set off the beacon so that you can pinpoint my position and give me the shortest path back," he said.

"Do not broadcast the beacon. We have a situation here," replied Dr. Zeek. "We have spotted an incoming battle cruiser so keep it terse from now on," he said. The webphones, webpods, and webpagers used a set of randomized encryption codes, but the warship would easily recognize and decrypt the encoded transmissions once the cruiser was within range. Dr. Zeek figured the battle cruiser was still out of range from their local web of communications, but he could not be sure. He did not want to take chances.

"What is next?" asked Ami, as they watched the approaching warship battle cruiser on the radar console.

"Are the remaining thermonuclear warheads ready for launch?" asked Dr. Zeek urgently.

"You cannot be serious," replied Ami, in shock. "We will all be destroyed if we launch them. The warship is inside the magnetosphere now and will be entering our atmosphere soon," said Ami.

"Of course I do not plan to detonate a thermonuclear warhead within this atmosphere, Ami, but it is too late for us to put this ship back together to escape. They have obviously spotted us. Our ship has been stripped of its radar and optics equipment. All that valuable equipment was used to build the dinometers. We are totally exposed. The major components of our guidance modules are out there up in trees monitoring the perimeter of our camp, and besides that, they would perceive any move on our part as an attack and they would counter. We had better just sit tight and wait but if they attack, we are doomed. What choices do we have?" asked Dr. Zeek.

"Doc, just listen to reason for a minute," replied Ami. We have thermonuclear warheads each capable of a five thousand megaton blast. Just one will easily destroy everything within one thousand kilometers. They were designed for defense in deep space, and only deep space," retorted Ami, furiously.

"I know the capacities of our nuclear warheads and what they were designed for, Ami, and of course we do not want to detonate anything within this atmosphere," replied Dr. Zeek, attempting to calm her fears. "Let's just hope they don't plan on detonating anything either," he said. "The only defense that we now have is the fact that we do possess warheads," he finished.

Up in the warship cruiser, the commandant and his generals studied the locations of the many sources of spacecraft radar lying in wait upon the planetary surface, spanning a radius of several kilometers at ground level. He begrudgingly conceded that the use of nukes was out of the question. They could not use thermonuclear forces against the cluster of spacecrafts down below. They wanted an inhabitable planet, not a barren wasteland. The ideal weapon of choice in situations such as this one, where precise locations of targets could easily be determined, was focused beams of high energy radiation. This was an appealing option but there were drawbacks. The energy requirements for simultaneously producing multitudes of focused radiation beams was immense, and it was required that all targets be hit simultaneously. He needed an answer from engineering regarding the feasibility of this option and they were busily working on an answer. He was not completely sure of the exact number of ships down there or if there were any ships at all. The radars could easily be decoys. The spacecraft down there had wisely remained on the ground. If this battle could have taken place out in the vast space arena, this elite commandant would have been in his element and it all would have been over with quickly.

A webphone buzzed in the control room of the warship cruiser and the alerted military command crew was shocked to realize that it was an outside call, one not originating from inside the ship. The brigadier general currently at the helm of the warship cruiser touched the communication screen and acknowledged the connection. The video screen sphere remained blank. The audio receiver crackled and a voice from the surface of the planet vibrated across the distance separating it from the control room of the warship. It was Dr. Zeek broadcasting from inside the Solarion. "State your business," began Dr. Zeek sharply.

"State my business?" replied the brigadier general in incredulous sarcasm. "My business is none of your business. Who the hell is this?" he demanded. The brigadier general had the war room paged where the higher ranking generals and the commandant were in conference, and they were conferenced into the call.

The commandant sat in the war room rubbing his temples to ease the pain in his head while he and his generals waited for a response.

"Let's be rational," started Dr. Zeek, and paused to let the connection crackle. "We have nukes and we can both destroy each other, and this planet along with us. Why are you here?" asked Dr. Zeek.

"You know damn well why we are here!" shouted the top general from the war room webphone speaker. "Our home planet is gone and we are here to assume control of this one. We have owned this planet for decades and it is off limits to the teracorps. Our claim to this planet is valid and has been in place for years," said the general. The lieutenant general nodded his head in support. The supreme commandant said nothing and merely massaged his throbbing temples and stared into the webphone speaker.

"We have not seen any evidence of a claim," replied Dr. Zeek "Have you been to this planet before? It does not appear so. You have no right to claim planets that you have never even traveled to before. Where can we go to find your claim?" asked Dr. Zeek. He and the Solarion crew were stunned by the comment that their home planet was no more, but they did not let on that it was news to them.

"Do not play dumb with me!" shouted the top general from the war room. "How did you beat us here and how were you able to steal so many FTL ships? Which teracorp do you belong to? The teracorps are still loyal to us and we will find out soon enough!" fumed the general. The veins in his forehead were bulging and his face flushed red. He could not hold his temper any longer.

The commandant put the webphone speaker on mute. "Control your anger, and the information that you freely give these renegades," said the commandant to his top general. "We will determine their weaknesses and soon they will be just a memory," he managed. He then reached into his pocket and fished for another pill to ease his headache. He crunched the bitter pill hoping relief would come quickly from the superluminal lag. There was another tense pause as they waited for a response from the aggravating early bird arrivals there on the ground, these indignant planetary inhabitants.

The audible communication webphone receiver then crackled and popped. "We owe loyalty to no one and we do not belong to a teracorp. Just bring your ship down so that we can talk. We do not want to do battle in the atmosphere for obvious reasons, but if you strike then we will strike back. We want to reach a mutual agreement rather than committing mutual suicide. This planet is big enough for us all so land your ship and we will negotiate," said Dr. Zeek to those in the warship cruiser, and with that he hung up the webphone.

The commandant beeped the engineering room and the news was not good. There was no way that they could take out all ships at the same time with simultaneous focused beams of high energy radiation directed at each ship on the ground. Too much energy was required. It was too risky and there was no guarantee that other ships were not hidden from them. After the attack and with so much energy expended, the warship would then be extremely vulnerable.

The commandant looked at his generals and shrugged. "Take us down. We will play their game for now. Once we land, send in the ground troops but only five battalions. The other five stay onboard. These homesteaders must be teracorp renegades, and if so then it is doubtful that they even possess handheld weapons. We are not sharing this planet with anyone. We will take care of this situation on the ground quickly before it gets out of hand," said the commandant to his generals.

The Solarion crew contemplated their next move. They realized the warship was not about to surrender, but the prospect of becoming subjugated and enslaved once again was totally gut wrenching. "They have not pinpointed our exact location, or they would have used a focused radiation beam attack," said Dr. Zeek.

"Did you hear the one ask us how we had stolen so many FTL ships? They think we have a fleet of ships," replied Ami, thoughtfully.

"What are you saying? Why would they think that?" asked Benny.

"I see now what is going on," Dr. Zeek whistled as the realization hit him. "The dinometers are each using a ship radar module. They think each radar module is a different spaceship. They believe we have a fleet of ships down here," said Dr. Zeek.

"The dinometers are acting as decoys," said Ami, as realization dawned on them all. Ami was an astute observer. They were bluffing but not even aware of the bluff until now.

"They will be sending in their ground troops," said Dr. Zeek. "You can bet they are not going to share this planet with us or anyone else," he said.

"The dinometers have loudspeakers built into them," started Ami, and she immediately captivated their undivided attention. "Doc, you were building an archive of dinosaur calls and sounds. After the attacks that we have witnessed here, your archive of recordings has grown very extensive. Do you think some of those sounds might possibly attract predators into the perimeter?" asked Ami.

"That is a possibility, Ami," replied Dr. Zeek. "I do have recordings now in support of the dinosaur defense system. My work was intended to chase predators off rather than lure them in, but you may be on to something," said Dr. Zeek.

"We could isolate calling sounds, sounds from acro and raptor fights, sounds of the pterodactyls over a kill scene, and anything else. We could broadcast whatever recordings that we have collected to possibly attract velociraptors and other predators into the perimeter," said Ami.

"That covers one of the senses. We could also appeal to the predator sense of smell in some way," said Dr. Zeek now thinking aloud. "Of the five senses, these creatures rely on hearing, smell, and vision to hunt down prey, so we cannot hope to draw them in with sounds alone. I was able to salvage sizeable blood samples after the recent acro attack, and have the dinosaur blood stored in the lab. A blood bomb may provide scent enough to lure them in," said Dr. Zeek. He was not totally convinced that they could successfully rally wild packs of predators into the base camp perimeter in order to meet attacking ground troops but they did not have a better plan at the moment.

"The blood bomb sounds good, Doc," replied Ami. "You work on the blood bomb," she said. "Benny will compose a dinosaur symphony for us. We must make this perimeter so attractive that the raptors will come running to the party," said Ami.

"A dinosaur symphony," mused Benny. "This will take my music to another level," he added.

"We do not have much choice," replied Ami. "We can seduce the raptors into the perimeter to attack the global military troopers, or the troopers will run right to our door. Whatever we do, we need to get started now before they have time to land and send in the troops," she said.

Benny and Ami went to work isolating the calling sounds of the utahraptors, the sounds of the fights, the feeding sounds, and all other sounds they thought might possibly attract the predatory dinosaurs. It was a starry night on Planet P which was to their advantage. The dinosaurs would be out and roaming about. It was worth a try but it was also their only hope. The crew possessed no handheld weapons and no other viable options for defense. Benny put together a masterful dinosaur symphony and they set about piping it to the dinometer loudspeakers.

Dr. Zeek went to work in the lab. He used the dinosaur blood he had salvaged from the aftermath of numerous vicious encounters between the predators. He mixed the blood with an odorless catalyst and condensed the substance into hard cone shaped bricks. The blood bombs had the appearance of extremely large incense cones. He loaded them into the rover and soon had them positioned in strategic locations around the perimeter of the base camp, lighting each one as he went along. The large blood cones burned slowly and gave off a very strong pungent bloody aroma. The blood bombs certainly smelled like they were working. When he was done, the dinometers were all emanating the smell of blood within their vicinity. The slow burning cones were sure to last for many hours.

Derek was up on the mountaintop wondering what he should do. It was a clear night and he scanned the star drenched heavens in search of the approaching ship. There was rustling about in the night as the creatures of Planet P came out to play. He climbed a tree and sat there and brooded. He could travel by starlight, but he was not sure of his position and travel would be useless without a position fix. He was very tired but also very disturbed. He felt so alone but he knew he was not alone. He had his crew, and now there were dangerous visitors that he could not see. The night wind gently wailed. He had come so far from the bubble city of Wafton, the floating metropolis where he once had lived, and the place he had come to know Jenniper. Again he wondered what had happened to her.

55

The Attack

The battle cruiser slowly descended upon the land in the middle of the night, floating on churning billowing clouds of unearthly energy fields. The warship put down several kilometers from the outside perimeter of the dinosaur detection system, as dusty clouds of charged particles faded and flickered into the twinkling night. The hatch of the formidable cruiser unlocked with a hiss and pivoted down to the ground forming a large ramp. The five battalions of armored military troopers emerged wearing night vision helmets with weapons in hand. There were fifteen squadrons each with one hundred men.

The commandant had decided that there would be no negotiation or talk whatsoever. He decided this group of renegades had somehow managed to beat his battle cruiser to this claim, and they needed to die. He decided there was no way they could possibly possess any handheld weapons at all because sophisticated handheld weapons were unheard of outside the ranks of the military police force. He decided that they were also bluffing or they would have engaged his warship cruiser in space, rather than keeping their fleet of spacecraft grounded. He decided the renegades were probably using decoys and that there was only one ship to locate and destroy. That one ship was stripped and spread out to look like more, which explained why it did not launch. He decided to attack and waste no more time. Attack is always the best defense. The commandant was a smart and ruthless man, and had a very bad headache this evening.

The ground troops spread out to encircle the perimeter and moved on foot with scouts jetting ahead in excursion rovers weaving in and out of the trees searching for the enemy ships. They heard strange squawks and howls as they approached. There was an unusual salty bloody odor hanging thick in the air. Trigger fingers twitched, safety mechanisms were released, and rounds were pumped into the chambers of the handheld chemical weapons in anticipation. The chemical injection guns were loaded with doses that were designed to first stun the human body into temporary paralysis with one dose. In the event that it was needed, the second dose delivered enough chemical to kill. The chemical injection guns were highly effective weapons and much cleaner than obsolete bullets. The second dose was rarely needed for rounding up fugitive slaves. The salvage value of a fugitive was much higher alive than dead. The ground troops were instructed to stun on sight and kill only if necessary. The organs of the renegades were to be salvaged even if a second killing dose proved necessary.

As the ground troops trudged onward to the perimeter of the dinosaur detection system, the squawking howls were louder and clearer. They were split into fifteen squadrons, and this one particular squadron was now the closest to the dinometer perimeter from the warship cruiser. The others had a longer jog in order to circle wide and surround the perimeter. The plan was to circle and attack the perimeter from fifteen different points. There would be no escape. This one particular squadron arrived at the first dinometer and they stopped at the tree and looked up to find the source of the disturbing sounds. They could see the ship modules mounted in the thick branches. The colonel fiercely barked out a command to his troopers, "Scale the tree and examine the decoy!" he commanded. A trooper scrambled up the tree to take a closer look at the squawking decoy. "What do you have up there trooper?" yelled the colonel above the animal noises blasting from the loudspeaker of the decoy.

"Sir, we have a ship radar module, a solar panel, an optic module, a

loudspeaker, and a webphone," shouted the trooper above the strange
den of squawks pounding from the loudspeaker. "There is nothing up
here of any risk. We have confirmation that these are decoys. We have
got them now!" yelled the trooper above the squawking loudspeaker
down to the others below. The trooper stuck his face into the optic
module and he grinned and shouted, "We have got you! You worthless
renegade bastards!" He laughed hideously into the optics. The trooper
up in the tree looked out over the jungled wilderness and spotted a
white excursion rover approaching. It was floating slow and easily up
to the troop below the tree. He called out to the others below. "A scout
is returning! He can tell us where they are!"

The white excursion rover floated up and eased to a gentle stop,
levitating a little off the ground. There was no scout onboard. The
ground trooper in the tree sat on a branch and watched as the others
below cautiously approached the excursion rover. There was blood
dripping from the handlebars and a pile of steaming organs and entrails
were in the driver's seat. The white levitating vehicle was smeared and
washed in blood. The colonel choked and bellowed, "Man down! Hit
the ground!"

The squadron hit the ground just as the utahraptors were on them.
The chemical injection guns were of no use as troopers fired dose after
dose in horror only to be ripped and torn to shreds. The utahraptors had
indeed flocked to the beckoning calls of the dinometer loudspeakers
and the salty smell of blood wafting through the night air. The raptors
were also as mad as teased hornets when they could not find the source
of the bloody smells. The colonel struggled to issue another command
in the unfolding mayhem as a claw hook from the nearest utahraptor
sliced his throat to the spine. He gurgled and fell. The troop scattered
and ran in all directions. There was a disoriented panic to flee the
snapping, snarling, hopping mad utahraptors. The one lone trooper
who had climbed up in the tree was still there, crouched on the branch
against the trunk of the tree and remaining motionless. The squawking
loudspeaker was still in his ear but he could hear above it the screams
and shrieks of his fellow troopers down below. He witnessed in
breathless mind flooding horror as one hundred of his comrades were

killed within minutes. He clutched the tree in frozen fear and never moved throughout the massacre.

When the utahraptors were finished there was not much left so they trailed surviving troopers, those who had run off in different directions shrieking in confused mindless panic. A pack of utahraptors remained right below the trooper in the tree, crunching and breaking open the chest cavities of the twitching groaning remains of his dead comrades. They clawed and ripped to get to the delicious hot pulsating vital organs.

The trooper up in the tree heard a desperate scream cut through the night in the dark distance, followed by a long pitiful wail. He began shaking. The slaughter of his fellow comrades so suddenly and so horrendously was too much for his mind to comprehend. He began to lose his thin hold on sanity and he shook harder as fear took full hold. He began to shake violently and he desperately hung onto the tree knowing what was about to happen next.

A few survivors of the utahraptor attack made it all the way back to the battle cruiser in a dead run. These troopers were the lucky ones, the ones with a stellar sense of direction to run back through the dark twilight, but they were very few. The supreme commandant and his generals watched and witnessed in shock and disbelief. He cursed his formerly zealous confidence, and he painfully realized that he had just lost many good men in a very short period of time. A commander, no matter how callous, never enjoys losing his men, especially on such a large scale and in such a short time. He was to blame and it was no one's fault but his own, but he was not about to be told something he already knew.

A brigadier general looked up from the spherical consoles in the control room and motioned for the commandant to come and see. "I have got them," announced the brigadier general. "Right there," he said, and he pointed to the three dimensional topographical projection.

"How can you be sure?" asked the top general standing beside his commandant.

"It is the hub for their network," replied the brigadier general. "They have a star configuration network and there is the hub of their web, dead center of all the decoys," said the brigadier general confidently. "They are right there and I am sure of it," proclaimed the brigadier general confidently.

"I have heard that before. You better be damn sure," snarled the furious general, but his commandant said nothing and only studied the topographical console sphere. "I will not stand for anymore mistakes or surprises," threatened the general to those gathered.

"No one could have predicted those prehistoric creatures," replied the lieutenant general hesitantly to his commanding officer, the top general. He fearfully eyed the commandant, who again said nothing and only continued to study the topographical display.

"I would like to respectfully remind everyone that we are on an uncharted planet," said the brigadier general as the tension grew.

"Do not remind me of anything that I already know, you happy go lucky bastard," growled the top general to the brigadier general. "You just better be damn sure that they are right there just like you say they are," said the general. He was in a very foul mood and his commandant had a bad headache, and none of this was going well.

"That is a star based network communications hub and it is also the web control station. It is obvious from the webphone transmissions. I am sure of it," countered the brigadier general defensively.

The military rovers were loaded with all available troops from the five remaining battalions who had previously stayed onboard the ship. All troops were now to be deployed. The exact location of the camouflaged Solarion was targeted. The rovers took off through the dark forest vegetation to the Solarion. There was no stopping them now, creatures or no creatures. They were the best global military troops in the world, but they were out of their element in these jungles. They were trained for conflict and engagement within familiar space arenas, not in the wilds of unknown planets. That was not important to these troops. They were trained to carry out missions and that was the bottom line. Their mission was to capture these renegades and bring them back to the battleship cruiser, dead or alive. They would accomplish their mission at whatever cost.

They raced through the forested jungle on their rovers, past the hideous remains of their fallen comrades, through the thick salty smell of blood floating on the night air, and to a spacecraft hidden at the edge of a grassy field. The troops dodged leaping and lashing utahraptors and rode hard and fast, stopping for nothing. They whizzed past bloody driverless rovers now floating aimlessly. They heard chilling howls and spine wrenching wails deep in the night. They ascended upon the Solarion nestled at the edge of the jungle. The door to the Solarion was wide open and they quickly discovered that no one was inside. They entered the spacecraft and performed a routine search of the premises.

The major general in charge of the five remaining battalions got on the webphone to the warship. "The renegade crew has fled the premises of their spacecraft," said the major general. "There is only one spacecraft. It is confirmed. The rest were all decoys. We have lost all of the first five battalions, approximately 1500 men, to the blood hungry prehistoric predators. There is not much trace of anyone left. We cannot stay in one place for long. The creatures will hunt us down. What do we do next?" asked the major general of his superiors.

"I want a positive identification of the spacecraft," snapped the general from the battleship cruiser. "I want to know exactly where this thing came from and who was on the ship," barked the furious general.

"It is the Solarion," replied the major general. "I remember something about this craft. It was supposed to be a solar probe from what I remember. It was a shuttle designed for solar probes," added the major general to his superior officer.

"I thought that the Solarion was destroyed," replied the general across the webphone. "It was sent into the sun," he said.

"It contained four crew members and a droid," blurted another major general from the battle cruiser war room across the webphone speaker. "If my memory serves me right, one was a doctor of psychophysics, one was a female engineer, and the other two were common laborers. They were all misfits, refusing to adhere to corporate culture. They were all rebellious thinkers," he added.

"Track them down and bring them here once and for all," commanded the military general across the webphone. "I am not sure how they survived their trip into the sun, but they have caused the deaths of five good battalions. I do not want to lose another man to prehistoric planetary predators though, so exercise caution. Capture the renegades once you track them down, but be careful of the creatures, because your chemical injection guns are worthless against those things. We must find out what these renegades know," said the general.

"I am picking up a beacon signal," said the brigadier general from the control room across the webphone conference. "It has to be them. Someone is separated and calling for help," announced the brigadier general from the control room.

"Good," said the general from the war room across the webphone conference. "Get a positive position fix on the beacon," commanded the general to the brigadier general. The brigadier general rapidly announced the coordinates.

The general in the war room told the major general waiting at the Solarion, "I want you to secure the Solarion, and send all remaining rovers to the beacon location. Let's take them quickly. The commandant has a headache and we all need to get some rest. This has gone on long enough. Be careful though, and look out for those creatures because your chemical injection guns do not work against them as I told you already. We do not want to lose any more men," barked the general from the war room across the webphone conference call.

"Yes, sir!" replied the major general sharply and he followed with an enthusiastic, "Consider it done, sir!" He was young and cocky and was enjoying the excitement, the danger, and the thrill of leading these elite battalions on the ground. He had earlier cringed when they passed the old dead colonel whose bloody body lay lifeless but still warm. The Solarion was secured and the remaining five battalions took flight for the position of the beacon signal.

56

Karn

Derek stood high on the mountain waiting. He set off the beacon at sunrise. The sun was creeping over the ridge and he could wait no longer. He had not heard from his friends since initial communications were cut short the night before. He was not lost or wondering what to do anymore. He was ready to fight. He wanted to bring them on, whoever they were. His bow was across his chest, his quiver across his back, and the knife was strapped to his boot.

He had never told his crew about Reverend H, or about the space ark, or the cult migration which Jenniper had planned to join. He had never told them that Jenniper was bound for this very planet. He had trouble believing it himself. He had no idea that his lost love was here on this very same wild planet, locked up in the brig of the fearless warship cruiser. The one thing that he did know was that the ship that had arrived in the night was no space ark. He had witnessed the billowing energized clouds and heard the thundering graviton levitation engines from the mountaintop in the dead of night. It was a battleship cruiser. He knew that it was no rickety space ark built from meager contributions and an old man's dreams. The warship represented slavery and Derek was enraged. He was ready to fight and die for his precious morsel of new found freedom.

He figured they would come fast once the beacon was detected. He could not be sure of the fate of the others now. He looked down at the sled of packed meat. It would have made a great feast, but it was not meant to be. They could have enjoyed a good camp fire and told tall tales by the warm firelight. It was all over now. The meat was probably spoiled anyway. Derek knew very little about meat. He figured that he had given it his best with what he had learned in such a short time. He had learned that hunting was an activity requiring great precision if it was to be done well. He wanted to be a good hunter, but he was a modern man and far removed from this world of rugged wilderness. He wished he was from this land, and not from the dark world of drudgery. They would not take him back alive, not back to the world of drudgery.

He bent his knee and bowed his head to pray. He had prayed only once before in his life, that day he and Jenniper had visited the old cult leader. He was not one to pray but it was worth a try. He asked for help in taking this next step, this next step in defending this wild free land, help in defeating the troopers that he knew were on their way to him now. He asked for revenge, revenge for all the dark sorrows forced upon the old world. He asked that his crew be spared, his friends at the Solarion. He asked for surprise and power over the approaching military troopers. He asked for the impossible. He offered no justification for his desire for revenge because he figured his reasons were already known. He was finally thankful for his time once spent with Jenniper, and for his time spent here wandering free in this pristine world.

He looked down the mountain, past the canyon, and as far as he could see across the high grass. There was no sign of them. It would not be long. He threw the live beacon as hard as he could off the side of the sharp cliff into the rocks below. It bounced and tumbled and smacked its way to the bottom. He looked into the early morning sky. There were pterodactyls circling above, calling to each other and loosening their stiff wings for another day of hunting and scavenging. Some were swooping lower and taking a closer look at the youth standing alone at the top of the mountain.

One of the pterodactyls swooped very low to the ground and landed some twenty meters from Derek. Derek nocked an arrow and drew down on the prehistoric bird. He had never seen the big boned birds act so bravely before. This one was too close. Derek was about to release the arrow when he noticed a rope around the huge chest of the ancient fowl. He eased off from full draw. It was a harness. A man emerged from behind the pterodactyl. The man had a bow across his chest. Derek stood still not knowing what to think. The man walked up to him and looked at him directly and spoke.

"My name is Karn. I am from this land. We have watched you and your friends since you first arrived. We know you are in trouble," said the strange man. The man was clothed in skins and was brown from the sun and his body was hard and lean.

"You speak my language," replied Derek. He could not believe this man standing before him. This man was no military trooper. It was also difficult to accept that he and his crew had been watched all this time. He looked up at the pterodactyls gliding high in the morning sky.

"Yes, we speak the same language," said Karn. "We were taught by the one who came before," he said, and he looked up and waved as other big dinosaur birds swooped low and landed around them. "There is no time to explain. We must prepare to fight. Your enemy is our enemy. We will not let them take this land of ours," said Karn.

Pterodactyls by the hundreds were flying in and landing all around him and men were climbing off and positioning themselves in the trees, among the rocks, and in the bush. The pterodactyls were flying off into the morning sky after the men dismounted. Karn blew into a wooden tube, but the tube made no sound that Derek could hear. Karn blew on the wooden tube several times as he gazed out over the mountain edge across the high grass down in the valley below.

Derek then heard a voice in his mind. It was the voice of Dr. Zeek. "They have us, Derek. They are taking us back to the warship. I am sending this neuroton projection directly to your mind, in hopes that you will save yourself. I am afraid it is too late for us, Derek. They are taking us back to the warship now. They have the rover. Save yourself. They are coming for you now," said Dr. Zeek telepathically.

"Here they come!" shouted Karn. The military rovers appeared in formation. The global military police troopers had arrived. The pterodactyls above dove out of the sky like wasps from a disturbed hive, down upon the approaching rovers. Hundreds of the rovers swerved and stalled as the pterodactyls snagged troopers and pulled them out of their rovers. The troopers were firing their chemical injection guns into the huge prehistoric birds, with no effect. Rovers spun out of control and crashed into trees and looped up and dove down into the ground as troopers were plucked from their vehicles. The troopers were carried high into the morning sky by the hind claws of the pterodactyls and then dropped. There were screams as the sky rained troopers. They hurtled down by the hundreds, free falling, and slamming into the ground. Karn blew on the wooden tube again. The rovers were still coming, straight to the beacon at the bottom of the mountain. Karn stood on the mountain at the edge of the cliff and waved to the approaching rovers to get their attention. He laughed out loud when the troopers saw him. "We are up here you idiots!" he yelled to the troopers. The rovers split up and started up the mountain from all sides.

The rovers slid up the sides of the mountain levitating off the ground each filled with military troopers armed with chemical injection guns. The natives of Planet P were scantily clothed archers who moved with natural ease and agility in the wild world. The natives were everywhere and nowhere all at once. They hid themselves well and the troopers had no idea that such an ambush was waiting. The troopers were expecting the small band of renegades on the mountain, and one was a young man named Derek. They soon found out that they were terribly and fatally misinformed.

The arrows flew and troopers fell from their rovers. Soon the arrows were whistling in all directions, and the troopers died and dropped from their rovers in droves. The military troopers were not trained extensively in firing chemical injection guns from their rapidly moving rovers. The chemical injection shots went wild from the gliding rovers and the troopers missed their marks, time and time again. The arrows from the natives of Planet P were deadly and accurate. It was a hideous display of mismatched weaponry. The best of modern chemical injection gun technology was pitted against crude bows and arrows, and the crude weaponry proved to be the most effective weapon of the day.

Derek fought alongside the native archers, and did his part to punish the invading troopers. He leaned behind a tree to catch his breath and nock another arrow. A rover floated through the trees directly toward him. The rover was some twenty meters away when he stepped out from behind the tree at full draw and released his arrow. The arrow arched through the air and buried deep into the heart of the trooper behind the rover controls. The passenger sitting beside the now dead driver was the major general who had previously been so excited and thrilled to take command of these last five battalions. The major general tried to take careful aim and shoot the chemical injection gun, but the rover was now gliding erratically with a slumped worthless driver at the controls.

The major general fired and the shot missed Derek, and the major general tried to steady his aim and fire again. Derek threw down his bow and ran directly for the zigzagging rover where the major general struggled to frantically aim his chemical gun. Derek dove onto the man. The major general squeezed off another shot in desperation and it went straight up into the air. Derek grabbed the chemical injection gun, and they both ferociously fought to possess the weapon. The major general's finger was still on the trigger and he fired again and again. He fired the chemical injection gun blindly and desperately. Derek forced the muzzle of the wicked weapon back upon the major general as the major general continued firing. The major general shot himself several times before he realized what he was doing, but then it was too late. The ambitious major general would never have guessed that he of all people was going to commit suicide this morning.

Derek pulled the dying major general out onto the ground and grabbed the chemical injection gun from the dying man's frozen grasp. He then retrieved his own bow and climbed into the rover and pulled the dead pilot with the arrow through his heart over the side. He spun the craft around and drove the rover up to where Karn was positioned. "I need to help my friends. They have been captured," said Derek.

"Go. This battle is over." replied Karn.

Derek spun the rover around and drove it straight off the cliff. The levitation mechanisms adjusted to the temporary free falling and the rover settled before ever touching the ground at the base of the mountain and continued accelerating smoothly parallel to level ground. Derek gave it full throttle and the vehicle raced across the high grass and into the misty jungles of early morning. Derek covered ground with reckless fury and rage. He had to save the others. He would not let his crew remain in the murderous hands of the system war machine. They were true friends and he was going to die for them.

Derek covered several kilometers in moments. He dodged confused and dying troopers, but not one gave chase. He raced past grazing seismosaurs and spooked a herd of antlered prey. Zigzagging through redwood forests reaching for the sky, he maneuvered past a mad pack of utahraptors snarling and lunging for his speeding rover. They chased him as far as they were able. He ripped past the Solarion, now uncovered and exposed, looking unreal in this prehistoric world. He could see the battleship in the distance and he pushed the levitation vehicle as fast as it would go toward the open hatch of the formidable warship.

57

Miscalculation

The elderly commandant now felt a little better, as he stood before the Shareholders. His general was also there, sitting and looking very official next to where the commandant stood. The pills were doing their job, to counteract the horrible effects of superluminal lag, and his pounding headache had finally abated. He hated having to debrief these egomaniacs. He just wanted to do his job without unnecessary scrutiny. He secretly hated reporting to anyone. This was the real reason why he had become the supreme commandant, but these decadent ones were his superiors and regretfully they had the final word in all major decisions. He had made some unauthorized decisions back there in the war room in the heat of the battle, some of which had gone very badly.

He sought their approval to proceed, as a matter of personal damage control. He had no choice now but to debrief the Shareholders and break the bad news to them about what had transpired so far, here on their new planet. He falsely assumed that the situation was now under control, because he was confident that the renegade crew of the Solarion was all captured. The three crew members and the droid were in the brig behind bars. The one who had activated the beacon was undoubtedly in custody, and so he was also on his way back to the ship, dead or alive. It did not really matter at this point. This had been a terrible mess, and he planned to execute the renegades after this debriefing. He wished he could have killed them sooner, but the dinosaurs got in the way. The prisoners may have provided valuable information about this new world in a friendlier setting, but not after what he had been through with them. Good information was not enough to save their lives now. He wanted them dead.

"After encountering the prior arrivals to this planet, our immediate objective was to subjugate them," said the commandant. "They have now been captured and are held in the brig. The final one is being escorted back to the brig as we speak. I can happily say that this world is now ours. We have carried the finest modern technology with us upon this formidable warship cruiser, and now we have an inhabitable planet and an unlimited supply of natural resources at our disposal. There is only one minor miscalculation which requires our attention. This beautiful pristine planet is inhabited by prehistoric creatures. These creatures are very fearsome and we have lost good men to them. This will not happen again, I can assure you," said the commandant with confident authority.

"How many good men have you lost, commandant?" a Shareholder asked curiously.

"We lost a number of good men to the prehistoric creatures. This was a variable that we regretfully did not anticipate. It was a miscalculation," replied the commandant haltingly.

"You can do better than that, commandant. We want numbers," demanded another Shareholder. The commandant cast a nervous glance to his general sitting there stone faced and staring straight ahead into nothing. His loyal general appeared to have frozen up on him just when he was needed the most.

The commandant cleared his throat uneasily and paused. He was in dire need of sleep, and his emotions were not buried as deeply as he would have preferred. He felt a surge of rage at this cynical questioning. His rage was mixed with the remorse of losing good men all because he had failed to factor in the unexpected. "I am not sure of the exact count, but we have lost almost five battalions," he chokingly replied. He paused for the shocking revelation fully sink in. "It is unsafe to survey the damage until full daylight, but many troopers have been lost," said the commandant choking again, and clearing his throat.

A cloud of opium smoke wafted up and engulfed both the commandant and the general, adding insult to injury. "You lost half the regiment to prehistoric creatures and you tell us this planet is ours?" asked one smoking angry Shareholder shocked by what he had just been told. "Is it now safe to go outside?" asked the Shareholder.

"Have these creatures been eliminated?" asked another.

"Regretfully, the prehistoric predators are still out there, and it will take some time to destroy them all," replied the commandant. "The ground troops encountered many large packs of vicious fearless carnivores, and our chemical injection guns proved worthless against them. This planet may be crawling with them for all we know. We need more time. Our troops on foot were powerless against the predatory attacks. Most of the first five battalions have not returned, nor have they been heard from again. We sent the second half of our regiment to capture the remaining renegade, but the entire final half of the regiment was safely riding in rovers. They are out there now. Please keep in mind that we are a military space force, and we do not specialize in ground operations. These men have not been extensively trained in large scale terrestrial conflicts," explained the commandant.

Derek plunged through the spacious open hatch of the magnificent warship cruiser and docked his commandeered rover. He grabbed the deadly chemical injection gun and jumped out of the vehicle. His bow was across his chest and his quiver across his back. His knife was in its sheath strapped to his boot. He did not remotely resemble a military trooper. His clothes were ripped to shreds, caked with mud, and smeared in blood. When he jumped from the rover, he was immediately confronted by troopers. "Who the hell are you?" asked the lead trooper. Derek dropped them both before they could react. He hit them with a single stun dose and moved on. They would be out for hours which gave him plenty of time to do what he came to do. The chemical injection gun was deadly accurate on solid footing, but not very accurate when fired from a moving rover, as the last half of the regiment was discovering this morning. He held the chemical injection gun ready and made way for the main control room of the cruiser. He took out everyone he encountered without hesitation or words on his way to the main control room of the battle cruiser. The access cards the troopers wore around their necks were all confiscated along the way. The luxurious warship cruiser was nicely organized, with framed floor maps mounted on the walls. He had no trouble at all in locating the main control room. By the time he reached the main control room doors, he had a collection of access cards draped around his neck, and the doors slid open with the third card.

As the access doors to the main control room of the warship cruiser slid open, Derek entered to discover the brigadier general huddled over the webscreen spheres. He was alone. He never looked up from the webscreen projections as he was frantically talking into a webphone. "I said that we have a big problem on our hands," he spoke loudly into the webphone. "The battalions sent to the beacon are engaged in heavy combat with planetary natives. I have lost contact with the major general. He is down," he urgently informed someone at the other end. "I do not care if the commandant is not finished with the Shareholders!" he yelled. "Page him now! This is an emergency! This requires his immediate attention. Get him out of that debriefing and on the line. We are outnumbered and outgunned. This is a crisis!" shouted the brigadier general angrily into the webphone never looking up.

"Get up," ordered Derek. The brigadier general paused and took his ear off the webphone. He looked up to a voice he did not recognize, and he was staring down the barrel of a chemical injection gun. "Hang up the phone," ordered Derek as the stunned brigadier general stared into the barrel of the gun pointed between his eyes. The brigadier general hit the disconnect button on the webphone. He recognized Derek.

"You!" said the shocked brigadier general, "You are the young man who was sent into the sun with the Solarion crew. When we realized that it was your ship, we pulled up your bios. How did you disappear from us?" asked the brigadier general.

"Get up," said Derek, ignoring the question. "We are going to the Shareholders now," he told the military officer. "Take me to them immediately or die where you sit," said Derek.

"Have it your way, son," retorted the brigadier general in a condescending tone. "Obviously I have no choice in the matter," mumbled the shaken military man.

"You are not used to choices," replied Derek. The young man with yellow eyes blazing in fury looked wildly out of place standing in front of this military man. They walked through the mazes and corridors of the ship. They encountered troopers and guards along the way, and Derek shot quickly before words crossed lips. He gave them stun doses good to last for hours. Not one guard had a chance to return fire, because the first thing they saw was the brigadier general and the last thing they saw was the floor. The paralyzing doses were all that he needed, so he conserved his rounds of chemical injections. The uniformed personnel were in no way prepared for hostile encounters within their own ship. The brigadier general scanned his card and they took a transfer cube to the floor of the Shareholders conference room. The transfer cube slid open and at the end of the hall were another set of doors. This hall was empty except for one lone figure standing in front of the doors.

"Here we are," said the brigadier general. "Now all you have to do is get through those doors," he smirked. "What are you going to do to me now, son?" asked the brigadier general.

"Where is my crew?" asked Derek.

"They are in the brig with the others. The brig has special security and lowly generals like me do not have access," the brigadier general lied to the young man and put on the best poker face he could muster. "Of course the commandant has access to everything," added the brigadier general. "Son, the commandant and his loyal general are with the Shareholders now, as you may have heard," he said to the young renegade slave.

"Yes I heard," replied Derek as he drove a knotted fist deep into the poker face of the brigadier general, loudly cracking his jaw bone. The brigadier general sank to the floor halfway out of the transfer cube and out into the hallway. Derek left the man lying unconscious on the floor, his body holding the transfer cube open. The lone hulking figure standing in front of the doors to the chamber was a bodybuilder android. Derek stepped out of the transfer cube and walked toward the doors of the chamber. The bodybuilder android watched him coming, unmoving and unflinching.

Derek fired his chemical injection gun into the chest of the bodybuilder android. It had no effect on him at all. The bodybuilder android grinned as the youth approached. Derek threw the chemical injection gun down. He drew an arrow from his quiver, nocked and released. The android caught the arrow in midair, with reflexes so fast that his motions were blurred. Derek put the bow and quiver down. He charged and slammed into the android. They both went down. Derek rolled across the body of the android and was back on his feet and poised. The android shook off the blow and spun around and crouched to face the youth. Derek charged again, but the android ducked lower and flipped Derek.

Derek landed on his back on the floor. The android pounced on top and began choking the human. Derek looked into murderous android eyes without a soul. The android was enjoying this. Derek could not pry the android hands from his neck. He could not breathe and the android gripped his neck and choked with crushing strength. He kicked the android hard between the legs several times but the android only grinned and said, "There is nothing to hurt me there." The android growled then let out an insane laugh, and Derek was out of air.

Derek clapped the palms of his hands together viciously, with the android head in the middle, over and over. The android shook his head and Derek continued the assault. He could feel the synthesized skull begin to cave in. He felt ooze on his hands as the head began to rupture and leak. He continued the killing blows, and began to breathe again. The android grip was loosening. The android suddenly stood up. The synthetic being appeared to be in shock, and gingerly felt the oily ooze seeping from both sides of its head. Shock turned to horror, then to rage. Derek reached for his knife as the android dove on him but landed on top of the blade. He gripped the handle of the blade with both hands and ripped the android open. The oily bodily fluids spewed and flooded the floor. Derek rolled the android off of him.

The bodybuilder android looked down at his horrible wound and moaned. Derek gripped the android's head in a hammer lock and twisted it until it snapped. He braced his boot on the shoulder of the android and pulled with all his might until the head tore loose. The android's headless fighting body squirmed on the floor.

Derek grabbed his quiver and bow and chemical injection gun and used the brigadier general's card to scan the entrance pad to the Shareholder chamber. He stepped in. He now held the bodybuilder android head in one hand.

The Shareholders were there with the commandant and the general. The commandant stood at a webscreen projection sphere and stopped in mid-sentence. Derek tossed the head of the bodybuilder android across the room, as it slung fluids and slime and then rolled on the floor. It left a greasy trail, stopping at the feet of the commandant.

"Release all of the prisoners now," said Derek.

Shock gave way to realization, and then a cold dark expression graced the countenance of the supreme commandant. "How did you escape my battalions?" asked the commandant.

"They are all dead," replied Derek. "Your battalions have all been destroyed. Release all prisoners now or I will kill you where you stand," said Derek and he pointed the chemical injection gun at the heart of the hardened commandant. The loyal general was poised to aide his commandant but he dared not move. There was nothing they could do.

"I will let the prisoners go," said the commandant. "We do not need them anyway. We have adequate cloning facilities to meet our needs," said the commandant. He entered a code sequence into the webphone speaker which connected to the brig.

"Brig here," answered the captain of the brig.

"This is the commandant speaking," said the commandant into the webphone speaker. "We have a situation here. I order you to release the prisoners now. Load them back into the space ark and release the ark immediately," barked the commandant.

"Sir, yes, sir," replied the captain of the brig.

As Derek heard these words, he realized that the commandant had miscalculated again. Derek had no idea that the space ark had been taken prisoner. He listened and his heart pounded. His mind raced. A jolt shot through his being. It could not be so. He now hoped Jenniper had left with the cult. The cult was captured and taken prisoner during their migration to Eridani. He hoped beyond reason that she would come some day. He had kept his reasons for wanting to come to Epsilon Eridani to himself, although there were not many other options at the time. He had almost given up hope and had almost forgotten the reasons, after all that had happened here in this wild world. The reasons why came flooding back. He was here in Eridani for a reason. He was waiting for Jenniper.

He eyed the wretched Shareholders, and they were sitting stupid and speechless. The room was thick with smoke and little naked androids stood among their masters, staring back at this strange man. The wicked Shareholders were shocked silly. They were the hideous and pathetic products of too much excess. Modern technology was the only thing keeping these disgusting monsters alive. They were the result of decades of decadence, and decades of surgical and cosmetic repair. All eyes were fixed on him, this muscled young man with blazing yellow eyes. Fear was upon them as they eyed the young warrior.

"He is the one," hissed the new god through trembling lips. She alone appeared to be unspoiled, and she looked out of place among the other hideous Shareholders. "He is the one from the dream," she cried. "He is going to kill us all," whimpered the new god. She sat in the middle of them and started to weep. The Shareholders were petrified by this revelation from the new god, but they did not comfort her. They eyed the wild youth and panic grew in their coal black synthetic hearts. There was no one to call for help on this wild planet filled with fearsome prehistoric creatures. There were no reinforcements. All battalions were dead. The elite military regiment was no more. Many troopers lay paralyzed in the wake of this wild intruder. They could only sit and wait, and helplessly imagine what would happen next.

"The space ark will be loaded and released very shortly now," grumbled the grizzled old commandant. "What more do you want from us?" he asked, looking down the barrel of the injection gun.

"Only after the ark is loaded and released, and all prisoners are safe," said Derek. "Then you will find out what else I want," said the young warrior.

The dazed brigadier general with the broken jaw staggered into the doorway. He drunkenly hoped the young man would be dead by now. He had stepped over the android corpse in the hall, and he should have known not to enter the chamber, but he was not thinking straight. There was blood trickling from his mouth, and his broken jaw was huge and swollen. He tried to speak, but no one understood. He realized too late. Derek hammered the butt of the chemical injection gun across his nose. He fell hard and did not get up. In a flash, the youth then smashed the conference room webphone with the butt of his gun.

"To the control room," said Derek and he motioned for the commandant and general to lead the way. With the door open, he smashed the access panel on the inside, closed the door from the outside, and smashed the access panel on the outside. The Shareholders were trapped. The general drew a small pistol, but he was not quick enough and before he could squeeze the trigger, Derek peppered the man with the chemical injection gun. The general died before his body hit the floor. He fell with a hollow thud on top of the headless bodybuilder android.

The bloody young warrior and the commandant took the transfer cube up and marched back through the corridors to the central control room of the battle cruiser with the commandant in front. Derek followed with his chemical injection gun trained on the commandant.

The Shareholders sat dumbfounded and trapped in their smoke filled chamber. They knew not how to alter this terrible turn of events. They relied totally upon the support staff and the elite military unit, and they frantically tried to make contact with anyone but the access panels were useless. They pounded on the walls but no one answered their cries. The naked miniature android servants huddled in the corner, like spider monkeys trapped in a cage of wild gorillas. The Shareholders were not accustomed to such harsh treatment or such uncomfortable uncertainties. They were at the mercy of this wild young renegade, their former slave.

58

Prophecy Fulfilled

The commandant and Derek entered the control room. Derek blocked outside access to the room from the inside access panel. A surviving major general sat at a webterm console trying desperately to make contact with the missing troopers. It was no use. He looked up and his eyes widened.

"You will not reach them. They are no more," said the commandant to the major general. The commandant was not dull and he knew this young man would not have a chemical injection gun pointed at his head if it were not so. Before the major general could respond, Derek gave him a single dose from the chemical injection gun and he sank in his chair.

"Login to the system console with full access privileges, and bring up the flight scheduler," ordered Derek to the commandant. He rested the barrel of the chemical gun against the temple of the commandant who nodded in compliance. He sat down to the main control terminal and touched a panel then placed his index finger on a pad. A small cylinder emerged from the panel and from inside the cylinder emerged a smoking sphere. The commandant breathed moist breath onto the sphere and the sphere retracted into the cylinder. The cylinder then retracted back into the system terminal panel. The unique DNA of the commandant was verified and the terminal displayed the superuser login prompt. The commandant looked back at Derek and grimaced, then slowly turned and entered the superuser password.

The commandant accessed the graphical flight scheduler routines which displayed in three dimensions before them. "What could you possibly want with these?" he asked incredulously, looking back at Derek who carefully watched the commandant. The commandant did not know what this wild looking youth was up to, but he was gambling that the youth did not possess the knowledge to destroy system control routines. Derek studied the displays.

"Once the prisoners are safe, you will find out," replied Derek. The commandant was bothered by this young man's confidence, and he then began to worry that this boy may know more than his wild look revealed. "While we are waiting for the prisoners to be safely released, bring up the user administration graphical," ordered young Derek. The commandant grimaced again but grudgingly opened the list of valid login identities. "Delete all user logins and the associated DNA profiles," ordered Derek.

"I cannot do that," replied the commandant angrily.

"Let me show you how," said Derek, and he grabbed the wireless touchpad from the commandant, while holding the gun on him. The youth wiped out all user logins and DNA profiles in a flash. The commandant began to sweat, but the chemical injection gun was pointed between his eyes and he was powerless to act. Derek then proceeded to change the password for the one remaining superuser login. "The user logins are deleted, and the password to the remaining login is known only to me. I will now block remote access and remote command execution and disable remote control of the ship," said Derek as he tapped on the wireless touchpad dragging, dropping, and deleting. "Finally, I will synchronize with all redundant servers so that my changes are populated across the cluster, and I will delete all system backups so that recovery is not possible," added Derek as he continued to work at the touchpad.

The commandant suddenly felt doomed. He helplessly watched in agony as Derek cleanly locked down all outside access to the ship supercomputer in short order. As a final insult, Derek entered his own personal DNA profile so that only he could access the one and only superuser login. The yellow eyed youth breathed into the smoking sphere. The smoking sphere retracted and his personal DNA profile was recorded. Derek performed a final logoff to slam the door on all access.

"You are now the only one who can access the controls of this warship. What more do you want?" asked the stupefied commandant.

The control room webphone turned on. "This is the brig captain and the ark has now been loaded with all prisoners, including those three renegades and the droid, captured from the Solarion," stated the captain.

"Tell him to release the ark immediately," ordered Derek.

The commandant touched the webphone and barked the command, "Release the ark and let the prisoners go, ASAP." There was a brief pause.

"Roger that, the ark is now free," replied the captain.

"Patch us through to the ark," commanded Derek. The commandant barked the command to the brig captain who patched them through. The webscreen projection sphere came to life with the images of those inside the space ark control room.

Derek looked into the webcam. "This is Derek," he announced to the space ark control room. "What is your status?" he queried.

Dr. Zeek appeared in the grainy sphere of the webscreen hologram. "Derek, we are all in the ark and we are pulling away from the warship cruiser now. We have full control of the ark. It is fully operational," replied Dr. Zeek.

"Put it wherever you desire," responded young Derek. "I will be there shortly," he said.

"What is going on?" asked Dr. Zeek.

"I am in the control room of the warship, and I have full access to the ship supercomputer controls. I have a plan, but only after the ark is completely free and clear," he said. They waited.

"We are now clear of the warship and navigating the ark without difficulty. We will put it down in a safe place," said Dr. Zeek. "There is someone onboard anxious to see you," he added.

The heart of young Derek raced wildly. He glanced at the troubled and helpless commandant sitting and uncomfortably waiting. His next move was crucial. Derek did not want any mistakes now. He initiated superuser login, breathed his DNA into the sphere and it verified. He entered his password at the superuser login prompt and it was accepted. He was in. He opened the flight scheduler graphical configuration display. The flight database projection screen displayed the surrounding planetary solar system in three dimensions. He drug an icon for flight destination one into the center of Epsilon Eridani and dropped. He moved an icon for flight destination two into the center of another sun further out, and dropped. He picked another sun further out to place the icon for flight destination three. He selected sun after sun, dropping successive flight destination leg icons, and then placing a flight destination icon deep on the other side of the galaxy.

He then selected neighboring galaxies, first the Draco galaxy, then Ursa Minor, then M33, and finally Andromeda. He proceeded to drop destination legs into sun after sun, placing the final destination deep into unknown parts of the universe. The commandant groaned. Derek saved the flight projection. He then opened the initialization sequence dialog.

The warped gravity track detection console generated an alert and Derek tensely eyed the spherical webscreen display. "Confirm the alert, and read the details," ordered Derek to the commandant.

The commandant complied and the warped gravity track detection console displayed the details of a massive disturbance. "It is Sol," said the old commandant sullenly. "Sol has been destroyed by the solar implosion bomb. Our great empire is lost. The resulting supernova has caused a massive disturbance," said the commandant.

"The great empire was lost long ago," replied Derek, but he also felt a great sadness sweep through his soul. Mankind did not possess the technology to predictably travel into the knowable past in order to change things for the right. There was no righting the wrong, and no changing the past. The Earth and Sun were gone, along with the billions of nameless slaves who had suffered and died.

The space ark webscreen projection crackled again. "We are landing now, and we are safe," said Dr. Zeek. "The cult congregation has a message to deliver. They do not wish to take revenge upon the Shareholders. They desire to live a healthy life in this new world which is revenge enough," he finished.

Derek completed the initialization sequence dialog. He entered a five minute countdown into the sequence display and put the ship at maximum graviton induction upon entry into Epsilon Eridani. He set the flight mode to autonomous and promiscuous to instruct the ship to operate on autopilot and automatically investigate the most inviting path to the next programmed flight destination leg. He saved the launch sequence and logged out of the warship supercomputer. He turned to walk out of the room.

"What have you done?" yelled the commandant.

"I have sent you into the sun," the youth replied. "You may survive to live a long life, but you will live it inside this ship for the rest of your days. You will journey through the universe from sun to sun, through stargate after stargate," said Derek as he left the control room.

Derek ran through the corridors to the dock. There were wounded panicked troopers at the dock trading tales of the wild things they had seen. He ducked past them just as one looked up and yelled. He jumped into his rover and sped out into the jungles as the hatch door closed down behind.

The warship engines revved and billowing clouds of charged particles belched across the land. Derek gave his rover full throttle as the warship screamed in mounting acceleration. The graviton generators whirred into a high pitched wail. The warship cruiser launched and ascended higher and higher then streaked deep into the sky and rapidly disappeared into the black clouds of the night. The land was soon quiet and the warship cruiser was gone, destined for the heart of Epsilon Eridani. Derek had more important things on his mind.

Jenniper was there at the space ark. Derek floated smoothly up to the gathering. Derek jumped out of his rover and ran to Jenniper, as she also ran to him. They embraced. They were together again in this new and dangerous world. Years would pass before the supernova light from the old world would reach their eyes, but their old Earth and Sun were gone forever. This lost world of prehistoric creatures was now their new home, and they must learn to survive together. They held each other tight and were as close as two people can be.

59

Death of a Sun

The sun went from its normal bright yellow brilliance to a more muted shade of orange and this was amazing to everyone on Earth. People could comfortably look directly into the sun, and many did so because the new color was intriguing. The solar colors continued changing and darkened until the sun then became a deep dark purple. The billions of bewildered slaves left behind were then told not to look directly into the sun even through the ultraviolet-filtered domes. Everyone hid from the sun and scientists watched through massive filtered telescopes in fascination. This was indeed a baffling and yet remarkable historic event, reasoned the scientific community, and one that must be meticulously documented. They were not yet aware of the antiquark implosion bomb. They were not privy to elegant cover-ups and such secret intelligence. There was speculation of an alien intervention, but the growing consensus from the religious community was that this was the final second coming.

The curious astronomers, cosmologists, and solar scientists studied the purple sun and its core appeared to be shrinking. They positively confirmed that the internal core of the sun was indeed contracting. The outer shells of the sun began to rapidly expand, and the purple core continued to collapse. They became extremely alarmed when they realized that the historic astronomical event that they were witnessing was the death of their own sun. The core shrank and turned from dark purple to dark gray while the outer shell expanded further.

They soon believed that the sun was evolving into a red giant star before their very eyes. They could not understand why the sun appeared to be aging so rapidly. They were shocked again when the core of the sun continued collapsing and morphing into something other than a typical carbon cored red giant star. The core became smaller and smaller, and darker and darker, until it was coal black, and the outer layers of the sun become more unstable as massive shreds tore off and reached out and enveloped Mercury. The scientists feared the sun was somehow becoming a super giant star, which was not supposed to ever happen to stars the size of the sun. Their fears were soon confirmed. Panic spread throughout the world.

The Shareholders were nowhere to be found. The people of the world waited in anticipation for official word from the Shareholders, but no word came. The global military space force aggressively searched for the Shareholders, but realized their supreme leaders were gone. Renegade corporate slaves abandoned their posts and positions, joined together, and commandeered ships. There was widespread looting and rioting. Stolen spaceships were stocked with pilfered provisions, and were launched in search of safety beyond the solar system. There was mass hysteria and mayhem. In the absence of old leaders, new leaders took charge. They were not sure of where they would go but they knew they had to get away. The tanker shuttles bound for Alpha Centauri, Sirius, Wolf 359, and Delta Pavonis were stuffed beyond their capacity with frightened refugees. Ships around the world blasted off to the unknowns in frantic desperation.

The religious community was convinced that the end was finally here. They prayed for a place in heaven, an invitation to the everlasting party, a reservation to be among the chosen ones. This was finally the glorious end. Countless religious leaders throughout history had preached, prophesied, and predicted that this day would eventually come. This was the day they had longed for, the day the wretched world of evil would finally be destroyed, and the saved would be separated from the damned for all eternity. They openly prayed for a home in the gated community above. They expected to see the almighty riding the clouds to receive the righteous chosen ones, but they dared not look at the sun or blindness soon followed. They searched the night sky for divine processions. They gave all they owned to the poor in final displays of unselfish generosity. They prayed for forgiveness and begged for mercy. So much of their lives had been spent in the service to corporations, rather than in service to the world of people in need. Mankind was not going to solve this one in time. The almighty would surely intervene.

Earth was rocked from its steady orbit as the magnetic poles reversed. Continents froze while others scorched. The bubble worlds of floating oceanic cities were torn from umbilical cords once anchoring them to ocean floors against the constant storms. The solid land based bubble cities were ripped apart, crushed and buried in rock and mud slides, and lost in bottomless sink holes. Earthquakes split continents and gave birth to sky scraping tidal waves. Molten lava oozed from continental ruptures, and ocean waters rushed in and steamed the entire atmosphere. Tunnels and tubes on and under both land and water, connecting the eggshell worlds, were crushed, melted, broken, and flooded. Thousands upon thousands of massive satellites and space stations crashed to earth. Clouds the size of cities froze solid and pummeled the ground below.

The webscreens, webterms, webpods, and webcams went blank and the web went down for good. There were no longer invasive eyes to worry about. Many loyal corporate slaves vainly attempted to report to their production complexes for work, to continue as if nothing had changed. This was the only life they knew or wanted to know. They trusted the scientific community and trusted the ability of mankind to find a solution to all problems.

The supernova explosion came quickly. The outer shells of the sun burst and blew off in blinding light, heat, and radiation, engulfing the solar system completely. The sun temporarily became the brightest star in the galaxy. No one was protected from the resulting ionizing radiation energy. All people were fatally damaged no matter how well they were hidden, no matter how thick their lead shelters. It was over for all inhabitants of Earth. The sun rapidly died, and in cruel retaliation, the sun lashed out to flame-broil all planets of the solar system. In the wake of the engulfing supernova blast, a rapidly spinning synthetic neutron star remained and a new pulsar was formed.

Billions died instantly. The handful to survive the initial supernova explosion suffered through the three classical stages of terminal radiation poisoning. The first stage was the bodily reaction to the intense ionizing gamma and cosmic radiation. There were few to survive the first stage which lasted only hours, as the living dead suffered traumatic burns, fever, nausea, and shock. The second stage lasted only days as hair fell out, nausea persisted, fever rose, gums bled, and wounds worsened. The last stage for those hiding in the best possible bomb shelters began with an overreaction of the body to compensate for low levels of white and red blood cells. The burns turned into pinkish rubbery scars and fatal internal infections set in. The bodies of the dead floated in the waters, and rotted in the dark chambers of the lead walled bomb shelters. Those who survived to the third stage wished death would come soon and finally it did.

60

Thanksgiving Dinner

Later that evening, the cult and the Solarion crew built a large fire and sat around the blaze telling stories and watching the stars. The crew of the Solarion told their tales of this unspoiled world, untouched by mass extinctions, and inhabited by dangerous predators and wary prey living and evolving together. Young Derek told the cult refugees of how he had happened upon the arrow, and how he had fashioned more arrows in the likeness of the one and then carved a bow. He told them how he learned to hunt with stick and string, and how the natives had shown themselves and saved him up on the mountaintop when he was out of ideas and in desperate need of help.

The cult refugees listened to the tales with fascination. They were somewhat fearful hearing the descriptions of this pristine but deadly world, one that was now to be their new home. There were daunting challenges waiting for them here in this lost world, but they had been through so much together, and had faced so many great obstacles to be where they were now. The refugees told of their visionary leader and now lost martyr, the Reverend H, who was mercilessly crucified at the evil hands of the Shareholders. A lonely duckbilled dinosaur many kilometers away honked several times and the long echoing calls broke the stillness and the newcomers listened in wonder to the strange sounds and gazed into a wondrous star filled night sky.

Derek held hands with Jenniper, and her radiant blue eyes twinkled by the firelight. He knew not what lay in store for them but he knew that he felt more warmth and happiness now than he had ever known. They could not stop smiling at one another. There was peace and love in the heart of an untamed wilderness. They whispered and shared the secrets of two people who were deeply in love. They passionately and openly embraced and the refugees and crew of the Solarion howled, hooted, clapped, and cheered. This was a first for everyone, an open display of affection without fear of retaliation.

Karn emerged from the dark shadows of the night with many natives walking with him. They were clothed in skins and hides and appeared to be very fit and healthy. The pterodactyls were gliding down from the night sky as the natives climbed off of the beasts, and many natives were landing around the roaring campfire blaze. The crowd grew much larger. Karn smiled sheepishly and announced, "We welcome you to our home and we have brought to you a gift that we hope you will enjoy." The natives brought the gift forward and into the light of the campfire.

Derek was the first to reply. "Karn, you and your people have saved our lives today. We are thankful for what you have done for us, and we are grateful for your courage and kindness. We are thankful that you have come to share this fire with us, and we hope to become good friends," said Derek. "What is the gift you have brought to us?" asked Derek.

"This is something that you were forced to leave behind," replied Karn. "It is something that we hope you will now enjoy," he said. The natives presented the new arrivals with large piping hot platters steaming with sizzling grilled and smoked cuts of seasoned and spiced meat. This was the same meat Derek had been forced to leave behind, packed on the sled before the attack. The natives also carried in hot platters of cooked vegetables and cool platters of fresh fruits. The aroma of the smoked meat and cooked vegetables was delightful. The natives quickly spread the food down before the new arrivals and they all then shared in the partaking. The cult refugees, solar survivors, and planetary natives all enjoyed getting to know one another and they gave thanks for the delicious dinner. The sizzling cuts of grilled, smoked and seasoned meat were a delightful new taste experience for the newcomers. Cookie brought out a steaming platter of the rainbow colored fish, courtesy of Benny. They would one day speak of this their first dinner together as thanksgiving dinner.

The natives listened in wonder and horror to the stories of how life was on Earth, so far away. The natives were told of the New World Order and the life of slavery and surveillance from which they had fled. The refugees recounted the permanently destructive actions of monopolistic teracorps in unsustainable pursuit of exploitable resources, and profit and growth without bounds. They were told how the short-sighted global teracorporations left a ruined world and a deteriorated environment in their insatiable wake, riddled with constant fierce storms of continental proportions, forcing all people to resort to living their lives within the protection of the bubble cities. The refugees described the web, the network which delivered the endless steady flood of misinformation, propaganda, and commercials which all were forced to endure. The natives were finally told of the wretched Shareholders who owned everything.

The natives of Planet P told their own stories of the dangers of living in a lush land crawling with deadly creatures, the prehistoric carnivorous predators. They told tales of courage, struggle, and heartache. They told of how they had learned to survive here in this lost world, and how their own battles to be free from the fear of attack had helped them to evolve and adapt to this beautiful yet deadly habitat. They conveyed an inherent love for nature, and they carried the untamed spirit of the wild. There was a unique strength and wisdom expressed by these natives as they shared their stories around the roaring campfire.

They sat around the fire and counted shooting stars until late into the night. Benny played his laser axe in soft rich enchanting tones. The refugees looked ahead to a new future and new chance. They were aware that this new world was a very dangerous place, but it was also rich and unspoiled, and they knew they could rely upon each other.

They were all free for the first time in their lives, and they had formed a strong bond with the wise natives of this land.

"Karn, can you tell us about the one who taught your people our language, the one who came before?" asked Derek with curiosity.

Karn looked into the twinkling starlit sky and sighed. "There is so much we do not know," he said. "We only know this world, the world you call Planet P where we have always lived. We learned much from the one who came before. My father knew him well. He was very kind to us, and many of the ancient ones remember him well, but I was only a boy then. He came from the sky as you and the others came. He was a teacher and he taught us the language that you speak, and he taught us about medicine. He said that others would come, but they never came and it has become only a legend now. The others never came and we have been alone all this time. We thought that you were the ones but it has been so long now. He taught us to grow vegetables from the ground and to store them for the winter. We hoped that you were the others who would come, the ones the legends spoke of. We hoped you were the ones, but it has been so long now," he finished.

"Karn, can you remember what the one who came before looked like?" asked Jenniper, with growing interest.

"It has been a long time but I can still remember him well," replied Karn. "He was young and handsome and wore his hair braided and long. He spoke much of the creator. His name was Reverend H but he left when I was very young. We hoped you were the ones he had spoken of who would come, because he spoke highly of the ones who were coming to live with us," finished Karn. The refugees were shocked and moved by this revelation.

"We are the ones," replied Jenniper. "We came with Reverend H to build our home here, and he was our teacher also. He is no longer with us. We lost him in the journey but he is still in our hearts. The world we came from is no more, and we are all saddened by the end of our world, but we have learned many valuable lessons. We hope to build our new home here, in this world with your people," she said.

The expression on Karn's face changed; as he listened to Jenniper speaking. "You are the ones," he exclaimed with excitement. "We have waited for you for all of our lives. We will build a home together, your people and my people. There is so much we have to do. The Reverend H spoke highly of you, and we hope to learn much together. We will teach you all about our world," said Karn. The natives grew joyful and excited. "You have made my people very happy," smiled Karn. "We must go now and leave you to rest, but we will work together and help you build your home here. There is much to do and so much to say," said Karn as they mounted their winged prehistoric birds and were off into the night. Karn called down from above, "We welcome you all to our world! Peace with you all!" Karn and the natives disappeared into the darkness. The flap of pterodactyl wings silhouetted the starlit sky.

Derek and Jenniper said goodnight to everyone and left the glowing embers of the campfire. Benny yawned and stretched and took his laser axe and headed to the Solarion to his apartment module. He did not feel so alone anymore. The cult refugees also said their goodnights and retired back to the space ark for the evening.

"Ami, what should we start to work on next?" asked Dr. Zeek, sitting by the dying fire, after the others had all left them.

"I was thinking that it would be a good idea for us to disarm those thermonuclear warheads. Those things bother me," replied Ami.

"That is an excellent idea, Ami," replied Dr. Zeek. "This project will keep us busy for awhile. We can start to work first thing in the morning. I think we are going to make it out here." he said.

"I feel better about everything too." replied Ami.

Somewhere far away in the distance, a lonely howl floated upon the night air and sent chills through everyone who heard the mournful cry.

The End

CPSIA information can be obtained at www.ICGtesting.com
Printed in the USA
BVOW082056110712

294995BV00002B/8/P